Light Singer

KINGDOM OF RUNES

LIGHT SINGER

AUDREY GREY

ISBN: 978-1-7349479-4-6

For the Greylings — you guys rock.

SOLISSIA

THE
MOTHER'S
SEA

COURT
OF
NINE

THE
GREAT
STEPPES

ASHARI

KINGDOM
OF
ICE

ISLE
OF
MIST

DRAGON-T
STRAIT

THE FLOATING
CITY OF
TYR

ASGARD

MORGANI
ISLANDS

GU
THR

FEYRA'S
SPEAR

THE
DESERT OF
BALDR

THE
SELKIE
SEA

DROT

EYIA

BAY OF SHADOWS

DARKLING BAY

SPIREFALL CASTLE

SHADOW KINGDOM

THE RUINLANDS

SCRED TREE OF LIFE

FEYRA'S TEMPLE

BLOOD BONE MOUNTAINS

THE WITCHWOOD

GLITTERING SEA

KINDOM OF VERDURE

THE BANE

DEVOURER'S CAMP

E SUN COURT

MANASSES

FENDIER

DEAD MAN'S STRAIT

ASHIVIER

PERTH

FALLEN KINGDOM OF LORWYNFELL

THE EENS

MUIRWOOD FOREST

CROMWELL

UNE

EN

E

RUNE WALL

KINGDOM OF PENRYTH

VENASSIAN OCEAN

VESERACK

THE MORTAL LANDS

*"When night roams the lands as a wolf and the moon howls beside it,
He will rise again to consume the world."*

~ blood augur prediction, last year of the Shadow War

PROLOGUE

Stolas Darkshade stifled the urge to prowl from the worn stone chair holding him captive, unfurl his restless wings, and ride one of the blasts of howling wind into the steely sky. Only his mother's gaze, flinty and crackling with power, convinced him what a bad idea that would be. Perched on a dark throne made to accommodate her glorious midnight wings, the Seraphian Empress commanded the head of the circular onyx table—and the rapt attention of every single guest.

The empress's laugh carried on the violent breeze, and Stolas slid his bored gaze to his mother. As always, her wings drew his focus.

Five attendants were required nightly to clean and oil them, and when a quill was shed, it was burned in the eternal fires deep below their palace, in the hollow caves made by the first Noctis.

Clad in delicate armor as dark as her onyx feathers, her razor-sharp features were trained on the Demon Lord to her right, Kazaack Nightfell, and his son, Raziel, the Prince of Ash.

But his mother's attention was solely on him.

Leave this table, she purred into his mind, *and I will strip those soft downy things you call wings and leave them nothing more than shreds of leather and bone.*

The warning in her voice couldn't quite mask her affection for him. It was no secret that he was his mother's favorite. Perhaps because she hated these affairs as much as he did.

Not everyone shares your scathing assessment of my appendages, he teased, sliding a look toward Lord Kazaack's mistress. The demonai female to his right had stared openly at Stolas since she was seated.

Her lips tilted upward, revealing the sharp silver teeth all demonai sported. Dark red clung to the silver.

The practice of *sangui mortus,* or blood-letting of lesser creatures, had been shunned by the Seraphians since ancient times. But those from the Demon Realm of Niefgard still practiced the savage custom.

His nostrils flared as he caught the scent of the half-congealed blood settled inside the demonai's glass. Solis, by the floral and coppery scent. Laden with copious amounts of fear.

A sharp prick in his gums heralded the descent of his fangs.

She noticed the change, a look of triumph overcoming her face.

He returned the smile, taking great pleasure in imagining the sound her bones would make as he snapped them. The only thing more satisfying would be the fear in her eyes as he tossed her into the void and then watched her body break upon the rocks below.

Hide your loathing, son, his mother purred, *or I will pluck out those beautiful eyes from your useless head.*

How can you tolerate them? They're almost as loathsome as the Golemites.

The Golemites were the parasitical creatures who scurried in the deepest recesses of the Netherworld. They lived off the magick of souls and blood of the living, off fear and terror and every emotion in between.

They serve a purpose, his mother reminded him. *When that purpose is done, they will slink back to their realm.*

Downing a pull of his spiced wine, Stolas turned his attention to Lord Kazaack. The Demon Lord had finally gotten past the pleasantries and was discussing the reason they were all gathered: trading for more demons to aid in their never-ending war with the Solis and mortals.

As he neared the end of the negotiations, his features softened, his voice changing, becoming more melodic.

The negotiation price was much more favorable to the Seraphians than it should have been.

"Why would you offer such agreeable terms?" His mother's question hung in the cool, briny air, thick with lethal promise.

If this was a trick, the Demon Lord, his son, and his entire court's black blood would feed the greedy sea below.

Kazaack's son, the Prince of Ash, drew his lips back in a bland smile. "We want *all* of your *prisoners.*"

So the notorious Prince Raziel speaks.

Raziel's mastery of the Seraphian language was flawless, his features pleasant and voice honeyed and soothing. Yet none of that changed the enormity of what the Court of Nightfell was asking.

To trade with only one of the Demon Lords would be an act bordering on war.

Stolas studied the Demon Prince carefully.

All of the Demon Lords and their retinue took great care to hide their true natures and features from those in this realm, masking both behind layers of magick. To every eye but the most powerful, they appeared almost human.

The Prince of Ash had chosen the façade of a golden-haired boy with kind brown eyes and a mouth quick to smile. His tunic, while finely made, was a simple onyx silk.

No embellishments.

No glint of weapons in waistbands or pockets.

His movements were soft, tentative, unthreatening. His gentle, lilting voice a reminder of how harmless he was.

How mortal and weak and trustworthy.

All lies, of course.

His mother's silence filled the tempestuous air. Stolas had seen more powerful males than this crumble beneath her stare, but the Demon Prince simply stared back into those twin pools of darkness.

His mother ran a delicate finger over her chin. "Your request puts my kingdom at great risk."

Raziel hesitated before responding, "I was told the Wolf of the Skies feared no one."

Insolent bastard.

Violence poured from his mother's very being as she leaned forward in her throne, her head ticking to the side. "Princeling, the endless magick of this land surges through my veins. Only Odin and Freya possess more power. But the Demon Lords' fury would spill over to my people, and I very much doubt your offer could compensate for their bloodshed."

"And if it could?" the Prince of Ash purred with that melodic voice and those warm, alluring eyes.

Stolas caught the faint feathering in his mother's sharp jaw.

"Look around you, Demon Prince." The empress's hand glided over the air to indicate the vast sweep of land around them; a mist-shrouded territory of jagged, snowy peaks as black as the sea. The famed Castle Starpiercer protruded from the ocean of clouds and mist like a dark spear. "What can you possibly have that we do not already possess in abundance?"

For a heartbeat, the glamour around the Prince of Ash faltered. Long enough for Stolas to make out the strangely otherworldly face; ethereal and haunting features that would undoubtedly appeal to any female in this realm—if not for the inhuman yellow eyes, bluish-silver skin, and slender pointed ears.

"They claim your teeth are as jagged as these peaks," Raziel purred. "Your appetite for blood and carnage as eternal as the waves below. And yet . . . I see what you desire above all else."

The empress's eyes glittered with violent delight as she arched a graceful silver-white brow. "And what is that, Princeling?"

If Raziel guessed wrong, it would be an insult. And his mother would end him and be done with this foolish game.

Stolas's incisors glided into position, his throat tight with need. He'd never tasted a Demon Lord's magick before.

The Prince of Ash must have felt the danger swirling around him. And yet . . . the bastard grinned as he answered, "Peace. The Wolf of the Skies longs for peace."

Stolas would have laughed—almost did laugh—if not for the strange look in his mother's face.

Her wings flared, sending cups flying to topple into the void, and she surged into the sky with such force that the mountains around them shook.

It was all the answer the Demon Lord would get tonight. But Stolas was left feeling slightly untethered.

Peace. The word ricocheted through his skull like a curse.

Peace.

Peace was dangerous. Treasonous. A death sentence. Peace meant no more battles. No more prisoners to trade to the Demon Lords. If they discovered his mother's longing for an end to the Shadow War . . . if Odin suspected . . .

Or his favorite pet, Morgryth—

Snarling, Stolas took to the sky, unable to shake the heavy feeling of fate locking into place like a chain slowly, *slowly* sliding around his neck.

ONE

By the time the booming ring of the giant bells atop the guard towers reached Haven Ashwood, she was already out of bed and clad in her knee-high boots, wool-lined pants, and long-sleeved tunic. Demelza said nothing as she helped Haven outfit her weapons, which had been conveniently laid out last night on her bedside table.

Demelza's rare silence was almost as unnerving as the peal of the bells. It was a macabre ritual, unfortunately. One that Haven prayed every night never came. So far, her prayers had gone mostly unanswered.

But tonight was the first night there were screams. Which meant the intruders had broken past the tower wards . . .

"Faster," Haven hissed as Demelza plunged the final weapon—a short sword—into the leather sheath at her thigh.

Haven spun around to face Demelza. The woman's tight curls haloed a face weary from nights such as this. The deep grooves marching across her craggy forehead and spiderwebbing the corners of her eyes were noticeably deeper, her thin lips bracketed by worried lines.

"Must you go out again?" her lady's maid asked.

"I must. But you'll be safe here." Haven nodded to the shadows flickering outside the windows.

The Seraphian guards who protected this tower were under strict orders to keep Haven safe at all costs. And they wouldn't know she had left until the attack was over.

"And you?" Demelza clucked her tongue. "Who will keep you safe?"

Haven winked, forcing her dry lips into a smile as she patted the iron pommel sticking from her waist sheath. "The Gods. Haven't you heard? They kind of like me."

Clucking louder, the poor woman just barely had time to slip a fur-lined cloak over Haven's shoulders before she was heading for the door.

"Be careful," Demelza called, and when Haven glanced over her shoulder and saw the worry inside the woman's dark eyes, an ache opened inside her chest that left her momentarily dizzy.

"I'll be fine, Demelza." Haven turned before the woman could see the emotion welling in her eyes.

The moment they'd landed on the high-cliffed shores of this mist-shrouded island, the attacks started. Every mercenary and cutthroat assassin for hire from the Ruinlands to the Selkie Sea had taken up Archeron's bounty on her head.

But it wasn't just Haven. Archeron promised thousands of runestones for the death of each member of her entourage. Her people. The very souls in the rambling city below who needed her help right now.

Stolas had worked tirelessly to restore a few of the guard tower wards to functioning level, but that still left a large part of the shoreline unprotected.

Pulling her emerald-green cloak tightly around her body, Haven slid into the shadowy corridor—and startled to see two glowing pairs of lavender eyes appraising her.

Her sister-in-arms, Surai, shifted impatiently from foot to foot, ready for action.

She'd already dispatched the sentinels guarding Haven's chamber, thank the Goddess. One less thing Haven had to worry about. It would have taken precious time to convince them to let her leave her room.

"Figured you would refuse to stay locked inside your gilded cage," Surai purred.

"Bell's going to be furious." Haven grinned at that.

Bell was in charge of her protection—an irony that didn't escape her. She was supposed to stay hidden inside her chamber during these attacks. Protected high in the night sky inside a nearly unscalable tower.

It's as if he didn't know her at all.

In the distance, another scream carried on the breeze. A shared fury passed between them. Haven's lips bared in a tamped down snarl as they raced down the hallway on silent feet, serenaded by the *clink* of their weapons. Windows shaped like stars were carved into the onyx stone walls. Between each opening was a torch held between the fangs of an iron wolf's head. A shimmering topaz blue, the flames flickered as Haven passed.

Haven took the winding stairwell five steps at a time, her boots hardly making a sound as she landed. Jumped. Landed.

Beside her, Surai had already shifted into her raven form.

At the bottom landing, the stairwell walls fell away to an open bridge that connected the tower to the main palace.

"Go!" Haven ordered, jerking her chin toward the dark expanse below. "Help Ember."

Surai hesitated, swooping around Haven's head in circles.

"I'll find a way down," Haven promised.

Satisfied, Surai cawed twice before diving into the swirling mist toward the western tower.

Normally, Stolas would have already found her and flown her to the fight, but the Seraphian Prince had taken a handful of his sentinels

8

earlier in the evening to confront the armada outside Shadoria's coastline. The blockade was a gift from Archeron, meant to starve their fledging kingdom. Not a hard feat when spies had already infiltrated the island's porous defenses and destroyed the few rare strips of fertile land.

Bastard.

And the Seraphians were just as likely to force her back to her tower than take her to the battle. Every single member of Shadoria had sworn an oath to protect her, which didn't always work in her favor.

A winged rune? No, the last one she tried had ended with her nearly plummeting to an ignominious death on the courtyard below. Every darkcaster resident here fed off her light magick, making certain spells unpredictable.

She was going to have to get down the old fashioned way. Haven narrowed her eyes, refocusing her frustration at the thin, rail-less bridge.

Runes, she hated bridges.

Castle Starpiercer had been built for the Seraphians. And winged creatures had very little need for railings or easy access to the ground. Which is why the castle was a series of interconnecting towers and structures that stretched to the clouds, an indomitable relic of the time Seraphians ruled the skies.

After the Shadow War and fall of Odin, when Morgryth and her kingdom had been sent back to the Netherworld and the first true King of the Nine claimed the palace, builders added stairs to many of the looming towers—but not all.

There was, however, a small servant's portal she'd discovered, a remnant of when mortal slaves served here, that would take her to the main market in the city. From there, the coastline was a hard sprint away.

The only sound as she crossed the bridge and then leapt onto the closest ledge was the whipping of her cloak behind her. She leapt from balcony to balcony until the slender towers gave way to parapets and crumbling stone.

Dark shapes stirred the murky air as the Seraphian sentinels patrolled the sky, sifting through the clouds for the intruders.

So they were winged, this time.

Shadowlings? Morgryth's Golemites? Gremwyrs? The list of possible enemy intruders was as vast as the city spread out below. A city full of innocent civilians who had followed her here with the blind faith that she could protect them.

And yet, here she was, scrabbling and lurching down the castle, a single misstep from death.

Grunting, she forced her movements into a dangerous pace. Any fear she might have felt was overcome by anger.

A dark, glittering rage.

When the ground peeked from the mist only a few stories high, she leapt, rolling to break the fall. Her bones groaned on impact, reminding her she was mortal. Flesh and blood.

Completely, annoyingly breakable.

But the flames of magick surging from her open palms were anything but human as she speared into the city that honeycombed the hills. The nightly storms that frequented Shadoria's coasts lit up the sky; dark, inhumanly fast shapes streaked against the violet jags of lightning over the water.

The intruders had been pushed back from the city.

Resolved to keep it that way, Haven cut through the main street, sprinting past newly opened shops and small homes carved from the onyx mountainside. Runelights flickered from windows as the people who had given up everything to follow her hunkered behind their walls. Their bitter terror choked the night air, as pungent and real as their muffled cries.

Haven was supposed to protect them. To keep them safe. And so far she'd failed at that.

A great swell of fury nearly blinded her. Twisting her fingers, she drew a newly learned swift rune into the air. The moment the final tail of the spiraling symbol disappeared, the world around her smeared into streaks of light.

Her speed ripped the air from her lungs. She hardly had time to blink before the cobblestoned streets gave way to bone-white sand so pale it nearly glowed. The tang of blood permeated the sea breeze. Haven whipped her gaze skyward to the shadows fighting high above.

A frustrated growl ripped from her throat as she paced below, boots sinking into the shifting sand.

If only she had the Seraphians' wings.

A thud drew her attention to the cliffs behind her where the luminous white hair of Seraphian soldiers bobbed against the dark rocks like flames. She collected more details as she stalked closer. A female Seraphian lay crumpled on her side, her beautiful glossy wings limp against the bloodstained sand.

There was something horrifying about seeing those wings, which were always moving, always outstretching and curling and so full of power, now lifeless and inert.

The other female knelt beside her friend tending to her obvious wounds. A thick white braid snaked down her back, and when she whipped her head to regard Haven . . .

"Delphine?" Haven called, rushing over.

Delphine turned back to her friend, her deft fingers working a series of dark runes into the air, while her free hand stroked her friend's cheek. Haven dropped to the sand beside them, ignoring the feel of blood as it seeped through her pant fabric and into her knees. She started to do a new healing light rune she'd just learned when Delphine lifted her eyes to Haven and shook her head.

That's when Haven realized Delphine wasn't performing healing runes; it was obvious the female was too far gone. These symbols were different. Some sort of last rites the Seraphians performed before death.

The dying Seraphian lifted her head. Her muted black armor, so dark it swallowed the moonlight, creaked softly.

It was painted in bright smears of blood and the scattered feathers of its dying owner.

As soon as the female recognized Haven, a strange serenity calmed the chaos inside her ebbing eyes.

With a silent gasp, the female used the final moment of her life to stretch a trembling finger toward the nearest tower to the east, away from the fight.

"What's over there?" she asked Delphine.

But Delphine couldn't speak, and the string of signs she created with her hands meant nothing to Haven.

She was embarrassed to admit that she didn't pick up on the twins' muteness until on the boat toward Shadoria. Only then did she notice that instead of speaking, the pair made a vast array of symbols with their hands.

She thought it might have been a code they'd developed during their enslavement to Morgryth, to keep her from intruding on their internal conversations.

The brutal truth was far darker.

As Stolas had explained, the Seraphians had been forbidden from communicating in any fashion. Cruel, savage magick was used to crush the part of the minds Seraphians used to soulspeak.

Any Seraphian caught talking aloud to their brethren had their tongues ripped out.

Haven shivered, her gaze flicking to the east and whatever awaited her before returning to Delphine. If only Haven knew how to read her signs, and she made a note to learn the next time she had a few hours to herself.

Stolas's friend made three signs, finishing the statement with a fist clapped over her heart, and then exploded into the sky. Her shadowy form soon joined the battle over the sea.

Time to find out what awaited her to the east. Haven's sword pommel was cool beneath her palm as she stalked toward the looming tower. The shadows of the cliffs easily hid her approach. Whatever the dying Seraphian directed her toward, Haven would face it alone.

There were no Seraphians here. Nothing but the soft crash of waves, the lulling song of the sea drowning out the cacophony of violence and death at her back.

She wasn't foolish enough to mistake the quiet for safety.

Thunder rumbled in the distance, an angry god awoken from its slumber. A few drops of cool rain pattered against her cheeks.

The dancing glow of a green portal lit up the beach, painting the pale sand a soft, sickly death-hue. Five Asgardian warriors guarded the portal, their armor glinting. And when she saw the creature that slithered from the portal's gaping mouth, its rider's massive axe already raised as the terrifying duo took to the skies—

A shiver of horror wracked her core. Death Raiders from the Asgardian nation. Known for defending the floating city of Tyr in Asgard on battle dragons, their battalions had slaughtered thousands in the Shadow War.

Their mounts were hardly larger than an Alpacian steed. Muscled and thick, with stubby wings meant for low-level fighting and scaled hides near-impossible to pierce, the domesticated wyrm hybrids had been bred for strength and stamina.

Combined with the skill of the Asgardian warriors they were absolutely lethal. And now they hunted the inhabitants of Shadoria.

Ice stung her veins. If the Death Raiders reached the city again—

That will never happen. Never.

A sword of blinding-white lightning emblazoned the sky, momentarily crippling the Asgardian's night vision. She counted to three, timing her attack with the earth-shattering crack of thunder that followed. The warriors protecting the portal neither saw nor heard Haven until her longsword tasted their blood.

A regular sword would have barely penetrated their flesh. But the rare *night ash* blade—forged from demon-fire and infused with raven's blood—turned their immortal flesh as soft as the ripened moon pears that permeated the island.

Three died immediately, crumpling to the ground in the eerie silence that followed the thunder.

The last two managed to throw up their iron shields, deflecting her powerful blows. Each shield was decorated with an image of the male's first dragon mount.

Metal clanged against metal in time with the booming thunder. The impact exploded up her wrist and arm, the pain slamming the breath from her lungs and keeping her sharp.

She ducked as the deathly-fine edge of an axe whistled through the air. A prickle of adrenaline warmed her chest and ratcheted her heart into a pounding rhythm.

Bjorn had kept his own axe honed to a killing edge. Memories of what it had done to the muscled, leathery body of Shadowlings surfaced . . .

Not for the first time, she cursed her mortal flesh and bones. If one thing was certain about this whole prophecy, it was that being called the descendant of a Goddess while being caged in a frail mortal body was cruel.

The air whined, and she pivoted sideways as the axe blade flashed beside her cheek, severing a long strand of rose-gold hair. A second later and her head would have been rolling over the sand instead.

Pushing the grim thought away, she danced out of their reach, laughing, drawing them closer. The waves crashed at their back. A timid rain fell, wetting their armor and hair and making a soft pattering song in the sand.

Satisfied that without the element of surprise, she no longer posed a threat, the Asgardians lowered their brutish weapons to their waist.

After all, she was worth more to them alive than dead.

That was Archeron's first mistake. She would never let herself become a slave again. Never.

TWO

H er nostrils flared as she quickly studied the males. They were towering, beyond seven feet in height, and most certainly Death Raiders turned cutthroats for hire. Tongues of their famed green light magick licked and crackled around them, scenting the stormy air with roses and myrrh.

Her sword hand spasmed tighter. Like Bjorn, both were handsome, almost God-like. Their flesh the color of dark Ashari pearls. Their light magick bursting from their mythical forms and dancing over their alluring visages as they closed in.

Just like she wanted them too.

That was Archeron's second mistake. Using battle-hardened Asgardians whose huge egos made them easy to lull into a false sense of power.

Her mortality meant they would never see her as a true threat.

"So this is the Shadeling's bastard," the tallest Asgardian said. There was no malice in his voice. No hatred. Only a cold, disdainful curiosity as his peridot green eyes, the same color as his magick, raked over her. "You're no descendant of the Goddess. I can sense your ruinous aura from here, infected with Odin's darkness."

The words scraped open an old wound. Haven fought against the rush of pain as Archeron's words whispered across the storm-winds. *Killing you is an act of mercy. I am saving you from what you would become.*

"You might be right." A taunting smile played over her face as she twirled her sword in a circle, her chest bubbling with anticipation. The edges of her cloak curled around her legs, buffeted by the wind. Strips of her rose-gold hair clawed across her cheeks and forehead, painted ashen-pink by the portal's light. "But if you call off your riders and leave now, that darkness will stay locked away, and that's a mercy you do not deserve."

The greedy thing inside her raged at the thought of letting them escape. She could feel it swelling against her breastbone, tapping and clawing and begging for release.

Every ounce of her power was used to keep it chained. If she spared them, if she could convince them somehow to join her and the others against Archeron and the Shadeling . . .

"And why would you offer such generous terms?" A taunting humor dripped from the closest Death Raider's words.

"Because the Shadeling is coming. And when he reaches your kingdom, it won't matter how many runestones and gold line your pockets." The tendons of his thick neck corded at the mention of the Shadeling, and she allowed herself a whisper of hope as she added, "We need allies to fight against him. Together, our nations could stand a chance against the invasion."

"Children of Freya and Odin and man together? Under your poisonous rule?" The Asgardian's laugh boomed across the beach, the axe blade reflecting the green flames circling him as he twirled it. "Even if the Sun Sovereign wasn't offering a hundred powerrunes for your capture, you would still be my enemy, you blasphemous bitch."

Anger coiled inside her. She expected the Solis resistance. The hostility and distrust. But not to this degree. Archeron was spreading tales of her trickery, claiming she was involved in the attack on Solethenia. That she did it all to steal the Godkiller.

No wonder they despised her.

Biting back a frustrated growl, she ground out, "Enemy or not, I offer more mercy than the Shadeling will."

"Every word you spew reeks of treachery. You claim to be descended from the Goddess, but your flesh is mortal and your magick twisted by your dark Noctis lover. The Sun Sovereign is right; you're an abomination and the deceiver's weapon. If the Sun King did not want to wield you himself, I would kill you where you stand."

The word Archeron used against her awoke the near-constant thorn of agony buried deep in her heart. *Abomination.*

She flexed her shoulders to hide the discomfort, forcing out a calming breath. "He's offering one hundred powerrunes now? He must be getting desperate."

She shifted her gaze to the other Asgardian. Perhaps he would think differently . . . his sneer shattered the last remnants of hope she had for an alliance.

A cold, vengeful part of her was glad.

There would be no talk of alliance tonight.

No mercy.

Only death.

The screams from earlier eddied around her mind. Innocent people slain. *Her* people terrified and slaughtered, and for what?

She could feel herself changing. Feel her light magick smoldering. She met the Asgardian's haughty stare, taking satisfaction in the flicker of fear that sparked behind his peridot eyes.

They both felt the darkness inside her awaken, stretching out its tendrils of power as she loosened her hold over it.

Her lips tipped up in a grin.

"Why are you smiling?" Sand crunched as the nearest male slowly drew closer. Centuries of defending the floating city of Tyr, of being heralded as legendary warriors who fought against the Noctis in the Shadow Wars, made him foolishly disregard the power he'd sensed. "Or are you enjoying the thought of what the Sun Sovereign is going to do to you?"

"Mortal whore," the other one spat. "No daughter of the Goddess would be in league with the Lord of the Netherworld, nor be foolish enough to stumble right into Death Raiders' arms."

Warmth kissed her palm, sending golden light dancing over the sloping steel of his breastplate. His eyes flicked lazily down to the magick dancing just above her fingers as he slid to the left, the fluid stealth with which he moved driving home these were Sun Lords, powerful ones. Used to killing monsters bigger and scarier than her with ease.

Well, if that's what they were used to . . .

Distracted by her light magick, both males missed the faint flicker of fiery blue twining between her fingertips. And when they did see it, see what it was becoming . . . when their eyes stretched into all white orbs of surprise and then filled with fear—it was too late.

Serpentine shadows writhed and churned around the Asgardians, a cruel cage greedily devouring their light magick. Sucking it from them with startling efficiency.

The portal guttered and then died, its magick feeding her monster.

Their skin turned ashen and sickly as they swung their weapons. Over and over and over. Slicing uselessly at the dark magick that was slowly, methodically killing them.

She could see it in their desperate faces: they knew their fate was sealed. They would die on this rocky coast for the promise of powerrunes and greed.

Their eyes jerked wide as the shifting obsidian cage began to change.

Solidifying as its sinewy body curled outward, tendrils of darkness sprouting into the air.

Something about its intelligent movements were different than all the times she'd practiced this trick before.

What in the Netherworld?

A strange panic skipped in her chest. Despite the cool storm winds, a trickle of sweat slid between her shoulder blades as she watched her dark magick take shape, torn between fascination and horror.

It was becoming something. Stretching and pulsing through the air, limbs slowly appearing from the nebulous shadows—

Goddess Above.

Stolas had warned her there was a small chance this could happen, but seeing it now . . . the terrible brutality seeping from its form . . .

She stumbled back as shards of ice burrowed into her core.

Every Seraphian had a Shadow Familiar, a creature born of dark magick that eventually manifested itself outside its host. The third night here, during Archeron's first wave of attack on the island, Haven had spotted a massive shadow blotting out the stars as it circled the night sky.

Its bellows were loud enough to wake the entire city.

Assuming the thing was sent by Archeron, she'd alerted Stolas.

Only to discover it was Nasira's Shadow Familiar, a firedrake dragon.

And that's when Stolas had mentioned the possibility that Haven might also have a familiar. He'd said it so casually that she had assumed the possibility was dismal at best.

Which is why she hadn't paid much attention when he explained what that meant.

In his words, the moment she entered the shores of Shadoria, if the Shadeling had passed on the same gift to her, the sacred transition might be awoken.

Whenever she had entertained the possibility, her mind had conjured a sleek, beautiful dragon, ferocious yet majestic.

This—this thing growing before her eyes was anything but majestic.

She shuddered as a long snout sprouted from a massive head, the darkness condensing into legs and talons and a serpentine tail that whipped with enough force to crack boulders. Skeletal wings sprouted from its misshapen back and sent shadows skittering across the sand. Horns grew and twisted like snakes all over its muscular body.

Bellowing snarls ripped from the crooked, bent creature, the gut-curdling sounds straight from the Netherworld.

She tried to wet her lips but discovered her mouth dry as sand.

How could that . . . thing be a part of her?

The grotesque entity hesitated, waiting for a command.

She could feel its thirst for blood warring with its need to please her. Its primordial desire for pain and destruction tempered by its desire to obey.

But that hold she had over it was fraying every second she waited. She knew she could end them herself. Could wrap them in suffocating darkness.

They wouldn't feel pain.

Their death would be quick.

But she didn't *want* to end them quickly. There had to be consequences for what they had done.

She wasn't aware she'd made a decision until it surged across that tenuous tether between her and the monstrous creature. With a pleased growl, the beast lifted over the Death Raiders, an amalgamation of Haven's nightmares.

Her every terror, every buried fear set free to form this sadistic, loathsome thing.

"What in the name of the holy Goddess are you?" the closest Asgardian shrieked as he swung his weapon again and again, blind to the wasted effort.

Haven wished she knew. There was supposed to be some

distinguishable form but—she would worry about that later.

The Asgardian's panicked eyes latched onto hers. "Mercy, Goddess-Born!"

Haven felt nothing as she said, "I offered you mercy, but you refused. I offered you peace, but you chose death. Now every one of your men will follow you to the Netherworld."

It was true. With the portal closed to reinforcements, the Death Raiders were doomed. Even now, their wounded and dying dragons crashed into the sea all around them. Their dying screeches reverberated off the cliff walls and tugged at her heart.

It didn't have to be this way. The dragons were only doing their masters bidding, but the Asgardians had been given a choice.

They chose wrong.

She waited until the last Asgardian and his mount death-spiraled across the stars and disappeared into the black ocean. Only once the Asgardians knew that the last of their men would die with them, once that haunting finality made them drop their weapons, did she fully unleash her spectral beast.

She felt nothing as it descended on the males. Nothing as their screams began.

Nothing as the cry of snapped metal and bone pierced the night.

But she had to turn away when they pleaded to the Goddess for mercy.

Mercy they'd refused from her. Spat back at her like poison.

She focused on the storm in the distance as the familiar pang of doubt nagged at her.

Perhaps the prophecy was wrong.

Perhaps she wasn't born of the Goddess, only the Shadeling, and the monk saw what he wanted to see.

Perhaps *she* only saw what she wanted to see.

Why else had her mother never tried to reach out to her?

Perhaps what Haven offered wasn't mercy, but a fool's errand. An impossible idea. The mortal, Noctis, and Solis nations had warred since the dawn of time.

What made her think she could unite them when even Freya had failed?

Something—a twinge in her belly, a dance of shadow across the cliff's jagged face—dragged her attention to the dark shape landing softly on a nearby boulder.

Bright red eyes pulsed from the shadows. Stolas. Something also told her he'd been watching her for a while.

Her devoted protector looked every bit the predator as he crouched low, his glorious dark wings crowning the sky, his moon-white wavy hair in sharp contrast to his midnight-black armor. His lips curved with pride as he took in the beast she'd created.

As if recognizing another monster, her dark magick lifted its nebulous black head from its gluttonous feeding to watch the dark prince.

Gravely wounded, the surviving Asgardian dragged himself across the sand until he met the cliff wall. Trapped, his panicked gaze darted between the magickal monster and the real one.

Both were equally bloodthirsty—and equally hers.

THREE

Stolas drew a quick rune, the electric blue lines sizzling in the air, and the dark beast became a nebulous mist that funneled painlessly back inside her.

Rage slaked, she turned to him, surprised to find she was breathing hard.

Stolas tucked his wings tight to his body as he leapt gracefully from the boulder and prowled toward her. A jagged black crown rose from his white locks, the only indication of his status.

Otherwise, he wore the same standard issue armor as the rest of the Seraphian sentinels that patrolled these skies, every inch of the once glossy material covered in blood and gore.

"Beastie." His voice was soft, gentle, tempering the otherwise overwhelming savagery that poured from his being. The red circling his irises faded as concern flickered in those silver depths. "Is this the first time your Shadow Familiar has tried to form?"

She nodded as she worked to hide her unease. Familiars were

supposed to resemble animal forms. Stolas and his mother both had dire wolf familiars. The rest of the Darkshade line were gifted dragon familiars similar to Nasira's firedrake.

Yet knowing hadn't made it any less unsettling. Especially considering the terrifying form her beast had taken. If children with dark magick inherited their Shadow Familiars from their parents, that meant hers came directly from the Shadeling himself.

"Give it time," Stolas said, his soft command cutting through her fears. "Sometimes your familiar takes months to commit to its final shape. In the meantime we must work to draw it out slowly, let the bond between you strengthen."

Despite his gentle tone, his mouth was tight. After Stolas had warned her of the possibility she might have a familiar, she'd teased him about his until she caught the suppressed pain in his eyes.

His simple explanation—that his was dormant—wasn't the whole story, but she hadn't pushed for more.

He would tell her when he was ready.

"So you're saying there's a chance I won't have something living inside me that looks like the spawn of Lorrack and a demon?" she quipped, keeping her voice low in case it could hear her.

"I am saying, Beastie, that whatever creature your familiar decides to manifest, it will be a part of you and therefore exquisite."

She swallowed, desperate for another subject. "The blockade?"

"We sank four ships, but the attack here called us back."

Haven felt her shoulders sag as the realization took hold. "They were waiting for you to attack the ships. It was a ruse to draw you away from the island."

As she said the words, icy fingers seemed to squeeze around her spine. It was like Archeron was one step ahead of them. He had the power and wealth of the mighty Sun Court behind him while they were a struggling nation of outcasts.

A nation that had nearly perished tonight. If the Death Raiders had broken through their defenses and entered the city . . .

Stolas brushed an errant strand of her hair behind her ear. "When was the last time you actually slept?"

"I'm fine."

"Or ate for that matter?"

Her jaw flexed. "We're all busy. Besides, I don't recall seeing you scarfing down food in the meal hall."

The strong column of his throat dipped, and too late, she remembered why. "I don't require the same *kind* of sustenance as you."

Kind. Right. Because he did require sustenance, just not mortal food.

When he was Lord of the Netherworld, he had a vast array of souls to feed from. But here . . . well she hadn't built up the nerve yet to ask how he was satisfying those needs.

"I'll eat afterward," she promised, the lie hovering between them.

He arched an ash-colored brow, his eyes flashing as if he wanted to argue further, but then he simply said, "I thought King Bell ordered you safe and protected inside the north tower?"

"Ordered?" she scoffed, ignoring the way his teasing voice gathered low and hot in her belly. "I think you know better than anyone how well I respond to commands."

His grin was devastating. "Indeed." His attention slipped to her lips as he traced a finger over the fine edge of her jaw. "Just as your King Bell should know by now that you could never hide behind tower walls while innocents are being slaughtered."

Her throat clenched. "How many?"

The planes of his face sharpened with controlled anger, and she wondered what it would be like to experience the unleashed version of that infinite rage. "We've found ten houses so far."

Houses. Not people. He was trying to shield her from the details. Trying to make this easier for her.

But she didn't want easy.

"How *many?*"

"Twenty-three." The muscles beneath his temples trembled as he looked beyond her to the edge of the city, where people still hunkered behind their walls and the illusion of safety. "But there will be more."

"Children?"

His throat bobbed. "Nine. Four of which came from one house. Only the father survived, but by the look in his face, I doubt he'll live much long after."

An ache formed beneath her sternum, guilt and shame and anger converging into a cold, hollow mass. "And the other city quadrants?"

The cities set into the mountains at the base of the palace were split into quadrants, each with its own watchtower and wards. If this one had been attacked, she assumed the others had as well.

"Nasira took out the portal near the southern tower. Bell and Xandrian handled the east. Surai and Ember the north."

The fury-edged pain in his eyes made her look away. She didn't dare ask how many casualties for the other quarters. She would learn soon enough when she visited the grieving families later today.

A bone-weary fatigue came over her. Each night brought new terrors. Each attack was worse than the last. The feeling of total failure threatened to overcome her.

Dragging the hair back from her forehead, she slid her gaze to the Asgardian raider where he slumped against the cliff's base.

"What will you do with him?" Stolas asked, a wicked gleam in his eyes as he shifted his stare to the Asgardian. There was a tightening around Stolas's mouth, a delicate flaring of his nostrils as he took in the wounded male's scent.

A scent no doubt permeated with fear.

The silver of Stolas's eyes darkened as the red glow began to throb, a soft growling purr vibrating his throat.

The fine hair at the nape of her neck lifted. If she had any doubt what the red color meant, the beastly growl dispelled them.

The night's battle had left him with a deep, unrelenting hunger.

As soon as Stolas's attention fell on the wounded male, fear tugged at his pain-wrenched face.

Haven stepped over the corpses of his brethren as she approached the male, whose eyes remained firmly on Stolas behind her.

"What would you do?" Haven asked the ravenous prince, never taking her eyes off the Asgardian. "Offer mercy?"

A dark chuckle. "As I recall, he rejected your mercy. Rather rudely."

So Stolas *had* been watching.

"Please." Blood trickled from the Death Raider's lips as he begged. "It was nothing personal. I . . . I was only following orders."

Haven stared down at him. Before Shadoria, before she carried the heavy burden of her lineage and the prophecy, she might have ordered him bandaged and healed. Might have tried again to stubbornly broker an alliance.

Before the deaths of her people, she might have even naïvely thought saving him would convince the realm she was good.

But her goodness wouldn't keep her people safe. Only fear would do that.

If they were expecting the Shadeling's daughter, she might as well play the part. "Was it personal when your raiders slaughtered the children sleeping in their beds?"

Fear sparked inside his eyes. "Those were . . ."

"A transaction?" Her fingers clenched and unclenched at her sides. "How much did you say he paid for each death again?"

His chest heaved with ragged breaths. "That wasn't—"

"Personal?"

He blinked.

She looked to Stolas. Her protector. Her friend. And, yes, in every sense of the word, a monster. But she was starting to learn there were very different kinds of monsters.

Once, she would have shied away from his nature. From the hunger she recognized inside his eyes as he drank in the Asgardian. The spark of *excitement* similar to a cat watching a wounded bird.

After draining his dark magick in battle, he would be ravenous for light magick.

"Tell the Sun Sovereign and the fools tempted by his offers that death awaits anyone who comes here uninvited. Tell him—" Her throat tightened as she remembered Archeron as he once had been, wounded— but full of hope. "Tell him that we don't have to be enemies."

Realizing he was being spared death, the Asgardian raider relaxed against the stone wall and closed his eyes. "I will. Now, please. I am bleeding out. I need a healer."

Haven turned on her heels to go.

"Wait. Don't leave me with him. He's a—"

"Monster?" Haven finished before meeting Stolas's stare.

Stolas's eyes flared wide with surprise as he realized she was letting him *fully* off his leash.

A wicked grin brightened his face, showing off ivory fangs she'd only glimpsed a few times before. He'd always been so careful to hide this side of himself from her.

To protect her from it.

But she refused to avert her gaze, to cringe from the primordial instincts that were part of him.

Another flicker of surprise—followed by a vulnerable emotion she didn't dare name.

But whatever passed between them, it was almost instantly devoured by the beast he let himself become. His pupils elongated into thin, feline slashes, his fingers unsheathing black talons.

That hungry gaze fixed on his prey. "Did you think you could sneak uninvited into my kingdom, the sacred home of my ancestors, and there would be no consequences? That you could murder children sleeping in their beds without facing my wrath?"

The wild terror in the Asgardian's half-rolled back eyes reminded Haven how truly feared Stolas was. Those glassy eyes shifted to Haven. "Please, Goddess-Born. Not him."

"So it's Goddess-Born now? What was it you called her before?" Stolas's voice came out in a low, rumbling snarl more beast than human. "A mortal whore?"

"No. I will carry your message to the Sun Sovereign—"

"I have my own message for the Sun Lord, but you may not like what it says."

Even Haven had the good sense to still as Stolas quietly glided toward the Asgardian.

The male began to pray. Stolas was silent, wholly focused on the hunt. The low, purring growl he made reminded Haven of the feral stable cats in Penryth after they'd been thrown leftover pheasant legs.

How long can I play with him? Stolas drawled into her mind.

As long as you want. Just . . . keep him alive enough to relay my message. Is that . . . possible?

Possible, yes. With the right amount of control. Although he will be ruined for anything beyond that simple task.

Haven didn't even want to know what that entailed.

A pause and then Stolas murmured, *Thank you.*

She nearly laughed at the façade. As if she could deign to give him permission for anything. He could take what he wanted, when he wanted. Especially here, in his own lands, where his powers thrived so strongly that sometimes she felt his roiling magick all the way on the other side of the castle, a living, breathing creature.

His insistence that she command him was for ceremony, to convince the world—or herself—that she was a descendant of the Goddess.

But his gratitude wasn't for her permission. In the Netherworld, he'd had a steady supply of souls to meet his needs, and she was never confronted with his dark hunger or the actual act.

He thanked her because she had recognized his hunger and hadn't cringed from it.

Truthfully, a part of her was curious how the draining of light magick worked. What it looked like. Felt like.

She knew from previous conversations that Stolas could make the act pleasurable, almost euphoric—if he wanted.

But when he didn't . . .

She made it barely twenty feet before the first scream began. And it continued until she was out of earshot.

FOUR

B y the time Haven trudged to the dining hall for a quick, tasteless meal of tepid oats, washed down by a scalding cup of ale, her weariness ran soul deep.

The hours after the attack raced past in a numb blur. There was so much to do before the approach of night and threat of new attacks. The wards inside the towers had to be checked, the weakened ones reinforced. Centuries before, during the Darkshade reign, the towers drew their power from the eternal demon fires that had been gifted by the Demon Lords.

But the fires had long since guttered out, and the ancient runes carved into the dark stone towers were eroded, worn away by the battering waves and ferocious storms surrounding the island.

The few rune scholars on the island spent their days and nights in the subterranean libraries below the city, scouring every ancient tome for the proper spells to fortify the wards once more—but less than half had been discovered.

Which meant every night when the silvery, ethereal light that blanketed Shadoria drained behind the Ravenite Mountains, fresh horrors followed.

And every morning in that magickal hour of dawn when the Goddess's light spilled over the mist-shrouded city, Haven forced her tired body through the streets to visit the families of the dead.

There was the cobbler's son, newly married with a baby on the way. The elderly couple who had been together for nearly sixty years. The family of six, slaughtered before they could leave the bed they all shared. They were still wrapped around each other as if sleeping, legs and arms entwined around the woolen covers.

Haven had rushed from the stone dwelling overlooking a dilapidated courtyard, disturbed not just by their tragic deaths, but by the way they had lived. The easy love that was evident in the way the mother held the eldest daughter close to her chest, the two youngest boys clinging to their father's legs.

A warm, familial love Haven would never know.

It was in that moment, surrounded by the leftover carnage from the night, the crush of citizens who'd come out to see her, their eyes still somehow, *somehow* adoring despite her utter failure to protect them, that Haven felt more alone than she ever had before.

Every offering they'd tried to press into her bloodstained hands, every precious herb or beloved trinket or bit of coin they tried to gift her felt like a lie.

Pulling her cloak over her head, she'd fled to the palace, hoping a meal would ease the hollow gnawing in her breast. Thankfully the long communal tables where the Seraphian sentinels and the rest of the Chosen ate were near empty. With her unusual rose-gold hair hidden, and the iridescent fleshrunes that mapped her skin covered beneath layers of clothing, the one table of soldiers hardly spared her a second glance.

She ate in silence. Even if the soggy, watered down oats were quite possibly the foulest thing she'd ever tasted, the food helped.

When was the last time she'd eaten? Or had a full night's sleep for that matter?

It was easy to forget she was mortal when the world seemed to be crashing down around her daily.

Her silver spoon scraped the bottom of her bowl. A rumble in her belly demanded more, but the need to wash the sweat and gore from the morning won out.

The sulfurous tang of the communal baths wafted through the corridors as she neared the huge chambers. The large rectangular pools were fed from the hot springs that traversed the island, the steaming water a crisp, inviting teal.

Her eyebrows gathered as she took in the amount of soldiers in the first pool, their laughter reverberating through the high-ceilinged chamber.

The baths were busy today.

No surprise. After each grueling attack, the Seraphians and Chosen needed time to unwind. The bathhouses were nothing like the clear, winding pools of the Sun Court. Rivers deep inside the island's core fed the irregularly shaped pools. The dark teal waters were revered for their healing properties, but it was the subtle shimmer of magick sparking across its steaming surface that enticed Haven.

Her boots splashed through the puddles pooled on the stone floor as she crossed to the second bath, where the Solis and members of the Order of Soltari congregated.

Silence overtook the light din of voices as she passed, trying not to make eye contact. The reverence in their faces always left her feeling unsettled.

Unworthy.

The final bathhouse was the smallest, its winding pool set deep into the glassy-smooth black stone that made up most of the island. Beastly creatures were carved into the face of the towering columns supporting the roof. Beyond those columns was a breathtaking view. The Ravenite Mountains a jagged cutout of obsidian and cream on one side; the ferocious Obsidian Sea on the other.

"Haven!" a familiar voice called, dragging her from the fog of battle and death.

As Haven took in Bellamy's features, his easy smile and vibrant topaz eyes, a weight lifted from her tight shoulders. Surai and Ember were with him, deeply engaged in a conversation Haven couldn't hear. The water's magick glistened off their skin and seemed to irradiate the intricate web of runemarks covering their muscled flesh.

Bell splashed at her as she approached. He was leaned against the side of the pool, basking in a rare beam of sunshine streaming through a skylight. The steam had loosened his curls so that his hair fell tousled and wild to one side.

A bruise was already darkening his high cheekbone, and more mapped his upper chest and back, along with a nasty cut on his shoulder.

The wound had already closed under the healing water's touch, the angry red line fading into his taupe skin. It was said the magickal properties of the hot springs came from deep within the earth, leeching from the same source that created the crystals.

"I hope the other guy looks worse," she remarked as she stripped off her boots, pants, and finally her tunic. Surai looked up from her conversation, her lips tilting at the corners as she saw Haven's reluctance to shed her underclothes.

Everyone else was fully naked, even Bell. But Haven had yet to acclimate to the Seraphian custom of bathing together daily.

Only the royal Seraphians had their own bathing chambers, smaller versions of this set high atop the palace. Stolas had offered Haven his . . . but the others already looked at her differently.

Special privileges would only widen that chasm she felt slowly yawning between them.

Ember's tawny cheeks were mottled and red from the heat, and they lifted beneath her grin as she took in Haven's underclothes. "Why hide the body the Goddess gave you?"

Ever protective, Surai cut her eyes at Ember. "Mortals teach their women to be ashamed of their bodies."

Ember didn't appear surprised at the explanation, but she didn't remark further on it.

Ignoring them both, Haven sunk into the water's blissfully warm embrace. A moan fled her lips as the heat worked its way into her muscles. Her eyelids dragged shut.

Bell chuckled beside her. "The look on your face is the same one you have when you eat sticky buns."

"If only the Seraphians made those." She sank deeper into the water, resting her head on the edge of the pool. One eye slid open. "So your magick worked then?"

"You should have seen me." Pride sparked inside his bright blue eyes. "I mean, Xandrian was there the whole time, and my threading was a disaster—even with help from my acrum. But I used a fire spell *and* managed to nick one of the Asgardians with my dagger."

Behind Bell, Ember and Surai forced back grins. Bragging about nicking an enemy in battle must seem so silly to warriors such as them.

Surai tweaked his ear. "Careful being such a badass or they'll write songs about your exploits."

"I bet they already have with these muscles," Haven teased, squeezing his arm. Bell would never be huge, but his training had reshaped his slender body, coaxing out muscles she never knew he had.

A sheepish grin brightened his face. She could almost see his happiness seeping across the water and into her breast, thawing the cold fist that seemed permanently wrapped around her heart.

Bell was flourishing under Xandrian's expert tutelage, but it wasn't just his runecasting that had improved. The Sun Lord's swordplay lessons focused on Bell's innate talents—agility and speed—a sharp contrast to his father's stubborn insistence that Bell learn to fight using brute strength.

His magick was coming along slower than he'd like, but according to Xandrian, for a mortal from the House Nine, that was to be expected. His magick had been dormant for years. Once they narrowed down his type of power, it would be easier.

"I heard you destroyed a portal," Bell remarked, and Haven stiffened, remembering the Asgardians' screams. "I thought we agreed you would stay inside the tower, where you're protected?"

"I agreed that the tower was the safest place for me, but I never promised to stay there during an attack."

"Smartass." Bell rolled his eyes.

"Droob."

"If the monk were here, you would stay put."

"Possibly," she admitted, cringing as she imagined the disappointed way he would quietly stare at her, his judgment cutting in its silence. If it were up to the monk, she would be in the temple every waking hour, praying for direction from the Goddess. "When he returns, maybe don't mention last night?"

The monk—they still had yet to learn a name—was traveling around Solissia gathering Order of Soltari recruits.

"I made an oath, Haven." The grooves around his mouth deepened as his voice grew solemn. "An oath to protect you. So let me. You know what would happen if Archeron captures you . . ."

Surai's face darkened. "We no longer use that name. It belonged to my brother-in-arms, and he's passed to the Nihl."

"The new *Sun Sovereign*," Bell corrected, "won't stop until he has Haven. If I was ruler of Penryth, I could offer her more protection—"

A muscle in Bell's jaw ticked, and she noticed how his fingers curled and uncurled at the mention of his stolen kingdom. "Until we hear back from the emissaries, this island remains too unprotected."

They'd sent out emissaries over two weeks ago to every corner of the realm. All of Haven's hopes rested on building alliances, hopes that deteriorated more and more each day the emissaries failed to return.

Surai's face was achingly empty of emotion as she said, "Every one of us would die before we let him take her."

Ember arched an eyebrow, the teasing gesture so painfully similar to Rook's that Haven's breath caught. "If only the new Sun Sovereign had enough peach-fuzz on those little balls of his to come to Shadoria instead of sending hired mercenaries."

Haven tried to smile at the joke, but the wounds Archeron had left were still too fresh. Every mention of him dragged his face to the surface.

His arrogant smile. His rich, always teasing voice. That fiery hope he'd always carried inside him to chase away the unrelenting darkness.

Little Mortal.

The air around her thinned. Her chest heaved as she tried to drag in a breath, the world spinning in loose, jarring circles. Despite the sweltering heat, a deep aching chill slithered along her bones and settled beneath her sternum.

Do you still love me now that I am no longer beautiful?

Her teeth slammed together as the bland oats from earlier threatened to come up. Eyes watering, she dunked her hands into the water to hide their shaking and looked out into the onyx stretch of sea.

Haven had never felt such deep shame as she did now.

Everyone had suffered the last few months. Surai had lost her mate and brother-in-arms. Bell's father had been murdered, his kingdom and title stolen. Xandrian had committed treason against the Sun Court when he chose to follow her here, and now faced a lifetime of being hunted by his own kingdom. Even Ember had been disavowed by her mother, her title to the throne stripped.

Yet they all remained strong. Disciplined. Uncomplaining.

Only Haven seemed unable to fight off the pain—pain that sometimes felt like waves of agony slowly drowning her.

Her inability to push past the trauma and wounds inflicted in Solethenia was a weakness, an insult to her friends.

She vowed to do better.

The delicate lines of Surai's forehead softened as she watched Haven quietly struggle to compose herself. Haven might be able to mask her emotions from Bell, but Surai had lived thousands of years, and the annoyingly clever Ashari scout picked up on everything.

"The Archeron we knew died when he broke the dark magick tethering his soul to the king's," Surai said softly. "Remember that this . . . tyrant who kills innocents and hunts us down like dogs is not him." Surai ran a hand down her glossy black hair, fiddling with the ends as her eyes darkened to amethyst. "If we ever meet again, I will not hesitate to end him."

After that, the talk moved to lighter subjects, and Haven tried to at least *look* like she was enjoying herself. But she couldn't stop thinking about Archeron.

Every night in Haven's dreams, the Sun Lord appeared. Sometimes he was gentle, kissing her lips and teasing her as he promised not to hurt her—if only she would come back to him.

Sometimes he said nothing, just watching her from the shadows. On the worst nights, he whispered how he would hunt down and murder each of her friends until she gave herself to him.

And every morning she woke with the memory of ramming the Godkiller into his chest.

But no matter how many times she plunged that dagger through his heart, no matter how many times she unleashed her fury on the Sun Lord, he always returned, a haunting specter of the man she once nearly loved.

FIVE

Dusk came as it did every night to Shadoria in an explosion of mauve and tangerine. In the hour before the sun rose and set, the normally silvery half-glow of the island became a breathtaking display of the most brilliant, most ethereal light Haven had ever seen. The dark amethyst crystals embedded in the natural obsidian of the island lit up like jagged sparks flickering over the ashen landscape.

The Seraphians called these two periods of delicate, shimmering light—when the sun shone beneath the layer of clouds and fog above the city—the hour of the soul.

According to their culture, that was when the old Gods could hear their voices. Before their fall, the Seraphian people spent those hours in the temples dotting the highest mountain peaks, praying to those long dead entities.

Haven could almost believe the Gods listened, especially inside Stolas's favorite temple, built for Odin's aunt and their namesake, Seraphina. Like most of the buildings here, the temple had been carved from the mountainside, a collection of slender black towers with open windows that all connected to a high-domed center.

The towers had long collapsed, leaving only the husk of walls like the snapped bones of an animal sticking up from the snow. By the Goddess's luck, the dome of the temple where Haven trained with Stolas remained intact—mostly. The far end of the ceiling had collapsed, and snow blew in from the mountaintops and collected in the ruined stairs that wound through the cavernous structure.

It seemed only fitting that Stolas's favorite place on the island was atop the highest mountain, impossible to reach without wings, and hidden from view by a magickal ward still etched across the dark stone floors.

Of course, that's where he would insist on training every evening. Although training was a mild term to describe the dangerous dance they performed.

"Stolas?" she murmured as the darkness inside her stirred. A startling combination of anticipation and primal fear worked its way into her chest, more potent than the aching cold.

Haven's boots squeaked over a dilapidated set of spiraling stairs that halted ten feet above the ground, as if a giant had scooped out the bottom half. Shafts of glorious light spilled from the temple windows into the space below, refracting off the glassy crystals embedded in the high walls.

Every evening, Stolas had a secret portal created just for her that took her from her tower to the mountaintop. She never knew the exact location it would lead.

Only that once she stepped through to the other side, she had to be ready.

Thighs bunching, she leapt from the final stair and landed hard on the stone floor. Snow collected in the corners. Her breath came out in cloudy puffs. Other than the muted howling of the wind outside, silence reigned.

A rush of air was the only warning of Stolas's attack. An orb of golden light was ready on her palm by the time she whipped to meet him, her cloak swirling around her legs and sword held high. Flames of magick rushed down the steel in an impressive whoosh.

A cruel smile carved Stolas's angular jaw, nearly distracting her from the onslaught of shadowy magick rushing at her face.

The fiery orb she released to counter his attack guttered out along with the flames of her sword.

"Focus," he demanded. "Use your dark magick to protect your light."

She tried again, but the flames of her powers died before she could fully wrap it in darkness. He was feeding off it. Devouring every bit of magick she conjured.

A wave of anger rose up inside her. Anger at herself. At her pain. Her inability to protect the people in the city below. At Archeron. Her father.

The whole damned world.

A blast of light wrapped in darkness exploded from her fingers, serpents of ink and gold slithering toward the Shade Lord. He slipped sideways, the ease of his movements infuriating. The magick slammed into the dark wall behind him, rattling the temple and cracking in the icy air.

Stolas grinned in delight as bits of stone and snow rained down over them.

"Better. Next time actually hit me."

Sword held high, she lunged for the Shade Lord. Steel flashed. He waited until her weapon was a hair's breadth from meeting his body. Waited until she felt the rush of triumph followed by the sting of fear . . .

Before gliding just out of reach again. Still wearing that infuriatingly wicked smile. Still moving with that impossible fluidity and otherworldly grace.

He moved so fast she lost track of him. She whirled, cloak tangling her ankles, boots slipping on the wet floor.

Where are you?

She was going to rip him apart with her bare hands—

"There's the Beastie I know." His cool breath shivered against her neck from behind. She snarled as she pivoted to face him—

A rush of wing beats and he was gliding in the shafts of plum-tinged light above. Lightning bolts of magick flashed toward her.

She dove, rolled over her shoulder, and uncoiled to her feet. Only to dive again as his powers crackled over her, whispering death against her mortal skin.

"Come back down here and face me," she growled, spittle dotting her lips, "or are you afraid?"

A dark chuckle echoed off the high ceiling. "Careful what you wish for, Beastie."

They fell into a steady rhythm of lunges and magick, steel and fury, as she stormed after him, this Lord of Darkness, and he flickered just out of reach—a taunting shadow.

She knew what he was doing. She'd figured out early on that the training sessions weren't just to advance her magick.

They were an outlet. For her magick, her rage and grief.

But admitting that also meant admitting he picked up on her emotions. That he was fine-tuned to her moods despite the hundred other things that occupied his attention.

Rebuilding his home. Fixing the wards. Smuggling food past Archeron's blockade. Taming Nasira. Working to create order and ranks and purpose again in the Seraphians sentinels, many of whom were physically broken from countless years of slavery and torture. Their wings hobbled and warped. Eyes blinded. Tongues carved out.

Those were the lucky ones. The Seraphian citizens whose small wings had made them ineligible as soldiers were used as servants to the Noctis. Their wounds were on the inside, invisible, but when Haven passed them in the halls, she always felt a chill at the emptiness in their eyes.

Every one of those things plus a thousand more occupied Stolas's entire being. She wasn't even sure he'd slept since they arrived.

And yet, he carved out precious time he didn't have to help her work out her pain.

A low growl dragged her focus to Stolas's leg . . . sweeping toward her feet. Her sword jerked from her fingers and clattered across the floor. She tumbled backward.

A column knocked the air from her lungs.

Before she could move, he claimed the space between them. Reminding her that he owned every bit of this land from the tallest peak to the caverns below.

His arms pinned on either side of her face, a sinewy cage of muscle and dark, glittering magick. It was times like this that she remembered just how much bigger he was than her. His body taut with untamed power.

Diaphanous light ran down the length of his onyx horns and caught in his feathers, coaxing out a rainbow of colors that stole her breath.

"You are distracted." His accusation hung between them.

"No."

"You have been since we arrived." His ash-colored eyebrows gathered above yellow-rimmed silver eyes, his bowed lips softening. His concern for her felt like condemnation. A mark against her somehow. "I can feel your pain, Haven. The hurt and shame pouring from some ragged wound I cannot see, cannot mend."

"We're all struggling, but I can handle it." She pushed against his shoulders, but she might as well have been shoving stone. "Move. *Move*."

Snowflakes dislodged from his ash-white hair as he shook his head. "Not until you talk to me."

"And say what?" Her throat ached. Why was he forcing her to do this? "I told you, I'm fine—as fine as anyone else here."

"Your nightmares say otherwise."

She stifled beneath the weight of his concern. It was why she'd pushed him from her dreams. Why she'd eventually moved her chamber from the central part of the palace, where all the other Chosen stayed, to the far tower.

Her nightly screams were an embarrassment, a burden for her to deal with alone.

"Haven." She hated the sudden gentleness in his expression, the concern welling in his eyes as he brushed his thumb over her cheek—carefully, so damn carefully—as if she might break apart. "I have been where you are now. The anger. The bitterness and confusion and rage and . . . shame. If you don't release the feelings, they will fester inside you like a poison."

Her chest squeezed so tight that it was all she could do to draw in a breath.

"You are not responsible for what happened in Solethenia. For what he did. For what he's doing now."

A well of ragged emotions surged to swallow her. She closed her eyes against the burn of tears. "Stop. Please."

"Archeron chose his path. He chose to betray you and his people."

"Stolas"—Why was he doing this to her? Why couldn't he see she was drowning?—"Stop." White-hot shame enveloped her, the pain searing her insides, consuming her.

She should have been there for Archeron. Should have recognized his pain.

"It's not your fault, Haven. Do you understand? None of this is."

Isn't it? a voice countered inside her head. She saw the family slaughtered in their bed. Saw Archeron's mangled face and haunted eyes. Saw Rook's mournful expression as she was dragged into the sky to her death. The finality in Bjorn's eyes right before he was incinerated.

So much death and destruction, and for what? It felt like it was never going to end, and she didn't know how to stop it.

She was powerless.

Helpless.

"Enough."

The pain and guilt was too much. It was swirling through her mind, her ribs, a whirlwind of accusation. It was devouring her whole.

"Release your pain, Haven."

"No. *No.*"

"You're safe with me."

"Please."

"You cannot hurt me."

Her last vestige of control shattered as she felt something inside her break open. The explosion rocked her to the core. Dark magick thundered from her entire body, pouring every ounce of her rage and guilt into—

Oh, Goddess, no.

Her powers slammed into Stolas like a thousand fists.

SIX

Even though Stolas had been ready for it, this all-powerful male who could destroy mountains with a single flick of his finger was flung violently backward.

The force was so strong she feared it would shatter every bone in his beautiful body. An ear-splitting boom rocked the temple as Stolas's wings snapped out, slowing his momentum. He skidded to a halt mere inches from crashing into the opposite wall, legs spread wide. The stone beneath his boots was cracked and pitted where his feet had dug in for support.

She threw a hand over her mouth. "Stolas—"

"I'm fine." His face was tight, body rigid from displacing the force she'd slammed into him—but . . . she scoured his body for injuries, blood, any sign she'd wounded him.

He was telling the truth. Thank the Goddess for that. Her relief gave way to fury as she took in his amusement. Those damned lips wrenched into a *smile*.

"Haven—"

She hurled herself at him, slamming wind and golden fire and snow and anything else she could use to pin him against the wall. Anger seared through her as she neared—

He vanished. Moving so fast that her mortal eyes couldn't track him. Too late, she whirled to meet him, but he speared through the air like mist.

"You provoked me," she snarled, leaping toward the flash of darkness to her left.

"Yes." His breath caressed her neck.

Anticipating his movements, she pounced to the left and pivoted, ready to slam her fist into anything she could connect with—

In one smooth movement, he had her on the ground, her back pressed into the cold stone floor, his massive body flush against hers.

With a burst of pure power, she slammed her palm into his shoulder, the impact ratcheting up her elbow, arm, and into her chest. At the same time, she swung her leg up and over, turning him.

She straddled his waist and stared triumphantly down at him. Her chest heaved violently, her ragged breath coming out in milky bursts.

He grinned, that lupine smile only enraging her as he laughed. *Laughed*, for rune's sake. As if this were all a game.

"You provoked me." She slammed her hands on either side of his head, just above the top edges of his wings. "Forced me to use powerful magick on you."

"Yes. And I will do it again and again, if I have to."

"I'm not a toy," she whispered, leaning down so that her lips were close to his, "to wind up for your entertainment."

"No." His focus darted to her mouth. "You are the child of the Gods. Perhaps the most powerful being in existence. I am simply reminding you of that fact."

"I do remember. Every second of every day. How could I not when everyone looks at me differently?"

"I don't."

She was suddenly, almost painfully aware of his body beneath hers. The startling warmth. The powerful muscles that curled and writhed with his every movement. The dark prickle of energy that called to her.

And those lips—lips that had kissed her with their own powerful magick, a magick that had made her body forget its pain. Forget anything but him and that raw ache she felt in his presence.

She could give in to that longing now. Use Stolas to once again forget her pain. Because that's all it was, right? A way to forget.

But she didn't want to forget because without the pain she feared she would feel nothing, and that terrified her more than anything.

She pushed off him. "Maybe you should."

Something flickered in his expression as he uncoiled to his feet, eyes never leaving hers—

His gaze snapped to the temple doors just as they slammed open. Before Haven could process what was happening, he had positioned himself between her and the guest.

A bitter irony considering the violent powers she'd unleashed moments ago.

As Stolas took in Bane and Delphine, the tension fled his wide shoulders, his wings relaxing at his back. The twin Seraphian sentinels—and once his closest friends—were still dressed in the bloodied armor from this morning, and Haven wondered if they'd been tending to their wounded this whole time.

And here was Stolas, their lord and commander, tending to *her* wounds rather than those of his people.

All because she was weak. Unable to accept who she was or what happened in Effendier.

A fresh round of shame hit, as icy as the cool air rushing in through the open doors.

The Seraphians bowed in unison, first to Stolas and then to her. Their snowy-white hair was pulled back in loose braids that hung between their shoulder blades. Their wings—smaller, less vibrant versions of Stolas's—were tucked tightly behind them, something she'd noticed all Seraphians did in Stolas and Nasira's presence.

Bane was the first one to start signing. Just like his sister, his tongue had been removed by Morgryth. The Seraphian sentinel's fingers deftly maneuvered at chest level to form symbols Haven could only guess at. Stolas did the same, his long fingers performing short, quick signs in response.

Delphine interrupted her brother, the quick, frustrated signs she made conveying her distress. Stolas's jaw was taut as he schooled his face into an emotionless mask, trying to hide his reaction to the news from Haven.

A sliver of fear wormed its way into her heart.

Countless scenarios arrived unbidden in her mind. Another attack. Another food shipment sunk. Perhaps Morgryth had found a way around the island's magick.

From the snippets of explanation she'd pieced together from Stolas and Nasira, every Seraphian Empress was gifted the mystical powers of the island. Somehow Morgryth had discovered a way to steal that power from the last empress and take it for herself.

But, once the Noctis were thrown into the Netherworld after the end of the war and the island regained its power, it realized it had been tricked.

Now no Golemite could get within a mile of Shadoria's shores without suffering the island's wrath.

Otherwise, their fledging nation wouldn't have lasted this long. They could barely withstand Archeron's forces alone, and if Morgryth found a way to get past the island's defenses, they were doomed.

Her heart was in her throat as the twins left and Stolas met her gaze. He seemed torn between continuing their conversation from before and dealing with this new information.

He held out his hand. "There's been a . . . development with the emissaries. Everyone is meeting in the Hall of Light."

Everyone? Coils of tension formed between her shoulder blades. If that were true then it must be more than bad. "How many emissaries returned?"

"All of them."

His cryptic answer unsettled her. He was trying to protect her from less than positive news. If only for a moment. Time enough for her to prepare herself for the dread she felt rising in her gut like the mist of Shadoria at sunset. Growing heavier, denser, consuming everything until it was all she could see.

Forcing the fear from her mind, Haven followed Stolas out the door just as the last dregs of light slithered over the jagged mountains. This high above the city, ice crusted the peaks and storms were as frequent as Stolas's wicked grins.

Snow crunched beneath her boots, and she pulled her cloak tighter around her body, fingers already growing numb.

She never thought she'd be so thankful for an active volcano. The mercurial formation, aptly named Death Spewer, was part of a massive network of magma rivers running beneath the city. The heat from those molten arteries of fire meant the streets were always warm, the houses each equipped with archaic runes that drew that heat into them. Even the beaches were gifted heat—

Stealthy as always, she felt rather than heard Stolas position himself behind her. Before she could prepare herself for his touch, his arms glided around her waist, and a sharp tug of yearning sliced through her.

One hand banded low and firm over her hip, the other high above her navel.

It was all she could do not to sigh.

There was a sudden *snap* as his massive wings unfurled to catch the powerful gusts of wind slamming down from the dark gray mountains.

"You have to stop provoking me." She leaned against his chest, the solid curve of his muscles trembling at the contact, and tilted her chin back so that her words reached him. "If I hurt you . . ."

A hoarse chuckle brushed against her ear. "Hurt me? What you did back there was a mere puff of wind. You are going to have to try a lot harder than that to injure me."

The smugness in his voice did make her want to try—right this instant. "Is that a challenge?"

"If you would like it to be."

The abrupt shift in his tone from taunting and playful to sultry and *vulnerable* made her dizzy. His body reacted instinctively to her shiver, wrapping tighter around her, his long fingers curving over her hips and ribcage as if holding her in place.

Even through the fabric of her clothes, fire barreled from his fingertips into her flesh.

She fought the sudden, overwhelming urge to melt into him. To give herself to the safety she felt in his primordial embrace. The memory of that evening in Solethenia after the ball curled into her mind like a flame, and she fought to douse it before the fire spread.

Did Stolas think about that night at all? He hadn't mentioned what had happened between them.

Not once.

They were busy, after all. Trying to resurrect a long-dead kingdom and its defenses and basically stay alive. An impossible feat when half the realm wanted them dead and the other half had just realized she would make an invaluable weapon. Especially with the Godkiller under her command.

As the days and nights blurred into a numb stream of fighting and rebuilding, the details of that evening became lost, distorted by time and trauma and reliving it over and over. Until, like a beloved blanket, the edges frayed and fabric thinned and she couldn't quite remember what it looked like before.

Had she forced Stolas to kiss her somehow, or had he *wanted* to?

Perhaps the act had been impersonal to him, a means to ease her pain and keep her going to achieve their shared goal. Perhaps knowing—or suspecting—who she was, he couldn't say no.

Or, worse, he found her a curiosity. Seducing a goddess trapped inside a mortal body had to be something a male could notch onto his belt with pride.

The idea stung more than she thought it would, but she rejected it almost immediately. Stolas was a lot of things—but weak, bragging male wasn't one of them. And he could have done so much *more* that night . . . if he'd wanted.

If he'd wanted.

She remembered Stolas right before he fed from the Asgardian. That ferocious intensity as he stalked his prey. There was no way a male like that would have stopped himself from going further—if he *wanted* to.

A sinking feeling weighed down her gut.

She ignored the disappointment. It would be easier this way. Her heart was already ravaged from one heartbreak—immediately opening it to another was beyond dangerous.

Especially when that person was Stolas Darkshade.

When the spires of Starpiercer Castle rose from the mist below, she forced Stolas from her mind altogether and prepared herself for the news.

SEVEN

The heads were wrapped in fine emerald silk and placed in gorgeously crafted boxes of abalone, brass, and rosewood. Seven, to be exact. Someone had lined them up neatly on the marble table in the center of the large chamber. Their eyes were open and eerily alert as they stared out at their audience, their faces molded into expressions of calm interest, as if they found this entire ordeal amusing.

They must have been drained of blood and preserved by magick after death because their skin was the exact color of porcelain, and there wasn't a single sign of blood or decay.

Bell half-expected the heads to blink at some point or call out a greeting.

That was the intent, of course.

His gaze fell to the Sun Court sigil, a sun with flowering vines, stamped into the burgundy velvet lining of the box lid.

Bell swallowed before turning to Xandrian. "Sick bastard. What sort of ruler hides their sigil on the inside of something like this?"

If it had been on the outside, they would have had warning, at least, as to what to expect.

The only sign of Xandrian's distaste for the grim display was a slight curl to his upper lip, as if he scented something foul.

Perhaps he did.

Perhaps no amount of magick could truly mask the aroma of death when a Sun Lord was concerned.

"All of the Sun Sovereigns have flirted with some degree of cruelty; it's a prerequisite of survival. But this . . ." His pale blue gaze flitted over each face peering from its exquisite box, and although he didn't so much as blink, Bell felt his disquiet. "To assassinate emissaries during peacetime is an affront to the Goddess's law."

Goddess knows how Xandrian was still surprised by his cousin's increasingly depraved actions. The Sun Lord had tried to murder Haven, after all. He'd sent spies to poison the fertile fields on the island and assassins to kill innocent citizens.

And now, he was murdering emissaries and presenting their smiling heads.

Really, it had only been a matter of time before Archeron graduated to severing heads. It was a once-favored tactic of his father's—

Don't think about him.

The far double doors swung open and Surai entered, shadowed by Ember. Both were quietly laughing, and Bell hated knowing their rare bit of happiness was about to disappear.

Before he could warn them, they halted halfway across the room, each reacting to whatever perverted magick or decay Xandrian had picked up on.

Surai sucked in a breath before looking to Bell. "Where's Haven?"

"With Stolas." One of Surai's elegant black brows arched at that, and Bell felt the need to add, "Training. The twins are alerting them."

Bell didn't know where they trained; that was a closely guarded secret.

Only that reaching the spot required wings.

Ember whistled as she circled the heads, studying Archeron's handiwork. "Who knew the pretty Sun Lord had it in him?" Her rich brown, amber-flecked eyes drifted to Xandrian. "Does bloodlust and insanity run in the family?"

Xandrian glided two fingers down his doublet. "Only when the moon is full."

It was supposed to be a joke, but no one laughed or even cracked a smile. Well, except the heads.

When the boxes arrived, Bell and Xandrian had been below, inside the subterranean library that runs the length of the palace. A vault more than a true library, the cavernous interconnecting chambers that housed the Seraphian treasures was different than the glorious library of Bell's childhood. Instead of sunlight and rich maple wood and dust, the leather-bound books and scrolls below were nestled in cool alcoves carved deep inside the earth, the soft glow of sunlight traded for the cold ethereal blue of the dark magick veining the stone.

Still, it was one of Bell's favorite places here in Shadoria. As luck would have it, he and Xandrian were in the chamber directly below when news came of the emissaries.

Or, perhaps that was unlucky, considering.

They were the first to arrive in the Hall of Light. Any other time, Bell loved this area of the castle. The windows were cut to form herringbone and other strange patterns that emblazed Shadoria's purple-tinged light along the black walls and mosaic floors.

But it was the stunning magenta and amethyst crystal chandelier that filled the space above that Bell loved the most.

The first day they entered the Hall of Light, Xandrian had noticed Bell gazing at the masterpiece, thousands of crystals cut to look like feathers inside a massive display of wings.

He explained that the crystals used in the chandelier and all throughout the palace were a natural gemstone found in the island's bedrock.

The crystal contained the highest concentration of naturally occurring light magick in any organic matter, save living things.

It didn't take much to deduce the rest. That the Seraphians drew from the crystals to fuel their dark magick. Bell had always assumed they solely relied on living donors, just as he'd always assumed Shadoria would be a dark, dismal, crude place.

He'd been wrong on both counts. Thank the Goddess for that, considering this might very well be his home for the rest of his mortal life, however brief that life would be.

A ferocious laugh dragged Bell's attention to the soaring walls. At least nine stories high, the vast chamber claimed the usual balconies and alcoves and passages that he'd learned made up most of the palace.

Any given day, in nearly any given room of the castle, one could look up and spot Seraphians nestled above, watching the commotion below, preening their feathers, even sleeping.

But the shadowy form soaring above was no ordinary Seraphian. Nasira Darkshade dove toward them at frightening speed, only to halt seconds before slamming into Surai, her silky black wings flaring out to stop the collision.

Midair, Nasira cocked her head, sniffed, her childlike expression shifting to predatory in that way Bell found unnerving. "Pretty. Can I have one? Perhaps the handsome head in the middle? He would look dashing on my bedside table, and his eyes match my bedspread."

"No, Nasira."

Bell recognized Nasira's reaction—not exactly fear, but definitely subservience—before he did the elegant but firm voice, and he managed to drop to a knee beside the others as Stolas and Haven prowled across the hall.

The tension between the two bled into the air. Had they been arguing?

No—not exactly arguing, Bell decided as he studied them beneath his dark lashes.

But . . . there was something about both their energies, like two contaminated barrels of plum wine about to burst.

Haven caught his stare before nodding at the group. The signal to stand. Only someone who knew her well could detect her unease at her new status.

To everyone else, she appeared regal and fierce, every bit the Goddess they claimed, a powerful being comfortable with the bows of her friends. The rose-gold hair he loved was pulled into a tight braid that fell mid-back, wispy strands framing her face. Even in dark leather pants, a loose tunic, and knee-high boots that had seen better days, she was radiant. Her eyes so gold they nearly glowed.

But beneath her confident smile and steady gaze, her jaw flexed.

Slowly, she swept her wary stare over the boxes.

He caught the shadow of surprise and then disappointment ripple over her carefully composed mask. The one she wore nearly all the time now.

A violent wave of *something* too quick to read fractured her controlled visage, cracks of emotion spiderwebbing over that veiled surface, breaking open to reveal a seething anger.

Her spine snapped taut. Her nostrils flared, her hands fisting and relaxing as she worked to compose herself. Behind her Bell noticed Stolas inch closer, his gliding movements so smooth he hardly appeared to move at all.

The Shade Lord had enough sense not to try and touch her.

Not in public, at least. Was it different in private? Bell couldn't be the only one who noticed the way she subconsciously positioned her body toward Stolas whenever he was near. The way she smiled more around him. *Laughed* more around him. Even Stolas's ability to provoke her in a way few could was telling.

The first time the unusual bond between them became apparent was in Solethenia during the trials. But it was now, mired in the pain of Archeron's betrayal and confusion of her lineage, that her reliance on Stolas as more than a mentor was apparent to everyone.

Everyone but perhaps Haven herself.

Maybe that was why one of the monks of the Order of Soltari frowned as he stepped forward, eyes trained on the Shade Lord even though he addressed Haven.

"Goddess-Born, all but one emissary were caught by Sun Court assassins, tortured, and murdered." The monk's calm tone was at odds with the severity of his words. All the monks spoke in that emotionless voice.

Did the man actually possess emotions, or had they been magicked away somehow along with his hair and personality?

Turning her back on the gruesome display, Haven matched the monk's calm as she said, "I'd like to see him."

"Unfortunately, he died minutes after arriving. Solis healers tried to save him, but he was gravely wounded." Disappointment dragged Haven's dusky rose brows together until the monk added, "the brave soul did manage to deliver a letter from the King of the Broken Three."

A jolt of interest rocked Bell.

King Eros Elhaem—the newly appointed mortal ruler of The Broken Three: Dune, Drothian, and Veserack, the three neighboring territories to the west of Penryth.

Penryth. Penryth. Penryth.

The name shivered through him like a song, a lullaby he'd memorized from birth—

Don't think about that. There's no point.

But of course it was all he thought about as one of the men from the Order of Soltari procured the letter, a tattered parchment splattered with what had to be blood.

Blood. He saw his father's panicked eyes as he lay dying, the whites stained bright red with blood.

No. Inhaling deeply, he centered himself on his new life. Protect Haven.

Nothing else mattered.

You are no longer a prince, or a king. You are part of her Chosen, selected by the Goddess herself.

It had been surprisingly easy to slip off his identity as crown prince and heir to the largest mortal throne in Eritreyia and simply become Bellamy, Chosen protector of the Goddess-Born.

It was all he thought about. Honing his magick. Honing his weaponry skills. Training for hours upon hours from predawn to nightfall and then soaking his battered body in the hot baths.

It was all he *allowed* himself to think about.

Not his father's face, twisted in a grimace of pain as he died. Not the greedy laws Renk had already undoubtedly enacted to benefit himself while the citizens suffered. Not the lies Renk whispered about Bell's treachery that rippled across the realm, solidifying Bell as a coward and murderer.

Especially not his new name—Kinslayer.

But now . . . an ache yawned open in his chest, and with it came the smell of jasmine and burning tallow of the castle, the tall forests and meadows of his youth, the feel of the Penrythian sun on his face.

His body was Haven's, heart and soul, but a part of that soul was still embedded in Penryth, the same as Archeron's had been trapped inside his father's ring. And only taking back his rightful throne and killing Renk would make him whole again.

From his periphery, Bell noticed Xandrian watching him with that quiet perceptiveness, and he refocused on his new, simple life.

Haven was just beginning to read the letter. It was short, and when she was done, she carefully folded the parchment, fit it into her pocket, and sighed.

"King Eros Elhaem offers a meeting in Veserack to discuss terms of an alliance."

Ember snorted. Bell hadn't known her sister, Rook, but if she was anything like Ember, he probably would have liked her. "Does this mortal king think the Goddess-Born daughter of Freya is going to travel to his Shadeling-forsaken little fiefdom?"

Haven squared her shoulders, drawing them back in a way that told him she'd already made a decision. "That mortal king controls three once-powerful mortal houses. More importantly, he controls the entire southwestern coastline of the mortal continent, which means he commands all the trade coming in from Asgard." Her golden eyes flicked to him. "What do you know about this new king, Bell?"

As all eyes drifted his way, he scoured the dregs of his memory. "Not much. He only recently claimed dominion over the three broken kingdoms." King Eros would have never declared himself ruler of the Broken Three if Bell's father had been alive. But with the weakling Renk on the throne and both Lord Thendryft and Eleeza dead, the vacuum of power on the southern tip of the mortal continent had changed everything. "He was a trader before the Curse was broken, I believe, the fifth or sixth son from House Coventry. I only remember hearing rumblings that his ships were suspected of piracy. The Asgardians across the sea call him the Ridere Felionous." He broke into a grin. "It means the Smiling Cat."

Surai arched an eyebrow. "A pirate king named after a grinning feline? And he expects us to come to him?"

"He knows our other options have recently become rather limited." Haven regarded the *options* she mentioned, all trussed up in their boxes.

"Don't we?" Xandrian drawled, picking at some invisible piece of dust on his lapel. Sometimes Bell forgot how grating Xandrian's arrogance could be. It seemed to come with being a Sun Lord. "Perhaps he knows precisely that because he helped my cousin kill the emissaries and now plans a trap for us. Your mortal kings are notoriously greedy."

Xandrian did have a point.

"I say we go see this mortal king," Nasira purred, her fascination with the macabre display finally shifting to the conversation, "and then see how his head looks inside a pretty box."

If anyone else had suggested this, Bell would have been annoyed. But coming from Nasira, with her huge silver-blue eyes and beaming smile, it was, well, cute . . . in a way.

After that suggestion, everyone looked to Stolas for his opinion on the matter. The Shade Lord had gone preternaturally still in that alarming way of his that commanded the attention of the entire room.

Even knowing the less savage side of Stolas—which couldn't quite be called noble or gentle—Bell felt fear prickle beneath his skin.

Stolas raked his intense stare over them one by one, his lips twitching as more than a few forgot to breathe. "Beneath these hallowed lights of my ancestors, I see the daughters of queens, the sons of sovereigns. I see a king twice over chosen by Freya herself, a Seraphian Empress who terrifies even the Shadeling, and a Goddess so ferocious even the heavens tremble when she's angry."

Haven traded a dark look with Stolas, and that twitching mouth finally committed to a dark grin. Reminding Bell that Stolas had many smiles, most of which were anything but joyful. "I vote," Stolas continued, "we accept this would-be-ruler's invitation to enter his territory. If indeed it is a trap, we show the kingdoms of the realm what happens when they forget their manners around Freya's daughter."

The softening lines bracketing Haven's mouth said that was exactly the answer she was hoping for. Not that Bell was surprised.

Sitting in one place waiting for her enemies to attack wasn't Haven's style.

Now that the decision was made, the heaviness in the air gave way to purpose, and they fell into the necessary details of protecting Shadoria while they were away. Haven wanted to leave as soon as possible, and it was decided that departing in the predawn hours was best.

A plan. A precarious, risky plan—but it was better than the hell of going to bed every night expecting carnage and death.

Night had fallen, the hall alive with luminous shards of moonlight and the crystals' pale-purple glow. It was probably his favorite time of day inside the castle. His mind was already on the upcoming sparring session with Xandrian on one of the mist-shrouded plateaus, so he only half-watched Haven from his periphery as she began closing the lids on the boxes, and only half-heard the soft clicking as each brass clasp was slid into place.

Xandrian would undoubtedly attack with one of the complex magick sequences he taught this morning. Bell was deep into playing out a defensive counter-attack maneuver when he had the odd sensation that *something was wrong.*

The torus of energy beneath his breastbone where he felt his magick suddenly spasmed.

Torn between his daydream and reality, he refocused on Haven as she went to shut the final lid. He became aware of a soft hissing. Something slithering against his senses. The framework of his magick.

An ancient, primordial language that scraped against his mortal bones and made his magick recoil.

Haven stiffened and jerked back her hand. The reason why became immediately clear: the head was staring at Haven, tracking her with alarming sentience, blinking and twitching and alive.

Alive. And the lips . . .

He understood with alarming clarity where the language came from.

Just as some rational part of him knew that it was too late.

Whatever dark curse the animated head was chanting had already been unleashed.

Stolas was the first to react. Talons out, he lunged for Haven so fast that by the time his snarl made it to Bell's ears, Stolas was already wrapping himself around Haven, using his powerful body, his massive wings, and roiling strands of his magick to form an impenetrable wall. Bell joined the others as they rushed to protect Haven.

But there was nothing to protect. A roar so loud it fractured some of the crystals above erupted from Stolas as he uncurled his wings and retracted his magick, blinking at the empty space before him.

The shattered look in his eyes could only mean—oh, Goddess, this couldn't be happening, but it was.

It was.

She was gone.

EIGHT

Wrapped in the complete darkness of Stolas's protection, Haven didn't notice at first when she shifted from that space to another. But the loss of Stolas's dark magick was almost painful, like being ripped from a deep, comforting sleep and tossed into a frigid sea. Wave after wave of foul magick washed over her. Her own powers drowned out beneath its contaminated ick.

Fighting for breath, gasping and clutching her chest, she sifted through the shadows to gather her bearings. She was in some sort of chamber. Oily fog layered the room, so dense she imagined she could peel it back with her fingers, but it was receding. Slipping away like the tide to reveal . . . windows?

Her eyes flicked desperately from the mosaic of tiles created into suns to the thick vines along the walls. This place was familiar but not. Nothing made sense. She was somewhere else, somewhere she'd been before, but behind a veil of a crude, horrible magick.

Everything felt empty. Sick. Wrong. Like the Ruinlands had before they broke the Curse. But worse. So, so much worse.

Because she finally recognized the three thrones. The male dominating the middle throne was clad in the finery of a god. Emeralds formed a runic pattern over his ash-dark waistcoat, his expensive knee-high leather boots decorated in silver and gold. A golden crown glittered from the shadows.

He watched her quietly, but her soul knew him even before he uncoiled to his feet and stalked toward her. It recognized her brother-in-arms before she found that comforting familiarity in his arrogant, prowling gait. Before her gaze shifted to his gorgeous face, once renowned for its rare beauty.

Not anymore.

The fabric of shadows seemed to part around Archeron as he halted in front of her, just close enough to touch her—or plunge a dagger through her heart. "Little Mortal."

His grin was a thing of nightmares, only it was half a grin. The other side of his visage was cloaked beneath a golden mask fitted so tightly, it could have been poured on. Emeralds and rubies decorated the adornment, but they couldn't hide the dark greenish blots blooming over the mask, as if the corruption within was bubbling to the surface.

"My advisers thought the jewels would make the mask more . . . palatable," he said conversationally. "What do you think? Does it do the trick?"

Her gaze was drawn to the eye watching her from the deep recesses of the mask. All-black, it seemed to come from a completely separate entity than the other eye, which was a brackish green similar to the corruption marring his mask.

She focused on that eye. That Archeron. "Did you receive my message of peace?"

"The Asgardian male delivered to my doorstep? He managed to relay your message, yes, along with a few other details my Gold Shadows pulled out of him."

She shivered as he drew closer. The shadows writhed around him like slippery eels. She searched for her powers, scrambling to draw upon them, to find a shred of something—

"Your magick doesn't work here."

Right. "And where is . . . here?"

"*You* are trapped in the Nether, while I am still in our realm."

Runes. That explained the oily strips of shadow floating around them and her inability to use magick. She should have picked up on that sooner.

"My mother hoarded wondrous treasures from all the Realms of Other," he continued. "I always thought her obsession with collecting rare powerrunes and dark spells was a vain preoccupation, but I'm finding certain things have their uses."

Despite his conversational tone, her heart ratcheted into a thundering beat. Stolas had explained that the Nether was the layer that separated realms. A slippery stratum positioned between each realm, Stolas had likened the Nether to oil used on a carriage wheel.

It allowed soulwalking and was used by powerful lightcasters like Xandrian to thread. Although when portaling wasn't done precisely right, one could get trapped in the Nether. Unable to use magick to return home.

Or something. She probably should have paid better attention at the time.

Could Archeron harm her here? If—no, when she made it back to Stolas, she'd ask for another lesson on this place and endure his scowl of annoyance.

Archeron closed another inch of space between them, and she became startlingly aware that she couldn't move from her position. Runes were positioned around her in a circle, their pale orange forms pulsing against the marble tiles. While she didn't recognize them, they were obviously some sort of magickal cage that prevented her from moving.

Her hands and face, on the other hand . . .

She drew the training dagger at her hip, the handle still wet from her sweat earlier, and bared her lips in a snarl.

Amused eyes flicked to the blade. He laughed, the sound almost normal, almost warm. "What exactly do you plan to do with that?"

The blade arced for the stretch of bare neck just above his high collar—

And slid through him like he was made of mist. Shadeling Below. "How I've missed that savage ferocity. That . . . mortal rashness."

Was that affection in his voice? If steel didn't work, she could use that. Could grasp the remnants of humanity still clinging to the husk of Archeron and weaponize it.

She forced her gaze to meet his eyes, drowning the flicker of disgust at what she saw there, and looked at him the way she used to. "Join with us, Archeron. I am not your enemy. I still . . ." She blinked, throat clenched as she forced the words to form, to release. "I still care about you. I see you in my dreams—I—"

The words shriveled to ash on her tongue as she took in his expression. Not disgust, but an emptiness that pitted in her heart.

"I dream about you, too," he admitted softly. She blinked. A part of her even wanted to protect the sudden vulnerability in his eyes. "I see now you are the key to Effendier's future."

She swallowed. Was he suggesting an alliance? Even after everything he'd done, hope burgeoned inside her chest like a flame roaring to life. "So you'll fight with us against the Shadeling?"

"Fight . . . with you?" Haughty amusement lanced his tone, an arrogance she'd once found charming. Now it sliced to the bone. "No, Haven. You are an abomination, a flagrant insult to the Goddess herself."

He was toying with her, another habit she'd once found charming and now—now she would gouge his eyes out if she could move.

"Have you heard of Aramos's wolves of war?" He took her silence as a no and continued. "The late Sovereign owned them. They weren't actually wolves, at least not the kind we have in our realm. They were from Neifgard, a present from one of the Demon Lords. Just as you'd expect from that realm, they were ferocious creatures, and left to their bloodthirsty natures, they would have slaughtered their way across the kingdom.

"Aramos understood he had to either kill them or find a way to control them. So he took all but two females and killed them in front of their mates. Then he put the wolves into pits alone until they nearly died from the separation. And finally, he broke them physically."

Haven had heard of the wolves of war. In fact, there had been a painting in the museum in Solethenia, and Stolas had spent a lot of time talking lovingly about the creatures. The terrifying beasts were known to form a protective vanguard around the Sun Sovereign in battle, and they answered to a magickal whistle that he wore around his neck.

A damned whistle, for Goddess's sake.

"I'm not going to fight *beside* you, Little Mortal," he explained softly, and the bastard actually had the audacity to look mournful. "No, I'm going to break you, leash you, and wield you like the beast you are."

Through the whirlwind of emotions battering her mind, the hurt and rage, she managed to hiss, "You will never break me. Never."

True agony twisted the uninjured side of his face, and that was almost worse than the emptiness, because she understood then that he still cared for her. That she couldn't blame this on someone else.

This was still Archeron. Her Archeron. Twisted and perverted with darkness, but he was still there.

"That fighting spirit is what I liked most about you." He was so close, she didn't see him lift his hand until he was already sliding his thumb over the sharp edge of her jaw. Where his fingers would have touched on the other side, a tingle formed, like the lightest silk fabric brushing past. "But there's a time for stubbornness, Little Mortal, and there's a time for accepting your fate."

"Don't use that name," she snarled, recoiling from the emotions attached to it.

Happiness had no place here.

"Why? Because you believe a radical faction who's convinced you that you're the daughter of the Goddess?"

The disdain in his voice was like a jagged knife slowly worming into her flesh.

"Don't forget the Shadeling."

He blinked, and she took a dark satisfaction in the tremor of disgust that soured his expression. "Believe whatever lies you want. If you refuse to become a weapon *for* Effendier then you are its enemy, and I will use my vast resources to end you."

The pain engraved into his features as he said this, the familiar caress of his thumb as it stroked gently back and forth over her bottom lip—it was all too much.

I can't take this. She couldn't breathe. The shadows seemed to thicken, the air turning to sand in her lungs.

She couldn't *breathe.*

Archeron slid his other arm behind her waist, a prickly sensation dancing across the small of her back where his fingers splayed. He might not be able to physically touch her from the other side, but he was doing *something.* Controlling her body somehow.

The tingling along her chin turned to aching pressure as he tightened his grip, tilted her face up to hold his stare. She could feel his magick building around them. Feel the runes etched into the floor shiver and pulse with growing energy.

Ribbons of pale green magick swirled inside his good eye and darted between the shadows, making the jewels inside his mask twinkle. But his black eye appeared even darker, a hungry pit gobbling the light instead of reflecting it.

"You allowed the Lord of the Netherworld to *drink* from a Solis under my protection." There was a cruelty in his voice that unsettled her. "Have you let him drink from you too?"

"Stop."

"Is that how he keeps you in his thrall? In his bed?" The dark blots on his mask seemed to spread as his rage swelled, roiling outward like a hungry beast of its own. "Are you his *whore* now?"

"Screw you!" Haven found herself panting with anger to match his own, the words spilling out between furious gulps of air. "I'm no one's whore. Although I almost became yours once, didn't I? Is that what this is about? Your ego?"

He jerked as if she'd hit him.

"Your mercenaries killed innocent people. Entire families mutilated beyond recognition, children dragged into the streets. Archeron, please. This isn't you. It's the work of a . . . a monster."

The anger in his eyes shifted to something colder. "A monster? You mean like the thing that slithered out of you? Before he went completely mute, the Asgardian managed to tell me how you smiled as you watched it slaughter his friend. How it was like a demon called up from the Netherworld."

A shiver skittered through her as she remembered the carnage. The undeniable bloodlust.

His thumb stroked her cheek. "You are just full of surprises, aren't you? What else are you hiding from me?"

"Why don't you meet me in the real world and find out?" she snarled.

"Soon," he promised. "For now, I need you to return and tell your Shade Lord I'm gifting Shadoria two weeks of peace, a little taste of what I can offer for your return to me."

Despite her panic, she clung to that word.

Return.

That meant he was sending her back—although by the swell of his magick she wouldn't return unharmed.

"You're wasting your breath. Stolas will never negotiate with you."

"Then remind him that no matter how much of yourself you give to him, you belong to me, and I can reach you anywhere. Anytime."

Bracing herself for the worst, she was surprised when he drew her close to him. It was too comforting, too familiar.

Her heart wobbled as his scent enveloped her—leather and sandalwood. His lips brushed her ear, her body remembering all the times he'd done that before. Remembering how he'd once so very gently kissed her behind her knee.

That was the night she'd admitted to trying to end her life in the desert, and the night he admitted his love for a mother who could never love him back and a kingdom that would never be his.

How very wrong they had both been.

"Consider this my final warning," Archeron murmured. "You need to understand what will happen to your friends if you don't surrender. What will happen to *Surai*, Haven. Their suffering, their torment and death—I need you to really see it, to understand the consequences of the foolish game you play."

"Game?" A bitter sound formed in her throat. "Surai swore an oath to the Goddess to protect her daughter. They all did. Even if I willingly surrendered, they would die trying to save me. Surely you still remember what honor is?"

He chuckled darkly, his breath reaching through the Nether and caressing her neck. "You're not Goddess-Born, Haven; you're mortal, from the corrupted race despised equally by Noctis and Solis. Even Freya knew that too much power would be misused by your kind, which is why there are laws against abominations like you. Tell me, why would she do that if you were her daughter?"

She didn't have an answer.

"Stolas is using you as a pawn. Even he knows the kingdoms of Solissia will never bow to a mortal, no matter how much magick you possess. It's cruel, the way he lets you hope. At least I offer the truth."

Doubt crept over her. The Asgardian had said as much.

"Stolas is parading you around like his own personal pet. Just like the wolves after the war ended, you're a novelty, kept in a little cage as entertainment. Perhaps you don't see the cage yet because he lets you out on occasion, because he throws you just enough scraps of power to stay fed, but it's still there. One of these days you'll realize better a cage you can see than one you can't."

A calm rage took over, her body going hot and cold. There was still so much about Stolas that he guarded from her, but she knew one thing with absolute surety: he would never try to cage her.

Archeron drew back enough that he could see her face. Perhaps he was expecting her to appear conflicted. Instead, whatever he saw chipped away at that arrogant grin until it died a glorious death.

"Did you forget what happened to the poor caged wolves, *Sun Sovereign?*" She practically spat his title; he didn't deserve it. "One day, bored of their howls and expensive appetites, the Sun Sovereign decided he would impress visiting royals by hunting the wolves. The Sovereign still had his whistle, after all. He thought he was in control."

The flex of Archeron's jaw said he knew how this story ended.

"But the wolves were bored too," she continued, "and when the hunt began, the sovereign quickly realized his mistake. One hundred Solis died before the Gold Shadows killed the wolves. Aramos himself lost part of his arm to the attack." She held his stare, remembering Stolas's wicked delight as he told the tale of the foolish Sun Sovereign. "You see, the wolves had only been following the Sovereign's orders in battle because his interests aligned with theirs: killing. In his arrogance, Aramos thought he could control them. He imagined himself as a predator and the wolves as prey—but it had always been the other way around."

His eyes tightened at the corners as her meaning took hold. Was that a twinge of . . . fear? Then he grinned and whispered a promise into her ear. "I have a beautiful cage waiting for you, Little Mortal. You have two weeks to decide if you want to come willingly, or at the cost of everyone you care about."

She tried to close her eyes against what came next, but she couldn't stop the onslaught of visions that barreled through her skull. Each one so vibrant, so real that she immediately forgot where she had been. She forgot about Archeron. Forgot that the visions were just that—visions—forgot that there would be an end to all of this.

Each hallucination was experienced as if it were happening.

They *were* happening.

Oh, Goddess, she couldn't stop it.

Bell. Surai. Stolas. Nasira. Xandrian. Ember. Demelza.

Each one died horribly, the torment stretched out for what felt like weeks. Months. Lifetimes. She was unable to look away for even a moment. Unable to cry or scream or do anything but watch as they called for her, as they begged and pleaded, to watch and watch and watch until something inside her cracked open.

NINE

The moment Stolas felt Haven ripped from this realm, the searing heat of her light magick going cold and dead against his chest, something ancient awoke inside him. He reared back as his mind reordered the situation.

Taken.

She was taken.

He took her.

Icy rage slammed into him. Shutting his eyes, he flung his senses over the entire realm, scouring for that flicker of white-hot fire that was Haven.

Gone—she was gone. Her light hidden beneath layers and layers of shadow and murk and—

A bellow tore from his throat as he understood where Archeron had taken her. But the roar wasn't from rage.

It was a warning.

He had only felt this way one other time. The day the Shade Queen forced him with magick to kill his mother.

Only then, he was ready for his Shadow Familiar. It took every ounce of his magick to lock it away. He had only just begun to learn to control his wolf with his mother's help, but somehow he had pushed it deeper and deeper inside him, starving it until it withered into a wisp of shadow and magick.

Dead—he'd thought it was dead.

Now it thrashed against its cage of muscle and bone, very much alive, its power reverberating through his rib cage like boulders colliding. If he had known it was still inside him he could have erected the shields necessary to keep it caged—

Blinding pain seared his middle as claws ripped through his hastily erected walls. He tried to cry out another warning but could only manage a snarl as the last of his defenses were shredded. The pressure in his torso released, his familiar's form shaping itself in the air.

The ground shook beneath the creature's massive black paws. Once he had been able to control it, but now—now it was ravenous and feral and half-mad with fury, a wild animal caged for too long.

A wild animal feeding off his hatred for Archeron. Off his rage and helplessness and pain. Its mind was linked to his, and Stolas felt the creature's focus whirl to the Solis and their light magick, so similar to Archeron's.

No.

Focusing every bit of his vicious rage, Stolas honed it on the one thing that might interest his shadow wolf: the glorious crystals. Crystals his ancestors had carefully embedded into these walls themselves. Crystals gifted by Freya and prized by his people.

The crystals inside the hall were the rarest found on the island. Each one precious beyond words. Right before her death, his mother had used their collective magick to draw enough strength to soulspeak one last message to him.

And yet, to save Haven's friends, he would willingly destroy them all. So he let his wolf sate its vicious fury on the hall his mother loved. The chandelier she designed and built herself. The shattering sound every glorious jewel made as it was rent in pieces burrowed into his heart.

When at last his wolf's lust for destruction had been tempered, he found the tether that leashed the beast to himself and forced it, snarling and whining, back into its immortal cage of magick, sinew, and bone.

And when Haven reappeared right afterward, writhing and screaming atop the rubble of crystals and stone, two of the things he loved broken and twisted together, every thought, every feeling went out of Stolas.

Save one. *Protect Haven.*

If any of the others had tried to stop him from taking her, they would be dead. He acted on pure instinct as he rushed her through the mist and clouds to the safest place in Shadoria: his room in the sky.

He didn't notice Nasira or Surai in the room as he settled Haven in his bed and curled his body around hers, using every bit of his powers to take away the pain festering inside her. A dull sort of terror threatened to take hold as he scented the demonic tang of the demented magick mixed with her fear.

Her eyes were open, glassy and unseeing, her flesh cold as the air outside. Her arms clawing like a wild animal. Body bucking and thrashing and emitting gurgling wails—

He was going to tear Archeron apart for this.

And he would take a long time to do it.

But first—gently, so gently, he held her still. "You're safe, Haven. Safe. Nothing can hurt you now."

She shred through the bedspread and then turned her nails on him. Gouging blindly. Choking and coughing as she tried to breathe through her terror. Ignoring the mindless attack, he focused on infusing his magick into her. Steadying his mind as he pushed his euphoria into her with rhythmic pulses, letting her get used to the feeling, waiting until he felt her open up to him. Waiting for her to recognize his presence. To accept the safety and relief he was offering her.

When he felt her body thaw, her wails turning to soft, pleading moans, he guided her to the meadow in their shared dreamscape. And then, just as she had once comforted him, he held her in his lap beneath the sprawling tree, whispering poems from his youth or favorite stories, anything he could think of to bring her back to him.

Until finally, the demented magick lost its hold on her mind, and whatever horrors she experienced bled away. Then she rested limp and quiet against his chest, breathing softly.

And he counted every breath the way some might stars, whispering his gratitude to the Goddess or the heavens or whoever the Netherworld was listening for her safe return.

TEN

Destroyed—the Hall of Light was destroyed. Giant craters of stone remained where crystals once glinted. They'd been torn from the walls. The floor. Ripped from alcoves. Shattered. As if that creature Stolas released couldn't stand the light.

Shards of the multi-faceted crystals that once hung from the millennium-old chandelier above scattered across the floor, among other wreckage. Furniture, paintings, tapestries—nothing had been spared Stolas's wrath.

Except them, of course. Just barely.

Xandrian bent on one knee beside Bell, picked up a sliver of crystal, and shook his head. "So much waste."

"Did you know he could do that?"

"There were rumors, but the Seraphian royals have always been very secretive about their gifts."

Bell scoffed. "Gift?"

Whatever that thing was, gift was too pleasant a word.

Hours had passed since Haven reappeared in the Hall of Light. But just as the hall she returned to was not the same, the Haven who returned was not the one who left. Her body had been curled violently into itself, her skin white as the moon peeking from the windows, limbs jerking so hard he thought the marble floor might crack.

And the god-awful screams that clawed from her throat as she lay helpless and writhing in the shattered rubble . . .

He had thought she was dying.

Bell realized that his hands were shaking, and he slammed them into his pockets. But it wasn't fear that moved him almost violently; it was anger.

The entire thing still felt like a nightmare. Watching Haven slip from their grasp. In front of her Chosen. In front of *him*. While he'd been busy daydreaming about training, he should have noticed the wrongness of the box. Should have reacted sooner.

He should have done something.

Xandrian squeezed his shoulder lightly, dragging Bell from his ruminations. "Is she still sleeping?"

Bell nodded, aware of how quick Xandrian was to remove his hand. Xandrian never touched him outside of training, so if he was making an effort now, it meant Bell probably looked just as horrible as he felt.

The moment Haven was returned to them, Stolas swept her into his arms and exploded into the night. Surai shifted to follow them, while Xandrian threaded to the nearest portals, taking them as high into the palace as they could go. The uppermost point of the palace was warded to outsiders. Only Seraphians of royal blood could pass through.

Surai had found them waiting what felt like an eternity later. Her lavender eyes were faded and hollow, but she promised Haven would be okay. Stolas was tending to her—whatever the Shadeling that meant.

That didn't satisfy Bell. Only after Surai relayed Bell's threat—to destroy the exquisite paintings and sculptures lining the halls—did

Stolas lower the wards to his chamber so they could enter.

The topmost floor of the castle loomed well above the clouds. Instead of rooms there was one giant chamber open to the night sky. Impressive columns with wolves carved into their sides propped up a domed ceiling painted like the heavens.

Inside that otherworldly room, surrounded by that breathtaking view of the heavens, Haven had looked so small. Especially tucked into the massive four poster bed at the center—massive to fit his wings, Bell assumed, and not the orgies the dark prince was once rumored to prefer—her hair swept across an ivory pillow like paint. The charcoal strips of silk that hung above the bed swirled in the breeze.

Stolas was perched on a ledge near a skylight. His eyes never left Haven as Bell entered, but he knew the Shade Lord was aware of his presence. Knew that if anyone but Bell or one of the Chosen entered, they wouldn't even see him coming until it was too late.

After what had happened in the Hall of Light, Bell had enough sense to feel a newfound fear near the Shade Lord.

Nasira met him at the head of the four poster marble bed.

"What did Archeron do to her?" Bell demanded.

"He dragged her into the Nether, trapped her there, and then afflicted her with some sort of nasty torment spell."

Bell fought the urge to hit something. "She's better now?"

"Stolas was able to break the spell and then calm her."

Nasira spoke as if Haven's affliction had been a fever, not some perversion inflicted on her by a madman.

After everything that Haven had been through in her life, all the tragedy and rejection and hurt, the thought of her suffering more made him physically ill. "I'm going to kill Archeron."

"Get in line." Nasira's eyes flicked to Stolas and back to Bell. "What you saw in the hall after Haven disappeared . . ." Another darting glance at her brother. "Has Haven explained to you what that was?"

"Was?" Bell said numbly, because he couldn't imagine there was a name for something so terrible, so monstrously savage as the thing Stolas had released.

"Every Seraphian royal has a Shadow Familiar." Nasira's wings fluttered with excitement as she continued explaining the phenomenon, as if the creature that had destroyed the most beautiful place Bell had ever visited in the span of a breath was something to be proud of. "My brother shares my mother's Shadow Form, the dire wolf."

Wolf. Everything clicked into place, the traumatic memories from earlier solidifying. At the time, he was in survival mode like the others, more focused on finding refuge from the shadowy creature tearing stone with its bare teeth than cataloging it.

But now the long snout dripping with fangs formed in his mind. The luxurious black pelt and fiery red eyes and bunched, coiled muscle. Nasira knew what was happening and had thrown up a shield to protect them as the creature rampaged.

It was like the most violent, most powerful storm imaginable had been forced into a wolf the size of a cottage. Everything it touched was ruined. If not for Nasira's quick thinking, the carnage would have included more than just furniture and stone.

"Stolas had barely discovered his form before Morgryth killed our parents," Nasira said, softly, almost as if she were speaking to herself, "so it was still a secret. Rather than let Morgryth use it as a weapon, he kept his familiar locked deep inside him, tightly chained, hidden and . . . and starved. He lied and told her it never came. If a darkcaster experiences major stress during their transition years, their familiars have been known to go dormant, sometimes indefinitely. She didn't believe him, of course. But no matter how long that hag tortured him, he kept it caged until . . . it withered into shadow and ash. We thought it was dead."

Bell exhaled. He could only imagine the things Ravenna and the

Shade Queen would have done with a monster that powerful. Then his mind circled back to her earlier comment. "You said every Seraphian royal has a Shadow Familiar. If Haven is descended from the Shadeling himself, does that mean Haven has one of those . . . things inside her?"

Nasira's grin confirmed his suspicion.

Enough. He could only handle so much. He'd find a way to compartmentalize that later.

Bell finally dared to look at Haven, part of him already flinching from the pain he expected to see.

Beads of sweat glistened over her upper lip and brow. Her head was thrown back to expose the pale center of her delicate neck, the silver sheets bunched between her curled fingers. But her features were soft, her mouth unlined and parted, breathing gentle and slow. Dusky rose-gold eyelashes fluttered as if she dreamed.

He relaxed. Compared to her desperate condition earlier, she almost seemed like a different person.

"What did Stolas do to her?"

Nasira shrugged. "Fixed her."

Translation: you don't want to know the details. And he didn't. Not right now, at least. It was yet another thing to mull over later, when his nerves didn't feel like they'd been frayed with razor blades.

Wings fluttered high above as Bell leaned toward Haven, brushing a damp strand of hair from her forehead. "I'm sorry. You deserve so much better than what he did to you, but you're the toughest person I know, and you will get through this." He kissed her cheek, and she stirred. "I—I love you."

He could have sworn the ghost of a smile twitched her lips. If she were awake, she'd give him so much crap.

Nasira was cocking her head at him as he straightened, but she didn't tease him like he expected.

No, her strange silver-blue eyes regarded him for a long, curious moment. Then she waved a tiny hand and said, "Go sleep, pretty mortal king. Someone will get you when she wakes."

After he got over his usual shock of being ordered around by the tiny Seraphian empress, he obeyed, but he knew he couldn't sleep so he'd come back to the destroyed Hall of Light.

Xandrian was there already, just staring at the destruction with that impassive gaze of his. Wordlessly they'd begun trying to salvage what they could, if for no other reason than to do something to forget how easily Archeron had breached their defenses.

Bell knew Haven was fine now. Whatever Stolas had done, he'd somehow halted the magick battering her mind, but he hadn't erased it. As Bell slowly gathered up the shattered crystal pieces, he couldn't shake the feeling that, just like the broken chandelier above, whatever Archeron had done to Haven couldn't be undone. *Unseen.*

Searing pain throbbed in Bell's hand, and he was shocked to see a shard of crystal clenched beneath his fingers, blood dripping onto the stone floor. He waved off Xandrian's offer to heal. The sharp sting of his cut distracted him.

"King." Xandrian startled Bell by taking his hand and wrapping an ice-blue sash around the cut. When he was finished, his hand lingered. "You should rest. We leave for the mortal lands as soon as Haven is ready, and I expect you to help with the threading."

Any other time, Bell would have felt excitement over the upcoming test of skill. Threading was one of the most complex skills a runecaster could hone; even Haven, with all her vast access to power, couldn't manage it. And now that Stolas was no longer the Lord of the Netherworld, neither could he.

Any other time, he might have also let his thoughts drift to Xandrian's fingers still lightly curled over his hand.

But only one thought clanged inside his skull: Archeron was never going to stop until he possessed Haven or killed her.

Bell pulled away from Xandrian's gentle touch. "I want to train."

"Now?" Xandrian's scoff turned to pity as he shook his head. "Don't. Don't punish yourself for what happened earlier. We all bear responsibility for that."

"This isn't a punishment. I'm going to be ready the next time that bastard comes for her—but I understand if you need your beauty rest, Sun Lord."

Bell's challenge wiped the sympathy from Xandrian's face; his lips tugged into a soft, punishing smile as he waved a hand toward the double doors. "After you."

Xandrian would make him pay for that remark, but Bell welcomed the pain.

He was discovering that was the best distraction of all.

ELEVEN

"I'm going to rip Archeron's head from his body," Stolas snarled, pacing along the length of the rough stone balcony he and Nasira stood upon. Humid warmth from the royal baths wafted over his cool skin. The sound of Haven's lady's maid humming floated over the wind, where she brushed out Haven's vibrant rose-gold hair.

Haven had awoken weak and mired in sweat. In her typical obstinate fashion, she had tried to get up, pretending she was fine. But the hollowness in her eyes said otherwise.

And when she slid from bed and nearly collapsed—

He hadn't rushed to her aid, as much as it killed him not to. She would have hated that. Thinking about it now made his blood boil.

How he had to watch her struggle to stand. To walk. How she used the little energy she had to hide the haunted look in her eyes. With the assistance of Demelza and Nasira, he had talked Haven into a bath and breakfast.

Two hours—it had taken two hours of her staggering and pausing to make it to his personal bathhouse. Every second watching her struggle while pretending to be fine twisted the dagger of pain and rage deeper into his heart.

Nasira stretched out her wings, face tilted to catch the first light of dawn. Like his mother, she was short compared to most Seraphians, her face strikingly beautiful, with an undercurrent of savagery that only added to the allure.

She yawned, flashing the canines she never retracted. "I can't believe I'm the one pointing this out, but killing the Sun Sovereign goes against Haven's plan."

"Debatable."

"Not really. She wants to unite the nations, remember? Or were you not present for the same boring speech I was?"

"I fail to see how that has to do with removing Archeron's head."

"Because removing the head of the largest Solissian kingdom's ruler would go against our new peace and love theme." She shrugged her bird-boned shoulders. "I am all for the idea, mind you, especially if I get to *keep* the head. It's so much more interesting now that half his face is hideous and the other beautiful, plus I always thought the notion of allying all the nations was ridiculous."

"So then this speech is . . . what? You arguing for the sake of arguing?"

"I just feel the need to point out that Haven will be furious . . . since you seem to care about that."

He felt his teeth bare in a ridiculous smile. "I do, strangely. As should you since you swore an oath as her Chosen."

"Swearing an oath to protect her with my life does not mean I care about her moods." She leaned back, stretching her wings. "And how long must we keep playing nice with the Solis nations, exactly?"

"As long as Haven wants."

"Begging for alliances? Pleading to be acknowledged as the daughter of Freya? Our mother didn't ask for permission to be respected, she demanded it. Disrespect was answered with immediate violence."

"Not in the end."

Nasira's eyes flashed. "And look what happened."

That was my fault. The words clumped in his throat, unspoken. Nasira would never say as much, but she didn't have to.

And now, the thought of the same thing happening to Haven . . .

A growl rumbled his chest. "She won't tell me what he did to her."

Nasira's gray-blue eyes took on a haunted quality as she met his furious stare. "Remember when they used to drag us away from our cells while the other watched?" She exhaled, shifting her focus to the purple and gold haze gilding the stringy clouds. "When you returned, covered in blood and bruises and worse, your eyes terrifyingly vacant, I would ask you what happened, remember?"

The memories pushed to the surface, poisoning his thoughts until he forced them back down. Today was not the day to revisit those particular horrors.

"I didn't understand then why you wouldn't answer me, but I do now." Nasira met his eyes again, the pain inside her face making his gut twist. "You were protecting me, Stol. You *always* protected me, no matter the price that safety cost you."

He let his attention slide to Haven. Done bathing, Demelza had a plush white towel wrapped around Haven's thin body. "She doesn't need to shield me from what happened."

"No? After she disappeared—Stol, the last time I saw you like that was when—"

"Don't. Don't say it."

He could still see his mother's silver eyes, rimmed gold like his, as they jerked wide. They flashed in his dreams, his nightmares. Her mouth parting. The gold ring fading and silver turning to soot as the life left her.

That was the last time he felt that angry, that afraid, his emotions tangled and raw and all-consuming.

"Are you sure she's worth all of this?" The wind nearly swallowed Nasira's soft voice.

Without hesitation, he replied, "Yes."

They both turned to watch Haven. She seemed to have regained most of her strength, evident by the animated way she argued with Demelza—something about demons?

And yet . . . his gaze riveted to the jaggedness of her collarbones and arms. The gauntness of her cheeks.

That wasn't caused overnight.

A swell of concern rose inside him, followed by a scowl. After centuries of smothering every emotion, every whisper of feeling beyond unfettered rage, the vulnerability that came with caring for another being was . . . uncomfortable.

Even with his sister, he had managed to detach himself from worrying over her. Probably because she was half-feral and most times it was whomever she came into contact with that suffered.

With Haven, though . . . there was no detaching himself. No severing the strange bond between them. Not now. He could no more cage his feelings for her than he could his Shadow Wolf.

Both had grown too powerful for that.

He followed her with his gaze, frowning as he made out the shadows that settled between the sharp knobs of her spine.

The demands of his kingdom made it impossible to ensure she made time to eat. At first, he'd assumed she was simply too busy and had the cooks begin delivering her food to that tiny, desolate room she insisted on using.

But they informed him the plates returned uneaten.

Assuming she was simply being picky, he spoke to Bell and had the poor Seraphian cooks spend two days learning to bake the pastries she loved.

Those also returned largely untouched. Along with her favorite soup, a tomato bisque. Her favorite breakfast food, biscuits lathered in gravy. All of it untouched.

She was starving herself.

If he wasn't trying to at least *appear* civilized for the others' sake, he would throw her over his shoulder and force her to eat. To stop punishing herself for what happened in Solethenia. To forgive herself for Archeron's betrayal. To stop blaming herself for every death that bastard claimed in her name.

But he couldn't do that *for* her, and as much as he wanted to lock her away in a room and force her to take care of herself, he at least had the presence of mind to know what a terrible idea that was.

"Is it her?" Nasira's voice drew him from his ruminations.

"What? Freya's daughter?"

"No." The skin around Nasira's eyes tightened. "You know who I mean. Her. The one the blood augur mentioned."

He went still. Completely, utterly still. "You know the rule. We don't speak of that."

"She is not immortal and—"

He growled.

"Stolas—"

"Enough."

She flinched at his warning tone. Flinched—but stubbornly continued. "I refuse to let that happen. I don't care what that lying augur said . . ."

Her words trailed away as Haven approached, and his shoulders loosened as he focused his attention on her. Some of the bruising beneath her eyes had faded, the healing waters working to mend her physical flesh, at least.

What lay beyond, though, that would take time. And he would be there for every step. Whatever she needed.

"Can you be ready to leave soon?" she asked by way of greeting. Of course she was trying to completely skip over what happened last night.

He narrowed his gaze at her. "The question is, can you?"

"I'm fine." She ignored the string of skeptical grunts and curses Demelza uttered. The woman really did make cursing an art form.

"First we eat breakfast." She went to argue, and all his plans to remain a gentleman fled. "You are going to eat, Haven, if I have to hold you down and force the food into that stubborn mouth of yours."

Well, there it was, and he wasn't sorry.

In his periphery he caught Nasira's grin. Demelza stopped mid-grunt and gaped at him, her expression either furious or impressed—it was hard to read the damned woman.

Haven's eyes flashed fire. "I'd like to see you try."

"Would you now? Because we can arrange that . . . or you can simply march your obstinate ass to the food hall, give your mortal body what it so constantly requires—sustenance—and go about our day."

"Would you have me go as is . . ." she tugged on the corner of the towel, highlighting how precariously it was wrapped around her body, "or can I at least dress first?"

He arched a brow. "Your choice. Although, Shadeling knows, the soldiers need something to wake them up this morning."

Incredulity stretched those beautiful golden eyes wide, and he barely refrained from cracking a smile. That would only infuriate her more—an amusing but ultimately unhelpful turn of events that would defeat the purpose of this standoff.

When her chin lifted, he prepared for more verbal sparring, but she turned on her heels and marched toward the doors. A few minutes later, she showed up in the hall, fully dressed, and polished off every single thing on her plate.

Afterward, those stubborn lips—now covered in honeyed pastry flakes—grinned ferociously at him.

And he only imagined what those soft, sweet lips would taste like for a ragged breath before pushing the fantasy away and returning her smile.

He would take anger over the haunted look he'd witnessed when she first clawed awake anytime. If that's what it took to make her take care of herself, to soothe the inflamed wound she kept hidden from everyone, he would gladly fill that role.

TWELVE

Haven wiped a sweat-damp strand of hair from her forehead as she stared up at the newly reestablished wards shimmering high above the stacked stone wall circling the city of Luthaire.

Stolas tucked his wings against his back. The white hair at his temples had darkened with sweat to a light silver, and he glared against the bright sunlight as he swept his gaze over the perimeter. "The wall we expected, but the ward is . . . new."

New wasn't exactly the right word. The capital city of Veserack was once the seat of power over the Broken Three Kingdoms, and its wards had once been just as impressive. As old as the runewall in Penryth and gifted by an Asgardian King, the powerful shield had kept out even the most cunning intruders—until it cracked and then faded into history years ago.

A mass exodus of the city had followed.

"It must have flared back to life after the Curse was broken," Haven said as she unbuttoned the top of her blouse, which was already sodden with perspiration. "I should have guessed."

Even from here, she could feel the shield's defensive magick prickling the moist air. And Goddess knew it was humid. She'd forgotten it was the middle of summer in the mortal continents, the southern tip a cauldron of wet, balmy heat.

She almost envied Surai and Delphine as they roamed the skies above, catching the sea breeze. They were assessing the city and surrounding territories in search of potential entry points—as well as traps.

"Am I the only one who thought coming here unannounced was a bad idea?" Xandrian asked, picking an invisible speck from the sleek silver vest he wore. "There is a decorum to these things, after all."

"You thought coming here period was a bad idea, Sun Lord," Surai called as she appeared from the nearest ash trees. "But we're here now so stop pouting like a mortal and deal with it."

It was times like these that Haven wondered if her friends remembered she and Bell *were* mortal.

The hard planes of Xandrian's face schooled into an aggrieved scowl. "I *am*. Who do you think got us here?"

Behind him, the portal he and Bell had opened sparkled softly between two large boulders, rimmed by pale green fire.

Haven frowned. "Should we do something to hide that?"

Bell's face took on a scholarly expression that meant he was about to teach her something. "The spells woven into the portal's makeup are incredibly complex. We included everything from longevity runes to masking runes."

"Explain it to me like I know nothing about portal creation."

A proud grin revealed his perfectly straight white teeth. "This particular artery between Shadoria and Veserack will last for weeks, possibly months, and it can only be seen by its original travelers: us."

"At most," Xandrian added, "anyone passing by would mistake it for a mirage of heat."

"An entirely believable occurrence," Stolas murmured, obviously loving the tropical temperatures as much as Haven.

"How astute," Xandrian muttered. "Perhaps now you can find a way inside those walls. Unless," his stare settled on Surai, "you discovered something useful, raven-shifter?"

Haven's stomach dropped a little as Surai gave a subtle shake of her head. "Nothing. The city and port are remarkably secure. This new king must have put all his resources toward defenses first."

Her voice held a note of respect that Haven was beginning to share. Most kings would have diverted their attention toward flashier improvements meant to show their wealth and power.

"No sign of hidden reinforcements or traps?" Stolas asked.

Surai again shook her head. "Delphine is still checking a few areas, but overall, it looks safe."

What are you playing at, King? Haven wondered as they all turned toward Luthaire. The port-city formed a crescent around a large man-made harbor. Haven faintly recalled visiting with Bell and the court years ago right before the city fell. Despite trade between the Solis and mortals being all but dried up, there were nearly thirty ships in the sparkling topaz harbor.

Once impressive sandstone buildings lined the ivory coast, their crumbling architecture hidden beneath scaffolding and ladders. Pale smoke drifted from the red-roofed houses as servants prepared for the evening meal.

During the Curse's reign, the city had been abandoned as factions broke off into clans and citizens fled to the mountains to hide. Without the masonry guild's constant upkeep and the wards to buffer the sea's destructive embrace, the great city of Luthaire had fallen into natural disrepair.

Now that the wards were working again and the harbor was filled with white-sailed warships and trading vessels, the citizens had returned and begun rebuilding.

Cradled by walls of the vast city and the calm bay, the sea-palace rose from the city's center, a monolith of sandy-white stone parapets and towers bleached by salty air and the sun. Like a beast washed up on shore, it extended out over the water on a complex system of stilts.

When the gate at the mouth of the harbor was closed during high tide, the palace and city was accessible by ships and smaller boats.

But when they were opened, the water drained, leaving the entire city completely out of reach to would be attackers. From land and water, at least.

Surai frowned at the palace. "Perhaps we enter from the harbor mouth? I didn't check that far out."

"The bay is guarded by a giant gate," Bell answered, sliding a slender bronze instrument into a pearl-inlaid silver sheath at his waist. "It would be easier to slip past the few guarded entrances on land—although that's not saying much."

The device was an acrum, a tool that aided lightcasters in piercing the Realms of Other as they carved a path through the invisible planes. One end was pointed like a needle, the other tipped with a black radiant-cut sapphire surrounded by tourmaline.

Acrums were what lightcasters of old used to create the ancient portals that used to connect all the continents. She knew this because Bell had spent an entire evening telling her all about the rare tools, and how it had taken twenty lightcasters with acrums an entire year to create one of those ancient portals.

According to Surai, there were only a handful of acrum needles left in all the realm. Which probably explained Bell's beaming grin and the extra flourish in his movements when he wielded it.

"Oh, wonderful," Xandrian murmured. "Anyone fancy taking a mid-afternoon stroll through this charming city?"

The rankle of his long, straight nose highlighted his sarcasm, in case the disdain dripping from his every word wasn't clear.

Stolas chuckled. "We could go to all that trouble, or we could simply bypass the formalities and arrive in the throne room."

Xandrian's light blue gaze slid to Stolas's wings, which were spread casually so that the indigo feathers crowning the tips brushed the soft grass. "Asgardian spells are woven into every inch of that shield. Last I checked, wings can't break through wards this complex."

"No, but *I* can. Or did you forget I am the son of the last Seraphian Empress?"

"Who can forget when you remind everyone?" Xandrian murmured.

"Asgardians are cunning. Any ward walls they built for other kingdoms always contain a tiny signature by its maker, a little door in case the kingdom becomes an enemy of Asgard." Stolas's arrogant grin bordered on suicidal glee as he added, "I've already located that section, now it's a matter of convincing the sentient ward that I am its master."

"It's that easy, is it?"

"It is when you're me," Stolas promised, his smug tone making her wonder if he was *trying* to rile Xandrian.

Xandrian clicked his tongue. "Even if that were true, is it a good idea to just show up inside this king's home? Uninvited?"

"Technically we were invited. But if you would rather ask for permission first, be my guest."

His dark gaze slid to Haven, and her chest swelled a little as she realized he was waiting for her input. She skipped her focus over her friends.

Each of her Chosen was willing to walk straight into a trap for her.
To die for her.

It had been decided that the others would stay in Shadoria in case Archeron's promise of peace was a trick. But all of them would have come despite knowing the risks.

They knew Haven was hunted, that the bounty on her head made her a target. A shadow of horror fell over her as her visions clawed to life, the screams and terror so real—

No. Archeron is trying to use fear to control you. Do not let him.

Jaw clenched against the memory of Archeron's depraved hallucinations, she exhaled through her nose as a cold finality came over her. "I'm tired of asking permission. If this king doesn't like it, he can tell me himself."

Surprised delight lit Stolas's eyes, and then he turned his attention back to Xandrian. "Are you and your little needle up to the task?"

"Some needles are more powerful than others."

Surai snorted before taking to the skies, where she would watch with Delphine for outside threats.

On the way here, Xandrian had let Bell thread the portals, an arduous process that required setting countless portals on every tiny outcropping of land they could find. Xandrian had been surprisingly patient as he gently corrected Bell's technique. Repositioning his fingers on the acrum or pointing out runes to deal with the humidity, which apparently messed with a portal's longevity.

Now there was no question who was creating the next portal. Xandrian winked, puffing out his chest as his sour mood shifted into cocky pride. "Watch and learn, Noctis."

Shadeling Below, there wasn't enough room in this realm for both their egos. As soon as Stolas tore a rift in the ward, Xandrian followed through on his arrogance with a portal that took them straight through the breach and . . .

Into King Elhaem's throne room.

THIRTEEN

The move went just as expected.

The second they were dumped, rather unceremoniously, into that airy room of ivory, sun-kissed marble and gold, King Elhaem's guards descended. The soldiers wore loose white clothes tied with purple sashes, and they tapped the butts of their spears into the floor as they approached.

By the runic prayer tattoos to the Selkie Queen covering their dark arms, they were former sailors.

Haven almost felt sorry for the men as the realization of who—and what—they were about to fight dawned on them. It didn't help that Xandrian curled his two fingers and suddenly a wall of frothy waves rose outside the open walls. Ready to crash down at his command. Or that Stolas's wings were flared so wide that the tips on either side scraped the walls, the points of his incisors peeking below a curled upper lip.

To their credit, the men didn't waver. If it came to a fight, she decided, she would end them mercifully.

"Whoa, easy, everyone. Easy!" Bell pushed forward, hands held up as he tried to calm the guards. Using every scrap he probably knew of Sancrit, the common language of the Broken Three Kingdoms, he explained who they were.

When Bell was finished, the sailor-turned-guards raked their gazes over Haven before settling again on Stolas. Their spears lowered a few inches, the charms hanging from the base of the spear tips tinkling.

It was progress, at least. All they would get if Stolas kept goading them with that taunting grin.

Provoking poor mortal guards? she said, soulspeaking into his mind. *They would hardly be worth the fight.*

What? he purred innocently back. *I'm smiling at them. I thought mortals liked that?*

If by smiling you mean baring your fangs like a mountain cat about to pounce, then yeah, you're nailing it.

Then what should I look like?

Less like yourself, she snapped.

"Bravo." Everyone's attention jerked to King Elhaem. He was striding down the dais steps toward them, clapping softly. Sunlight sparked inside the rubies and diamonds of the rings adorning each finger.

The proclaimed King of the Broken Three territories was nothing like Haven expected. Eros Elhaem was young, no more than a decade older than her, for starters. And unlike King Horace, whose body had been bloated and spoiled by too many delicacies and not enough stairs, King Eros moved with the lithe grace of a man who had lived off fish and little else for years.

This king was very capable of wielding a sword—or an army, she would bet.

A brocade silk tunic in gold and turquoise draped almost to his knees, as was the mortal fashion, but failed to hide the muscular swell of his thighs. Tapered at the waist by a belt of abalone shells, the tunic's colors were striking against his tanned olive-brown skin. Instead of the long, elaborate braid plaited in gold that sailors preferred, his onyx hair was cut short, two thick, simple braids cresting his skull.

A single gold hoop dangled from his ear—the only hint he'd ever hunted over the open sea.

And he was handsome—shockingly so. Those dark eyes teeming with a feline intelligence that made his nickname suddenly seem . . . imposing instead of silly.

The Smiling Cat indeed.

Eros appraised Stolas first, those cunning eyes taking their time as they shifted to Bell, Xandrian, and finally Haven.

There his gaze lingered, long enough to conjure a low growl from Stolas. And when Eros finally flashed his teeth in a smile, it was anything *but* welcoming. "How lucky we are to have a visit from four of the most infamous players in the realm. A fallen Lord of the Netherworld, a traitorous Sun Lord, a kinslaying would-be king, and a—"

"Careful how you address her," Stolas drawled, the grave warning beneath that mannered tone making even Haven shiver. "The ivory walls of this room have a wonderful airiness that would be lost if I had to paint them with your blood."

Xandrian cursed under his breath, and she caught the spark of magick flickering inside Bell's half-closed palm.

Subtle, she snapped, slamming her words into his mind, hard enough that his jaw ticked.

This king doesn't respond to subtly, was the only reply she got.

Perhaps breaking in had been a mistake. Perhaps—

Distant laughter broke her thoughts. Childlike laughter. If she could hear it then . . . she discreetly cut her eyes at Stolas, following his rapt attention to a balcony on the other side of the chamber.

Two small children in expensive silk dress similar to the king's sat on the tiles, oblivious to the intruders as they played. The girl couldn't be older than four, the boy probably six or seven. At least nine guards surrounded them, facing outward to deflect any surprise threats.

His children. The king was guarded because his children were near.

Understanding dawned just as a strikingly beautiful woman clad in loose emerald silk draped over long, muscular limbs approached to stand beside the king. Her skin was the rich, bronzed color of the region, her dark hair shorn close to her scalp, showing off a long neck devoid of jewels. "Yes, Eros. Where are your manners?" The woman turned her wide eyes to regard Haven, a surprising ferocity brimming in their deep brown depths as she angled herself to hide the children from view. "I am sure our guests are not here to harm anyone, isn't that right, Goddess-Born?"

This was King Eros's wife and mother to the kids on the balcony. Haven nodded, never breaking the mother's stare. "I apologize for the abrupt entrance, but . . . I'm having trouble trusting lately."

"As you should." The woman smiled, making up for Eros's cold grin with blinding warmth. "I am Neri, Queen of the Broken Three, and my husband was just about to offer you all the comforts of Luthaire, starting with some of our famed wine."

Eros's jaw was tight as he gritted out, "Of course. Where are my manners?"

A flick of his fingers summoned servants into the room to lay out a spread of food and drink onto a long serving table. The guards melted back against the walls, one on each side of the countless balconies overlooking the sea. Their impeccable organization and obvious training was another notch for Eros, who Haven was beginning to suspect was so much more than just a pirate who'd confiscated a throne.

The cry of seagulls filled the ensuing silence. Xandrian must have concluded the threat was past because he loosened his grip on the sea outside, the waves merging back into the still bay, and ambled over to sample the wine.

The coil of tension inside Haven's chest eased as she glanced over the throne room. Centered above the deepest part of the bay, the fin-like structure floated at the heart of the castle, held aloft by countless covered walkways that led to different wings. The entire chamber was constructed of white slanted marble strips, like the bleached bones of a whale, the opening allowing the briny ocean breeze to stir through the room.

From afar, the structure made the sea-palace look like some long dead oceanic skeleton rising from the bay.

King Elhaem noticed Haven's curious stare, and she was surprised to see a real smile touch his lips. "Marvelous, is it not? When I was younger, I used to pass outside the walls of the bay and marvel at the daringness of such a place. The beauty like a direct insult to the Gods."

Before Haven could answer, Stolas began prowling over the chamber, his face schooled into a studious expression as he inspected the architecture. Of course, he was perfectly aware of how every single courtier froze as he passed.

The king arched a dark eyebrow at Haven. "Does the Lord of the Netherworld enjoy the arts?"

"He does, indeed," Stolas answered, not bothering to look away from a sculpture that was made with sea-glass, shells, and coral.

Wonderful. Stolas was talking about himself in third person now.

"Then perhaps a tour of my city before we discuss more serious matters?" Eros suggested.

Haven frowned, cutting her eyes at Bell. Penryth was only a day's hard ride through the mountains away. If Renk heard that Bell was here, or worse, if Renk was part of a trap to lure them here . . .

Understanding dawned on Eros's face, and he tilted his head to address Bell. "While within these walls, *everyone* under my protection is safe."

Xandrian, who had been perfectly happy watching the scene from the rim of his near-empty wine glass, barked out a bitter laugh. "Right.

Every Solis in Effendier knows that the words of mortals are filled with lies. Your kind hold nothing sacred except the greed inside your hearts. How do we know there won't be assassins waiting in the alleyways? The bounty on the Ruler of the Nine's head alone could fund the renovations for this entire city."

Neri went rigid beside King Eros, and Haven hated watching the hurt flash over her proud expression.

Stolas glanced over his shoulder at her, his look saying, *It's not me this time.*

Runes and shadowfangs. Before she could try to smooth things over, King Elhaem gave a curt nod. "It is no secret the mortal kings of our land have acted dishonorably in the past, but not every man should be judged by their ancestors."

"Perhaps if some of your mortal kings were queens you wouldn't have this problem," Stolas idly pointed out, not even bothering to look away from his current fascination—a cord that, when tugged, draped the slats in the ceiling with golden curtains to block the light.

If they were in private, she might have kissed him.

Neri's lips twitched, and when her dark brown eyes drifted to Haven again, there was a newfound light there.

"Perhaps." Eros took in the fleshrunes glowing softly over Haven's bare arms. "But I think you will find, where honor is concerned, gender or race have very little to do with it."

The servants froze as Stolas padded on silent feet to the refreshment table and poured himself a glass of sparkling wine. "A pirate waxing poetic about honor?"

Eros's wide shoulders stiffened at the insult, and Haven gritted her jaw. What the Netherfire was Stolas doing?

But Neri didn't look surprised as she slid a calming hand down the king's side, a honeyed smile on her tight face. "Pirate would imply stealing something that isn't yours. After the former ruler of Luthaire fell and the kingdoms broke into chaos, King Boteler sent mercenaries to take command of our shipping fleet. Naïvely, we thought he was helping us. But as soon as he controlled the trade routes, he diverted all of the food and resources to Penryth."

Bell's brows gathered. "That's—that's not true. He had to take control or the warring factions would have destroyed all trade south of the runewall."

"That was your father's claim, yes, but not the truth." Neri regarded Bell for a heartbeat. Was it just Haven or did the fierce lines around her eyes soften? "I imagine during the Curse's reign you were well fed? Well clothed? You had clean water and spices and medicines, tallow for your candles, oils and perfumes to smell nice?"

Bell blinked. "Of course, as did the southern kingdoms. The ruling nobles south of the wall came to Fenwick every month and I assure you, they lacked for nothing."

That was absolutely true. Haven always knew when the southern lords were visiting by the cloying perfumes and ladies garbed in the latest fashion.

"The nobles who visited Penryth struck a deal with your father. Their absolute support for a few scraps of food and fabric, just enough to keep them accustomed to their opulent lifestyles."

Bell's throat dipped as he worked out what she didn't say. "But not enough for the people under their rule."

Something dark rippled over her expression, there and gone. "When you've seen a child die of starvation, you do things you might never have done otherwise. Eros started with one ship. Then two. Slowly, he took back what belonged to the people knowing he would be branded an outlaw, his reputation forever soiled. Everything he raided from King Horace's shipping line was given to the people. He is the only reason most of us survived, and the reason every single citizen here remains loyal to him."

Us. That explained the raw edge in her tone. Haven had assumed by Neri's well-spoken manners and grace she was noble-born, but perhaps not. Most noble-born mortal females didn't speak their mind, and they certainly didn't challenge their husbands.

"If that's true," Bell began, "then I am deeply sorry, and I will do whatever it takes to right that wrong . . ."

His mouth clamped shut, as if he was just now remembering that he was no longer in a position to make such a declaration.

Haven's heart clenched. If she could take that pain away from him somehow—but no, just as she had to deal with her own wounds, he had to mend his.

A squeal drew the group's attention to Stolas and something . . . no, *someone* tugging on his wing? When Haven's mind wrapped itself around what was happening, she couldn't hold back her laugh.

Eros and Neri's youngest child had escaped her guards and was tugging on one of Stolas's long wing feathers. Her black hair was pulled into tight braids all around her head and secured with green and yellow ribbons, and she was screeching something in Sancrit as she jumped up and down, completely oblivious to the danger right next to her.

Stolas had gone completely still, as if not moving would somehow hide him.

In the time that Haven had known Stolas, she'd never seen him appear so . . . torn between amusement and terror. As if he didn't know how to catalogue this creature.

For a tense breath, all eyes watched to see how the Shade Lord would react. The guards were halted around him in a circle, ready to protect the princess, while her parents were frozen in fear.

A memory of the Bane floated uninvited into Haven's head. One of the captive girls in the Devourer's camp had stumbled and fallen into the pit where Damius kept a poor snow leopard he'd bought from a Solis trader. Haven could still remember the absolute silence from the girls as they gathered around the pit, unable to move or do anything but pray the cat had been recently fed.

It hadn't.

She saw the same paralyzing fear on Neri and Eros's faces now, and she widened her stance, prepared for all hell to break loose.

FOURTEEN

Before Haven could say a word to calm the king and queen's fears and prevent the guards from doing something rash, a hoarse laugh boomed across the room.

Laughing—Stolas was laughing. His eyes lit up in a rare shade of green she'd never seen before as he leaned down until he was on the little girl's level, opened his palm, and released a spark of dark magick. The fiery blue flame broke off into a school of silver and orange fish that raced around her. The girl squealed with delight, smashing as many of the fish as she could with her tiny little fists.

Cursing in her native tongue, Neri chased after her daughter while Eros shook his head. "My son never gives us a moment's trouble, but that one?" Eros's sharp gaze softened as it drifted to the little girl, who was still somehow evading both a very agile Neri and at least ten flustered soldiers. A flicker of pride sparked inside his eyes. "Goddess help the man she marries."

"And if she doesn't want to marry?"

Eros blinked in surprise. "What sort of female doesn't dream of becoming a wife and having children?"

It took everything in her not to snort. From across the room, she felt Stolas's attention sharpen on her. "Some of us have other dreams, King."

"Even a princess cannot escape her duties to her kingdom." The king ran his thumb over a gold button just below his collar. "Surely you know that?"

"Are you still speaking about your daughter or me?"

"I am merely pointing out that in chaotic times such as these, great sacrifice is required from everyone."

A stab of disappointment throbbed in her chest. What was she expecting? This was the mortal realm, after all, and the entire continent was in massive upheaval. Securing alliances through marriage was the quickest, most efficient way to shore up power and protect territories.

And yet, the idea of being forced into marriage with a stranger. Worse. Someone you despised . . . "Who is your daughter promised to? Dune or Drothian?"

A muscle in his neck jumped. "Dune. My son is promised to the Drothian ruler's daughter."

That's how he took control of all three territories so quickly. A flicker of anger sparked inside her. How was using children to control territories any different than King Horace using food and resources?

"I suppose it's fortuitous then that you have two children to marry off to the two territories under your control." Her tone was razor sharp.

"Yes." He held her stare, unflinching. "The Goddess blessed us in that regard."

Haven stiffened. She believed Eros was an honorable man, but just like any ruler, he had to be cunning to survive. Until they knew *why* he risked both Archeron and Renk's wrath by meeting with her, she couldn't trust him.

"Why did you invite me here, King Elhaem? You know the risks of this meeting and you have much to lose."

Xandrian and Bell raised their eyebrows at the bluntness in her question, but she was tired of dancing around the subject.

A fleeting emotion too brief to catalogue—vulnerability? Fear?—darkened his visage. Then he swept out an elegant arm toward the mainland behind him. "Take that tour of the city. We will speak again tonight during dinner, Haven Ashwood."

Not Goddess-Born, but Haven didn't feel as if the name was meant to slight her. Rather, Eros seemed like someone who gave respect after it was earned, and she had yet to do anything but break into his throne room and insult him.

"We look forward to it. In the meantime, where should we start on our tour?"

"What foods do you favor?"

Bell laughed. "That's easy. Anything sweet enough to rot her teeth."

"And for him?" Eros glanced at Stolas, who was examining what appeared to be a bottle of very old, probably very expensive wine he'd somehow talked a nervous servant into procuring. "Or would he rather stay here and deplete my expensive wine collection?"

There was no animosity in his tone. Perhaps he was relieved that Stolas seemed more interested in draining the wine than the servants themselves.

But how long would that last? Other than the Asgardian she let him have, Haven had no idea how he was staying fed. The crystals in Shadoria kept him nourished but not . . . sated. She knew that much.

And now that they were here, would it be enough to siphon light magick from the wards and spells hewn into the city, or would he need to be taken care of somehow?

As a servant led them to their rooms, Haven realized how very little she knew about Stolas Darkshade.

Her need to compartmentalize him as Lord of the Netherworld started first as necessity, and then, because it was easier when pretending he didn't have feelings and desires, to keep him at a safe distance.

But now . . .

She jerked from her thoughts to see Stolas at the end of the sun-filled corridor, the rare bottle of wine all but forgotten in his hand as he watched her quietly. Something in his raw gaze sent heat rushing up to sear her cheeks.

She wet her suddenly dry lips as she mentally asked, *Do you trust him?*

His intensity shifted to caution as he shrugged. *He withstood my provocations when most mortal males would have reacted. That alone makes him worth more than half the kings in Eritreyia. And . . . he has impeccable taste in wine.*

She rolled her eyes, murmuring aloud, "You spoiled royals and your love of old, overpriced grape juice."

He tsked, and then something warm and liquid smoldered inside his silver eyes. "Join me for a drink and I will show you how marvelously wrong you are."

Her pulse quickened. Other than last night, when was the last time she was truly alone with Stolas? Training, but that didn't count. All her concentration was focused on conjuring the correct magick and avoiding his brutal attacks.

If she entered his room, there would be nothing between them to hide behind. Only the warm sea breeze and endless sunlight and calming rush of the ocean below. At least during training her high heart rate could be explained away.

But here, without the constant threat of attack or demands of Shadoria, there was no hiding the building feelings she had for him.

And that terrified her for two reasons.

First, he could reject her, and she wasn't ready for that kind of pain. Not from him.

But if he didn't reject her, if he felt the same way . . . if something happened between them, Archeron would know.

Somehow, he would *know*. And he would turn all of the resources of his kingdom from hunting Haven to assassinating Stolas—

No! A violent shock of horror and fear slammed through her, the visions of Stolas's death hurtling to the surface of her mind. It was Stolas's slow, agonizing end that still invaded her thoughts. Still tormented her whenever she closed her eyes. Infecting her like a plague that had settled deep inside every part of her being.

Archeron had seen to that. Whatever magick he used to craft the nightmare, it had been so real. So painfully real . . . almost like a prophecy of the future.

No. In some ways, Stolas knew her better than anyone here, even Bell. Stolas was the only one who could understand the darkness that lived inside her.

She couldn't lose him. Terror and agony ripped at her heart just imagining a life without him.

A cold finality came over her.

Doing her best to look tired, she gave Stolas a bland smile. "Another time. I—I need to freshen up before the tour."

The fleeting disappointment in his eyes was so brief she could have imagined it.

Stolas was her friend. Her mentor and protector.

That was enough—it had to be.

FIFTEEN

The few hours before dinner passed by in a blur of cafés and shops. Neri sent two of her cousins to take Haven and the others around the city using the slender little boats that glided down the winding canals. When Haven had asked what they did when the gate was fully opened and the water let out, one of the cousins simply explained if that happened, they had bigger problems.

Haven tried to glean information from the cousins that would paint a better picture on King Elhaem's relationship with the new Penryth court and ruler, but whenever she tried, they feigned not understanding her, even when she used the Solissian common tongue.

Why was it important to see the city before dinner? Especially knowing the risks of leaving the protection of the palace? By now, Haven felt she understood enough about Eros and Neri to see that they were nothing like King Horace.

If they promised Haven and Bell were safe within these walls, they meant it.

But . . . Archeron was the Sun Sovereign, and the wards of this city no match for his power and influence. And Renk, while not the brightest, possessed a lethal cunning that, when combined with his cruelty, was every bit as dangerous as King Horace had been.

Because of that, she never relaxed during the tour.

Not when they were taken through a winery and given samples of a sparkling honey-gold wine that tasted like heaven. Not when they stopped in the shops to be fitted for the light, airy clothes for the evening—a present from Eros.

Not even during their last stop, at an oceanside restaurant overlooking the harbor, where they were served crab legs and lobster fresh from the sea. She sat on a stone bench near the balcony next to Bell and Surai, unable to enjoy the food as she scanned the horizon for any signs of danger.

Stolas noticed, and he raised an ash-colored eyebrow until she snapped the hard shell of a crab leg, dipped the delicate white meat into a ramekin of red sauce, and crammed the entire thing into her mouth.

Satisfied? she demanded into his mind.

Not nearly. He grinned, that dark gaze going to her mouth. *You have some . . . sauce on your bottom lip.*

Ignoring him, she forced the rest of the meal into her mouth, her body grateful for the sustenance even if she could hardly taste it.

When she glanced back at Stolas, prepared to continue their private barb session, he was deep into his own private conversation with Delphine.

Haven couldn't tear her eyes from the two as they signed back and forth. Stolas was leaned in close, his eyes alight, smiling in a way that shouldn't bother Haven—but did. His hand made a series of symbols, and Delphine's face jerked into silent, hysterical laughter, tears glistening the corners of her eyes.

Even dressed in normal clothes, with their wings magicked away, it was obvious they were Seraphian by their moon-white hair, pale skin, and ever-changing eye colors. While Delphine was smaller—as most Seraphian females seemed to be—and didn't possess the horns that only royal Seraphians sported, she could very well be his sister.

Or lover.

Her last bite lodged in her throat.

Was that what he wanted? What he needed? Someone who understood him, his customs and language and history. Delphine knew exactly how he stayed fed.

And instead of looking away when he did, she would probably *join* him.

She released a shaky breath, a strange, twisting sensation grinding in her chest.

If Stolas didn't have to spend all his time training Haven, worrying about her, perhaps he and Delphine—

"You okay?" Surai asked suddenly. She was dabbing at her lips with the corner of a white linen after somehow polishing off a giant mountain of crab legs.

"Yeah." Haven forced a smile. "Just, you know, being so close to Penryth is . . . hard."

Surai slid her knowing gaze to Stolas and Delphine and then back to her. "Hmm." Her lavender eyes darkened. "You are sure you're up for dinner tonight? We can postpone, King Eros—"

"No. Tonight has to happen."

Surai and Bell exchanged a quick look of concern. They hadn't stopped watching her since she met them this morning for breakfast. She had been vague about what Archeron had done, desperate to spare her friends the worry.

It was hard to say that every time she looked into their eyes, the gruesome reenactment of their death played out before her, so real she couldn't breathe. Harder still to face the reality that, when she first woke

up, a part of her was ready to give herself to Archeron just to spare them.
Which was what Archeron wanted.

"Haven." It was Bell's turn to plead with her, his bright blue eyes the same color as the sea below. "No one would blame you if you needed a day to recover from—"

"The only way to protect me, to protect *all* of us from Archeron is alliances, and I plan to do just that tonight, looking gorgeous, by the way."

The lines bracketing Bell's mouth smoothed out at the joke, just as she knew it would, and soon she had him discussing his wardrobe for the evening. The tension cleared as Xandrian joined in, followed by Surai.

They didn't even notice when Haven quietly removed herself from the conversation, relieved to no longer have to pretend to be excited about her dress or the evening or . . . anything, really.

Because when she peeled back the superficial emotions she plastered around her like a wall, all she felt was fury.

Fury and *fear*.

She was just finishing wiping her mouth on a napkin when something drew her attention to Stolas, who was watching her while the others debated silk versus linen.

His chin was dipped forward, his silver eyes more blue than normal as they studied her beneath heavy lashes.

On instinct, she began the process of lifting her lips in a smile when he said into her mind, *Don't.*

Her poor attempt at a grin faltered, died. *Don't what? Grin at you? Fine.*

Not when it's a lie. I'd rather you rake your nails across my face than feel the need to deceive me.

For some reason, shame seized her chest, followed by that all too familiar anger. At Archeron. At the Shadeling. Her mother. *Herself.*

And then, a slow, creeping bitterness at Stolas for not letting her deal with her trauma her own way. For insisting she show him beneath the happy veneer to the monstrous, unfettered rage and trauma beneath.

Fingers curling into fists, she flicked a dark look his way, scowling, letting him feel the roiling darkness skimming beneath the surface.

If that's what he wanted, fine. He could have it. All of it. *Better?*

She expected him to recoil. But he held her stare.

And when his wide, full lips slowly lifted into a wolfish grin, there was no doubt the emotion was real.

Immensely.

SIXTEEN

The dinner King Eros planned for them was elaborate but thankfully private. Other than the attendants who summoned them at dusk and the few servants bustling in and out, only Eros, Neri, and Haven's party attended.

Haven nearly balked as she followed her attendant through a series of corridors and then down an impossibly long, deep stairwell. The sensation of the ocean pressing in on them grew until she could almost hear the deep waters rushing in and around the bricked tunnel they passed through.

On the other side, she was rewarded with a huge conical chamber made of the clearest glass she'd ever seen. And hopefully the thickest, considering they were situated in a deep basin on the bottom of the harbor's sandy floor, surrounded by turquoise water.

Enchanted, Haven pressed her fingers against the curved wall, watching the orange and silver schools of fish dart past. Coral of every color rose like a city around them, a home to sea creatures beyond her wildest imagination.

Neri joined Haven. The blue silk draped over the queen's lithe body was the same color as the ocean, and it flowed with her every graceful movement. "This is perhaps my favorite place in all the kingdom."

"I can see why." A smile flitted over Haven's lips as a metallic blue-green jellyfish undulated past them in the current. "It's like they don't even notice us . . . or care how much power and magick we might have. They live in an entirely different world, with different rules and hierarchies."

Neri blinked, her surprise turning to approval before she slid her attention to the reef. "If we're lucky we might even see the enormous white-fin sharks that hunt in these waters."

Bell, who was the final one in their party to arrive, flashed a scholarly smile that meant he was about to give one of his lectures. "According to old accounts from the record books, the reef was all but decimated after the last court fled. Years of living without mortals near the ocean let it thrive again."

"Very good," Neri murmured, this time not bothering to mask her approval.

"We do have a penchant for ruining things," Haven added.

With a sigh, Haven tore her gaze from the colorful scene and followed Neri and Bell. A long table had been set up to accommodate their party, and Haven was pleasantly surprised to see that Eros had set a chair next to his at the table's head for Neri.

Most mortal kings would never dream of putting their wife at the head position. But after hearing they were undeserving of a male's respect from birth, most mortal queens wouldn't know *how* to fill the prominent spot, especially when entertaining a powerful party such as theirs.

Unsurprisingly, Neri didn't have that problem. Head held high to show off a long, elegant neck, she slid into the high-backed wooden chair and immediately began peppering Xandrian with questions about his time in Effendier.

King Eros nodded his head as Haven took the seat opposite Bell's, next to the king. Surai and Delphine sat together on the opposite side, and Haven bit back a grin as she noticed Surai had picked up enough signs to carry on a conversation.

That left Stolas to her right. A quick glance revealed he looked gorgeous in a long, expertly cut gold and black tunic that matched the kingdom's style.

Something tossed and turned inside her chest, and she ignored the wicked grin he flashed, quickly refocusing on the king.

But even without looking, she felt Stolas's razor-sharp focus prickle over her skin—particularly along the bare flesh of her back. The sinfully thin fabric of her emerald-green dress draped seductively over her collarbone and shoulders, held together by two exquisite pink-diamond encrusted seahorse jewels.

Neri gave Eros a triumphant grin. "I told you the emerald color would be perfect on her."

Eros chuckled. "Neri chose all your clothes. She has quite the eye for that sort of thing."

"I was a royal seamstress and clothier's assistant in Ashiviere, before . . . all of this." Surprise widened Haven's eyes, and Neri met her stare. "How do you find the dress compared to the fashion in Penryth?"

If everything didn't rest on Haven convincing them she was Goddess-Born, she would have snorted. "Different. There's—well, there's definitely less of it, for starters."

Neri's tinkling laugh filled the air. "The nobles of the previous court kept to the old, cloistered fashion, even after the citizens adopted the Asgardian's more practical loose fitting silks and linens."

"But you changed that tradition?" Haven asked as an attendant poured water into her cup. Inside their cylindrical glass enclosure, everything—from the rush of water in her glass to her voice—seemed amplified.

"We changed a lot of things." Neri flicked up her dark eyebrows almost mischievously. "In a time of such upheaval, it makes sense to question the more archaic rules of the past."

Neri's gaze pointedly lowered to Haven's arms and chest. With so much of her skin exposed, her fleshmarks glittered like the golden rays of fading sunlight that flickered through the water's depths.

Eros didn't bother hiding his fascination with them.

"Were you born with the marks?" he inquired, as two bronze-skinned attendants poured decanters of golden wine into their glasses.

She shook her head. "They were given to me by . . ." Her throat tightened, and she caught Surai's gaze before meeting the king's stare once more. "By friends."

"Those must have been powerful friends."

"They were." The moisture fled her throat, and she took a steadying breath before sipping the wine. The cool drink tasted of apricots, grass, and lemon. "They didn't know then who I was or, well, I imagine they would have refused."

Lie. Bjorn knew. Or suspected. And Surai would have still gone through with the plan regardless of who Haven was.

But Archeron . . . he had begged her not to do it.

Did some dark, ancient part of him know it would come to this?

She realized her fingers were trembling slightly around the stem of her wine glass. Stilling her hand, Haven took another practiced sip.

"And have you always possessed both kinds of magick?" he continued, his hands steepled together beneath his chin, his wine untouched. The look in his rich brown eyes was curiosity, nothing more—but she hadn't been ready for such broad examination, and something inside her recoiled from the questions. The memories they dredged up.

Teeth gritted, she shrugged. "They showed up around the same time."

"And when did you learn of your . . . unique lineage?"

Warm sweat trickled between her shoulder blades. How to answer that? When she was bound and nearly killed by Archeron, her almost lover and the new Sun Sovereign?

Beside her, Stolas took the world's most theatrical sip, swirled the wine around in his mouth, and sighed loudly. "This wine is almost as exquisite as your wife, Eros. Where is the vineyard, did you say?"

As the king begrudgingly tore his focus from Haven, she felt the muscles of her jaw unclench. *You didn't have to save me,* she mentally shot to Stolas, annoyed more at herself than him.

She should have expected these types of questions. Should have been more prepared.

Your scent says otherwise.

The king was savvy enough to know what was happening, but he kept the questioning benign after that, falling into an easy conversation with Bell over trade tariffs during their course of shellfish stew. When Renk was brought up, the king navigated away from the tricky subject with an ease only an experienced ruler could manage.

Neri was curious about the magickal tournament in Solethenia, and Bell was more than happy to regale the table with tales of the trials and infamous Sun Court.

Unsurprisingly, he left out the part about the end when the old Sun Sovereign had Haven imprisoned and then Archeron tried to kill her.

It was a strange dance, watching everyone tell stories while skirting around certain topics, of which there seemed no end.

Still, despite the abundance of wine and conversation, Haven could feel the king growing restless.

Once the desserts were handed out—a rich, glazed custard topped with raspberries inside gilded clam shells—Haven knew she couldn't put off his questions any longer. "I apologize if I didn't seem forthcoming earlier," she began, stirring her spoon inside her custard. "My past has a few . . . unpleasant memories."

Eros was quiet for a moment. When his eyes met hers, they were almost kind. "I, too, have memories I would rather not revisit. But I have to know who I am allying with."

"The Goddess-Born of prophecy," Xandrian answered, casually swirling a finger around the rim of his wine glass. Up until now he'd been content picking at his food and making it abundantly clear how lacking he found everything.

Everything but the wine, apparently.

"And I should just . . . take your word for it?" King Eros arched a thick brow at the Sun Lord, his saccharine smile doing little to mask his sarcasm.

"Yes." Xandrian took a bite of his custard, dabbed his mouth with a seafoam green napkin, and met the king's stare. "Have you heard of the Order of Soltari?" The way the king stilled, he had. "We've been searching for Freya's daughter for years. Scouring every Goddess-forsaken mortal city, risking torture and death in the process, and I can tell you, unequivocally, the female sitting to your right is her."

The king's eyes narrowed as they took Haven in once more. This time, there was no flicker of kindness, only the shrewd intelligence that had gotten him this far.

"She is beautiful, and there is no question of the power inside her. Even I can feel it crackling off her skin like the air right before a storm. It's an intoxicating combination, looks and power. Unfortunately, beneath those curves, she is still very much *mortal*. So if that is all you have to offer, a beautiful female who possesses rare magick and can fill out a dress, I am afraid it's not enough to risk the safety of my kingdom and family."

Frustration swept over Haven. And then, perhaps because she was tired of being spoken about like she wasn't there, or of being assessed and prodded like an oddity, she fixed her gaze on the king until he met her seething stare. "Who said *I* agreed to the alliance? I have yet to be convinced by *you*, mortal king. Or did you think a nice custard inside a shell and an expensive bottle of wine was enough to win over the daughter of Freya?"

He straightened, that handsome face twisting a little in shock as he blinked at her, his lips parting as he prepared a response—

"I'm not done," she snapped. "I've seen rulers more powerful than you come and go. I've personally helped vanquish some of them, including the Shade Queen not once, but twice. So, while I suppose I enjoy being ogled and flattered as much as the next girl, if you think calling me 'beautiful' is all it takes for me to choose to ally with *you*, you're just as dim as all the other mortal kings that came before you, and you'll last just as long."

The silence that followed made it hard to breathe, but Haven felt . . . better. Remarkably so.

King Eros cleared his throat, pushed gently back in his chair, and stood. Then he turned and left without a word, his soft footfalls echoing off the walls.

The others stood, and Haven did the same, her chest constricting. She meant every word she said, and yet . . . all her hopes had been riding on this alliance. On Eros being different than other mortal kings.

"Was it the attack on his wine?" Stolas purred, sliding his lethally calm gaze toward Neri, "or the custard? Which is perfectly acceptable, I might add, even if the presentation was a bit ostentatious."

Neri kept her face neutral as she regarded Stolas, but her hands clenched and unclenched at her sides, her chest trembling with every inhalation. "He is under enormous pressure. The decisions he has to make have huge—"

"Do you think Haven is under any less pressure?" Stolas interrupted softly. "That her decisions are any easier? Her losses any less painful? As we speak, her people, *our* people may be dying under yet another attack from the Sun Sovereign. Our choice to travel here left them at great risk, and now innocent civilians may be suffering for that choice. Tell me, did we make a mistake?"

The muscles in Neri's neck were taut, her delicate nostrils flaring. "You don't understand. If you did . . ." She exhaled, her fingers loosening as she met Haven's stare. "I will talk with him. In the meantime, there's a reception in the Stargazer Hall for you. All of you. Perhaps after a few more drinks, we can begin again?"

As soon as the queen disappeared, Xandrian impaled a raspberry on his fork and twirled it in the air. "That went well. I vote we keep insulting him and see how long until he has us imprisoned."

"Or tries, at least," Bell added, earning an amused—but pleased— look from Xandrian.

Stolas ran a finger over the rim of his mostly untouched wine. "The king insulted Haven. For all we know, that was a test. One that she passed rather amusingly."

Xandrian said, "Yes, I imagine he rather enjoyed being called dim. And questioning his ability to rule—males love that."

"If only the negotiations were left to the females," Surai groaned, her lavender gaze pointedly settling on Xandrian, "we wouldn't have to play this mine-is-bigger-than-yours game."

"Other males don't play those games," Xandrian corrected with a sly grin. "Not when Sun Lords are present. Otherwise, they would never win."

Haven's groan mirrored Surai's, and when Delphine responded, holding her thumb and pointer finger out to represent a less than impressive length, Haven didn't need to be fluent in signing to recognize the meaning of the gesture.

Or to laugh along with the others. But just like earlier, the emotion felt hollow. Forced. There was no question in her mind now that if they stood alone against Archeron, every single one of her visions would turn into reality.

And every person in this room would die.

SEVENTEEN

Stargazer Hall was a dome situated over a shallow area of the bay, with countless alcoves and tunnels built into the walls. Moonlight streamed in from above, lighting up the floor, which Haven was delighted to discover was made of thick glass that clicked beneath her heels and gave a direct view into the ocean beneath. A light crowd of people gathered in the ballroom, drinking from tall flutes and pretending not to stare at Haven, Stolas, and the others.

Although their attention was mainly reserved for Stolas. The females, especially, stared with doe eyes as he made a show of tasting the wines and pretending he didn't know he was the fascination of every single mortal in the room.

She convinced herself it was because of his wings—oiled and brushed into a glorious sheen—and not the devastating smile he flashed. A smile that when combined with his sumptuous onyx and silver suit, powerful body, and horns, made him look like a God of old.

"Why does he keep smiling at them?" Bell whispered into her ear as they watched Stolas dazzle yet another female.

"Why does a cat toy with a mouse even when it's not hungry?" she quipped, surprised by the acid in her tone. Stolas was free to smile at whomever. "He can't help himself."

"Goddess help the fools," Surai muttered from her perch against a column wrapped in tiny seahorse-shaped runelights.

Haven forced her gaze off the spectacle. In truth, if not for the prospect of talking to Eros again, she would have retreated to her room and the giant porcelain bath that was calling her name. It was becoming harder to force a smile and pretend she was fine when every time she looked into her friends' faces, she saw how they died.

Perhaps that was part of the dark magick. That even now, long after Stolas broke the visions, she relived that in the faces of those she loved most.

King Eros and Neri had yet to appear, so Haven grabbed a flute of the chilled white wine, broke off from the others, and took the moment to gather her thoughts.

The ballroom was huge and probably once entertained all the mortal lords of the continent. A few runelight sconces in the shape of seahorses were positioned around the spherical chamber, but most of the light came from the star-shaped cutout above.

She thought at first that was why the hall was called Stargazer . . . until she peered down into the glass and realized the sea life was *glowing*, illuminated by magick or some other phenomenon, thousands of tiny sea creatures flowing by like a river of sparks beneath her feet.

No, like a river of stars. Glowing, wriggling stars.

The bell-shaped form of a jellyfish danced past, its vibrant purple tentacles pressing into the glass, sliding and wiggling as they tried in vain to wrap around her ankles and carry her under. Giving up, the hungry creature moved on to a school of fish, and she followed it through the hall, passing couples pressed into alcoves until she was alone in the tunnel.

The incline of the path was so subtle that she hardly noticed they were entirely undersea—just like the room they dined in earlier—until the runelights disappeared and the walls became a winding maze of glass tunnels.

This part of the ocean was deeper, darker. And something about the darkness, the soft glow of the alien sea life floating past, calmed her.

"That particular type of jellyfish is called the white-death," a familiar voice drawled behind her. "One brush of its tentacles could kill one hundred mortal men."

She turned to face Stolas, her back pressed into the pale wall of the alcove, stomach tightened against the rush of heat she'd come to expect at his presence. "Are there a lot of those on the coast of Shadoria?"

"No, they prefer the warmer waters of the mortal coasts." He studied the jellyfish a few heartbeats longer before sliding that intense focus to her, her heart ratcheting into an erratic beat. "But I met many souls that ran afoul of the white-death's lethal sting. Once an entire crew of shipwrecked sailors, in fact." One corner of his mouth twitched. "I liked the sailors. They possessed a wonderfully crass sense of humor."

Oh. After a few weeks of freedom, it was easy to forget what he had been before. The souls he'd spent countless years tormenting. "It almost sounds like you admire the jellyfish."

"Perhaps I have a soft spot for murderous creatures."

Something in his voice, or perhaps in the way he stared at her, made it suddenly very hard to breathe, and she felt just like those women he smiled at—one smile and she would melt. "Did you get tired of flirting with the females in the ballroom?"

"Was that what I was doing?" A flash of dark emotion glinted in his eyes, there and gone. "It was better than sensing their fear whenever I passed."

The delicate light of a passing fish glinted along the dark blue feathers of his wings, held loose behind him. They flared a little as he took a step toward her.

On instinct, she tried to put space between them—only to remember there was nowhere to go. The cool glass pressed into her bare back as she flattened against it, Stolas closing the distance until he was nearly touching her.

Nearly, but not quite. As if an invisible barrier held him back.

All around them the sea life gathered, as if drawn by the powerful magick they felt oozing from Haven and Stolas.

"Are you afraid of me too, Beastie?" His breath caressed her lips.

The smell of him—irises and blood mandarin and musk—filled her senses and made her dizzy. Her heart pounded wildly against her sternum.

"No."

"But you are afraid of something whenever I'm near. If not me, then what?"

His question caught her off guard because—because he was *right*. Her heart was racing, her chest trembling with every inhalation, the muscles of her thighs and core gathering power, ready to flee. It happened every time he drew too near.

Every time they were alone, even briefly, and he looked at her the way he did now.

Stolas didn't scare her, but this thing between them, the way her body reacted to his nearness, his scent, his magick—

She crossed her arms, not ready to deal with this tonight. "I'm not afraid, just tired."

The lie came so easily. But she couldn't do this. Not right now. Not with so much at stake and her nightmares still so close to the surface, ready to rip through her confident façade and ravage everything she cared about.

The tangle of emotions beneath her chest threatened to unravel any moment, as if tugging on one thread—any thread—would bring it all crashing down.

Archeron had seen to that. Just the thought of the visions prickled her skin with sweat, the image of Stolas hurt, Stolas dying, her heart shattering over and over as she relived losing him . . . *runes.*

"Tired. Right." He inhaled deeply. "King Eros was right about one thing. Your flesh is still very much mortal, which means you can't lie to me, nor can you mask your fear."

Dammit.

"Maybe that's why I'm afraid. No matter how much magick I possess, or how beautifully I dress the part, I will always be mortal, my fragile body slowly decaying, growing older, one mistake away from death."

"We are all one mistake from death." His full lips parted slightly as his heavy-lidded gaze swept down her dress, clinging to the curves. "But fragile and decaying are not words I would use to describe you."

"Not yet, but the Solis and Noctis? That's all they'll think about when they look at me. Perhaps King Eros told the truth."

A wicked grin carved into his jaw. "Oh, he most certainly did. You *are* mortal. You *are* beautiful. And you do fill out that dress—although he failed to mention how *exquisitely.* But that is not why your heart races, is it?"

Her dry throat scraped together as she tried to swallow. That thing inside her—the thing that twisted a little each time she was around him—throbbed almost painfully, cutting into flesh and bone with each turn.

Bad idea—this was a bad idea.

"There it is again." His fingers were cool as they took her chin, delicately, as if she might indeed break, and tilted her eyes up to meet his. The ring of golden fire rimming his strange eyes danced light over the high cliffs of his cheekbones, his thick eyelashes casting long shadows. "What could make the most magnificent creature I've ever met afraid?"

As she looked into that cruelly handsome face, the familiar planes of his too-sharp jaw and straight nose, the devilish mouth perpetually twisted in some private jest, those haunted eyes so full of emotion and now brimming with delicate hope . . . she understood.

She could love him, this broken, monstrous, beautiful Shade Lord. That's what scared her.

She probably *did* love him. Probably had for a long time. Before Effendier. Before they broke the Curse. She must have known it when she said Stolas's name while with Archeron.

And then, when Archeron made her relive Stolas's death in her visions and she woke up to Stolas holding her, unaware she was awake, unaware she could witness the tenderness of his touch . . .

Everything had fallen into place.

But it had taken up until this moment to admit to herself the truth. Her mind reeled. When had that happened? How?

Maybe during one of their training sessions, which made absolutely zero sense because she had hated him and he had despised her and . . .

Runes. She loved him.

Shit. Shit. *Shit.*

She loved Stolas Darkshade. *Loved* him. And she was terrified because she knew what Archeron would do if he found out.

Just as she knew that there was a good chance that Stolas didn't feel the same way. Perhaps he wasn't even capable of love.

Agony tumbled through her at the next thought.

Perhaps he simply wasn't capable of loving *her.*

She heaved out a ragged breath, intending to push him away, but his stare dropped to her lips. Something dark flashed in his eyes as he took in her mouth, parted and trembling.

Head tilted, his eyes lifted once more to meet hers as, slowly, curiously, he flicked his thumb out and brushed the delicate swell of her bottom lip.

The contact sent a shiver of sensation hurtling through her so powerful that she thought he used magick at first.

His pupils swelled, a snarl of surprise rumbling his chest.

And then his gaze shifted to the curve of her shoulder and she followed his attention and—

She was glowing. Just like in Solethenia right before . . . oh, Goddess save her.

This wasn't happening.

EIGHTEEN

"**B**eastie." Stolas's normally elegant voice was husky as he ran a lazy finger down her shoulder, tracing her marks, leaving a path of icy-hot fire in his wake. "Is *this* what scares you?"

"I don't know what you're talking about."

Liar, her body accused. Molten fire burned through her core. Each wave that crashed over her, leaving her skin sensitive and aching, whispered the same.

Liar liar liar.

"Or this?" She gasped as his hand found the slit of fabric along her skirt, his fingertips sliding beneath that too-thin silk and over the burning flesh of her thigh, stroking, teasing.

Promising.

Her back arched, her body reacting wildly to his touch, to the cold magic that was so similar to the magnetic powers crashing through her own veins.

A part of her could almost feel the monster inside him calling to hers, that primordial beast of shadow and rage, hunger and desire. Could almost feel its rumbling snarl echo inside her bones.

Even now, with the world crashing down around her, she knew she could lose herself in this—whatever this was. Could lose herself to Stolas.

"Why does," his thumb made contact with the inside of her thigh, "this," he circled higher, higher, *higher*, "scare you?"

"Stolas." His name came out pleading, a whispered incantation to . . . what? Stop? Keep going? Both?

Both. But she couldn't say anything as those hands continued exploring her flesh, running along her runes like he was memorizing them . . . like they belonged to him, and the memory of what those fingers could *do* . . .

Fear and longing and a strange, breathless panic constricted her spine. Her heart slammed and whirled and, runes, he could probably *hear* her body freaking out. Could feel it responding to his touch. The inner muscles of her thigh twitching and leaping beneath the teasing flick of his thumb.

Every muscle she possessed jerked rigid as he suddenly brushed his nose over her neck. "If I kiss you," he murmured, his breath caressing the shell of her ear, "what will you taste like?"

The moment his lips collided with hers, surprisingly soft and gentle, her traitorous mouth parted for him. His tongue swept over hers, slowly, pressing deeper with each kiss.

He leaned back to study her, a strange look on his face. "It's even in your kiss, a sweet note of panic layered with the wine from earlier."

"Does that excite you?" she whispered, because she couldn't think of anything else to say to distract him from the truth. And she knew when he'd fed from the Asgardian, his fear had most certainly roused Stolas—for lack of a more fitting word.

"Excite? I'm not feeding from you Haven. At least . . ." A pause. "Not in *that* way."

Sweet Goddess and everything holy.

"So you can separate the two?"

"It takes . . . effort," he admitted in that husky, remorseless voice. "When I was young and foolish, I mixed sating my hunger with other pleasures, but that was a mistake."

"And now?"

"Now, I'm simply curious to know why my presence makes your body pulse with fear, when it also makes you feel *other* things."

"Things?" Odin strike her down where she stood. "How can you be so sure?"

Biting her lower lip, she willed her damn thigh to stop trembling.

His smile was devastating. And apparently a distraction. His free hand slid around her hip, splayed out flat against the small of her back, and gently tugged her forward.

Her right leg spread out to steady herself—

His thumb flicked over the space in between, there and gone, and what he found there . . .

"Because," he growled into her ear, "fear doesn't usually do *that.*"

Shadeling Below.

"What is it that scares you, Haven? Are you afraid of *how* I make you feel? Of losing control? Are you afraid of *me?*"

Her throat clenched, and she pressed deeper into the coolness of the glass wall as heat danced over her skin. Her body was inflamed. On *fire.* The relentless light of her runemarks glinted off the glass enclosure, drawing even more sea creatures until the water around them glittered.

"I told you I am yours, Beastie. Your monster. Your protector. Say the word and I'll take you away from here. I'll take you wherever you want to go."

"And do . . . what?" Nethergates, she sounded like such an idiot. But she needed him to spell it out. No—she needed him to confirm he felt the same way she did.

That this wasn't just quenching physical desire.

He chuckled, his lips curling in feline delight. "If memory serves, I've already answered that question before. Thoroughly."

Goddess save her. The fluttering in her chest migrated to her belly.

"And the king?"

"Is not invited." His stare slid to her lips. "Granted, he is handsome, but I don't like to share."

She flicked up her brows in exasperation.

"The king is an idiot. Making him wait a night—or three—would teach him some manners. He wants this alliance as much as we do, I just need to figure out why."

"So it would be a negotiation tactic?" Something warm and languid unfurled deep in her lower belly as she imagined doing what he proposed for three whole nights. And yet . . . "The people of Shadoria? What happens to them in the meantime?"

His jaw flexed. "These types of alliances take weeks to build. I wouldn't have come if I didn't trust my sister and the others to take care of them, but . . . I didn't swear my allegiance to them, Haven. I swore it to you. And I'll do whatever is necessary to ease your pain."

"My pain?" She blinked.

"Yes, the same pain I took from you last night. The pain you try to hide from everyone. Surely you know by now that my duty is to protect *you* and no one else, whatever the cost."

Bombarded by his touch and his smell and the promise of so much more, it took a few hazy seconds for his answers to sink in.

But when they did, when her mind grasped onto the meaning behind what he said . . .

A chill skittered over her shoulders. He couldn't have doused the inferno raging inside her any more efficiently than if he'd thrown a bucket of ice water in her face. She inhaled deeply as his words clanged against her skull.

Allegiance. I swore it to you. Whatever it takes. Ease your pain.

My duty is to protect you—whatever the cost.

Like it was his command. His *duty* to touch her. To make her feel this way.

To make her—

No.

Those were the words of a soldier, not someone taken by passion. Certainly not someone . . . someone in love.

Love. In that instant, she knew how foolish she had been. To bring an emotion like love into the equation, especially now—what the Nethergates had she been thinking?

Fighting for breath, she retreated into the wall, away from him. From his touch and the traitorous way her flesh still clung to it. To *him*.

The air between them dimmed as light from her runemarks faded to their usual iridescent glow.

Any other time she would have still found them marvelous, but now they seemed muted and . . . cold. Containing a mere fraction of their brilliance from before.

For a painfully stretched out second, he stared at her, a questioning, almost vulnerable look in his silver eyes making the whole situation even more unbearable.

And then, as if recognizing the full magnitude of her discomfort, his hands fell to his sides and he retreated an inch, but it was enough to sever the spell.

Stupid, to think the son of the late Seraphian Empress could fall in love with a mortal. Not when there were so many of his own kind for him to choose from. Females with wings as glorious as his who could tear through the sky as his equal. Who would live thousands upon thousands of years, while she . . . she flamed out in the blink of an eye.

Love. Really, what had she been thinking?

Bitterness welled in her chest, sharp and biting, followed by the realization that it didn't matter if he loved her back. Actually, it was best that he didn't.

After last night, she understood her love was a curse. A death sentence.

A look of determination gritted his jaw, and he planted his hands on either side of her face, although he was careful not to touch her. "Tell me what I did to offend you."

She shook her head, unable to find the words to cover her shame. His eyes narrowed. Runes, he wasn't going to let this go until she fully embarrassed herself with the truth.

The inescapable, stupid truth.

I love you, idiot. And you just offered to service me like a whore.

No way she was saying that aloud, ever. He could soulread her and probably discover enough to understand, but for some reason, he was respecting her privacy—as much as that seemed to pain him.

That was . . . new.

"Haven—"

She darted under his arm, ignoring the raw confusion in his voice as she pretended to study a small octopus clinging to the glass. This whole thing felt like a mortifying nightmare, worse than the dreams she used to have where she showed up at court without a stitch of clothing and then tried to hide behind her sword.

But there was nothing to hide behind now. Nothing but the humiliation surely reddening her cheeks. The absolute mortification that, for a wild heartbeat, she thought his touch was *real*. That he wanted her the same way she wanted him.

That his offer of intimacy wasn't fueled by his duty to fix her brokenness so she could present herself to the world as the Goddess-Born, infallible and strong and perfect.

My duty is to protect you—whatever the cost.

Nausea bubbled up her in chest as her understanding grew. Of course he felt obligated to take her pain away through physical pleasure. That's exactly what she asked him to do last time, and it's not like she had any expectations then beyond forgetting.

But this time . . . cheap and cold all over—that's how his *obligation* made her feel now.

That familiar prickle cascaded over her bare shoulder blades as he came up behind her. She could feel his questioning stare, the loaded silence that hung heavy between them.

Her dutiful protector, even now. Sworn to keep her safe from everything—including her own foolish heart.

Netherworld take her. What if he thought he *had* to pleasure her?

A fresh wave of horror crashed over her as the implication sank in. What if, in some cruel twist, he now felt bound to her in the same way he had been bound to Ravenna?

Runes. Why didn't she know any spells for disappearing? Suffocating shame slid down her throat, her chest tight and airless and—

"Beastie, look at me." Gathering her courage, she met his unreadable gaze in the glass's reflection. His voice held the ever-constant amused lilt, but there was an undercurrent of vulnerability that made her throat clench. "If you think—"

"Goddess-Born?"

Stolas's head snapped toward the voice with a booming snarl, his wings whooshing out and sending the swarm of fish behind the glass darting away. Grateful for the intrusion, Haven quickly straightened her dress as she followed his stare.

The queen waited near the entrance to the alcove, somehow managing to stay in place when most mortals would have already fled under Stolas's foul mood. As her eyes adjusted to the darkness and she made out Stolas's intimate position behind Haven, one hand fluttered to her neck.

Her miss-nothing gaze swept over Haven, lingering on her flushed chest and the parted slit of her dress—pushed high up on her thigh—

before settling once again on Stolas.

Whatever she saw in his face caused her to blink—in surprise or something else, only the Goddess knew. "Eros has agreed to continue the meeting—unless I've caught you at a bad time?"

If only the queen knew how bad. Perhaps she did. She was mortal, not blind.

"No." Shoulders back, Haven strolled toward the queen, somehow managing to school her expression into a bored smile. "We're done here."

The arch of the queen's brow was just enough to hint at her suspicions, while the softness around her eyes said it was none of her business.

Still, Haven felt the quiet disapproval in the queen's too-long stare as she led them away from the ballroom. A completely understandable reaction considering mortals only knew Stolas as the Lord of the Netherworld, the monstrous being who waited for them in death and delighted in their screams.

Not to mention every royal child taken to feed Ravenna during the Curse's reign had been retrieved by Stolas. Mortals knew so little of the Noctis and their history. Most couldn't distinguish between a Seraphian and a Golemite, and they certainly weren't educated on the Darkshade court's fall to Morgryth.

No matter the truth, the realm would always see him as Morgryth's enforcer, not slave, a bloodthirsty creature as feared and reviled as the Shadeling.

Feeling anything other than disgust for someone like that—well, it had to seem strange to Neri. It certainly did to Haven.

You love a monster, and if you don't know it yet, you will.

Bell had seen what she couldn't. If only he could have also predicted that particular monster wouldn't love her back. That he would see caring for her physical needs as his job—a job that took him away from his people, his kingdom, and his new life.

If he had simply wanted to sleep with her for pleasure . . . *that* her ego could have handled. It wouldn't have been enough, not now knowing her true feelings for him.

But it wouldn't have felt like having her guts ripped out either.

Stolas was silent as he followed behind them. The dutiful soldier, ready to do whatever it took to keep her safe. Distract the king at the first hint of her discomfort. Force her to eat. Kiss her breathless. Hold her as nightmares ravaged her mind.

Bed her whenever she was sad.

Anything to keep her on track as the Goddess she was supposed to be instead of the mortal she was.

A bitter laugh surged up her throat as she realized he was hers to command in every way but the one she wanted. Head held high, she choked the emotion down, all too aware of Stolas's unrelenting stare.

His eyes were like a thousand suns on her back.

And on other areas . . .

Good. She might have let her hips sway a little more than normal. Might have tossed her hair over her shoulder in the silly habit she used to judge other females for.

If he was going to treat pleasuring her as his runeforsaken *duty*, then she was going to make sure he regretted every second he failed at that task.

NINETEEN

Haven expected King Eros to be waiting in another ostentatious room with rich foods and wines to regale her. So when Neri led them through a servant's hallway outside to a covered walkway and then to a corroded iron ladder, Haven nearly hesitated. Only Stolas's presence behind her, both comforting and a source of constant shame, pushed her to kick off her heels and scale the rungs to the edge of a copper roof.

The king sat a little ways down on the roof, his legs dangling over the edge like a child, staring out into the fleet of ships dotting the dark waters as waves crashed far below. There was only one way to scuttle across the roof in a dress, and it wasn't pretty. Haven managed to secure a spot next to Eros as Stolas took to the clouds above, his shadow making slow, pointed circles around them.

"Do you always keep the leash to your monster so short?" Eros asked as he poured dark wine into a simple steel tumbler and handed it to her.

If he was trying to get a rise out of her, it would take more than that. She accepted the glass and shrugged. "Only when half the realm is trying to kill me. I still haven't figured out which half you fall in."

"Neither have I."

She couldn't tell if he was joking or serious. "Would you rather I send him away? I will, if he makes you nervous."

"That is the point, yes? To make people nervous?" He craned his neck to study the clouds, a curious tilt to his mouth. "Did he tell you I sent him two females before dinner?"

Her eyebrows shot up in surprise, but she smoothed over her expression into one of boredom. "Only two?"

His lips curved at the edges, teasing a smile, but she didn't confuse that with anything close to warmth. "I had heard rumors, of course, but I wasn't sure."

"You weren't afraid he would hurt them?"

"I was cautiously optimistic he could restrain himself, considering we are in the middle of negotiating an alliance."

"Is that what this is?" she drawled.

"Aren't you curious if he behaved himself?"

Yes, yes she was. "Considering you haven't thrown us out yet, I assume he didn't hurt them. The rest is none of my business."

He ran his thumb over the top of his leather boot, just above his knee. "Every ruler has their necessary evils. You've seen him feed then, I take it?"

"Only once," she admitted.

"And? Was his victim alive at the end?"

A pit of unease formed in her gut as she remembered the screams. "Yes. In a sense."

His glass clinked against hers. "To necessary evils."

She nearly choked as the harsh red liquid hit her mouth, burning all the way into her stomach. *Good.* It reminded her to drink with care, unlike the heavenly wines he'd served at dinner that went down much too easily for her comfort.

Around a man like Eros, she needed her wits completely intact.

She thought he would jump right in with more questions like at dinner, but he was strangely quiet, his solemn gaze as he stared out into the harbor making him seem so much older than before. In the distance, a ship's foghorn cut through the cry of seagulls.

"Is this your plan?" She lifted her tumbler. "Get me drunk on cheap wine and then push me off the roof? Because, if so, it has some serious flaws and we should probably discuss that."

A smile—perhaps the first real one she'd seen—graced his face, reminding Haven that when he wanted, he could be handsome *and* charming, a dangerous combination. "You know, you're nothing like I expected."

"I could say the same for you. I've had the misfortune of knowing a few mortal kings, and you're nothing like them. Then again, I've never met a king called the Smiling Cat."

Another grin. He really was beautiful when he smiled. Perhaps that's where he picked up the nickname, although she very much doubted it. More like his intense curiosity coupled with his razor-sharp cunning and disarming charm earned him that moniker.

A long stretch of silence followed as he sloshed the dark burgundy wine around in his cup. "When I was a captain, this was the only wine onboard. I swore the second my feet found the shore for good that I would never drink another drop of this swill. But here I am, sitting atop the most expensive collection of wine barrels in the entire mortal lands, and this is what I crave."

She took another drink, fighting the spasm that clenched her throat. "It does have its . . . charm after the fifth or sixth sip."

"The undersea room we dined in? I have ten more chambers just like it, filled with furniture and artifacts of solid gold. Elaborate rooms meant to impress Sun Lords. Even our royal bedroom is underwater.

And yet, the only place I feel normal is *here*, on the roof with the seagulls and rats."

Compared to his formality from earlier, his confession surprised her. Perhaps he was trying to disarm her with his sudden vulnerability, make her loosen up and make a mistake, but . . . it truly felt like he was being genuine.

"I think all of us find comfort in what we know." She watched the tall harbor gate in the distance slowly open to let a single, white-sailed vessel through. "I'm supposed to be the daughter of Freya, but I cling to mortal emotions and desires."

Stolas came to mind. The way he kissed her. The way her skin shivered at his slightest touch. Desire was too tame a word for what she felt around him.

A long stretch of quiet descended as they watched that solitary ship grow closer to the docks, Eros rhythmically tapping his forefinger over his cup.

When the tapping stopped, he turned to her. "What are your plans for the mortal lands?"

Haven blinked, not expecting the question. She had been so busy the last few weeks trying to survive that she hadn't thought what her plan was two weeks from now.

A month.

She watched the trading vessel dock and begin unloading their goods, wondering what it would be like to live such a simple life. "I have no plans other than allying Solis, mortal, and Noctis against the Shadeling."

"And afterward? Assuming there is a war against Odin and we are victorious, then what?"

"You mean, will I try to rule?"

It was his turn to blink.

"I don't want lands. I don't want gold or power or more magick, and I certainly don't lust after anyone's throne, yours included."

"Then what *do* you want?"

The same question she could ask of him. "I . . . want to live in a world free of fear."

"That's it?" If the almost comically arched brow didn't tell her, his voice made clear his skepticism. "And what of your Chosen, King Bellamy?"

"What about him?"

"Do you seek to reinstate him on the throne of Penryth?" His eyes were razor-sharp as he turned to her. "Mortals can overlook a lot, but a Kinslayer is universally reviled."

"You've met King Bellamy. Does he seem like the kind of king who would poison his own father?" Her cup clinked over the brass roof as she set it down, hard. "I imagine you've also met Renk by now, who as king is undoubtedly ten times worse than he was before—and he was already awful. So, tell me. How is that working out for you? Do you see a long and fruitful union with that tantrum-throwing tyrant?"

She had no idea if they'd actually met yet or what Eros thought of Renk, but the muscles flexing in his jaw said they had met—and it hadn't been an amicable affair.

"King Renk is . . . troublesome, but he is young and green enough that he is manageable."

"For now." Her hand fisted around the handle of her tumbler. Renk had hurt Bell their entire lives, but what he did in Effendier . . . that betrayal earned Renk a dagger with his name on it.

When the day came, she would help Bell twist it into the bastard's greedy black heart.

Eros unbuttoned the top of his collar and gave a long, tired exhale. "You know, what they don't tell you about being king is how utterly exhausting it is. I used to spend nights on the open sea with nothing but Neri and a bottle of wine and the stars."

"Who knew being a pirate was so romantic?" she teased.

He could have let himself take offense. Instead, he chuckled, but the sound lacked any real warmth. "Now I spend evenings up here. Sometimes all night. When the sun rises, I watch the families under my protection leave their homes and wonder, will my actions today condemn them to death?"

It was in that moment that Haven knew she liked Eros the pirate turned king. Even if his charm and looks and diplomacy was dangerous, even if he was possibly laying a trap for her . . . she liked the bastard.

Which made what she had to say that much harder.

"King, a war is coming. There's nothing you can do to stop it. You can't hide from it. You can't bargain out of it. People are going to die, yours and mine and others, so many others. The question is, which enemy will you fight against? Sure, you can placate Renk with gifts and beneficial trade deals and he might forget that he wants your lands and power—for now. But if Renk sits on the throne of Penryth when the Shadeling comes, Penryth and all the northern lands will fall. How long do you think it will take the Shadeling and his demon armies to cross the mountains and reach your kingdom?"

His eyebrows lifted at the turn in conversation, reminding her how young he was. She imagined Bell like this in ten years, tired, a bit disillusioned, but still full of fire to do the right thing for his people.

"When you put it that way . . ." Tipping back his head, he finished off his wine. "I should have brought the brandy."

"You know I speak the truth."

"No. I know you speak *a* truth, one that the oracles and seers and blood augurs have been predicting for centuries. Every year someone claims the dark God will break his chains and enter our world, and every year he remains trapped below—or dead, for all we know."

Haven shook her head. "He's alive. I can feel it here." She pushed her fist into her belly. "Morgryth woke him out of desperation and now he gathers an army."

"I cannot make decisions based on a feeling you have."

"No? What about what you know? Entire tribes have sworn allegiance to him. People under your control. They're heading north in droves. How do you explain that?"

"How does anyone explain madness in these times?"

She gave a frustrated grunt. "Are you always this obtuse?"

"According to my wife? Yes." A tight smile tugged his lips as he glanced to their left, where she undoubtedly waited for him. "I have a confession to make. I only invited you here to make her happy."

Haven fought back her own grin. "She seems like a queen who knows how to get her way, when it's important to her."

"You have no idea." He ran two fingers over the light stubble of his jaw. "As you may have already guessed, my wife is not from nobility, but she does claim distant blood ties to King Bellamy."

Those ties must have been very distant because Neri had never been around court. She looked to be possibly from Dune or even the Ashiviere region—where Bell's mother hailed from. But after Bell's mother died in childbirth, the Kingdom of Ashiviere lost their only ally in the Penrythian court and quickly fell out of favor with King Horace.

A rocky coastline with little resources or farmable land, it had always relied on trade from Effendier to sustain it. After Effendier completely cut off trade with its coastal neighbor, the kingdom fell into ruin.

"Because of that connection and . . . other reasons," the king continued, "she insisted I reach out to you."

Other reasons? There was no doubt Neri was persuasive when she wanted to be, but Eros would have never said yes to a meeting this risky over family ties. Whatever reasons he alluded to, they had little to do with family relations.

"Of course," he continued, "I assumed you would send a message back first, not appear in my throne room."

"And by the time the usual process of formalities had been exhausted, you would have talked her out of the idea, and this meeting would have never happened."

Another grin. "That was the hope, although she was so sure once I met you I would be convinced to offer my support."

"And?" Haven tilted her head as she met his stare. "Are you convinced?"

"Convinced that you are a divine creature with more powers than any mortal in this realm? Without a doubt. You, Haven Ashwood, are quite possibly the most stunning runecaster I've ever encountered, and I've traded up and down the Solis continents. Not only that, but you possess a rare combination of ferocity and kindness that in any other situation, in any other time, would make me bow before you myself." He dipped his head in reverence before meeting her eye again. "But none of that changes what you are: mortal."

She swallowed as disappointment hit. "The prophecy said Freya gave birth to a mortal child."

"Perhaps. But all the later texts use the word immortalis."

Immortal.

She blinked as she tried to process this new information. It was becoming clearer and clearer that, for being the supposed Goddess-Born, she knew very little about the prophecy itself.

Her disappointment gave way to a deep, growing frustration, and she rose to her feet. "You knew I was mortal before I came. Why go through this process then? Or was it that sailor's curiosity?" She ran her cold gaze over him. Perhaps he wasn't as deserving of her kindness as she thought. "The bored mortal king who discovered ruling wasn't as exciting as he thought and needed a distraction. Am I your entertainment?" She didn't bother veiling the threat in her tone. Nor did *he* bother trying to mask the flicker of fear that scuttled behind his tight smile as she added softly, "Because I can assure you, using me or my friends as playthings will not end well for you, even if I do really like your wife."

Calmly, he set down his wine, blotted his mouth on his finely tailored sleeve, and stood—favoring his left hip. An old sailing injury?

"Everyone loves my wife. Or anyone that's worth something, anyway. And believe me, she would be first in line to remove my balls if she thought I had so much as disrespected you."

Yep. Haven adored Neri. But she pushed any feelings of affection for her aside as she said, "Then what do you call this? It's starting to feel like a game, and if I didn't make it clear upon our arrival, I despise those."

"Then you are going to be in for a world of disappointment because that's all this is. Securing alliances. Forging unions between kingdoms. All one complex, deadly game of deceit that even the daughter of Freya has to play."

She met his eyes. "It doesn't have to be."

"Of course, you're one of those. An idealist." Eros sighed, running a hand through his short cropped black hair. "When I was a child, my family lived far from the city in a walled-off manor. My father, a lord by title only, he was an idealist too, in his own way. He thought the scraps of wealth and power thrown to us by the Penrythian King could keep the Curse out. For a while, we lived as if the Curse never happened, with servants and attendants and monthly balls to distract from the dying people all around us. My favorite servant was my nanny from Asgard. She used to tell these enchanting tales before bed of the Gods, but it was the story of Freya's hidden child that fascinated me the most."

Haven felt herself still. Very few in the mortal realm had ever heard of the prophecy. The waves continued to crash below, the seagulls continued to caw and the briny wind continued its soft rustling through the bay.

But all she could hear was the thrum of her pulse inside her skull as she asked, "Was it a story with a happy ending?"

"According to my nanny, the child would beckon a new age of war and death. But the Asgardians perceive fate and destiny as a river, and this child's future was uncertain, a stream trickling through mud and stone, looking for areas to carve itself into, to widen and thrive. Depending on the path the child's destiny took, the child would become a powerful river that would cut through the heart of the coming threat . . ."

He trailed off, and she prodded, "Or?"

"Or the prophesied child would join with their father and become a raging flood of annihilation for all mankind."

Haven shivered as invisible fingers of dread tapped down her spine. "What an awful bedtime story," she quipped, trying to hide how deeply it had affected her. "No wonder you have trust issues."

"From your surprised expression, I see the Order of Soltari hasn't divulged that lovely offshoot of the prophecy."

"It doesn't matter because I would never join my . . . the Shadeling."

The moonlight sparked inside the golden ring he wore as he toyed with his earring, his gaze fixed on the dark waters beyond. In that moment, with his unbuttoned collar, breath smelling of cheap tavern wine, and eyes loose with alcohol and probably days of little to no sleep, he didn't look like a king who could hold together The Broken Three for a single night, much less convince them to ally with her.

Then again, she cringed at what Eros saw in her. Her bare feet and loose, tangled hair, mostly free now of its pins and whipping in the gentle growing breeze; her own fatigue showing in the hollows beneath her eyes; the sharpness of her collarbone that gave her a half-wild look.

She probably more resembled a vengeful siren come to devour his heart than the Goddess-Born from his stories.

"You say you would never join the Shadeling," he said, "but just yesterday I swore I would never risk my kingdom to join with a mortal outlaw claiming to be the Goddess of prophecy."

Her heart lurched sideways. "And now?"

"Now, well now everything rests on this mortal proving she is who she claims."

"And how does she do that, exactly?"

His eyes were almost empathetic as he regarded her for a long moment. "Logic and history say that you are simply another heretic, neither savior nor destroyer. A mistake of nature being used by forces vying for control of the realm. But, if you *were* the prophesied child of Freya and Odin . . ."

He shook his head as if the idea was simply too far-fetched to entertain.

Then he picked up the near-empty bottle of wine, gathered the steel cups, and set off for the ladder, strolling uncomfortably close to the roof's edge. "Tomorrow, meet me at the docks at dusk."

"For what?"

"Your chance to prove yourself."

Wiping the dust from the back of her dress, she padded after him, the metal cool beneath her feet. She made sure to keep a safe distance from the edge. The last thing she needed was to fall and have Stolas save her. "So a test? And if I fail?"

He paused. His broad jawline came into view as he glanced back at her. "Then you leave the mortal lands immediately, sparing my wife any more of the cruel false hope you peddle, and promise to never return."

TWENTY

Despite the rhythmic lull of the waves outside her window, Haven slept fitfully. When she finally did slip into a deep, dreamless sleep, Bell woke her shortly after for training, which she forgot she'd promised.

He milled around her room as she yanked on her pants and boots, hopping from one foot to the next.

"Long night?" he teased. "You disappeared right after the dancing started and then, shortly afterward, so did the gorgeous winged male in the room."

Wedged against the wall, with her boot propped against the dresser, she finished tying the worn laces and threw him a dark look. "Was that before or after you and Xandrian fled to your own private balcony?"

She'd searched for Bell last night after the meeting with Eros, only to find Bell and Xandrian on a small balcony, huddled over a book and whispering. She'd waited until he came strolling back to his room hours later before divulging her conversation with the king.

Bell stopped examining an oil diffuser made from an abalone shell and cut his eyes at her. "Believe me, it's not like that. He's helping me refine the poison I discovered in Solethenia for our soldiers. We're close to finding a medium that would retain its potency but allow us to make one hundred times as much."

"Huh. Fascinating. For over two hours?"

He busied himself making her bed for her, tucking in the corners and fluffing her pillow. "Really. He made it painfully clear in Solethenia that he's incapable of a relationship." Bell shrugged, toying with a golden pillow tassel. "Which is fine because now that I know him, he's . . . he's . . ."

"A narcissistic, puffed up peacock with an inflated ego that probably doesn't match his you know what?"

Bell's head fell back in a startled laugh. "I was going to say emotionally unavailable, but that too." A knowing look came over his face. "Oh, you're good. I almost forgot I was interrogating *you*."

Haven sighed as she struggled with her hair. Bell had insisted that the daughter of Freya couldn't wear a simple braid, which just happened to be the only one she knew how to do. "There's nothing to interrogate. Stolas is bound to me the same way you and the others are, but his interest is purely out of duty."

Duty. She jerked on her hair so hard a few strands might have come out. She'd never hated a word more.

Bell snorted. "Are you braiding your hair or fighting it? Here, let me."

He came around the bed and took over, just like when they were younger. Normally that would have made her feel childish. But now, with everything changing so fast in both their lives, the old habit brought her a much needed sense of comfort.

"Nothing elaborate, okay?" she clarified as she settled on the bed, knowing otherwise he'd spend two hours making her hair into an elaborate bird's nest or something equally ridiculous.

"You're the Goddess-Born, Haven, and mortals are just as shallow and vain as the Solis. You need to look the part."

"Or I could just look like . . . me?"

He snorted as if that was the most awful idea he'd ever heard. Thankfully his hands worked fast, gently pulling and weaving strands of her rose-gold hair back from her face.

"You say his interest in you is simply duty," Bell began, circling back to their previous conversation, "but you didn't see the monstrous thing he released on the Hall of Light after you were taken."

She stiffened. "What monstrous thing? What happened?"

"Nasira called it his Shadow Familiar. Whatever it was, it might be the most terrifying thing I've ever witnessed. And as you know, I have a lot of experience in that department."

"What did it look like?"

"Like an inky mist at first, but then it grew gorgeous black fur and teeth and onyx talons long enough to gouge stone when it walked, which wasn't really walking but prowling, by the way. Its giant paws shook the floor with each footfall. It had these horrifying red eyes and it was *huge*, this massive . . . wolf, for lack of a better word." Reaching across her, he retrieved the black hair tie from her nightstand and secured the braid. "The thing was death in beast form, and I don't think he could control it. If not for Nasira it would have killed us all."

Haven shivered. "He told me his Shadow Familiar was dormant, all but dead, probably forever."

"Well apparently his familiar got bored of near-death and reanimated."

What would Bell think if he knew something possibly even worse lurked inside her? She met his bright blue eyes in the dressing mirror across the room, wondering how that conversation would go.

It has horns and wings and looks like demon-spawn, but it's nicer than it looks?

He caught her frown and smiled softly. "There. Now you look like you could be the daughter of Freya instead of a swamp creature. But I suggest brushing your teeth to solidify the look."

She swatted his arm, but she indeed brushed her teeth using the small basin of water by her bed. And when her gaze once again met her reflection, she could almost ignore the bruised crescents beneath her eyes.

The session took place in the small courtyard outside their rooms overlooking the bay. Xandrian, Delphine, and Surai showed up an hour later, and they sipped tea as they watched Haven and Bell work. Mostly swordplay with a bit of magick thrown in.

By the time the sun had risen well above the walls of the city, he'd proven proficient at both wielding the light rapiers he now preferred as well as spelling the weapons to inflict maximum damage and improve his aim.

He could only keep the magick flaring down the blade for a few seconds at a time, but that would improve with practice.

Haven savored the way her muscles burned and lungs seared as she sank into the table stools, covered in sweat. She'd pushed a grueling pace, using the ache of her body to distract her mind from last night's mortifying encounter.

"Where's the brooding bastard with the horns?" Xandrian asked by way of greeting.

Haven was sure her swallow was audible as she shrugged, praying her cheeks weren't bright red.

Delphine and Surai discussed something for a moment and then Surai explained, "Delphine said Stolas never returned to his room last night."

"Should we be worried?" Xandrian asked, eyeing the basket of biscuits as if a viper hid inside.

Another volley of signs passed between Delphine and Surai.

"He's Stolas," Surai said, "I don't think it's *him* we should be worried about."

Delphine passed Haven the tray of fruit. Grateful for the distraction, Haven quickly performed the sign that Surai taught her for thank you. When she was sure she hadn't accidentally told Delphine to screw off instead, she filled her plate with figs, half a grapefruit, and two hard biscuits.

Xandrian clapped as Bell finished putting away his gear and joined them. "Not as skillful as when I train him," Xandrian drawled, glancing at Haven, "but you helped expose his weakness telegraphing the lunge, so it served a purpose nonetheless."

Surai shared an amused look with Haven while Delphine performed a sign that Haven suspected meant *cocky bastard* or something very similar, considering she only used it after Xandrian spoke.

They had all gotten used to Xandrian's arrogance, a trait Haven was beginning to suspect most Sun Lord's possessed. Actually, most immortals with powerful magick, regardless if they were Noctis or Solis, seemed to be endowed with an overly large and inflated sense of importance. Take Stolas for—

No. She frowned at the poached egg on her plate, trying to scrub the Shade Lord from her thoughts. She refused to think about him this morning. Refused to wonder where he was or, worse . . . if he was off somewhere sleeping in someone else's bed.

Perhaps the king had sent him more . . . *sustenance.*

Knowing Eros and his insatiable curiosity, that sustenance would be gorgeous.

Her gut clenched as her appetite shriveled to nothing. Stolas had said he didn't mix feeding with pleasure, but he was a male, after all.

A male who'd just earned his freedom after years of imprisonment. A male who spent every waking moment either trying to build up his kingdom or tending to her instead of his own needs.

She forced a plump fig into her mouth. Forced herself to focus on the food as conversation swirled around her.

Chew. Swallow. Nod on occasion. Smile.

Pretend she's not thinking about him.

Because thinking about *him* meant reliving last evening, which she'd already done all night, tossing and turning in bed as she replayed his words. His touch. The meaning behind both twisting and contorting until she couldn't trust what was real or imagined.

"Any idea what the test might be?" Surai was asking Xandrian now.

Haven refocused on that question, the other thing that had kept her up most of the night. After informing Bell of the king's plans last evening, she'd found Surai and Delphine in Surai's room, gorging on a plate of shellfish, and told them the same.

No one seemed to have any clue how King Eros would test her.

Xandrian poked at his egg, nose wrinkled as he stared down the delicacy. "How would I know? Mortal kings are a mystery to me on the best of days. When they're not predictably stabbing one another in the back over trinkets of gold and silver, they're acting unpredictably, guided by emotion."

"No one at this table needs a lesson on mortal kings," she reminded him, her tone coming out grumpier than intended. "But you're the only one here who has firsthand knowledge of the prophecy."

Last night had all but confirmed her growing suspicion that she was purposefully kept uninformed about certain elements of the myth surrounding the Goddess-Born.

Xandrian dragged his disdainful gaze from the poor egg on his plate to her. "The prophecy? Not every answer lies in the texts."

"How would I know that? I've yet to see any of them."

"Neither have I. My work for the order was as a spy, meaning I had very little contact with any of the sacred scrolls over the years. But even if my dangerous position didn't prevent me from such information, they're scattered around the continents in secret places. Some have been translated and therefore changed, minutely, but still. Others are considered apocryphal works that are yet to be confirmed, while some highly guarded scrolls that were once considered gospel are now regarded as fakes."

Haven pinched the bridge of her nose. The monk had been even less helpful on the few occasions she managed to corner him before he left. "Eros mentioned an offshoot of the prophecy last night. One that was considerably darker than what you've alluded to."

Xandrian's ice-blue eyes narrowed. "Perhaps you shouldn't listen to those who have reason to manipulate and trick you."

"Perhaps if you gave me more information, I would know who to trust." A white gull hopped over the cobblestones toward their table, and she tossed it her biscuit, uneaten. "When the texts mention me, do they speak of me as mortal or . . . immortal?"

Bell, Delphine, and Surai all exchanged glances. Steepling his hands under his chin, Xandrian sighed. "That's complicated."

"It's not, though. Not really. It's a word."

"A word that may have been translated ten times over through the centuries, therefore changing. Again, minutely, but the word mortal and immortal in any language is very similar, enough that a scribe or a monk, half-starved and hiding in near darkness, might confuse the two."

"Then how do I know any of it is real?"

The others went still, forks poised over their plates.

It was the first time she'd ever allowed herself to question aloud the prophecy, but the words had been loaded on her tongue for weeks.

Bell tucked a strand of his curly black hair behind his ear. "Perhaps if you explained how the prophecy originated in the first place, we could better understand it."

Xandrian swept a longing glance over his fruit, sighed, and pushed the plate away. "Most people think the prophecy came from Freya herself, but it first originated from Varyssian's most trusted blood augur. Most of the original foundation of the prophecy came from the augur. It was because of what this augur told Freya about your pivotal role in the future, along with Freya's desire for a true child, that convinced her to die so that you could live."

Haven's throat went dry, as it did every time there was mention of her mother's sacrifice.

"Most of the actual texts were recorded before she was transmuted into stone. First on sacred tablets that were broken and hidden and then, years later, on paper. But after she was awoken to have you, before she died, some claim she added more to the prophecy."

"And where are those texts?"

"Not texts. Paintings. In her final days before she gave birth, she created a series of three paintings. No one knows why. If those paintings were simply an outlet for her madness after being asleep for so long, or a distraction during the first pains of labor, or . . . if they were part of the prophecy itself."

An ache of longing welled inside her heart. Painted—her mother painted. "Where are they now?"

"Their existence caused such a rift in the order that they were eventually slated for destruction. The first painting was destroyed, but before the other two suffered the same fate, they were stolen."

Haven took a long sip of her pomegranate juice to hide the sudden, overwhelming relief. Just the idea that something her mother created, something tangible and unique as a painting, existed made her feel lightheaded. "Stolen? Who? Why?"

"The who we don't know. The why is . . . complicated. There are rumors, but nothing concrete."

Haven lifted an eyebrow. "Rumors? Such as?"

"Such as, the paintings held a secret."

"A secret?" Her pulse quickened. Why couldn't he just spit it out already? "To what?"

"To immortality. Or, rather," Xandrian clarified as he stabbed a fig with his fork and held it up for inspection, "the secret to obtaining immortality for those not blessed with it."

Immortality for mortals.

Whatever Haven was expecting, it wasn't that. And yet, the moment the words spilled from his lips, everything seemed to click into place. The problem she'd been turning over in her mind trying to solve suddenly had a solution.

Her mother knew Haven would be born mortal, just as she knew she would have to become immortal.

"She painted them for me," Haven murmured.

Surai flicked Xandrian a dark glare before turning to Haven. "We do not know what the paintings really mean or where they are, or even if they still exist. Putting all our hopes into a rumor—no, the *hint* of a rumor—can only lead to disappointment."

Of course Surai was being logical and cautious. And yet the idea of artwork created by Haven's mother with instructions on how to become immortal seemed too fortuitous to overlook.

"Bell," she said, talking quickly, "have you ever heard of such paintings?"

If there was anything about the secret to immortality in the history books, Bell would have surely found it.

She tried to stifle her disappointment as he shook his head. "Never. Not a single passage in any book I've ever read. And if such a thing existed, immortality for mortals, it would be mentioned somewhere."

Runes, he was right. If King Horace or any of the other lords had stumbled upon even the tiniest inkling immortality was possible, they would have traded their entire kingdoms for the chance to hunt it down.

Surai couldn't hide the concern behind her soft smile as she said, "Immortality is beyond the scope of magick, *Soror*. If such a thing existed, undoubtedly it would have been used by now."

"Delphine?" Haven asked, wishing Stolas were here. With his wealth of knowledge gathered from years interrogating souls from every kingdom, he might have heard something.

Haven's heart sunk even further as Delphine shook her head and mouthed, *Sorry.*

Immortality was not something that could be bought.

But Haven refused to give up on the idea entirely. "What if, what if someone has the paintings, but they don't know what they are? What if, whoever stole them gave them away to someone who had no idea what they have?"

"Right." Bell tossed the final crumbs of his breakfast to the seagull, who'd become rather aggressive. "That's actually really smart. Pass off the paintings as nothing special. They would be hidden in plain sight."

Xandrian gave an aggrieved sigh as he pushed his chair back and then stood. "Oh, good. We now have two paintings that may or may not exist. And if they do exist, they could be anywhere. On any wall or vault in any continent. How, exactly, does that help us?"

"Because, now that I know my mother left me a way to become immortal, I'm going to find it." She unfolded from her chair, arms crossed over her chest. "As is, I may be able to get a mortal king like Eros to ally with us. Maybe. But you know your kind and their prejudices against mine. As long as I remain mortal, they will never follow me."

He ran a hand through his long blond hair, fisting the ends as his brow furrowed. Finally he conceded to her point with a grim nod. "If the paintings are out there, I may be able to use my connections to narrow down who might possess such art, knowingly or accidentally."

Haven almost rounded the table and hugged him.

"But . . . we must keep this between us. If whoever owns these possessions learned of what they have—well such a thing would be priceless to the mortal lords of this realm. And dangerous, if they fell into the wrong hands."

Bell's face twisted into a grimace as he realized what a corrupt king like Renk could do with immortality. Even Eros, if he knew about such paintings, would probably covet them for his own kingdom.

She could see now why the Order of Soltari may have chosen to destroy the objects. In the wrong hands, the paintings could do irreparable damage.

TWENTY-ONE

After a hot bath, an attendant from the palace arrived offering another tour of the city, this time by Neri herself. The queen wore wide-leg cream breeches and an almond tunic, the loose, flowing fabric showing off her graceful movements as she strolled down the hilly streets. Her excitement to show off their city was infectious. Unlike yesterday's visit, which focused on popular landmarks and other formal—but incredibly boring—locations, the places Neri took them weren't on any of Haven's maps.

An underground market that trafficked in magickal artifacts and spells. A shop run by twin Asgardian females that featured ancient axes and spears. A tattoo parlor that specialized in forbidden runes.

They stopped at a café deep in the heart of the city, and just as Neri claimed, the crab cakes and chowder were the best Haven had ever tasted.

Every shop and market they visited made one thing clear. The people here adored their queen, and she adored them. It was an easy thing, to love Neri. With her infectious smile, kind eyes, and stubborn loyalty.

She reminded Haven so much of someone . . .

The last stop was a rum distillery nestled at the top of a cliff, run by priestesses from a nearby temple. The women proudly handed out samplings of their golden rum as one of them gave the history of their product.

Haven left the others and joined Neri outside, on a rocky overlook with a stunning view of the harbor. "Is it true?" Haven called. "King Eros drinks their rum every night before bed?"

Neri winked. "Only if the priestesses ask."

Haven tucked a strand of hair behind her ear. "It was kind of you to take us around. I'm sure you have a thousand other things you could be doing."

"My pleasure." Neri shrugged, and again . . . something about her gesture, her eyes, felt familiar.

"Eros said it was your idea to invite us here, so thank you."

Neri waved her hand as if it was nothing. "Sometimes men just need to be told it's okay to do something. Besides, I don't think Eros has had such a good time in years."

Haven raised her eyebrows. She was pretty sure their conversation last night, while interesting, hadn't made him lighthearted.

If anything, he was more conflicted.

"Oh, your Shade Lord didn't tell you?" A curious look passed over her dark eyes. "He talked Eros into taking him around last evening after you left. They've been out all morning and they're still going. According to the owner of the café, they've visited every museum and bar in the city."

Relief swept through Haven. He hadn't been in the arms of another woman. But that relief was replaced almost immediately by frustration, at herself, mostly. Stolas could spend his nights wherever he wanted.

Worrying about what he did—or who he did it with—was an unwelcome distraction.

"Did you think your Shade Lord was elsewhere?" Neri asked, and her teasing tone reminded Haven so much of Bell—

Goddess Above, that's who she reminded Haven of, and probably why Haven—and basically everyone—loved Neri.

It was the same way they loved Bell. That grin. That mischievous sparkle and rare kindness.

"The king said you and Bell were distantly related," Haven mused, watching Neri closely. "How distantly, exactly?"

A flicker of something—shock? Alarm?—passed over her face, and Neri turned toward the distillery. "We should return. Dinner will be served early tonight before your test, and you hardly touched your lunch."

Why would Neri be guarding her ties to Bell? As Haven followed Neri to collect the others, she couldn't help but think that secret, whatever it was, could also explain why Neri had invited them in the first place.

TWENTY-TWO

The dinner this time was held on a huge balcony overlooking the city. Long countless banquet tables had been set up to hold what seemed like the entire court of Veserack. Below, the streets thronged with people waving and cheering as they vied for a spot in the crowd.

"The people love the king and queen," Bell remarked as they took their seats at the royal table nearest the railing.

Haven searched his face for jealousy or bitterness, but found only awe and the bloodshot eyes of too much rum earlier. Still, it was hard not to compare the adoration the citizens of Veserack had for their king to the people of Penryth, who had never cheered like that for the Botelers, not even during Bell's runeday.

"He risked his life stealing food from your father to feed them during the Curse," Haven reminded gently.

Bell's habit of seeing the good in everyone meant he never truly recognized his father for the cunning tyrant he was. Forcing him to admit that now seemed cruel.

"I imagine Renk is furious that a pirate claimed the territories before he could put one of his own lords on the throne." Bell grinned. "A pirate king nicknamed after a cat."

"It's not as if your kings have set the bar very high," Xandrian muttered as he toyed with the amber wine in his glass, his fingers making little birds out of the liquid. Haven had almost forgotten that was one of his powers.

Xandrian was the only one seemingly unaffected by the rum. Surai and Delphine, on the other hand, were nursing their glasses of water, their food so far untouched. Both girls took turns running to the bathroom.

As the banquet dragged on, Haven could hardly look at her own plate. The test loomed larger every second the sun inched closer to the horizon, and neither the king nor Stolas had arrived yet.

Picking at the claw of a prawn in her fragrant white soup, she tried to be understanding. He'd just regained his freedom after years of imprisonment. And between training her, trying to feed and protect Shadoria, and Archeron breaching their defenses nightly, he had to feel stressed.

Goddess knows she did.

But tonight was important. Even if the king came back indebted to Stolas in every way possible, none of that would matter if she didn't pass whatever blasted test he had in store.

As if conjured by her worry, a trumpet announced the king and Stolas's arrival.

Still clad in the same clothes from the night before, they prowled toward the table with the easy confidence of males who could arrive as late as they pleased. Eros's booming laugh drifted on the cool breeze, and Stolas clapped him on the shoulder, both males ignoring the attendant who tried to take their jackets.

Neri couldn't hide the tightness in her lips as she watched them saunter their way, one elegant dark brow lifted at the scene.

"Someone's in trouble," Bell whispered to Haven, and Haven didn't dare remark that was the same furious look Bell got when he was angry.

Stolas wore a devilish grin as he slid into the chair across from her. His tunic was unbuttoned mid-chest, his high, severe cheekbones flushed, those lush lips pulled into that loose sardonic grin. His bone-white hair was tousled to the side, a few longer strands curling against his stiff black collar.

The scent of smoke, brandy, and something else—the cloying hint of perfume—clung to him, killing the last of her appetite

Stretching back in his seat, he folded his arms behind his head, causing his half-unbuttoned shirt to bare even more of his chest, and fixed her with a heavy-lidded gaze.

She held his stare, praying she looked indifferent.

You look . . . nice. His voice trickled into her mind, syrupy and warm and uninvited.

You look drunk.

Before he could respond, she imagined a black wall of dirt and rocks and sludge between them, forming it with her mind. Making it grow wider and wider until it lodged heavy and impenetrable between them. Stolas had insisted they spend at least half an hour every day practicing that very move, locking her up tight in the event that she was ever captured.

Using that very same technique against him felt oddly empowering, and she gazed placidly at him.

"Very good, Beastie."

Thank the Goddess, no one seemed to find it weird that he was having a one-sided conversation with her, probably because of his condition. Which wasn't really sloppy drunk. If most poisons couldn't kill him then it probably took a lot of alcohol to affect him, and even then, he would never be falling-down-drunk.

But his edges seemed softened somehow, his powerful body loose and at ease in a way she hadn't seen in a while.

Delphine was to his right, and her nose wrinkled as she leaned in and sniffed him. Then she balled her hand into a fist, hit into her open palm, and gestured as if drawing air into her nose.

"What is she saying?" Bell asked Surai.

Xandrian laughed. "Oh, I can answer that. I imagine she said he smells like a whorehouse."

Haven's gut tightened. Maybe that's why he looked so . . . content.

"I do hope Neri doesn't castrate Eros," Xandrian continued. "He's the first mortal ruler I've encountered who has any balls."

Everyone went quiet. Haven looked to Bell, but he was already rising from his seat, his jaw tight. "I'm going to get some air."

Too late, understanding dawned on Xandrian's face. He blinked. Cleared the flicker of emotion from his eyes.

And then, after a fleeting glance at Bell's retreating form, went back to making magickal creatures from his glass.

Haven's chair scraped against the marble floor as she rose. "I think I'll join him."

Ignoring Stolas's blistering stare, she caught up to Bell in the nearest alcove just outside the corridor. It didn't take long to find an empty balcony overlooking the docks, tucked away behind an overhanging wall of clematis and wisteria.

He snagged two flutes of champagne from a waiter passing by and then leaned against the marble railing. "Runes, this feels just like in Penryth when we used to escape those never-ending banquets Cressida held, remember?"

"Runes, that woman insisted on at least thirty courses," Haven groaned, sitting along the railing as she accepted the champagne. "You know Xandrian didn't mean it, right?"

"Yes, he did. But that's not why I left." Bell studied the bubbles in his glass as if they held the answers to life.

"Then why did you? And don't say it was the soup because I actually liked it."

Bell barked out a hollow laugh. "You like everything, so it doesn't count." He took a sip. "I left because everything Xandrian said was true. My ancestors, the kings I've been taught to look up to my entire life, they were terrible rulers, corrupt in almost every way." His knuckles whitened around the stem of his flute. "Now Renk holds that seat of power, and he's worse than all of them combined. So, yeah, I'm pissed. Pissed at the suffering he's going to cause. Pissed that I can't do more to stop it. And most of all, I'm furious that it took me this long to understand."

"Understand?"

"The difference I could have made back then. Instead, all I cared about was books and clothes and hiding from my duties. Renk doesn't deserve the throne, but maybe neither do I."

Her chest tightened at the pain and frustration dripping from his voice. "Trust me, we've all done things that we're not exactly proud of, me more than most, but those actions hold no bearing on who you are today. This very moment."

"Goddess Above, who are you and what have you done with my friend?" he teased.

"Shut up. You're not the only one who's changed."

He held out his hand, a spark of golden magick dancing from the center of his palm. "I was thinking about visiting my mother's court."

"You want to visit Ashiviere?" She carefully placed her untouched champagne on the railing. She needed her wits about her for the test.

"I know, it's been years since we heard anything from them, and they had no love for my father. But my grandfather, if he's still alive, would probably take a meeting with me. I am blood, after all, and if we can get their support against Renk, we might stand a chance."

"When do you plan on visiting?"

"After you pass this test and I help you find the location of the paintings. Unless you need me for something more."

After she passed—not if she passed. Because if she failed, none of them would be allowed back on the mortal continent.

That was the deal.

She nodded, ignoring the unease that crept over her shoulders at the thought of Bell in Eritreyia without her, alone against Renk's wrath. "If you think there's a possibility they could become allies, it's worth a shot."

"Wow," Bell teased, "you really have changed."

She definitely had. A few months ago, she would have balked at the idea, and not just because of the risks Bell faced, but the far-reaching consequences of his actions.

If Renk discovered Bell was here, if he captured him, or worse— she wouldn't hesitate to bring the entire might of her powers against that sniveling bastard and burn Penryth to the ground, screw the consequences.

Which, of course, would be severe.

Assassinating a mortal king—even one as deserving of death as Renk—would turn every mortal kingdom against her.

"Shadeling's shadow, you shouldn't be dealing with this right now," Bell said, brow furrowed. "Not with the test coming up soon."

"Oh, that." She made a flippant gesture in direct contrast to the anxiety nibbling her insides. "Haven't you heard? I'm the daughter of Freya. Mortal tests don't scare me."

"You're worse than Xandrian," he groaned as he pushed off the railing and headed to the arched doorway. "I'm going back in. Care to join me?"

His lighthearted tone couldn't hide the concern in his bright blue eyes.

"I need a few minutes to clear my head. Have them fetch me when it's time?"

His mouth parted as if to argue. Then he nodded, his worried gaze lingering on her for a heartbeat longer, and ducked under the banner of flowers.

He'd hardly left before her senses picked up on a heaviness in the air, a prickle of sensation.

Stolas.

TWENTY-THREE

Bell had been forced to duck under the canopy of vining flowers over the doorway, but as Stolas entered the suddenly too-small balcony, she could have sworn the honeysuckle flowers retreated to allow *him* passage.

Goddess save her, he was beautiful. Especially now, bathed in the ethereal light of dusk, his wings catching every bit of the sun's dying glow and refracting it in a kaleidoscope of colors. His hair was pushed to the side, a few silky strands more wavy than usual as they curled around the base of his horns.

Her fingers flexed against the need to run her fingers through his disheveled locks as she raised a brow. "Here to fetch me?"

"Fetch you?" He closed the space between them, his lips curled in amusement. "Are you a jacket to be retrieved? Moreover, do I look like the fetching kind?"

"You know what I mean." She wasn't going to play his games. Not tonight.

"The king will send for you in a few minutes, but," he suddenly reached forward, and she stiffened, his gaze pinning hers as he plucked her untouched champagne glass from the railing, "that is not why I'm here."

She swallowed, struggling not to react to his nearness. Not to gape at the smooth, muscled planes of his marble-hewn chest peeking from his unbuttoned tunic. The strong column of his throat.

If he knew how she felt about him, how her body was reacting even now with the test looming like a dark shadow, he might offer his *services* again.

And she couldn't take that raw humiliation.

Not tonight—not ever again.

"Then what do you want?"

He took a meticulous sip of the champagne, studying her over the rim of the glass with those amber-framed silver eyes. "Want? I want many things. But at this moment, I am simply endeavoring to divulge the information I gathered during my time with Eros."

"Information?" She settled against the railing as his motivation became clear. "That's why you invited him out?"

His eyes gleamed. "What other reason would there be?"

"And why you visited a whorehouse," she added, unable to let that bit go.

"Eros was beginning to sober so I may have accidentally guided him into a very classy establishment that just so happens to offer those services, yes."

The bitter tang of disappointment coated her mouth. "I didn't think Eros was the type."

"Oh, he's not. He remained faithful to Neri despite the many offers to service him for free. It seems being a king has its perks." She opened her mouth to question him, but he added, "I needed him drinking because I needed his lips to loosen, and any male, even a king, has trouble saying no to a shot of brandy when it's presented between a female's breasts."

Her brows flicked up as a hot ribbon of jealousy unfurled inside her.

The king might have restrained himself, but did you?

The words hung between them unspoken, even though she had no right to ask such a question. If he had tried soulreading her, he would have realized the true emotion on her face as she held his stare.

Instead, he mistook her pained expression as disgust.

"You disapprove?" He watched as her hand skimmed her throat, that razor-sharp gaze taking in her every movement. "I've never hidden what I am. I've never claimed to be good or decent, and I'm certainly not a gentleman. What I am is yours, a dangerous creature wholly devoted to one task: keeping you safe. And if that means frequenting brothels, debauching kings, or opening someone's throat, I will do it without hesitation."

You're mine in every way but the one I desire.

More words that she would never say aloud. She sucked in a lungful of salty air as she forced herself to admit the truth. She was being unfair, cruel, even. Everything he did was in service of her. And even if he had slept with one of the women who undoubtedly tempted him, so what?

It was his heart she wanted to claim, not his body.

Liar. She let her gaze dart over his chest again, imagining the hard lines of his stomach beneath. The way those rigid muscles would feel beneath her palms and . . .

All of him. She wanted all of him, and the idea of another female catching his eye, touching him—

"You're on fire."

"What?" She blinked as a flare of light drew her focus to the sleeve of her tunic. Her flaming tunic.

With a jerk of his fingers the flame snuffed out. "Who knew your disapproval would be so strong that you would catch fire?"

Shadeling's Shadow, this had to stop. She cleared her throat. "What did you learn during your time with the king?"

He tilted his head for a moment as if listening to ensure they were alone. "Eros is a clever man, and even intoxicated he gave up very little. But I was able to piece together the small details he did admit to weave together a working theory."

"Go on."

"Apparently little Renk has been busy enacting laws regarding magick. One such law stipulates that common mortals who possess forbidden magick will not be put to death if they declare themselves to House Boteler."

Her hands curled over the lip of the railing. "What? Why would Renk offer them a reprieve?"

"Not from the kindness of his heart, Shadeling knows. He claims the Curse completely depleted the Nine Houses of magick and that the exception to the Goddess's law is for the greater good."

Haven snorted. "Anyone who believes that is a fool. What does Eros think?"

"The king became cagey when pressed directly, despite having drank enough rye to stun a small dragon, but I managed to infer his suspicions." Stolas plucked a honeysuckle flower from a vine along the wall and twirled the tangerine petals between his deft fingers. "It seems recently there have been quite a few common mortals who develop magick, some well before they are of runeday age. No one knows why. Eros himself sent several common lightcasters to Penryth, a few as young as nine mortal years."

"And?"

"And the lightcasters from Veserack handed over to Renk all mysteriously vanish. Renk has excuses. One escaped, another didn't have magick after all, not that Renk needs explanations because most kingdoms never bother to check up on their citizens after they're handed over. They're simply glad to be rid of the problem."

The problem. A shiver skittered down her spine. Any common child not from a royal house found with magick was executed. That was the law. In times such as these, of course the kingdoms would give up any suspected outlaw lightcasters without asking too many questions.

"Renk probably never dreamed Eros would bother checking up on them," she muttered.

"That man has a dangerously curious mind. Since then, he's been covertly recording the fates of the lightcasters sent from other kingdoms."

"You must have used every ounce of charm you possess to pry all of that out of him."

"I can be incredibly charming, when necessary." His smile was positively wicked. "Do you doubt me?"

Goddess save her . . .

Willing her heart to stabilize, she said, "And? What did you learn?"

His voice quieted. "It's as if they vanished."

Another shiver engulfed her as she suddenly understood, although she wished she didn't. "I know what he's doing. He's draining their magick for himself the same way he tried to take Bell's."

Stolas's nostrils flared with barely suppressed anger. To those with magick, the act of stealing it—which was quite different than the temporary magick-letting he practiced—was blasphemous, beyond depraved. "Eros did not outright say as much, but I believe those are his suspicions, just as I believe Eros may now be harboring forbidden lightcasters. Soon after Renk passed that law, he gathered a council of the lords from surrounding territories and kingdoms and had another one passed. It is now a mortal offense for a kingdom to hide anyone with magick."

"That's why he wants the alliance." It wasn't a question. Exhaling, she leaned against the railing as a boulder of ice swelled in her gut. "If Renk truly is taking their magick for his own, it's only a matter of time before Renk is the most powerful mortal in Eritreyia. He'll be free to take whatever he wants, from whomever he wants. Eros is hiding them not from the goodness of his heart, but a matter of survival . . ."

She inhaled sharply as the ramifications of that became clear.

"Yes, that's my thinking."

"Then why keep this from us?" She couldn't help but feel they were still missing something. "If anything, knowing would make us more desperate to form an alliance."

His smile said that he was pleased she noticed. "I would have kept him out longer to learn the last piece to the puzzle, but I assumed if he missed dinner, Neri would publicly eviscerate him."

"She might yet," Haven murmured, remembering Neri's furious glare as her husband returned. "But before you dragged him to the . . . *after-hours* establishment, she was genuinely happy he was out enjoying himself. I think—I think it's been a long time since Eros has had a friend."

Stolas's ashen brows gathered as he looked out toward the bay. "I must admit, I like him much more than I thought I would. He's clever enough that when he sobers fully, he will put together my intentions, and then any friendship between us will be impossible. But I don't regret it."

His profile was to her, the last bit of light from the setting sun reflecting off the angular slopes of his cheekbones and highlighting the prominent sweep of his lashes. A light breeze ruffled his feathers.

She was about to speak, if only to break the sudden stretch of silence, when he turned back to her. "I will never regret what I do—or the sacrifices I make—for you, Beastie. Never."

It was the way he said it, or perhaps the way he looked at her, or maybe both that had her stomach dipping and her heart flip-flopping in her chest.

They both turned suddenly as footsteps sounded on the other side of the door. And when the king's attendant peeked his head beneath the tapestry of honeysuckle, Haven had managed to create space between her and Stolas.

After a quick bow—and a few terrified glances at Stolas—the attendant informed them that it was time.

As they left the privacy of the balcony and wound their way through the corridors toward the king, heralded by a gathering crowd of courtiers and servants, thoughts of Stolas or the way he had looked at her faded. Replaced by the rhythmic hammering of her heart and an ever-growing resolve.

However desperately Eros wanted this alliance, it was still a huge risk. One he would never take without validation that she was, in fact, the Goddess-Born.

Which meant passing this test using whatever means necessary.

TWENTY-FOUR

Whatever Haven had been expecting—a riddle, a magickal contest of sorts, a raw display of her power—none of it prepared her for what Eros actually had planned. It had taken them nearly an hour to trudge their way along the sandy coast, trailing a wide estuary that skirted the city and ran deep inland.

Eros led the way. He was accompanied by Neri, their children, a handful of advisors, and the same twelve royal guards that shadowed him everywhere. They halted at a large cove flanked by near-vertical limestone cliffs. A pale stretch of sand unfurled beneath their feet, strewn with boulders and blue grass.

While guards led the small crowd along a narrow path to the cliffs above, Haven craned her neck to peer at the clear night sky. Delphine and Surai were somewhere above, scouting the lands in case Eros wasn't as wise as she originally thought and this was some elaborate trap.

Once she spotted the two shadows engraved against the stars—one small and one large—she relaxed, sweeping her attention back to the cove, where the moon shone against the still-as-glass surface.

"Maybe it's a swimming contest," she muttered, forcing a smile to hide her nerves.

"Or some crude ceremony that involves swimming together naked," Xandrian quipped, not looking the least bit disturbed by the idea. He caught Stolas's raised brow and added, "Mortal kings are known to be depraved, and more than a few would love to claim a night with immortals such as ourselves."

Stolas clucked his tongue as his focus slid to the people watching above. "And the spectators?"

Xandrian lifted a shoulder. "Wouldn't be the first time a king wanted an audience."

Bell met her amused gaze. "Any sign of selkies?"

Goddess could only hope not. This far south, selkies and other water creatures typically stayed away from inland waters close to mortal cities. Nothing got men more roused to hunt than the whisper of a selkie infesting nearby waters.

And Haven still hadn't gotten over nearly drowning the last time she swam in selkie-infested waters, before Archeron—

She flung the thought away like it was fire, but not before it seared through the layers of defenses she'd constructed and allowed unwanted memories to surface. Archeron's arms steady and protective around her waist as he saved her from drowning, the fight they'd had afterward. She had wanted runemarks and he refused to entertain the idea because of the consequences. She thought he was being overly cautious and stubborn.

If only she had known—

Eros was approaching. Sending the unwelcome memories skittering back to the hole where she buried all things Archeron, Haven refocused on the king, squaring her shoulders as she did. "If I had known we were going to swim I would have brought my bathing suit."

His flash of teeth couldn't quite be considered a smile. "As you know, after the Curse fell, the city of Luthaire held out for hundreds of years before the chaos bled into the palace. The royals fled, taking with them their most precious belongings, mainly priceless magickal artifacts gifted from the Asgardians."

"Their sudden exodus is documented in the histories," Haven answered, wondering where he was going with the story.

"On the road they were set upon by thieves and criminals. Fearing the heirlooms passed down for millennia would be lost, they hid the most powerful of their belongings in caves and estuaries, with carefully spelled maps that detailed their locations."

Haven smoothed back a loose strand of her hair being blown around her face by the soft breeze. "You want me to retrieve one of those artifacts?"

Such an endeavor hardly seemed like a challenge, or worth their time.

He jerked his chin to the tallest cliff, and she followed his gaze to a shadowy area set halfway down the vertical face. "The final missing treasure is hidden deep inside that cave. Bring it to me and you shall have your alliance."

Haven swallowed as something nagged at her. Something important. "What will I be retrieving?"

"Look for an iron box covered in ancient runes." Her mouth parted to respond and he added, "The what is unimportant."

Something still tugged at her. A feeling of not quite rightness. Tucking the end of her tunic into her waistband, she studied the cove, senses flicking out, trying to discern what it was that bothered her—

"It's too quiet," she murmured. "There are no birds or fish, nothing in the water or the nearby trees."

She shifted her gaze back to the shore to find Stolas's eyes watching her, the fiery gold ring glowing in warning.

He felt it too.

"Oh. Did I fail to mention the sea orc that lives in the cave above? My apologies, I blame the copious amounts of whiskey and rye I consumed earlier."

If his cutting sarcasm in his words wasn't clear enough, the acidic tone left no doubt Eros knew he'd been used for information—and he wasn't pleased about it. Stolas arched an amused brow before throwing her an apologetic look.

Runes. "Did you also happen to forget how big this sea orc is?"

"Big enough that I haven't dared send any of my own men to retrieve the treasure."

Her hand fluttered to the hilt of her short sword—which suddenly felt like a toy against what she faced. "Bell, refresh my memory on sea orcs."

Bell's throat dipped. "They're an ancient species of dragon that lives off sea mammals, typically whales, sharks, seals, and the occasional hapless sailor. Their scaled bodies are long and serpentine, their wings smaller than most of its cousins. They prefer the water to land or air and only take flight in emergencies or when diving above the waves to spot their prey."

Her gut clenched. "Are they fire breathers?"

In some cosmic twist of luck, some dragons seemed incapable of using fire to kill their prey.

"The accounts I've read suggest they hunt by slamming into their prey from above water, stunning it, and then using their hind claws to eviscerate the animal."

Nethergates, Bell read way too much. "Wonderful. Any weaknesses or suggestions other than to avoid its talons?"

"On land they're clumsy and slow, especially if they've eaten recently." His eyes flicked to the shadowy mouth of the cave before meeting hers again. "In water, they are lethal killers."

"Stay away from water. Noted." Unfortunately the only way to the cave that she could see was up the rocky limestone cliff face. And the only way to the cliff face was *through* the water.

Frowning, she ran a few magickal scenarios through her head, only to dismiss them just as quickly. Damius's wyvern was attuned to even the slightest whiff of magick in the same way some creatures were attuned to vibrations or smells. It was one of the reasons Damius kept the beast despite the fortune he spent keeping it fed and hydrated.

The moment she used even a whisper of power, the dragon would feel it and know she was there.

Best-case scenario, she wouldn't have to use her powers, instead sneaking past the creature as it slumbered.

Ignoring the alternative *worst*-case scenario, she cracked her neck and stretched, wishing she'd thought to bring a bigger weapon. Then she bent over and unlaced first her boots then the top of her tunic, stripping to her bare feet, pants, and undershirt.

Stolas's lips twitched at the corners as she removed her belt . . .

Rolling her eyes, she tossed the heavy buckled accessory at his face and kept her pants *on*. Now substantially lighter and unencumbered, she dipped a toe in the dark jade water, fighting a shiver as the cold leached into her body.

"At least we know any selkies would have been eaten," she called out as she waded deeper into the murky pool.

No one responded. *Silver linings, Ashwood.*

The swim across was uneventful. By the time she reached a sloping jettison of pale flat rock at the base of the cliff, her body had adjusted to the coolness.

The water slicking her palms was deposited on the lichen clinging to a boulder. Then she craned her head as she followed the vertical rock face up with her gaze, quickly plotting the safest route with the most potential handholds.

Here goes nothing.

Her soggy leather pants creaked softly as she began her ascent. Her breath rushed in and out in time with the gentle rhythm of her heart. All she had to do was stay calm, sneak past the creature, and return with the box of treasure.

When the mouth of the cave came into view, she slowly lifted her head to peer into the darkness. The faint odor of rotting fish wafted from the enclave, masking a gamey, primal scent that coiled around her spine and coated her palms in sweat.

The reaction was an instinctive warning to retreat as an insistent voice whispered *run run run*.

Any other time she might have listened.

Damn Eros and his love of games. No doubt this was yet another experiment to satisfy his curiosity in the same way sending Stolas two females had been.

Gritting her jaw, she slid over the lip of the cave, her cheeks pressing against lichen and moss, and flowed silently to her feet. Once her eyes adjusted enough to make out the walls, she began the heart-pounding task of plunging deeper into the shadows. Each step was a study in willpower. Her body itched to turn around. Her muscles locked and loaded, ready to flee at the first hint of danger.

Crouched low, she moved toe to heel, keeping all her muscles engaged to ease the force of her footfalls. The task was made more arduous as she penetrated into a smaller chamber and came into contact with bones. The moonlight was a measly trickle this far in, so she navigated by touch and the delicate silver glow of her runemarks.

Her *fleshrunes*.

Her mistake hit her all at once.

The magick seeping from her runemarks was faint, a mere wisp of power perfuming the air. Same as the sea orc's scent, it was a warning to the few creatures who could pick up on it. Most never would. Even powerful Sun Lords lacked the ability to feel the trace of energy her runemarks constantly emitted.

But as one of the most ancient creatures in existence, dragons were highly sensitive to even a tinge of magick.

A tinge that now filled the enclosed space every second she remained.

A vibration entered her bare feet and speared into her chest, like something heavy and large moving over the walls. Scales scraped stone as something sniffed the air.

Close—it was too close. Possibly in this same chamber.

Possibly right next to her.

Entire body clenched against her overwhelming impulse to flee, she backtracked slowly, one hand on her sword hilt. The vibrations were coming from everywhere now. Loud enough to block out sounds and distort her senses. Her heart hammered in her ears. The stench of rotten fish clogged her throat and made her eyes water.

A wall nearly knocked the breath from her lungs. She froze, scouring the shadows for the opening that led back to the first chamber.

Was she turned around? Had she missed the exit?

The rumbling was deafening now. The dragon speeding through the tunnels as it grew louder.

No reason to hide her magick now; it knew she was here. An orb of gold flung from her wet palm into the air, chasing back shadows and illuminating the cave walls. Blinking, trying to get her bearings as the ground beneath her rocked and dirt and rocks rained from the ceiling, she whipped around and came face-to-face with an eye.

A slitted yellow eye the size of her head.

The elongated pupil contracted and dilated as hot, foul breath slammed into her face, blowing back her hair and bringing her close to retching.

For a stunned heartbeat, they regarded one another—beast and mortal, performing that age-old dance deciding who was the hunter and who the prey. It didn't take long for both to fall into their places on the food chain.

Prey. She was the prey.

The blast of light magick that burst from Haven's fingers rolled over the sea orc's head, revealing a magnificent creature straight from one of Bell's storybooks. Webbed jowls tipped in black talons flared over a serpentine body covered in slick viridian-blue skin. Thousands of iridescent teal and onyx scales flickered like jewels.

It was quite possibly the most beautiful creature she'd ever seen up close.

The beast's head jerked away from the light. Chunks of stone broke off as it smashed into the wall. Loosing another volley of singeing fire, she ducked beneath its swaying head and darted toward the shimmer of silver moonlight ahead.

If she could lure it out into the open somehow—

If she could somehow trick it into the water below while remaining above, long enough to erect a shield, seal off the entrance, and grab the loot—

Rock and dust exploded behind her. Something was biting at her neck. Stinging and burning as an orange glow danced over the walls and black smoke billowed over her head . . .

Fire. The damned thing breathed *fire*. Bell was never going to hear the end of this.

She tossed twin orbs of light and dark magick together and then drew a protective rune into the magickal sphere. It twined around her to form a shield as the full brunt of the orc's flames enveloped the chamber and burst from the cave entrance into the night.

She imagined Bell frowning at the evidence of his error as hungry red fire licked around her, pawing at the shield. Though erected in haste, the shield was solid. Still, the heat was so great that some of it seeped across the magickal barrier and turned the water from her clothes into steam.

Legs crouched and ready, she waited for the fire to recede back into the darkness and then plunged toward the sliver of sky in the distance. Her knee slammed into something hard but she hardly felt it.

Another kiss of fire on her neck. Another shield. She waited out the fire and then continued. The scent of singed clothing, hair, and moss choked the cave. A rage-filled bellow echoed through the chamber right behind her, shaking the walls of the cave.

The lip of the cave appeared suddenly. There was nowhere to go. Pivoting to face the oncoming beast, she drew her sword. Inky blue light spilled down the length of the blade as the dragon rounded the final corner.

Its huge head slowly came into view, bobbing up and down as its predatory gaze followed her magick, dark wisps of smoke trickling from its parted mouth.

"I don't want to kill you," she whispered. "I just . . . need something in this cave."

A low guttural rumbling drifted from the beast as it watched her. It was no longer approaching, the upper portion of its long serpentine body curled and stacked to block the entrance, its primordial eyes glowing softly.

The way the dragon blinked at her, watching, waiting—there was a vast intelligence there.

Perhaps it was sated from a recent meal, or didn't find her particularly appealing, but the creature was letting her leave. It only seemed to care about preventing her from entering the tunnels behind it.

Was it protecting the lost treasure? Some dragons became obsessed with collecting and guarding jewelry and other baubles. At least, according to myth.

A huff of hot, smoky air burst from its jaw and rolled over her. As if the beast couldn't understand why she was hesitating.

You and me both, buddy.

Killing the thing had seemed easy ten minutes ago. All Haven knew of dragon-kind was Damius's wyvern, Shadow, a cruel beast fully under its master's thrall. But now, face-to-face with the sea orc, its magnificence on full display and eyes brimming with human-like sentience, the thought of destroying it made her sick.

There were two options she could see, and neither were promising. She could kill the beautiful creature—or she could try to soulbind it.

Killing it would be mournfully easy. Her endless supply of magick saw to that. Soulbinding the thing would be near impossible. Unlike the primitive vorgraths, dragons were ancient, intelligent beings that took years to fully soulbind.

But only one path would let her sleep at night. With a dramatic sigh, she slid her sword back into its holster. The dragon flinched a little at the sound. Holding its stare, she rolled out her shoulders and slowly began to reach out with her mind. Searching. Prodding. Looking for a way inside its being. For anything she could grasp onto.

At the same time, she gently glided her thoughts toward it, little waves of comfort meant to lull.

I'm not here to hurt you.

Her mind crashed against a protective shell.

You are beautiful, magnificent.

The shell softened like leather beneath her words.

I am your friend.

The dragon's pupil constricted to a mere crescent of black as she felt the tiniest of holes breach that protective wall.

I am the daughter of the Goddess Above, the Goddess of all creatures big and small.

A soft huff sent charred dust and debris swirling around her feet.

I will not hurt you.

Quick as lightning, she speared past the breach and into its mind.

Instead of thoughts, smoke and sulfur and fire formed images that raced past. Hunting black whales deep in the gulf. Skirting the city where the men lived. Men that hunted it. Wanted to kill it.

And then Haven saw what the sea orc was hiding. Protecting.

Not jewels or treasure.

Something infinitely more beautiful and precious.

Dragonets. *Her* dragonets. They were somewhere safe in the recesses of the cavern. Somewhere—

A rage-filled screech split the air. Before Haven could react, she was ejected from the dragon's mind, so violently that for a heartbeat inside her own body, she couldn't see.

And when her vision returned a split second later, it was too late.

A churning wall of fire was racing toward her, the heat blistering in its absolute fury.

She had no choice but one—jump.

It was only as she tumbled through the air toward the cove that she remembered Bell's advice to stay *away* from the water.

TWENTY-FIVE

Haven had barely gulped a breath of air before the water slapped it from her lungs. She sank sank sank, legs kicking in hopes of finding sand to push off from and finding nothing. Clawing her way to the surface, she scoured the sky until she found the mouth of the cliff above.

If the Goddess was smiling down on her, the sea orc would decide she was no longer a threat and—

A curse fled her lips as she spotted the creature winding down the side of the cliff. The moonlight danced off its fishlike scales, painting its slick flesh a pale silvery-blue. Boulders crashed down in its wake, sending waves slamming over her head.

The dragon was pissed, understandably. As any good mother would be. Haven dived, tossing spheres of golden magick around her for light as she speared toward shore. The impact of the orc entering the cove reverberated through the water and then . . . silence.

In the water, they're absolutely lethal.

It would make no sound as it stalked her. The strike would be lightning fast, her death over before she could register the pain.

She had a few seconds, at best, to kill it first.

Unless . . .

The rune to control water was a simple figure eight and a five point star intertwined. The moment she finished the symbol, she latched onto the water with her mind. Imagined it curled around her fingers like seaweed, slick and pliable.

Then she flung both arms out. There was a great whooshing sound as the water surged to her right and left, parting around her in two growing waves.

When the waves were nearly as tall as the cliff and the path at least twenty feet wide, she lunged toward the shore, sand shoving between her toes and making her work twice as hard.

Now at least she would see the sea orc coming, buying Haven a few seconds before death.

Debris scattered the sandy path. Rocks, mounds of kelp, a few flopping minnows. She kept her eyes trained on the two walls of water as she leapt over trenches and skirted boulders, her sodden braid slapping up and down on her shoulder.

A long, serpentine shadow flickered against the dark green wall to her right. There and gone.

A sudden panic hit. What if it attacked the others?

No, they would have shields erected. Powerful, impenetrable shields fueled by their collective magick.

Twenty feet remained till shore. If she could just find solid ground before her spell wore off . . .

A burst of water jerked her attention to the right just in time to see the sea orc surging toward her. She ducked, rolling over her right shoulder, and popped to her feet on the other side of the orc.

The creature was so long that half of its body still remained in the water while the other half was coiled along the path. That enormous head—nearly the size of a carriage—bobbed back and forth. Short front legs dug into the sand with talons the length of her forearm, and smoke curled around glittering teeth.

Haven's sword hilt was cool and wet inside her palm. Her heart rocked her chest as her fingers curled around the metal, feet digging into the sand, and she began to draw her sword—

Don't, a small voice whispered into Haven's head. It was so soft she might have imagined it, until the voice repeated, *Don't. She's only protecting her babies.*

The voice was childish, brimming with raw, clumsy magick. Her first instinct was to erect defenses to prevent the intruder from entering her mind again, but something had her glance up instead. Toward the crowd at the top of the cliffs.

It was easy to spot Eros's children; they were the only ones surrounded by the royal guard above. Her gaze riveted to the older boy's, and his eyes widened as he realized he'd been caught.

Magick. Eros's children possessed magick.

Her attention dropped to the mouth of the cave—and the two pale dragon heads peeking out from the shadows. A shudder slammed through her knowing they would witness their mother's slaughter.

Her sword was half-pulled. Any second now, the sea orc would rain fire around her. She could use the water to shield herself, but then her hold on it would break and she'd be in the same predicament as before.

The only option left was to fight, but—

She tried to reach out into the dragon's mind once more only to recoil from what she felt.

Or, rather, saw.

Baby sea orcs, her babies, dead in the water. Speared by sailors. Their tiny bodies half-submerged.

More than once.

The mother's pain and sadness was like a wave of agony crashing over Haven. She saw the sea orc gently carrying her past dead babies to the cave. Saw her nudging them. Curling her body around them in a desperate attempt to bring them back to life.

Haven understood the emotion in the creature's eyes now. Not rage, not animalistic hatred, but a mother's protective instincts. She would do whatever it took—even give her life—to save the babies in the nest above.

Just like Haven's own mother.

And Haven knew with a sudden, raw clarity that she couldn't kill the dragon. Eros and this alliance be damned.

She wouldn't do it.

She held the dragon's intense stare as she fed her sword back into its sheath, then raised her empty hands.

"I'm sorry for what they did to your children," Haven whispered, willing her words over the distance. "No mother deserves that. But I promise you, from today forward, no citizen of Veserack will harm your children or you—as long as you do the same."

She would make Eros keep that promise. Threaten him with whatever it took. He might not want the alliance now but he wouldn't risk her ire over a dragon, even if the treasure inside her cavern was a powerful artifact.

He was too rational and cunning for that.

The sea orc huffed, sending sand and debris flying around Haven's bare feet, and tilted its head. The long row of spiky fins ridging its back jerked taut, and Haven's hand fisted as her heart rammed into her throat.

But she didn't draw her weapon.

With a guttural screech, the dragon whipped toward the water and speared into the depths. A moment later it was clawing noisily back toward its nest, its long finned tail swiping back and forth in the air in warning.

Haven peered at the nest, watching as the sea orc and babies disappeared, before relief loosened her shoulders. But her relief was short-lived.

Now she had to face Eros and then explain to the others why she had failed.

Every step toward the shore made the pain of defeat a little more cutting. She didn't regret sparing the mother dragon, but the price of that one life was hard to stomach. They would return to Shadoria empty handed, without the alliance that might have prevented more bloodshed and given them a chance.

The group was quiet as she approached. Eros had left to meet his family and advisors as they made the short trek down the cliffside path. He was probably trying to hide his disappointment from her.

Kelp and sand littered her hair, her pants creaking and groaning with every movement. She dared a look up to find Stolas already watching her, his eyes unreadable. And then he gave her a tender smile and something inside her nearly snapped in half.

She cleared the emotion from her throat. "I couldn't kill her. Stolas, she had babies—I couldn't do it."

"I would have been disappointed if you had," Stolas murmured, and her assumption that he was only saying that to make her feel better died when she noted the truth in his gold-rimmed eyes. "Now," his gaze slid over her body, "are you injured?"

Her chest clenched. If she hadn't admitted last night the true depth of her feelings for Stolas, there was no denying them now.

"I'm fine. Maybe missing some of my eyelashes"—she glanced pointedly at Bell—"but otherwise okay."

Bell dug a boot into the sandy shore. "The books never mentioned fire."

"Books can't tell you everything." Surai clapped Bell on the shoulder. "Life must be learned from experience."

"You couldn't soulbind it?" Xandrian asked, his gentle tone doing nothing to hide his frustration. She didn't blame him—she felt the exact same way.

"I tried. We can all see how that turned out."

"And you refuse to go back up there and kill it like we all know you can?"

Her teeth flashed. "No one touches her. I promised her she would be safe." She yanked a slimy strand of kelp from her collar as a coil of disappointment formed in her gut. "Now I get to inform Eros of that promise."

"Inform me of what?" Eros drawled behind her.

Slowly, still picking off bits of the cove's offerings from her tunic, she turned to face the king, her shoulders tightening at what she knew she'd find in his expression. "The sea orc. I promised her that she and her babies would be safe for as long as they remain in your lands."

Beneath the moonlight, Eros's face was hard to read. His gaze held hers, dark and brimming with an emotion she couldn't quite name, his mouth set into a hard line. Two marble-wide eyes blinked from beneath the king's arm as his son peered up at Haven.

She thought she heard his childish voice whisper, *thank you*, into her mind.

"You can talk to dragons now?" Eros had yet to blink. To do anything but stare in that strange way.

"I don't know if she understood my words, but she did understand my intentions. And if you or anyone here harms her or her children, I will personally return to deal with you."

Wonderful, Ashwood. Why don't you threaten him just to ensure any chance of an alliance is well and truly dead.

But her threat was real. She would come back if she had to, and the feathering of his jaw said he knew it.

"You would risk everything for a mere creature?" Eros prodded, that sharp curiosity on full display.

A breath slid from her throat. "I would."

Eros finally blinked. Then the expression on his face went from some nameless emotion to . . . to awe, and it was her turn to blink as, one by one, every person in his retinue dropped to their knees and lowered their heads.

The princess whined about the muck until Neri gave the girl a stern look that could make Sun Lords cower, and then queen and princess joined the rest.

Bowing—they were bowing. The entire royal family and trusted courtiers, even the royal guard. Their fine silk capes and linen pants were soiled in the muddy sand. Their eyes downcast, hands clasped together as if praying.

"I know mortals are strange," Xandrian murmured behind her, "but what in the Goddess's name are they doing?"

"Paying fealty to their one true Goddess-Born," Stolas answered.

And it was only then that she allowed herself to believe what she was witnessing.

To hope.

Swallowing, she looked to Eros. "I don't understand. I failed your test."

Eros rose, mud and water darkening his seafoam colored cape, and met her questioning stare. "There was no ancient artifact to retrieve."

"I don't—you lied?"

"Lie is a strong word. That cave did harbor the magickal jewels I mentioned, but I retrieved them the first day I arrived in Veserack." His eyes softened as they darted to the cave above before returning to her. "We were incredibly lucky, and the sea orc was out hunting. Her dragonets had yet to hatch."

"Then why send me in there at all? You knew I would have to fight. You knew—"

"He wasn't testing your ability to retrieve the artifact," Stolas informed her, and there was a begrudging respect in his voice. "He was testing *you*."

Eros stepped forward, his boots squelching in the wet sand. "I've known from the moment you entered my throne room that you were descended from the Goddess. When you've been around runecasters long enough, you recognize power, and yours is like nothing I've ever felt. What I didn't know is if you were capable of mercy."

Surprise made her voice come out sharper than intended. "Since when do mortal kings care about trivial things such as mercy?"

"I needed to know if allying with you would just be trading one monster for another."

One monster for another. She remembered his version of the prophecy, how her path could branch off toward the light—or into the darkness.

If she had been him, she might have done the same.

"So by sparing the dragon . . ." She waited, forcing him to say the words aloud. To make it real.

"You passed the test," he confirmed. "And earned the absolute allegiance of the kingdoms of the Broken Three. We are yours. Our armies. Our cities. My palace. For as long as I sit on the throne, Goddess-Born, we swear an oath of obedience to you."

This wasn't just an alliance. No. As full understanding dawned, a shiver ran through her.

King Eros had just given her full command of the Broken Three.

TWENTY-SIX

It was late when they returned to the city so they stayed a final night, despite Haven's protests that she was perfectly fine to travel. Now that they'd accomplished their task—and then some—her thoughts veered back to Shadoria and their people. Even after a gloriously hot bath, she tossed and turned in her bed, worrying.

The few times she slipped into her dreams, they were nightmarish. A horrifying repeat of Archeron's spelled visions replaying in her head. Every detail remained. Her senses overloaded with the scent of blood, the sound of screams, the taste of ash and destruction in the air.

At the first sign of the dawn creeping over the ivory floor, she shot up, dressed, and dragged herself to the king's personal dining balcony overlooking the port city.

A sleepy attendant let her by. The city was just waking up, and the squawk of gulls mixed with the calls of fisherman and captains, the occasional ship's horn, made her smile.

It was still dark enough that runelight sconces flickered over the white and gold-veined marble table, their soft glow gliding over the handsome face of her companion—King Eros.

He didn't appear surprised to see her as he swept his arm out, calling her to the seat across from his. Azure and gold cushions lined the bench, and she took the fluffiest one, arranging it beneath her. Magenta salvia stalks filled the table's center, scenting the briny sea air with an intoxicating aroma no perfumer could ever truly capture.

"They're Neri's favorite flower," Eros explained before lifting a thick brow. "Tea?"

She glared at the carafes steaming from a nearby platter, trying and failing to hide her distaste.

His chuckle echoed off the walls, causing a half-asleep attendant leaned against a pillar to jump to attention. "I never acquired a taste for the stuff either, even though all royals of the Broken Three are expected to drink nothing but the finest tea herbs, imported from all over Solissia. The cost of that assortment alone could feed five families."

She watched quietly as he poured her a cup of dark coffee, waving away the bleary-eyed attendant who tried to help. Her tongue prickled as the rich, loamy coffee aroma filled the air. They drank in silence, Haven not even caring that the liquid scalded her tongue.

When she downed enough coffee to feel semi-alive, she lifted her gaze to the king. "I know why you wanted the alliance. It took me a while, but I figured it out."

"No doubt with the help of a certain Shade Lord." Eros regarded her quietly over the rim of his mug. Then he set down his cup, flicked his fingers, and sent the attendants scurrying.

Once the last servant disappeared, she said, "How long have your children had magick?"

He blinked, a long callused finger tapping his coffee mug. Then he exhaled and looked out into the city. "My son showed signs first, about a month ago, right after the Praetori Fiernum ended. My daughter's powers awakened more recently."

The timing of that was . . . interesting. "Do you have a magickal lineage?"

The shake of his head was subtle, his gaze still snagged on some invisible point in the city. "None."

Eros was technically from a House of Nine, but many of the houses had fractured long ago, with hundreds of lesser nobles claiming Nine blood without ever having a prayer of magickal abilities.

"Then . . . where?" And yet as soon as the question left her lips, she knew the answer. "Neri. How closely is she related to Bell?"

When his eyes met hers, they looked almost umber in the dawn's growing light. His nostrils flared delicately. "King Bellamy's grandfather, the former ruler of Ashiviere, is her father."

Haven blinked, trying to fit that into what she already knew about the Ashiviere court—which was basically nothing. Contact with Penryth had ceased after Bell's mother's death, the nearby kingdom separated by a vast swath of wild woods and treacherous mountains.

"Technically, she's his bastard child, born in secret to one of the royal seamstresses. Neri's mother fled as soon as she realized she was with the king's child. It was rumored Prince Lorenth Ashiviere was consolidating power in a bid for his father's throne, and he would not have taken too kindly to a sibling with potential for magick, bastard or not."

Lorenth. Where did she know that name? Haven toyed with a golden tassel on her seat cushion, wishing she'd gotten more sleep last night. "Lorenth . . . that's Bell's . . ."

"Uncle," Eros answered, popping an olive into his mouth and chewing slowly. "Once King Boteler cut off ties with the kingdom, Lorenth soon came to power. He only recently passed, giving the kingdom over to his only son, Dram. As far as he's aware, his grandfather's magickal bloodline only seeded in Bell's mother."

Haven traced a swirl of gold in the table with her finger. This meant

Neri was Bell's aunt, even though she couldn't be more than seven or eight years older than him, and her children his cousins. She had recognized the resemblance earlier but now, knowing what she did, it was glaringly obvious.

And if she could see it . . .

"You're afraid Renk will figure out the connection eventually," Haven said slowly, watching his expression, "and try to take them."

His eyes flashed with anger. "King Renk's hunger for magick is insatiable. We think he's somehow carving out the magick of the children that come to him and then killing them, either in the process or to hide what he's doing. Although I suspect Stolas already informed you of this information."

She sucked in her lower lip, having the sense at least to appear contrite for the small betrayal.

"It's no matter," Eros continued, waving his hand in a flippant gesture. "I would have done the same in his shoes."

"If it helps, Stolas felt bad afterward."

A wry grin flashed across his face. "Did he now? A Shade Lord with a conscience is a rare creature indeed." His grin soured as he leaned across the table, eyes darkening to the color of his coffee. "If Renk knew who Neri really was, if he somehow discovered that our children have the same power running through their veins as King Bellamy, he would—he would—"

His fist suddenly hammered the table, causing the carafes to jump and the coffee in her mug to slosh over.

He exhaled, his eyes ashamed as they met hers. "I apologize for losing control. When it comes to my children and their safety, sometimes all rational thought flees."

Haven smiled despite the twinge of sadness she felt—and always felt—witnessing a parent's love for their child. "We will do whatever it takes to keep them safe. Especially now that I know they're Bell's family—which makes them mine."

A flicker of surprise rippled across his face, followed by gratitude. He bowed his head. "You truly are a marvel, Goddess-Born. Only Freya's daughter could possess such a kind heart beneath such ferocity."

"Careful, King Eros, or someone might hear and think you've gone soft."

His laugh was so much like Bell's that she was forced to remember his age, how young he was. This would be Bell in ten years, Goddess willing. With a partner at his side and wisdom beyond his years, ruling over Penryth and working with Eros to make the mortal lands a better place.

The vision swelled inside her until she thought she might burst, a bittersweet hope she barely dared grasp onto, barely dared pray for, in case she somehow cursed such a bright future with her greediness.

Soft footsteps echoed across the balcony as Neri approached, looking resplendent in a flowing sea-green silk robe and loose ivory gown that nipped at her bare feet. Tiny gilded seashells hung from her ears, tinkling as she strolled across the patio.

Even simply dressed and without shoes, she was every bit a queen.

Yawning, she assessed the empty balcony before turning an inquisitive stare toward Eros. "Where are the attendants, my love?"

"I sent them away so the Goddess-Born and I could talk privately," Eros explained.

Their shared gaze lingered, communicating in that silent way only lovers could before a knowing expression came over Neri's face.

Her eyes were no longer sleepy as they flicked to Haven. "My son spoke to you last night, at the cove." It wasn't a question so Haven merely waited. "I thought he might have by the way you looked up at him but . . ." She uttered what had to be a curse in her native tongue before switching back to Solissian. "He's going to be in so much trouble."

"Don't punish him too harshly," Haven said. "He's partially the reason I passed the test."

"Ah, I see he's already charmed you with those big puppy eyes and that impish smile. Too much like his father, that one." She slid onto the cushion nearest Haven, stretched like a cat, and sighed. "With all the attendants chased away, who will fetch me my breakfast?"

Haven suppressed her grin as, with a beleaguered groan, Eros left the table to procure Neri's food.

That, Haven decided. That's what she wanted someday. Someone who loved her the way Eros loved Neri. Who cherished her above all else and thought nothing of his ego when it came to making her happy.

Any other mortal king would have cast their wife aside when the opportunity to take the throne presented itself. Her shadowy lineage and common background would have made his ambition to take Veserack and hold the Broken Three nearly impossible.

Yet Haven had no doubt he would die before he let a single person insult his wife.

Someday, when they had more time, Haven would ask Neri the story of how she and Eros met.

Haven lifted her eyes to see Neri watching her as if she knew her thoughts. Perhaps she did, because her words were about love—of a kind. Just not between her and Eros. "Goddess-Born, I don't mean to cause hurt by what I say . . . but what I saw under the sea the first night here. You and the Shade Lord, Stolas Darkshade are . . ."

In love.

The unsaid words hung in the air between them, growing a life of their own with each second that passed. Taunting her with their inaccuracy because *in love* implied they both felt the same way.

And that was a lie.

Clearing her throat, Haven repeated the words that ran through her mind like a mantra. "He is my friend, my protector, and my most trusted soldier. That's all."

Neri's full lips pressed together as she seemed to weigh the best response before finally settling on the simple truth. "He's more than that to you."

Damn Neri's miss-nothing gaze. Haven suspected she'd learned that from being an illegitimate child on the run, her survival dependent on reading the room before anyone else.

Sizing up people quickly was a valuable skill—one that now served her well as queen.

Haven picked at a fleck of dried juice on the table. "It doesn't matter; he doesn't feel the same way toward me, and I respect that."

Neri snorted. Actually snorted. Looking less like a queen in that moment than a friend. A very annoying, very smug friend. "Haven, whenever you're in a room his eyes are on you every moment. His body positioned toward yours. He's aware of your every movement, every discomfort, every breath. There is no one else that can even catch his attention, and believe me, more than a few mortal females have tried."

A surge of hot anger flooded her at the thought, and she wet her lips with a glass of water. "He's very protective."

"No male is that attentive, not like that. Not every moment of every day, with females practically throwing themselves at his feet."

Her hands curled in her lap. Did Neri really have to keep mentioning all the women Stolas had access to?

"I think you're forgetting that it was Stolas who dragged your husband to a brothel."

"Yes, something I have yet to forgive him for. But Eros said Stolas didn't once look at the women, something even my husband, whom I trust implicitly, surely did not do." One of her sharply trimmed brows arched. "That is how Eros determined Stolas was using him for information, by the way. After he sobered, of course."

The relief Haven felt at hearing that was eclipsed by frustration. This was silly. Neri was making the same mistake Haven did, believing Stolas's unfettered loyalty was something more than it was. "You have to understand Stolas to make sense of his actions. He's the most dogged person I've ever met, singularly driven to his cause, and right now, I'm that cause. His duty is to protect me, but that's all I am to him—a cause."

Her heart kicked as she articulated the words aloud, breathing life into them.

For the first time, she wondered if Stolas might be throwing himself into the task of protecting her to distract himself from his demons.

Demons which she was beginning to suspect were the size of a small army.

By focusing his every waking moment on Haven, he didn't have to confront the mountain of trauma left over from centuries of tragedy and torture. He was, after all, now living in the same home where his entire family had been slaughtered in front of him. Where he'd been imprisoned, forced to marry his family's murderer.

Forced to become a monster.

Neri shook her head, her earrings tinkling softly. "For the daughter of the Goddess, there is so much about the heart—and desire—that you do not know." Her hand was warm as she placed it on Haven's wrist. "Just beware, in Eritreyia, the mortals despise Stolas. To them, he embodies the Curse, plague and affliction, and most of all, that one thing we mortals all fear: death. If you were to align yourself romantically with him, there are many who would not follow you."

Her statement sliced through Haven like a knife, made all the more painful because Haven knew Neri spoke the truth.

And yet . . . "You say that, but you know better than most that mortals can accept unlikely marriages that go against . . . *custom*."

"I do, and the obstacles my common birth and colorful background caused was almost enough to make me leave Eros, if only to spare him the trouble. But Haven, I promise you, it is not the same. If it were, if there were any chance—any at all—that the mortal kingdoms could accept such a union, I would support you even if I didn't understand it."

Haven's chest ached as if Neri's words had burrowed inside her, nestling deep as they carved out an ever-growing hole.

She glanced over the marble balcony, shielding her eyes, as if she just now felt the morning sun's fury. Sailors and fisherman swarmed the docks in controlled chaos. She let her gaze roam beyond, taking in the families holding hands. The shopkeepers sweeping their sidewalks. The restaurateurs washing down patios and setting out chairs for the breakfast crowd. The market vendors shooing gulls away from their stands.

This—this was what she was fighting for. A life beyond the Curse. A life protected from tyrants like Renk, where men like Eros and Bell ruled fairly. She swept her attention over it all, forcing herself for a single horrifying moment to imagine what the city would look like once her father reigned.

Ash. Ash and rubble and the charred bones of this wondrous city would be all that remained if the Shadeling reached these shores. And he would. If she couldn't convince the mortals and the Solis to follow her under one allied banner, the mortal continent would become a wasteland worse than the darkest recesses of the Netherworld.

Her mind rioted at the thought. She jerked her gaze away from the vibrant city and people, resolved to keep them safe no matter the cost. If giving up the foolish love she felt for Stolas meant saving them then her sacrifice was worth it.

It had to be.

TWENTY-SEVEN

Three days had passed since they left Luthaire with the promise of an alliance. True to his word, Archeron's assaults had ceased, and their return found Shadoria nearly rebuilt from the previous attacks.

The peace after so many nights of horror felt wrong somehow. A trick meant to lull them into a false sense of security. But Haven tried to enjoy the infectious hope that spread over the island as she walked the streets, marveling at how resilient the people here were. It was midday and those already done working were gathered around their neighbor's homes, helping erect fallen walls, patch roofs, and repair shattered doors. Some worked on the fountains in the town square, plastering the once stunning Seraphian statues and filling the pools with buckets of seawater.

The magick that made the fountains work was still present, and a few of the fountains were now up and running.

The aroma of yeasty bread and fish drew her gaze to the newly erected market, a maze of makeshift stalls cobbled together in the town square.

Vendors smiled as she passed. If they worried about their mostly empty stalls, their ebullient faces didn't show it.

"Goddess-Born," a woman with a young girl on her hip called. "Come take a charm for luck."

Word of Haven's presence spread like wildfire through the market until her name filled the air. They begged her to bless their homes, cure their sick children, heal their husband's wounds from fighting.

But it was their grateful prayers that sliced her open. Their calls of thanks.

Thanks.

If they only knew the truth . . .

She flicked a panicked look toward Bell where he bent over a row of shiny throwing daggers, inspecting the blades.

The air shriveled in her lungs. She couldn't do this. Look them in the eye and pretend she didn't know in another week their lives would be upended, their smiles replaced by the hollow-eyed look of people infected with never-ending fear.

Chest aching, she ducked into an alleyway where a few smaller vendors had set up shop, her head down. She focused on the uneven cobblestones as she worked to calm her mind. To breathe.

Bell quickly caught up with her. "They have fresh honey a few stalls down, Haven. Fresh. *Honey.*"

Any other time, that would have been enough to drag her back. Honey was the perfect food. It could be drizzled on biscuits and bread, added to bland gruel to sweeten it.

Runes, it even made Demelza's coffee palatable, and that alone was worth its weight in gold.

But every second she looked into the people's hopeful eyes broke open the scab inside her a little more. Their belief in her ability to keep them safe should have fueled her confidence.

Instead, it felt like a dark secret she was keeping.

She rested her weight against the stone wall on her left, grateful for the coolness that seeped into her arm and cheek. "This was a bad idea."

Coming here was supposed to be a *good* thing.

"I thought seeing this place would cheer you up," Bell said, and even though she kept her eyes trained on the city beyond the alleyway, she could tell he was frowning.

Fearing any second now the vendors would recognize her, she pushed off the wall and broke into a brisk stroll, Bell struggling to keep pace. "I did too," she admitted. "I just . . . I wasn't expecting them to be so grateful. They think the attacks stopped because of something I've done, not something I have yet to do."

Give herself up. Become Archeron's weapon.

The words hung heavy and cold between them until Bell gripped her sleeve, jerking her to a halt. "Stop. You have to let yourself enjoy their happiness."

She bristled at his touch, barely suppressing the urge to rip from his grasp and flee. "It just makes everything harder, Bell. I can't watch them rebuild knowing he's just going to shatter their hope all over again."

Which, of course, was exactly why Archeron had given them a short reprieve in the first place. Show them how wonderful life could be without her. Show her the *price* of her resistance.

This was the price, and it was only a small fraction of what would be taken from Shadoria, from her if she didn't return to him.

"We have to," he answered softly. "Our survival depends on being able to dream a future different from the dreadful one Archeron provides, even if it never comes to pass. Even if . . ." His jaw flexed. "Even if daring to imagine such a world leaves our hearts unprotected and vulnerable."

For a heartbeat, she looked at her friend. He had to know more than anyone what this felt like. To envision an impossible future so bright, so wonderful that it physically hurt to imagine it.

Jaw clenched, she tugged free, gliding inside the shadow of the building in hopes of anonymity as she strode toward the end of the alley.

No such luck. A man hawking a paltry little bucket of fruit recognized her. His eyes lit up as he waggled a bright green apple at her.

"I couldn't possibly," she said, patting her stomach to show she was full. A lie—she hadn't been able to stomach breakfast this morning, and lunch had been a few bites of a bread loaf and a sliver of white cheese. But the thought of eating now repulsed her.

Bell didn't have that problem. After insisting he pay for the apple—offering twice what the fruit was worth—he polished the fruit on his seafoam tunic and took a loud bite.

"You eat louder than our old tutor," she groaned as they passed through a crumbling gate and the stretch of black sea came into view. In the ethereal, purple-tinged afternoon light, she could see the water wasn't actually black but a dark, rich green.

"Shadeling's Shadow, I forgot about that." Bell chewed, making an effort not to be so noisy. "He was constantly munching on pecans and other fruit he stole from the garden, remember?"

"How could I forget? When Cressida discovered he'd been pilfering royal property, she tried to have him hung."

At Bell's insistence, he was only fired, not executed for his infraction. They discovered later he had seven children at home—three adopted—and could barely afford to feed them all on the pittance of a salary the king paid him.

Thinking about all those years ago made her chest ache tighter for some reason. Perhaps because things had been so much simpler then. Her only worries were keeping Bell safe, finding her parents, and not getting caught when she broke the rules—which was practically all the time.

Knowing now how many people had been suffering around them as a direct cause of King Boteler's rule was startling—and shameful.

Especially considering how selfishly oblivious she and Bell had been, caught up in their own bubble of wants and needs.

They found Xandrian waiting for Bell near a small cove. The shallow water glittered like one giant emerald, the edges dark blue and rippling with silver fish.

Xandrian's lips lifted as he saw Bell, only to reverse course into a frown when his gaze slid to Haven.

"What have you learned?" she called by way of greeting, picking up one of the rapiers on a tan blanket and testing its weight.

Xandrian raked a hand through his shoulder-length golden hair, and a small part of her ached at the resemblance to Archeron. Once she looked past the spun-gold hair, jewel-toned eyes, and sun-bronzed skin, they looked completely different.

But it always took a painfully long breath to realize he wasn't Archeron. His beauty more refined. Body lither. Whereas Archeron commanded any space he occupied, Xandrian had learned to move like water through a crowd. Only noticeable when he needed to be.

Xandrian's shirt was unbuttoned, the runemarks that mapped his chest a dark metallic pewter in the twilight. He'd tossed away his boots and was ankle deep in the ocean, a rapier held low and loose at his side. "Goddess-Born, I informed you yesterday that I would alert you the moment I learned anything tangible about the paintings."

"Yes, but yesterday you hadn't visited with the Ashari trader that came ashore."

It was no secret Xandrian still maintained hundreds of contacts he'd nurtured as a spy for the Order of Soltari, and normally she wouldn't bother discovering who he was meeting with. But now, with the paintings out there and time slipping by, she wasn't beyond using Bell to stay informed.

Xandrian's sea-blue eyes narrowed as they flicked to Bell. "I see news travels fast."

She tossed the weapon to Bell, proud of how easily he caught it. "You should probably know that Bell loses all reason when it comes to pretty clothes."

Xandrian cursed. "I should have guessed as soon as I saw him in his new silk vest this morning."

Bell rolled his eyes as he began a series of practice maneuvers, the last smoky-purple rays of light flickering off his blade. "I would have given her that information for free, but who am I to say no to a silk vest?"

Stabbing his rapier into the sand, Xandrian stalked close. "While your loyalty to one another is adorable, I didn't mention what I learned this morning because I have yet to substantiate it, and the first thing I learned as a spy is that I'm only as good as the information I provide."

Now that Archeron's blockade was temporarily removed, a few brave ships had begun trickling into their shores. Mainly King Eros's contacts from his time at sea, which meant the ships were undoubtedly peddling stolen goods.

Not that she cared where they procured their goods. She'd accept shiploads of fruit stolen from the Shadeling himself if it fed the people.

"Just give me something, Xandrian," she pleaded. "Do we have a location? Has the Ashari heard anything about the paintings rumored—"

"Whoa. Let's not get ahead of ourselves, Goddess-Born. The Ashari I met with happens to specialize in finding homes for certain types of misplaced luxury items. If anyone has heard of rare art stolen from the order, it would be him."

She arched an impatient brow "And?"

"And there were several possibilities." She must have raised the other brow because he added, "What? *Rehoming* rare art is a lucrative business. Anyway, judgement aside, one story piqued my interest."

"Spit it out, Sun Lord," she growled.

"Around the time the paintings were stolen, there was a rumor of a mortal noble who fled to the Morgani Islands. In exchange for refuge, he gave the Morgani Queen a painting—"

"Just one?"

"Just one," he confirmed, retrieving his sword from the sand. His back was to her as he added, "You see why I failed to mention it. It's flimsy at best. Not worth the risk of traveling to Solissia to investigate further. Not until I find something more conclusive."

"The noble could have sold the first painting for passage. And we know the queen wouldn't have accepted a painting as a gift unless she felt powerful magick inside the canvas—even if she didn't know where that magick came from or what it meant."

"Do you see now why I didn't tell you?" Xandrian murmured over his shoulder, the muscles of his back rippling against his form-fitting shirt as he moved through sword drills with Bell. "Now, don't you have a date with a certain horned bastard?"

Date wasn't exactly the word she would have used, but Xandrian was right. Stolas would be waiting for their nightly training sessions. And if his mood the last few evenings was any indication of his demeanor tonight, being late wasn't advisable.

TWENTY-EIGHT

As feared, the moment she tumbled from the portal and caught Stolas's black expression, she prepared herself for another long round of brutal training, curt responses, and tension so thick she could almost see it sucking the air from the room.

The most frustrating part of the entire thing was that she had no idea *why* he was upset. Was it something she said? Or perhaps the usual darkness she felt hovering around him when he was in Shadoria, especially inside the castle?

Especially now. Despite the effort he put into hiding his feelings, he was gutted by the destruction of the Hall of Light.

A few of the crystals could be mended, but most had been shattered beyond repair, their precious light magick lost.

All of those things could explain his sudden black mood, but a part of her worried it was more than that. That perhaps what had happened that night under the sea had irrevocably changed their relationship somehow.

Had she offended him when she refused his offer? Obviously that was the opposite of her intentions.

Before she could ruminate on the problem further, he was putting her through a grueling session of defensive maneuvers, each one requiring every ounce of her focus. Normally they trained inside the temple to escape the cold mountain winds, but not tonight.

As if he wanted the environment to match his emotions. Or perhaps he simply wanted to punish her because he was a bastard with sadistic tendencies and a black soul.

After a grueling hour of meeting his relentless onslaught of attacks, she almost moaned in relief when he stopped for a break. She found a spot between two snow-crusted boulders to conjure a fire, and this time she did moan as warmth worked its way back into her fingers.

"Next time wear gloves," he remarked behind her. She was startled by his closeness. Then again, she'd take anything that blocked the icy winds, even if it came in the form of a grumpy Shade Lord.

"I don't like gloves," she explained, thrusting her fingers darn near inside the flames. "They make my hands clumsy."

"Better clumsy than frozen off."

"Okay, well I assumed we'd be inside the temple again. You know, that place where my limbs don't fall off after a few minutes of exposure?"

"Assumptions are lazy," he growled.

Assumptions are lazy, she silently mimicked, grateful he couldn't see her face. She would have argued aloud, damn his reaction, but his boots crunched the snow-packed ground as he abruptly prowled in the opposite direction.

With a dramatic sigh, she left the warmth of the fire to catch up to him. "Are we done?"

Admittedly, she wanted to continue training. She just preferred somewhere . . . warmer.

He peered down at her for a stretched out second, and she found her heart doing strange little twists beneath that unreadable gaze.

"Since you're obviously struggling with the elements, we can end early for the evening. Or we can work on bonding with your familiar. It's up to you."

A lump lodged squarely at the base of her throat. In the days that had followed her familiar's appearance, she'd nearly succeeded in forgetting its monstrous appearance. Now that hideous image of sinewy black flesh and horns painted itself inside her mind with perfect clarity.

Forcing back a shudder, she said, "If I'm going to have this thing inside me, I have to learn to control it."

Too late, she realized he might have offered to continue training out of duty. That spending his entire evening fixing her issues probably wasn't his idea of fun. But when she dared meet his eyes, she caught approval flickering over his dark expression, there and gone.

"But," she added, rubbing her numb fingers together, "can we at least do it somewhere warm?"

"Is the Goddess-Born afraid of a little cold?"

"Yes—yes she is," Haven ground out between clacking teeth. "Because she's still mortal, remember?"

For some inexplicable reason, he flinched a little at that. Or did he? The tremor was so subtle she could have imagined it.

The first day they had returned, she explained the paintings and her suspicions about their purpose. He had gone quiet—so quiet, in fact, that she was now starting to suspect that her possible immortality was somehow contributed to his foul mood.

Which made zero sense, but sometimes Stolas was a complete enigma. Actually, most of the time Stolas was a complete enigma.

He was a Seraphian male in the prime of his life, and yet Eros had said Stolas hardly even glanced at the women in the brothel. All of his free time was spent with Haven, yet it was obvious his interest in her was fueled by duty alone and—

A gasp of surprise burst from her half-frozen lips as he slipped behind her, wrapped his arm around her waist, and took to the sky.

"A little warning next time," she hissed as his wings sent snow flying around them.

"Warning?" he drawled, that cold voice edged with amusement. "Perhaps if you weren't daydreaming then my intentions wouldn't have caught you off guard. What was running through that curious head of yours, Beastie?"

"A hot bath," she lied, knowing he probably sensed the lie and not caring. Let him wonder what she was really thinking about.

Some ridiculous instinct had her leaning back against him. Her flesh hummed where his hands pressed, flat palms radiating a teasing heat.

Warmth. Her eyes became slits as his magick poured into her. She'd forgotten he could do that. Warm her with his powers. He'd done it once before after the Woodwitch left her near death, and just like then, it was strangely . . . wonderful. Like falling from a bucket of ice water into velvety blankets of slick, glossy heat.

She shivered as the fiery tendrils pulsed through his splayed palms and into her belly, coiling and sliding through the hollow of her bones. The feeling was almost sensual, like a visceral caress of fire.

If she could have curled into him and fallen asleep, she might have in that moment. Even as a part of her recognized that a Noctis as deadly as Stolas possessing abilities to sooth and disarm was all kinds of unfair.

At least, to his prey—which was basically everyone in existence, except maybe the Shadeling and the Goddess.

No one should wield that amount of power. Even Stolas.

Especially Stolas.

For a wild heartbeat, she wondered how it would feel to have him use that euphoria on her while awake. Twice now, she'd received his gift while out of it. The first time in pain after the wyvern attack. The second time after Archeron's cruel vision spell.

All she could remember from the experience was a flood of warmth, although different than the physical warmth now cascading through her body. A bubbling, peaceful feeling, like molten sunlight gurgling through every part of her body.

Like liquid happiness.

Filling every wound, every jagged hole.

Mending the broken parts of her piece by piece.

Yes, she decided as they speared through the delicate layer of clouds and were enveloped in pure, diaphanous white. An immortal capable of both absolute pleasure and complete destruction was the most dangerous creature in existence.

You love a monster.

By the time she realized just how far up they were, the clouds were hundreds of feet below and Stolas was diving toward the highest tower of Castle Starpiercer. Her ears popped, muffling the squawks of the ravens that startled from the tower's domed roof. More huge black birds gathered on the wrought iron railing of the balcony that circled the chamber, watching them with keen alertness.

Stolas's chamber.

He whispered a spelled command as they dove toward the nearest balcony, and a fire flickered to life somewhere inside his room. The second her boots brushed the marble floor, she jerked free of his hold, scouring the chamber to distract herself from the wild urge to crawl back into his arms.

Curiosity quickly overwhelmed anything else she might have felt. His chamber was off limits to everyone. The one and only time she visited was right after Archeron's assault, and her memories between waking up and making it to the hot baths were fuzzy, at best.

The first thing she noticed was the warmth. This high up, the temperature was below freezing, the winds absolutely brutal. And yet despite boasting no walls, the pale silk drapes that hung from each column hardly moved at all. A fire crackled from a marble fireplace, veiled by a metal screen in the shape of wings.

Between the fire, whatever spells kept the wind out, and the warmth still radiating from Stolas, his room was bursting with heat.

She flicked up a brow. "Your chamber?"

"You said you wanted somewhere warm, and we need privacy, so it was either here or the lip of the volcano on the other side of the island."

A part of her suspected the volcano would have been less dangerous. She spun in a slow circle, skimming her gaze over the fur throws, scattered furniture, and books. "Do you always keep it this hot in here?"

"Only when entertaining guests."

"Did you entertain a lot in your old life?" she asked before wishing she hadn't.

If his mood was dark now, bringing up that painful part of his history surely wouldn't help. But this place was obviously built large enough to accommodate more than just Stolas. It was huge. The size of the library back in Penryth, at least.

And Goddess Above, that bed . . .

It came into view, a circular monstrosity of exotic furs, oversized pillows, and glossy sheets.

A sweep of goose bumps ridged her skin as her body recalled how it felt wrapped in those layers of luxury. The sheets gliding over her fevered skin, cool and silken. The furs plush and comforting. And Stolas all around her, his power, his scent, his breath as he whispered in her ear, those powerful limbs holding her still, caressing and—

Nope. Pivoting so that her back was to the poster bed, she developed a sudden interest in the armoire, a beautiful teakwood piece that looked well loved, despite appearing ancient. A large silver cage filled with shiny, stolen trinkets—a golden bracelet, a bent spoon, a few shards of glass—rested on top.

Ravius.

Her focus shifted to the leather-bound books with broken spines stacked atop a sofa table. More were crammed into a set of marble bookshelves to her right. A crystal decanter half-full of amber liquid glinted on a low table next to a single glass.

"In my old life, yes," Stolas finally answered in a clipped voice. "I entertained frequently, as was expected of a Seraphian prince. Although I preferred more . . . intimate gatherings to the large parties you're probably envisioning."

"Hmm." If he thought that was somehow more comforting to her, he was a fool. There were more than enough cream-colored sofas and chaise lounges to hint at what some of those intimate gatherings really were. "And how many guests were you *intimate* with?"

His jaw flexed as he followed her stare. "A few. Does that bother you?"

There was something guarded in his tone that made her blink.

Yes. A thousand times yes. "No." She shrugged. "You were young, and I'm guessing even more arrogant than you are now, if that's possible. I'm sure you loved having females throw themselves at you."

Did his lips just tilt up on one side?

"Throw themselves? I wasn't aware females did that. Tell me. Do you literally heave your body at a male or—"

"Shut up." But she was grinning, relishing the fiery spark of amusement in his eyes, however brief. "Is this how we're drawing my Shadow Familiar out? By teasing me until it appears just to make you stop talking?"

"As fun as that sounds, I was thinking I would help you connect with it first. Coax it out slowly after convincing your familiar that it can trust you. I'm rather fond of this room—particularly my bed—and would very much prefer it stays in one piece."

His lips definitely curled at the mention of his bed, his sharp gaze dancing over her as she struggled to remain composed.

For rune's sake, Ashwood. It's just a bed. A massive, sinfully soft cloud of a bed . . . but still. Who cares how many females he's entertained on it?

"So, how do we safely entice it out?" she asked.

"First off, it is not an *it*. Your Shadow Familiar is a highly revered, highly coveted companion. More than a few royal Seraphians who lost their Shadow Familiars in battle ended up dying shortly afterward of grief."

Her experience thus far did not support that statement, but she was trying to be positive about the whole thing. "Okay, how do we convince my highly revered familiar out?"

"We can start in a similar fashion to the process that I used to reach mine." Shucking off his boots, he slid to the ground, crossed his legs, and motioned for her to do the same.

Her mouth parted. "We're . . . sitting on the floor?"

"Would you rather my bed?" he purred innocently. "It's vastly more comfortable."

She snorted as she bent down to work on her boots. Her fingers were still sensitive from the cold earlier, and it took longer than it should have to unlace them. He watched silently as she tugged the last one free and then dropped to her bottom.

"Get comfortable," he ordered.

"I'm sitting on a hard floor, I can't—"

He suddenly maneuvered behind her, his muscular legs opening to wrap around her own as his cool breath slid over her neck and right jaw. "Comfortable now, Beastie?"

Her heart dipped before stuttering into a wild rhythm.

She should have chosen the volcano.

TWENTY-NINE

aven wasn't short by any means, but compared to his long limbs she suddenly felt tiny.

"Lean back." When she froze, he slid his arms around her waist, gently pulling her until she was fully reclined against him. "Better now?"

Yes.

And no.

It was complicated.

He took her silence as a yes. "Good. It's the only way this will work. Your familiar is hyper-sensitive to your moods. During the awakening process, if it feels tension or stress, even the slightest bit, it will flee. Now close your eyes."

She did, but her obedience earned her only silence.

"Am I supposed to—"

"Stop overthinking," he barked. "Actually, stop thinking at all. Focus on your breathing. Inhale through your nose and into your abdomen, *here*," he circled his thumb around her navel, seemingly oblivious to the shock of pleasure his touch sent straight into her core, "deep enough to lift my hands."

Settling her own hands into her lap, she did as instructed. Or *tried*.

There were too many things going on. Namely his body so close to hers. His scent everywhere. His breath drifting over her neck like a slow caress.

And how did he think splaying his fingers low over her belly was supposed to not distract her?

When she did finally tear her attention from Stolas, it veered straight to the painting.

What did it look like? Was it placed in a gilded frame or rolled up? Did the Morgani Queen know what she had?

She would have to ask Ember later if she'd ever seen such a painting. Even if Ember didn't know what it was, she would probably know where her mother kept prized art—

"Focus." His gravelly voice rumbled through her back and somehow gathered beneath his huge palms, as if his words were their own type of magick. "Don't fight your thoughts, let them roll through you with each breath. Release the tension I feel coiled tight in every muscle. Relax your jaw. Your eyelids."

His commands had the opposite effect. The more she concentrated on not tensing her shoulders and jaw, the more they seemed to contract on their own.

"This is pointless," she muttered as her eyes snapped open to . . . darkness.

Where were the stars? His bedroom? That gaudy, oversized bed—

Oh. His wings—they were draped around them like an inky cage of shadows. With her eyes narrowed she could make out the fine filaments of the glossy feathers, each one painfully beautiful, a masterpiece of indigos, greens, and purples.

Impulsively, she reached out two fingers to touch one—

A growl vibrated through Stolas and into her body, causing her to jerk back her hand. "Concentrate!"

She huffed out a frustrated breath. "I'm trying."

"Your attention span is alarmingly short."

Bell would agree, she decided. He'd also scold her for her defeatist attitude. Closing her eyes once more, she vowed to accomplish this task or spend all night trying.

This time she did as he suggested. Breathing in her thoughts and then letting them flow through her, a river of worries and stress raging across her mind. Funneling past until they all blended into one. Only this time, instead of trying to dam them, she relaxed and let them go.

Soon her rhythmic breaths drew her attention. She couldn't imagine what was fascinating about breathing, but once her mind fell into that steady in and out rhythm, a soft white calm descended.

She imagined opening her throat wide as she pushed her navel out, drawing the warm air deep deep *deep* into her chest.

With each full inhalation her belly rose, lifting Stolas's hands.

In and out.

In and out.

In the far recesses of her mind she became aware of her heart slowing, and Stolas's own heart punching softly at her back in time with hers.

The river of thoughts became darkness rushing through her. A soothing cascade of liquid nothingness. Time slowed. Her body growing lighter as her mind drifted on that river.

Drifted and drifted until she could feel the presence of *something* beneath the flowing rush of her consciousness. Something thick and hollow and hard . . . a cage of mud and stone.

And inside that hollow prison something stirred. A primordial presence.

She felt its wary excitement as she found the lock. Felt its gratefulness as the lock clicked open. Still breathing softly, still focused on nothing but the rush of that obsidian river of nothingness, she set it free.

A snap like hollow bones wrenched in two pulsed in the center of her sternum. Her eyelids flickered as she opened her eyes, blinking at the darkness. Stolas's wings were still blocking the light, so she reached an impatient hand out to quietly signal him to open them . . .

Only to watch her fingers glide through misty shadows. Shadows that playfully curled around her thumb and pinky.

They weren't wrapped in his wings; they were wrapped in her Shadow Familiar.

Heart racing, she watched it swirl hesitantly around them. Jet black tendrils resolved from the nebulous form, their touch like icy butterfly wings on her skin.

She felt Stolas stiffen behind her as the blackness reached out suddenly to stroke the ragged cliff of his cheekbone. The gentleness of that touch went against everything she witnessed the other night. It moved from his face to his horns. Touching. Exploring.

Trying to figure him out as it examined his feathers, even his pale hair—bone-white beneath the moonlight.

Stolas didn't move, not even to blink. And when her familiar finally left to explore the room, his only reaction was a soft exhale.

This creature was different than before. Instead of endless rage, it was oddly . . . inquisitive. And careful—it cataloged the room like a lone wolf in unfamiliar surroundings, one loud noise away from fleeing.

"I don't understand," she whispered, tilting her head so her cheek pressed into Stolas's chest and she could make out the lower half of his jaw. "It's so different now."

He angled his face toward her. "Your familiar is driven by your emotions. Your desires. It feeds off your pleasure and, when properly bonded, will do anything to please you even at great cost to itself."

She flicked her gaze back to her familiar to discover it hovering over Stolas's bed, inspecting the sheets. The pillows. The furs. Toying with the golden tassels on the pillow shams like a cat.

It spent an inordinate amount of time on the bed . . . but only when the shapeless thing began to rub itself over the covers—like a dog rolling on its back to mark its favorite spot—did Stolas's words finally have meaning.

It's driven by your emotions. Your desires.

Goddess kill me now.

Was that a chuckle she felt vibrate her shoulder blades?

"Obviously we're not bonded yet," she said, mentally trying to will it to another part of the room.

"Obviously."

Even without looking she could tell he was smiling. Wonderful. "So will it become part of my consciousness?"

"No. They are influenced by your will—and some Seraphians form such deep bonds with their familiar that they can sometimes see through their eyes—but your familiar is a separate entity."

"So I was . . . born with it?"

"They are very rare, only found in incredibly powerful darkcasters almost always from the Darkshade lineage, so there is very little known about their origin. Some scholars say they're souls of beasts from another realm trapped in the Nether, and only royal Seraphians are powerful enough to harness them. Others claim they're gifted by the Shadeling himself. The only thing we all agree upon is that their souls are eternally tethered to their darkcasters'."

"How do you know they have a soul?"

"I believe that every creature, however small or hideous, possesses a soul. Those who claim otherwise do so in order to justify their brutality against them."

She remembered the pixie. How all the creature wanted was territory of its own, and how, when Bell brought up the idea, the mortal lords laughed in his face.

"Careful, Shade Lord, or I might start to suspect you have a heart."

He was still holding her—she'd unpack that detail later—and she felt the muscles of his chest and arms go rigid around her. "Don't let my words confuse you. I'll never be the good guy, Beastie." A long pause followed. "I've always been very careful not to make you think otherwise."

"Then what are you?" she teased, trying to ease the sudden tension she felt between them.

"Merciless, Haven. That is what I am. And to those who would hurt the people I care about, I am worse. An unfathomable evil."

"But you *are* capable of caring," she persisted, thinking of the way he sacrificed himself for Nasira. "Which means you're not quite the villain you claim to be."

"I would argue that's what makes me the most dangerous. To protect those I love, I would do all manner of cruel, vile things. Things that would make me exactly what they say I am."

A monster.

You love a monster.

He was being painfully honest—that much she knew, but if he was trying to scare her away, it wasn't working.

Yet it didn't feel exactly like that. She had witnessed him right before he fed. Had given him permission. And while she suspected that barely scratched the surface of the savage nature he kept hidden from her, the fact that she hadn't cringed from the act was huge.

Maybe he was trying to prepare her for what he might have to become if things spiraled into war?

If that were true then he was wasting his breath. They would all be expected to do horrible things if it came to war, herself included.

"When I trained to become Bell's royal guardian," she said, resting her head against his chest, "they kept a brown bear in the barracks, locked inside this sad little cage. All the other students took turns poking the poor creature with sticks to make it growl like it was a toy for their amusement."

"I'm assuming there's a point to the story? Or am I the bear and you the stick?"

She rolled her eyes. "The point is, one day, the bear got tired of being poked and did what bears do. It killed four cadets and maimed countless more before escaping."

His arms tightened around her waist. "I like this bear already even if the point still eludes me."

"The bear wasn't to blame for the deaths; he was just a bear. They were."

He was quiet as he rested his chin on top of her head. She didn't know if he got the point of her story. She certainly didn't know how to feel about the way he held her—or the way her body responded.

The only thing she knew for sure was that every minute spent getting to know Stolas only reinforced the feeling that she didn't know him at all. Every shield he let down revealed another, even more impenetrable one erected. Every kind act was followed up by a reminder of his beastly nature.

And every lingering touch was tainted by his fierce and unwavering duty to her.

And yet, his choosing to be honest with her about who he was—and who he wasn't—felt like a promise of some sort.

Like a whisper of hope.

He was showing himself to her—all of himself. The good and the bad. The villainous parts as well as the pieces that were still, somehow, after everything he'd experienced, good.

Relatively speaking, of course.

She knew Stolas would never cling to the noble ideas that Archeron once had. He would never speak of honor as if the word was sacred, or shy away from cruelty because of notions of right and wrong.

Perhaps that's what the world needed right now. Not a golden hero, but a dark prince capable of meeting the Shadeling's evil with a little wickedness of his own.

Sighing, she sank even deeper into Stolas as they quietly watched her Shadow Familiar move around the room. It still had yet to choose a form, but there was something graceful in the way the oily-black mist glided around the columns and prodded the books. Something whimsical in its delicate, agile movements.

Maybe having a monster living inside her wasn't so bad after all.

And maybe loving one, even if that love wasn't returned, was forgivable.

THIRTY

Days passed. Waiting for word to spread of their new alliance. Waiting for Eros to confirm the kingdoms under his rule didn't object so they could begin preparing for the inevitable war with Penryth. Waiting for the ravens they sent—in lieu of emissaries this time—to elicit a response from the Solissian nations.

Waiting. Haven despised it.

She filled her time working around the castle, doing anything and everything to get through the day. Evenings were spent with Stolas, training first and then releasing her Shadow Familiar. Each time, Stolas slid behind her, holding her during the experience.

She'd figured out why last night. They were watching her familiar, and something—she still wasn't quite sure what—had triggered a memory of Archeron.

Everything had happened so fast. Her familiar reacted to her pain, transforming from an innocent blob of shadow into a rage-filled creature of talons and gleaming teeth. Before it could destroy the nearby column, a finger of pleasure stroked down her spine, filling her with mindless joy.

Her familiar calmed immediately, and nothing was destroyed.

It was only afterward, when she thrashed in bed remembering how he held her, that she understood.

He'd used his soothing powers to prevent her familiar from losing control.

To prevent *her* from losing control.

So she threw herself into even more work the next day.

No one objected when she put on an apron and scrubbed pots in the kitchen, to Demelza's absolute horror. She joined Surai to mend fishing nets, weaving the frayed strands of rope together with magick until her fingers blistered and bled. Helped Bell and Xandrian patch the wards on one of the failing towers dotting the coast. She even aided Delphine in the tiring process of conjuring crops to replace the ones poisoned by Archeron.

When Haven questioned why they couldn't simply conjure food to feed the people, she learned that magicked food held almost no substance, and it degraded ten times as fast.

They could summon an entire island full of fruit that would be rotted and inedible before they could finish distributing it.

Conjured plants, on the other hand, could produce normally if they were rooted into proper soil within the first few minutes of being summoned.

Delphine was already bent over, her wings a charcoal color in the ethereal light, silky white hair pulled back in a loose braid. Like the rest of the Seraphians here, she wore knee-high leather boots and gloves. Haven found out why a moment later when Delphine jerked her chin to a fly-ridden mound at their feet.

"What is that?" Haven asked, wrinkling her nose at the stench that wafted from the pile.

The Seraphians watched her with amused grins.

Delphine made a sign Haven had already learned. *Crap.*

Surai was teaching Haven the Seraphians' unique sign language in the mornings. It was yet another thing to help pass the time, but she also wanted to be able to communicate with the Seraphians who couldn't speak.

But surely Haven misread the sign. "I'm sorry, what?"

A few of the Seraphians chuckled.

Grinning, Delphine performed the sign again, the downy feathers along the base of her wings fluttering in the light breeze.

There was no confusion this time as Delphine performed the sign for excrement.

Fantastic.

The others were watching her to see if she balked.

So she drew a rudimentary rune to block the stench, rolled up her pants and sleeves, and began shoveling the excrement into the pre-dug holes.

It was mind-numbing work, but after an hour of working without complaint, there was a respect in Delphine's expression that wasn't there before. Haven even talked Delphine into teaching her a few snappy phrases.

The next time Stolas popped off with that smart mouth, she would surprise him with a comeback in sign language.

When they were finished, sweat had turned the black dirt covering her arms into sludge, and she desperately needed a bath. But she was meeting Nasira at the guarded entrance to the caves beneath the palace, and she was already late.

A deep purple gilded the clouds as night fell. Thanks to Delphine, Haven wasn't that late as she trudged down the slippery rock path to meet Nasira. The caves were hidden behind a sheltered cove, the entrance guarded by a gate so rusty it looked one touch away from crumbling to dust.

Not very impressive. Then again, it wasn't the corroded bars that kept intruders from passing beyond the threshold. It was the promise of having one's insides incinerated by Netherfire and burning alive that did the trick.

Nasira was perched on a small nearby ledge, throwing pebbles into the jade green water below. No one was allowed inside the vaults by themselves, even Stolas. The threat of someone getting their hands on the Godkiller was too great not to take every precaution.

She shivered. Even miles below the earth, she could feel the dark weapon's cold sentience. That odd prickling evil seeping from its tomb like pus from a wound. Hinting at something corrupted, something ancient and twisted and malignant beneath the surface.

Inhaling through her nose the way Stolas had taught her, she took several cleansing breaths. That horrible wrong feeling would only get worse the deeper they plunged toward the demonic dagger.

Nasira, on the other hand, looked completely at ease as she toyed with the fish below, ignoring Haven. After finally tiring of her game, she hopped from the ledge and approached.

Her pert nose wrinkled. "Why do you smell like a pig pen?"

Haven sighed. There was no question Nasira was loyal to Haven, but that's where their relationship ended. Haven was a little embarrassed to admit how the girl's cold demeanor stung. On the ship here, Nasira had seemed ready to trust Haven.

But when they arrived everything had gone back to the way it was before. If anything, Nasira's dislike for Haven had grown over their weeks here, if that were even possible.

Haven found a small pool of water and began rinsing the muck from her hands. "I was working, Nasira."

"Inside a waste bucket?"

Gritting her teeth to prevent saying something she'd regret, Haven dried her hands on her shirt and nodded to the entrance. "Ready?"

She wanted to get this over with. They all rotated on a schedule between the Chosen. Two people checked on the Godkiller in the morning and two in the evening. Considering it was the most powerful weapon in existence, *and* it was connected to the Shadeling, they had to be extra cautious.

Nasira entered first. Flattening her wings against her body, she drew the gate open with her magick and disappeared inside. Haven shuddered as she crossed the threshold and felt the sharp prick of the ward rake her entire being.

The sensation was extremely uncomfortable and always left her nerves achy and sensitive for hours afterward. Her lips curled at the dank stench of mud, stagnant water, and ancient magic.

Two hours. Then you'll be with Stolas. That was the only part of the day she looked forward to.

Goddess Above, please see fit to allow me time to shower before then.

Plucking a runelight torch from the cave wall, she darted down the spiraling stairs carved into the stone. Nasira's light bobbed around the curve. Pale blue runes flickered beneath Haven's boots. The protective magick inside each symbol rolled over her, their whispers scraping her skull.

Who are you?

Who are you?

Who are you?

The underground vaults honeycombed out in a maze of labyrinthine passageways and caves. Haven caught up to Nasira near the first vault, where the rare scrolls and books were kept. If only that's where the Godkiller was kept, but no. It was secured in the deepest vault, which meant racing down treacherous, crumbling steps two at a time for nearly an hour.

This deep in the earth, it was easy to lose track of time and surroundings. But Haven always knew when they approached the last vault. The Godkiller's cunning magick warped everything around it. The jet black walls. The air. Even the magick of her torch crackled and guttered beneath the corrupting pall of twisted power.

Heat blasted up the stairwell in waves.

Without a word, Nasira threw up a shield of cold to protect them from the fiery temperatures. The stairs became a single pathway tattooed with countless pale blue runes that glowed as they passed.

They stepped out onto a huge ledge, the air choked with smoke and embers.

All around them was a giant cavern big enough to fit Fenwick Castle and some of the gardens. A lake of fiery orange magma bubbled hundreds of feet below. In the middle of that ocean of flaming death was a stone pedestal, ringed by three pairs of massive stone wings.

And centered atop the wings, chained and bound by practically every protection spell in existence, was the Godkiller.

Any other weapon would have melted from the boiling miasma of heat. Then again, any other weapon wouldn't be casting out its senses like a net, each thread of that immense power glittering with razor-sharp barbs with one sole purpose: snare anything that breathed into complete subservience.

Part of her always hoped to find the weapon a little damaged. The eye not quite so bright or the wings over the hilt misshapen.

Something.

And always there the blasted thing waited, defiant and untouched, that red eye blinking merrily as it roved the cavern until it latched onto her.

I was looking forward to seeing you again, the Godkiller whispered. *He will be pleased.*

The tension in her chest softened as she realized the inhuman voice coming from the weapon wasn't the Shadeling's. Her father hadn't spoken to her from the dagger since the attack on Solethenia when she slid the blade into Stolas's chest.

When she killed him.

You shouldn't be, she spat back, refusing to flinch beneath the eye's unblinking stare. *If it were up to me I would have sunk you in the lava the first day here.*

Fire can't hurt me, child. Your mother learned that the hard way . . . right before my loving caress found her traitorous bitch heart.

The cruel words stuck a visceral reaction inside her, and she flashed teeth. *Something can. And when I discover what that is, I will end your miserable existence.*

Liar, the weapon whispered as its depraved magick slithered over her skin. Seeking purchase. A crack in her defenses. A foothold in her mind. *You crave me, I can feel it. You want to let me in. You need me—*

Blasting her light magick outward, she repulsed the blasphemous evil and was rewarded with . . . laughter. Horrible, malicious, wicked laughter that rocked the cavern and sent loose rocks splashing into the magma below.

"What was that?" Nasira demanded, her appraising gaze never leaving the weapon. "Did it say something to you?"

Haven's throat felt raw and sandy as she tried to swallow. No one else ever reported the dagger speaking to them, and admitting she shared a connection with the weapon felt . . . shameful. Like a dirty secret.

"The weapon's angry. Same as always."

"Of course it is," Nasira said. She had finally torn her curious gaze from the dagger and was busy turning nearby sparks into monstrous creatures of fire and ash. "The Godkiller is bored. Something this powerful was made to annihilate Gods, not live chained and bound."

Something in Nasira's voice made Haven uneasy.

The first night intruders breached their wards, Nasira had begged Haven to take the Godkiller and launch an assault on the Sun Court.

With Haven's growing powers and the weapon's untapped magick, there was a chance they could have succeeded.

Haven had toyed with the idea for longer than she cared to admit. Especially after the first child was killed in the raids.

But outright killing the new Sun Sovereign wouldn't make them safer from the Shadeling. In fact, the bloody, chaotic war that followed would destabilize their world, leaving it vulnerable to the Shadeling's army.

Even if the day came when outright murdering Archeron was their only choice, the thought of using the Godkiller made her stomach twist.

"Something this powerful shouldn't exist." Haven turned her back on the weapon, its demonic gaze cutting into her shoulder blades. "Let's test the last wards and be done."

Nasira frowned as she and Haven sent their magick out to probe the intricate meshwork of runed wards engraved into the cavern walls. Haven was nearly done with her probe when she felt something was *wrong*.

Like a dark presence near. Not the Godkiller. Someone else. Someone who shouldn't be here. A presence flickering in and out of the planes of her consciousness—

It hit her as darkness snapped through her mind just how confused she was. No one had broken inside the cavern.

She was somewhere else.

She blinked as hands came into view. Not her hands. A man's by the dusting of coarse dark hair and thick knuckles. A black and gold signet ring with a falcon holding a sword in its mouth flashed from the otherwise bare hand. The finger next to it was missing at the second knuckle.

She went to call out to Nasira but—Shadeling's Shadow, she couldn't speak.

His mind. She was inside the ring wearer's mind. Seeing through his eyes. Everything was blurry, out of focus. What was he doing? He was looking at something. Smoothing out tan parchments. Using a magnifying glass of some sort to read whatever was on that scroll—

Like the elastic of a waistband suddenly snapped, she was flung from the reader's mind and back into herself. Cold, clammy flesh and bone wrapped around her. A surge of sour heat flooded her throat, and she barely managed to hold back her puke.

What in the Goddess's name was that?

The cavern wobbled and listed in circles as her senses trickled back. Her hearing was last. When it returned, Nasira was hissing Haven's name.

"Haven! Did you hear me? I said some of the runes have been tampered with."

A pit of unease yawned open inside Haven, eclipsing her panic over jumping into someone's head. "I heard you. I'll finish checking mine." She quickly swept her magick out. "There's a chunk of wards missing on my side too."

Her pulse skipped into a frantic beat as she quickly assessed the extent of disarmed runes. More than should have been possible since the last check.

"Who could have done this?" Haven asked, talking through her panic. "The runes haven't been disturbed from the outside . . ." The air sucked from her chest as understanding hit. "The Godkiller. It's somehow found a way to disarm the wards from the inside."

It was working fast. The last check had been twelve hours ago. In twelve hours it had found a way to disarm almost a third of the runes in the lowest vault.

They quickly repaired the wards as Haven ignored the Godkiller's intense gaze, that unblinking eye watching them work with a smug curiosity.

It would try again, she knew. Becoming more and more efficient as it unraveled the wards from the inside out.

If it ever reached the final threshold . . .

No, she would never allow that to happen.

THIRTY-ONE

aven had almost forgotten how nice it was to spoil herself with a long, steaming bath. Now that the night raids were on hold, Demelza actually had time to lug water up to Haven's hammered brass tub—and Haven actually had time to soak in it, hair and everything.

That wasn't all. For the first time since stepping foot on Shadoria, they managed to arrange a sit-down dinner together. Haven was acutely aware of how her shiny rose-gold hair fell in silken waves around her shoulders and back, and just as aware of how the others stared.

Xandrian actually had the nerve to whistle when she arrived, last of course. Her skin still wrinkled from her bath.

It also happened to be the most magnificent evening. The clouds veiling the sky were more threadbare than usual, letting through glorious rays of warm sunlight. A soft breeze dragged the thermal heat of the city up to the balcony they dined on, warming her enough that she removed the scratchy wool shawl Demelza insisted she bring.

The balcony overlooked the hills where white tendrils of mist slithered over the land like spectral serpents. Every so often they would shift to reveal the glossy black sea below, unusually still for this time of day.

"From tonight onward," Stolas said, idly handing Ravius a chunk of bread from his plate, "we're increasing checks on the Godkiller to three times a day."

She shivered as his gaze swept over her . . . and coasted past. He had hardly looked at her since she arrived, his normally wicked half-smile replaced by a distant stoicism she couldn't pierce. His moods had been growing darker, and the only time she felt like she could truly reach him was that single hour in his bedroom when they released her familiar.

Ravius—perched on the Shade Lord's shoulder—seemed to sense the shift in his mood as well, and his black feathers ruffled anxiously.

Xandrian frowned down at the wine in his glass. "Is that really necessary? There are thousands of wards leading down into that hellhole. Even if the Godkiller managed to disarm some of them in the lower vaults, surely it couldn't inactivate them all in half a day?"

Stolas arched an ashen brow. "In twelve hours, the Godkiller managed to make it nearly a third of the way through the lower vault's defenses on its first try. It was testing them. Learning their pattern. Each time it will work a little quicker. So, yes, I would say it's necessary. But I can take your shift if you're too busy?"

Xandrian slid his wine glass away, untouched. She'd noticed he hardly ever actually drank the wine, just toyed with it, going through the motions of drinking, almost like a prop.

"And let you lord that over me?" Xandrian asked. "No thanks."

Delphine flashed a series of signs to Stolas, and Bane's mouth fell open in silent laughter.

"What are the twins going on about?" Xandrian asked drolly.

Stolas grinned. "Oh, they were commenting on the pleasant evening."

A snort worked its way up her throat, and she swallowed it down. That was absolutely not what they said.

Bell leaned back in his chair, the wind ruffling his dark curls. "Correct me if I'm mistaken, but the wards in the vaults below Starpiercer Castle are a unique combination of dark and light runes. For the Godkiller to counteract them so quickly, it would need access to the original creator's runebook."

"Very good." Stolas tented his hands beneath his sharp chin. "Every ward is really just a complex tapestry of runes. To maintain a ward over centuries, you need a map to know what goes where. Any good ward weaver will encrypt the map, but such encryptions can be broken."

"And where is the ward map for the vaults?" Surai asked. She was to Haven's right, her glossy black hair recently cut to her jawline.

"Not here. I checked the day we arrived." The muscles of his temples flickered beneath his pale skin. "All the ward maps—including the maps for the tower wards—were looted along with half our family's heirlooms."

"By whom?" Ember demanded, her brown eyes—a deep umber against the dark green of her tattooed band—burning with fury.

Haven imagined her family had countless troves of treasure passed down for generations. To lose even one piece would be devastating.

"Does anyone even have to ask?" Nasira murmured. "The Court of Nine didn't just invade our land and claim our ancestral home as theirs. They pillaged everything. Jewels that had been passed down for generations. Musical instruments once played by the Gods. Pearl-inlaid boxes that once housed a feather from every child born to our royal line."

The bitterness in her voice sent a rush of unease sweeping through Haven, and she imagined the mortal lords rifling through Stolas's family's belongings. Ancient, beloved items that deserved reverence and respect, not being appraised, picked apart, and then hawked for money.

"Luckily," Stolas continued, his face expressionless, "the mortals never did learn to grow wings, so the heirlooms in the highest towers still remain."

Bell's jaw was taut as he shook his head, disgust evident on his face. "They shouldn't have done that."

"No, they really shouldn't have. But what's done is done. The question remains, who has the map now and how are they feeding that information to the Godkiller?"

The food she was chewing suddenly became unappetizing. She choked it down and cleared her throat. "I think I know how. Or, at least, a piece to the puzzle."

The entire table's attention settled on her.

"When I held the dagger the first time, the Shadeling . . . he spoke to me."

Bell dropped his fork with a loud clang. Surai gasped, and Ember threw a hand over her mouth as everyone waited in stunned silence. The only person who didn't seem surprised was Stolas.

"It hasn't happened since, although the weapon can also speak, but that's another story."

Surai's dark eyebrows flicked up, and Haven felt a stab of guilt for not telling her.

"I'm sure the Shadeling can still communicate with the Godkiller," Haven continued. "Could Morgryth have found the map and given it to him?"

Stolas ran two fingers over the tip of his jet-black horn as he thought. "Highly unlikely. He may be free from his cage, but he's still trapped in the lower levels of the Netherworld, and ward maps cannot pass the threshold into the Netherworld. All ward maps are sensitive to even the slightest hint of magick. It's a failsafe in case the map falls into enemy hands, meant to prevent magick being used to unlock the encryption."

"So someone in this realm has the map and is slowly deciphering the encryption and then feeding the wards to the Shadeling somehow, who in turn works through the Godkiller?"

"That would be my assumption, yes."

245

Everyone at the table stilled at that. Of course Haven knew that forces would come for the Godkiller. Archeron. Morgryth.

But she hadn't expected the breach to come from the *inside*.

It was just another reminder of how vulnerable they were.

For a moment, she remembered the brief vision she saw in the caves. But everything had been blurry and she wasn't even sure what she saw now. Hands and possibly scrolls of some kind?

"Why not destroy the thing?" Demelza asked. She was seated to Haven's left, wrapped in both her heavy wool shawl and Haven's, her crooked body hunched over her beef stew trying to capture the escaping heat. Apparently the woman despised the cold, which seemed odd considering she was from the north and complained of hot flashes all the time.

"Powerful runecasters have tried," Xandrian explained. "It's like the abominable weapon is permanently coated in black ruin."

"Black ruin?" Haven looked to Bell as she waited for him to put on that scholarly face and explain.

He didn't disappoint. "Black ruin is a substance that's collected from the Nether and broken down into liquid form. It's very volatile. When an object comes in contact with the stuff, that object temporarily exists inside the Nether and is protected for a period of time, even if it can be seen in this realm still. But black ruin only works on an object for a few days, a week at the most."

Haven remembered the sticky substance that seemed to coat everything in the Nether a monochromatic gray.

Nasira's eyes brightened. "Didn't the Demon Lords gift us a vial of black ruin once?"

"Whatever you're thinking, Nasi," Stolas warned, cutting his eyes at her, "don't. Even mother knew not to touch that poisonous material. It has more uses than the Demon Lords let on."

Nasi? Haven was absolutely filing that away for later.

Now, though, her thoughts were riveted to decreasing their ever-growing list of enemies. Poking at the biscuit resting on the edge of her stew bowl, she said, "Nothing yet from the ravens?"

The silence gave her an answer—just not the one she wanted.

"I thought once word of our alliance spread . . . never mind. I'm sure it takes time to craft such a response."

Relinquishing her grip on her bowl, Demelza reached over and patted Haven's hand. "If these Solis rulers do not come to you, they are fools. Every one of them."

"My mother is one of those Solis rulers," Ember pointed out, her fierce pride reminding Haven so much of Rook.

"And if she does not come to Haven then she is a fool," Demelza bravely insisted.

For a tense heartbeat, no one dared to breathe as they awaited Ember's reaction. But the Morgani princess finally cracked a smile, her head falling back as she laughed. "Haven, I think your lady's maid was a Morgani warrior in a past life."

"Agreed." It was Haven's turn to squeeze her friend's hand. The kind of courage it took to follow an outlawed crew of immortals across the sea to a condemned land, and to not complain once . . . Haven could only pray she could be half as badass when it came to protecting her friends.

"There might be a reason my mother has not sent a carrier hawk back yet," Ember added. "My kingdom is in the middle of planning their Fertalis Amare festival."

Bell straightened in his chair as his face lit up. "I've read about that festival. It celebrates Freya's sister, the goddess of love and fertility, and ends with a contest, right?"

A look of intense longing sparked in Ember's eyes before guttering out. "This year it's an archery contest."

"Rook entered one year," Surai mused, her eyes darkening at the memory. "It was right after her mother stripped her of her title and forced her to leave. She wasn't allowed to take anything with her, but she desperately wanted a necklace her grandmother had gifted her before she passed."

Ember laughed, but the sound was closer to a sob. "I remember. Mother was furious. The rules of the festival and contest state that anyone can enter—mortals, Noctis, lesser Solis, anyone. She couldn't keep Rook from becoming a contestant."

"And when Rook won and claimed her prize?" Surai said, her gaze fixed on some distant spot in the misty horizon. "I've never seen your mother so angry. I think her face turned bright purple."

Both women burst into choking laughter, and Haven wished more than anything that Rook could have been here now to see her favorite sister and her mate as friends and allies.

"Wait," Haven said. "What was the prize?"

Surai wiped away tears of laughter as she said, "That was the best part. The winner of the contest can choose any item from the Morgani's closely guarded trove of ancient treasure. Rook could have picked priceless artifacts worth indescribable sums, but she chose her grandmother's necklace, and the Morgani Queen had to let her take it."

A rush of excitement swept through Haven. "The winner can choose . . . anything?"

"Anything," Ember confirmed.

Haven turned to Xandrian to find him already shaking his head.

"No, Haven," he murmured, his voice growing more insistent as he took in her grin. "I told you that information is unsubstantiated, a rumor at best. And we cannot risk everything over a rumor."

She lifted her chin. "I think we all know the Morgani Queen isn't waiting until after the festival to respond. None of the nations are. They're never going to ally with us . . . not while I'm still mortal."

Haven had always marveled at how Stolas could command the

attention of a crowd without uttering a word. Now, the Shade Lord unfolded his clasped hands and leaned forward, and every gaze jerked to him. "Will someone please tell me what's going on."

Even though his voice held the same mannered tone as always, his dark mood came through in his lowered brows and tight mouth. Ravius abandoned the Shade Lord's shoulder and took up a spot on the back of Haven's chair.

She tossed the insatiable bird a wheel of white cheese bigger than his head and then met Stolas's rapt gaze. "Xandrian found a connection to one of my mother's stolen paintings."

Surai gasped. "What?"

Xandrian started to protest but Haven continued, "We think the Morgani Queen unknowingly has it in her possession." She met Ember's startled eyes. "Have you ever seen anything that could be the stolen painting?"

"I . . . Haven, there's hundreds of pieces of art in the palace alone, and countless more stored in the troves. I wouldn't even know where to begin."

Haven released a ragged breath. "Still, it could be there, right? And if I win the contest I could claim it?"

"Are you mad?" Xandrian asked quietly. "You are the most hunted runecaster in the realm. All of us are now, actually, in case you've forgotten."

"Yes, but *anyone* can enter the contest. And Archeron wouldn't dare attack me while I was a guest of the Morgani Queen." She hoped. "He's too smart to cause an all-out war with the second most powerful nation in Solissia, even for me."

Again, she hoped.

"And Morgryth?" Xandrian pressed. "Or are we pretending the Shade Queen no longer poses a threat because she's been rather quiet lately? Because in my very extensive experience, when your enemy goes silent, it's not a good thing."

"I haven't forgotten the Shade Queen, nor have I forgotten my father. But playing it safe today simply translates to pushing back the inevitable." Inhaling, she swept her gaze over the table. "Without allies in Solissia, we will not survive. Does it really matter if our end comes in a few days or a few weeks?"

Ember grimaced as she stared down at her clasped fingers. "I mean, she does have a point."

Bell shot Xandrian a sidelong glance before looking back to Haven. "I agree. In fact, if the Morgani Queen's army is obligated to protect the contestants and their companions, I would argue we're actually safer there."

Xandrian flashed Bell a betrayed look.

Stolas, who had been watching quietly from the other side of the table, slid his unreadable gaze to Ember. "Is that true? Would your mother and her guard protect Haven from Archeron?"

"Anyone can enter," Ember admitted cautiously, "and contestants are considered guests under the protection of the Morgani nation, yes."

Stolas blinked. Looked to Haven. "And you think you could somehow recognize one of these paintings?"

Haven gave a slow nod. "They're the last things my mother gave me. Get me near them, that's all I'm asking. The paintings will do the rest."

She held her breath as she waited for Stolas to explain how foolish she was being. Without his support, the rest of them would follow suit. Which would be extremely inconvenient because she'd already decided in the last minute that she was going no matter what.

Deep inside, a quiet voice whispered this was the answer to everything.

Her mother had left a map to immortality for Haven and like hell she wasn't going to scour the realm for it.

Would anyone accompany her? Surai—she could talk Surai into sneaking away . . . probably. Possibly Ember and Bell. The rest were iffy.

And Stolas would get over it.

Probably.

All of her desperate plans came to a halt as Stolas stood, blotted his lips on a crisp white napkin, and said, "Then it's settled. We leave tomorrow."

Haven felt her eyebrows crawl up her forehead.

"Why does that surprise you?" he asked softly.

"Because I assumed you would say . . . no." That was only partway true. She had been thinking of Archeron and all the times he disapproved of her actions. All the times she'd had to fight tooth and nail for her opinions to matter.

Had to fight for him to *listen* to her. Not talk over her. Not explain over and over how she knew nothing of his world and how he knew best.

Really listen and let her be heard.

That experience had prepared her to battle for Stolas's approval.

A wry half-grin tempered the hard line of Stolas's mouth. "Would you have listened if I had disagreed?"

"No."

The chuckle that left his lips was soft, almost wicked, and inexplicably made her blush. "Then that's why."

"Because I would have left anyway?"

"Because finding the painting is obviously so important to you that you would risk going alone, and what is important to you is important to all of us. We rise and fall together, Haven. That is the only way we survive. Although I suggest in the future you remember you are the Goddess-Born and should never answer to anyone, even me."

His words took hold like nightfall inside her—slowly, and then all at once.

You should never answer to anyone, not even me.

Lips parted, every seemingly plausible reply faded on her tongue as she watched him turn to go.

To *go.*

"Wait," she called a little too eagerly. "What about our . . . training?"

Her stomach dropped as he murmured over his shoulder, "not tonight," without even turning around.

THIRTY-TWO

Stolas had barely left the table before Xandrian drawled, "Is it just me or does he seem moodier than usual?"

Nasira flashed her teeth at Xandrian. "What did you expect today of all days?"

He shrugged, swirling the untouched wine around in his glass. His golden blond hair was pulled back from his face by a silver ribbon, showing off his elegant brows and perfectly rounded cheekbones. "I mean, it's been hundreds and hundreds of years since the coup. I assumed the anniversary of the event would become just another day after, say, the second or third century."

Goddess Above, was today the day Morgryth took over Shadoria?

"Why don't I force you to push a blade through your mother's heart," Nasira whispered, voice strangely emotionless, "but slowly, so you get to watch her every expression, see her fear and pain and sadness as she dies knowing her children are all dead or enslaved? Then we can see how long your grief lasts."

The entire table quieted. Even the breeze seemed to die. Icy fingers wrapped around Haven's heart. She couldn't imagine watching her parents and siblings die in front of her to that depraved monster, but to be forced to end their lives . . . to have the memory of the act ingrained inside your soul . . . that was beyond horrifying.

No wonder Stolas was upset.

Unfortunately, the only person who didn't seem to empathize was Xandrian. "Considering my mother is now a ferocious creature with gills and an appetite for fish heads and sailors, I very much doubt my mourning period would be a protracted affair."

Bell's chair scraped the stone floor as he placed his napkin on the table and stood. "You know, Xandrian, I used to admire you. I thought . . . I thought you were everything I aspired to be."

"And what is that, exactly, Bellamy?"

"Handsome. Admired. Your name known to every courtier and citizen in your kingdom."

"And now?" Xandrian drawled, all arrogant callousness as he feigned more interest in his wine glass than Bell. But there was . . . something else in his tone too. A vulnerability behind that lazy smile.

"Now I see that, while on the outside you are all those things and more, on the inside you are empty, a fraud—and everything I aspire *not* to be."

Other than the subtle tic of a muscle at Xandrian's temple, his face remained as smug as always. "So . . . you admit you find me handsome?"

If Xandrian thought doubling down on the arrogance would work on Bell, he didn't know her friend like she did.

Bell swept his gaze over the table with a confidence that made him seem five years older. "Goodnight. Haven, you can come by later if you want to discuss tomorrow. I have some thoughts on the portals."

Nasira's wings unfolded as she went after Bell, the glossy tip of one of her feathers *accidentally* knocking Xandrian's wine into his lap.

Xandrian frowned at the spreading red stain. Then he casually reached for the crystal decanter and filled his glass again. "A shame," he said. "I rather liked these pants, although the wine is only so-so."

Ember snorted before getting to her feet. "I think I just remembered why there are no pompous males on our island."

"There are no males on your island period," Xandrian pointed out dryly. "It's quite literally against the law for one to enter your kingdom, except on holidays and festivals."

"Yes, well you just reminded me why." Upper lip curled in disgust, she snatched the decanter from in front of Xandrian and then waved it around like a trophy. "Anyone without a useless appendage between their legs want to join me in the hot baths?"

Delphine and Bane rose simultaneously. After a heated conversation, Delphine cast an annoyed look toward Surai and signed something too fast for Haven to decipher.

Surai grinned. "Delphine said that while her brother's appendage is most definitely useless, it's also quite small and shouldn't be a bother to anyone."

Bane shot his sister a murderous look.

Ember stared pointedly at the body part in question and then shrugged.

Surai moved to join them before glancing back at Haven. "Coming? It may be the last night we have for a while like this."

Without death and dying, Surai didn't say. She didn't have to. It was written over all their faces. The desperate need to enjoy tonight. To really live in this one rare, peaceful evening.

Haven wanted to go. It had been too long since they'd really hung out, or just talked like they used to.

In some ways, her life was so much lonelier now than before she was Goddess-Born.

But she couldn't stomach drinking and having fun knowing what today signified for Stolas. Knowing the despair he must feel, even hundreds of years later.

She shook her head. "No, I think I'll try to finally do that thing mortals call sleeping. But you guys have fun for me, okay? And take Demelza with you."

"No," her lady's maid protested, her curls blowing around her head as she shook it. "I will stay with you."

The way Demelza glared at Bane and Delphine, she probably suspected they were demons in disguise.

Haven gave Surai a pleading look. "Please? And make sure she has a good time."

Whether Demelza would admit it or not, this place had been hard on her, and she needed a break.

Surai came around the table and planted a kiss on Haven's head. "As you wish, *Soror*." Her lavender eyes darted to a cursing Demelza. "You owe me big time for this. Sure you don't want to come?"

Haven shook her head before she could change her mind.

"Fine. Just make sure this 'sleep' you mention doesn't come with twisted horns, gorgeous wings, and a dark, brooding scowl, okay?"

"I don't know what you're talking about," Haven teased, knowing full well her meaning.

Surai grunted beneath her breath as she hooked an arm under Demelza's and tugged, coaxing her from her chair. Surai gave Haven one final look, mouthed, *you owe me big time*, and wrestled the cursing woman across the patio as they caught up to the others.

Haven watched them go, not even bothering to hide her envy.

Are they marching the witch to her death? Ravius asked, hopping onto Haven's shoulder.

"Of course not," she snapped, taking her jealousy out on him.

Shame.

"Excuse me?" Xandrian said.

Oh, right. Sometimes Haven forgot no one else could hear Ravius, and she wasn't in the mood to explain to Xandrian. "Nothing."

"You should go with them. " Xandrian's eyes became sea-blue slits as he stared out into the misty ocean. "Goddess knows if I let every tragedy affect me, I would never enjoy myself."

"Is that what you're doing now? Enjoying yourself?"

"Oh, I am the very epitome of happiness, Goddess-Born."

Not in the mood for Xandrian's flippant cruelty, she went to leave . . . and hesitated.

"If you don't let anything get to you, what's your excuse?"

He flicked up a bored eyebrow. "Pardon?"

"For being a bastard? At least Stolas has a reason, what's yours?"

He chuckled, toying with one of the golden buttons of his vest. "Being a bastard has kept me alive in a court where I should have died hundreds of years ago. That's my excuse."

"Is that why you always have a glass of wine in your hand when you hardly even drink? Why you say the cruelest things to people you might actually like? I watched you in the Sun Court. You were always surrounded by the most beautiful people, but you never smiled. Not once."

"Is there a point to this?"

"You're not in the Sun Court, Xandrian. You don't have to play that role anymore."

"No?" An emotion flashed inside his guarded eyes, too quick to catalog. "What if, after pretending to be something for so long, I don't remember who I was before? What then?"

"I don't know. Start with not being a dick and go from there?"

He snorted. "Sorry, when I want advice from someone younger than the chair under my ass, I'll ask."

She sighed as she stood. The air had cooled considerably with the approaching dusk, but for once, the shrouds of mist were thin, allowing a view of the fiery orange sun as it dipped into the jet black sea. With the purple-tinged white layering the hills, the golds and pinks dancing across the frothy waves, Shadoria had never looked more beautiful.

It seemed odd that today of all days would choose to be glorious.

She planted her palms on the smooth marble table. "I may be young, but I know that Bell is the best of all of us. He's kind, and noble, and courageous, and he deserves so much more than this . . . whoever you are."

"That's definitely true, but give it twenty or thirty years and if he's still alive after everything, he will not be so kind or noble. This dangerous life of kings and tyrants will shape him into something harder, something darker, in the same way it will you. Come talk to me then, Goddess-Born, after you've lost nearly everyone you love."

Something about his words were like a knife tip ripping open the scar of Archeron's visions, and she flinched before she could stop herself.

"Oh. Did you think you could get through this unscathed?" What looked like true pity flickered across his face. "You poor, naïve girl."

Anger swept through her like a brushfire. She dragged her furious stare over his stained breeches before meeting his eyes. "You haven't quite lost him fully yet, but you will, Sun Lord. Forever."

Holding her stare, he took a long swig of his wine. "Who says I want to keep him?"

Haven shrugged, tossing the last of her plate to the ground for Ravius. "Don't say I didn't warn you."

As she strolled toward the set of doors leading inside, she waited for Xandrian's snappy comeback.

And waited and waited until the doors clicked shut behind her.

THIRTY-THREE

Stolas might not have wanted to train tonight, but he did have plans. She discovered what those plans were when she passed by the entrance to the Hall of Light on the way to bed. Night had fallen in the time it took to walk from the balcony on the far west side of the grounds to here—which was basically a testament to the size of Starpiercer Castle.

She hadn't meant to stop by the massive stone doors with door handles shaped like wolf heads, but something—a feeling, or perhaps the light trickling from beyond—made her stop.

Newly lit torches cast pale blue ovals of runelight over the cratered black walls of the massive chamber. Silver rectangles of moonlight crept across the floor.

And on his knees inside one of those swaths of ethereal light was Stolas. His wings hung tight and limp against his back, their tips brushing the dark floor.

She thought she might have heard him audibly sigh as she quietly crossed to his side. When she saw what he was doing, how delicately he collected the small shards of crystal in his palm and then transferred them to a folded piece of cloth . . . her heart felt similar to the shattered crystals he was trying to save.

"I thought the attendants would have collected all the pieces by now."

"I told them not to," he said without looking up.

"Why?"

"When my Shadow Familiar first awakened, I was too foolish to understand its danger to others. I thought I could control it without taking the time to bond first. That mistake cost a Seraphian citizen their leg. For an entire year afterward, my mother forced me to live with that man—a baker—as his servant. I fetched him his robe in the morning, his breakfast. I put so many loaves into that huge oven I swear I'll never look at bread the same."

She smiled a little as she imagined a young, privileged Stolas slaving away in front of an oven, his massive wings cramped inside the bakery.

Stolas Darkshade knew how to make bread. The idea was so ridiculous she almost laughed, but then again, so many things about Stolas were the opposite of what she expected.

He was a study in contrasts.

Sometimes the raw, unfettered power she sensed roiling beneath his flesh was overwhelming, like the midday Penrythian sun—too powerful, too bright. Other times his presence was like standing beneath a sky of falling stars—wholly mesmerizing.

"That must have been humiliating," she said.

"It was. But I learned a valuable lesson. I alone am responsible for fixing what I break."

She wasn't sure you could fix taking someone's leg away . . . but she got the point, and she was torn between scoffing and smiling.

Only Stolas could turn this situation into a lesson. He was always mentoring her in some way. And even if those lessons were typically delivered with impatience and a short temper, she appreciated them.

She glanced down at Stolas. He had yet to look at her, his attention focused on a tiny sliver of crystal caged between his long fingers. She understood why he took sole responsibility for cleaning the damage he'd done, but to do that tonight of all nights, alone . . .

"If you plan to stand there all evening with that pitying look then I'm going to ask you to leave," he murmured.

She didn't blame him for his curt response. The last thing he needed right now was pity from anyone. But he was wrong if he thought she would leave him alone to bear this burden.

Dropping to her knees, she tossed her hair over her shoulder and began searching the black tiles for the quick flicker of light that marked a nearby crystal fragment.

A lock of ivory hair, made whiter by the moonlight streaming down, fell over Stolas's brow as his head tilted so she could see his profile. "What are you doing?"

"What does it look like I'm doing?" she asked softly. "I'm helping."

"I didn't ask you to. This is my burden to bear alone."

"What about that speech you gave earlier about rising and falling together?"

Even with his face turned away, she knew he was rolling his eyes. "You're twisting my words."

"No, I'm literally repeating them back to you. And . . . I'm being a friend."

"A friend?" A gravelly chuckle cut through the hall. "Is that what we are to one another?"

Her fingernails stabbed into her palms. If she didn't know Stolas the way she did, his words would sting. But she did know him.

Whenever he felt someone getting too close, especially during a vulnerable moment, he did this.

Lashed out.

Pushed people away.

Tried to be the monster they claimed he was.

"You can't scare me, you know." She grunted as her knee, already sore from falling during a training session this week, caught on a jagged part of the floor. "I've seen you at your worst, remember?"

"Beastie, you haven't even scratched the surface on my worst."

She plucked a fingernail sized fragment of crystal from a crack in the floor and held it up to the light, fascinated by the glimmer of power she felt pulsating from its core. "I'll take my chances."

Apparently coming to the conclusion that she wasn't going to budge, he switched to ignoring her, and they gathered the pieces in silence. The only sounds were her soft breathing and the occasional ruffle of Stolas's feathers as his wings shifted, stretching and ruffling seemingly on their own accord.

More than once, she found herself watching him when he wasn't looking. Something about the way the soft light glided over his kneeling form was mesmerizing. Painted in those silvery beams, his skin luminescent and spun from the moon itself, feathers dancing with indigos and deep purples, he didn't look like the dark lord who had ruled the Netherworld for countless centuries.

No, he looked every bit a Seraphian prince.

"This was her favorite room in the entire castle." Stolas took a chunk of amethyst crystal the size of a nectarine and held it up to the moonlight. "She drew the plans for the chandelier herself. Picked out every single crystal with her bare hands."

A deep ache opened inside her as she imagined his Shadow Wolf destroying the magnificent light structure. Wiping her dirty palms on her pants, she said, "You were protecting them, weren't you? You directed your wolf to the crystals instead of Bell and the others?"

"Don't," he growled. "Don't make me the hero of this story. Please. Not tonight."

Frustration warmed her cheeks. "Stolas, if you hadn't chosen to sacrifice something you held dear, they would be dead."

"You give me too much credit."

"Do I?"

"It was right here in this very spot that I killed her." His words were so soft that she almost missed them. His back was still to her. Those glorious wings stretching to fill the space between them. Catching every bit of light as they did. "Still want to paint me as your hero?"

"You didn't kill her, Stolas," Haven corrected, inching closer. She pushed past the waves of inky darkness pulsing from him. "Morgryth did."

"I held the knife. I looked into her eyes as I positioned it over her heart. I might have whispered her name, I don't recall. But I do remember the sound she made when the blade first pierced her skin. Her magick had left her, she was completely unprotected. Unable to defend herself from her own son."

"You. Didn't. Kill. Her."

"Stop." He didn't raise his voice, but the warning was there in the softness of his tone and all the unspoken words in between.

Anyone else and Stolas would have already *made* them stop. She knew that. Knew she was hovering over a very dangerous line.

And yet . . . to let him continue this dark cycle of self-hatred and blame was cruel, and if she didn't at least try to break that cycle then she was a coward.

She scooted quietly closer. "Stolas, Morgryth murdered your family, not you."

"Haven, I need you to leave right now."

His voice was unrecognizable.

Gravelly. More beast than man.

His stillness was a preternatural thing that warned the most primitive parts of her to run.

Everything in her screamed to obey. To flee from this—this predator. But the idea of him in the hall where he killed his own mother, alone with his anger and shame and grief, hating himself more with every passing second . . .

"I can't, Stolas."

"Why?"

"Because—because I care about you."

The dark chuckle that rumbled from his chest was part laugh, part growl, and one hundred percent terrifying. The hairs along her arms went rigid as he finally . . . finally turned to face her.

And she suddenly knew why he hadn't fully looked at her before.

Nearly all black eyes fringed blood-red watched her above the longest incisors she'd ever seen on a Noctis. His normally elegant eyebrows were severely arched, his lush lips twisted cruelly.

"You care about me, Beastie?" His voice was unrecognizable. "And what if I told you that right this very second, I can sense your light magick throbbing inside your delicate veins. That it calls to me? That I want to gorge myself on it—on you?"

Hot, sticky fear clumped in her middle. No, this wasn't Stolas. Jaw gritted so hard she expected a molar to crack, she purged the terror from her body—but not fast enough.

His nostrils flared, picking up the scent she tried to hide. A wicked grin bared the full length of his fangs.

Panic bubbled up inside her—

A whisper of shadow slicing through moonlight—that's all she caught before he was upon her. She slammed the heel of her palm up on instinct, grazing the hard angle of his jaw.

It felt like ramming her flesh against the edge of a marble counter.

He didn't seem to feel it as he closed in. His eyes were black pits fringed in fire. Twin pools peering directly into the Netherworld.

"Stolas."

Nothing.

"Stolas!"

His silence was unnerving. The way he moved seemingly through the planes of this realm like smoke. She spun from his grasp. Her heart dipped and then ratcheted into a wild throbbing rhythm as she sensed him around her. Dancing in and out of the shadows. Moving too fast to catalog.

A brush of wing here. A caress of breath there. His dark magick tingling and pulsing and raking against her skin.

Something stroked her neck as laughter echoed off the walls.

Gathering her energy, she focused on that wicked, throaty chuckle. There. Before he could move again she blasted her light magick out—

And watched it drain into nothing.

She honed all her attention on his deadly presence. Waited until she felt it materialize—

Her kick was hard and unexpected. Her boot connected with something—his thigh?—and she winced as the impact reverberated up her shin and into her femur.

"That wasn't very nice, Beastie."

Too late, she felt the hands clamp around her waist. The arms like marble. That familiar scent of irises and blood mandarin and musk.

She rammed the heel of her boot into his shin.

Once. Twice.

Countless times until the floor disappeared and her stomach hollowed out and—

They were high above the Hall of Light where the chandelier once hung. Suspended in a shaft of delicate moonlight. Flecks of dust sparkled as they swirled lazily around them. Giant windows offered views of the mist-laden hills, the soft glow of runelanterns pulsing beneath that ivory veil where the city slumbered.

The beauty of it all could almost convince her she was dreaming.

But this wasn't a dream—it was a nightmare.

One arm was slung low over her belly.

The other brushed the wild tangle of her hair, his knuckles sending shivers through her inflamed skin as he positioned it out of the way.

Baring her neck.

Her n*eck.*

She froze as his cool breath fluttered over her jaw.

Closed her eyes as he dragged the tips of his fangs over the tender spot just below her ear.

"You don't like the taste of blood," she said, stupidly.

"Don't I?" His lips vibrated with laughter as they took turns with his fangs, exploring her flesh.

Shock and confusion clouded her actions. Was he trying to teach her another lesson? "Why are you doing this?"

"It's obvious our nights together have made you forget what I am. I think you need a reminder."

"Screw"—she grabbed his free arm—"you."

She wrenched his forearm close to her mouth.

And bit.

Hard.

The second she felt his grip loosen on her waist, she rammed her elbow into his abdomen and twisted.

Her cage of muscle and bone became open air.

She threw out her magick—or tried.

It was gone.

Runes.

Eyes slammed shut, she braced for impact . . . only to blink in surprise as she was halted mere inches from the ground.

Before she could react, she was flipped gently onto her back.

But there was nothing gentle in the hands pinning her wrists to the ground. And the eyes that stared down at her—there was nothing even close to gentle in those.

"That was stupid."

Her cheeks inflamed with hurt and anger as she glared up at him. "Take a single drop of my magick or blood without my permission and I will kill you."

"You've already killed me once. It didn't take."

Bastard.

Head canted to the side, he gathered both her wrists in one hand. The other hand pushed back a strand of hair from her forehead.

"Where were we? Oh, right. You were saying how much you care for me, and how much I *don't* like blood."

Furious, she drove her knee up, aiming for anything she could hit.

He twisted out of her reach, those predatory eyes gleaming in delight as he tsked. "That doesn't seem like caring, Beastie."

She bucked, jerking her hips. Trying to throw him off her. Trying to rip her hands from his grasp. Trying to escape the savagery raging from his being.

She'd always sensed that darkness lurking behind those beautiful manners . . . but it had always been tightly controlled.

It wasn't controlled anymore.

She reached out for her powers . . . only to find a cold, hollow hole in her chest where that roiling magick normally waited.

A noise tumbled from her throat, part snarl and part scream of rage. What the Netherworld was he doing?

"I could drink your magick by force," he murmured, trailing a fingertip down her cheek. "But then I do believe you would try to kill me. Such a murderous creature you are, Beastie."

Damn right.

She felt his power stir, felt it slowly reach out, a caress of euphoria that softened her mind. Another stroke of that horrible, wonderful emotion and her muscles relaxed as liquid heat rolled through her in waves.

Promising wholeness. Happiness. Pleasure—such pleasure.

"How long do you think you could resist before you do whatever I ask? Is that what you want?"

She clawed her way through the velvety layers of magick he'd wrapped all around her. Clawed and clawed until she surfaced from that promise of euphoria, half wild with fury.

"No," she gritted out.

"Good." His darkness receded as he pushed himself off her and stripped his powers away, leaving her cold and confused on the floor. "Next time you think you *care* for me, remember this moment."

She scrambled to her feet as the world seemed to spin around her. Leaving—he was leaving.

Her eyes burned.

Her throat ached.

She was undoubtedly in shock. Too numb to say a word as she watched him go. Those glorious wings caught the light and made her heart tug oddly as she remembered how beautiful he had looked just moments before.

Confusion blunted the full impact of the emotions ravaging her chest, but her body felt everything. The left side of her neck still stung from where the tips of his fangs had dragged. The flesh above her hipbones ached from the deep press of his fingertips. Even her lips were swollen, probably injured when she jerked his arm to her mouth.

To bite him. *Bite* him.

It didn't feel real. None of it felt even close to reality.

Even if the soreness from his attack—there was really no other word for it—faded in the next few minutes, the dull throbbing where his fingers had circled her wrists like manacles were already darkening.

A slice of pain tore open her middle as she realized his fingers had once done the same thing, holding her wrists above her head as he took complete control.

But this time there was no pleasure—only confusion and betrayal.

She reached out to rub her wrists and realized she was trembling. From the euphoria he'd infused into her, the adrenaline still slamming through her arteries, or her growing rage, she wasn't sure.

Probably all of those things.

She didn't find her voice until he was past the rectangles of silver light and masked in the deep shadows near the doors.

But she didn't need to see him to call him what he was. "Coward."

He froze. Every feather seemed to still. Every mote of dust swirling inside the pools of light suspending, if only for a moment. As if this place, broken and ruined as it was, tied to his emotions.

Then Stolas Darkshade prowled through the doors and disappeared.

And Haven forced her muscles to stop trembling. Forced her legs to take steady strides until the Hall of Light was far behind her.

Only then did she let Stolas back into her thoughts, just long enough to decide he was a cowardly bastard. A runeforsaken, Shade-damned bastard and *liar*.

In one night, he'd destroyed everything she thought they shared between them. The trust. The friendship.

The . . . feelings she'd kept hidden away.

Everything between them—*everything*—now broken and scattered like the shards of crystal on the floor.

And yet he wasn't here to pick up the pieces.

THIRTY-FOUR

Haven awoke to pounding on her bedchamber door. Archeron! He'd betrayed them. She sprang from bed, nearly tripping on the sheets tangled around her legs, and searched the pile of laundry on the floor for proper clothes.

Dammit, where were her pants?

A week of peaceful nights had made her groggy and unprepared. She whipped her head to the open windows, searching the sky for signs of the Seraphian guards. A thick tapestry of steel gray clouds greeted her, but no flickering shadows to hint at a battle.

Outside, the world was quiet. Still.

The pounding became more insistent. Demelza snorted, jerked awake, and rolled off the low cot in the corner and onto the dusty floor.

The last time Haven saw Demelza, she was being carried to bed by Surai and Delphine, singing the national anthem from whatever Curse-forsaken northern city she hailed at the top of her lungs. Haven had to help Surai pry a bottle of wine from her gnarled fingers.

"I'm awake," Demelza cried, using the bed frame as support to stumble to her feet. "Goddess-Born, what do you need?"

Haven was nearly dressed, Demelza clipping on her sword-belt, when the door splintered open with a booming crash. Haven flung up a half-hazard shield to protect Demelza and then lunged for the intruder, sword drawn—

"Haven, wait!"

On the other side of the door frame, Bell waved his hands trying to get her attention through the cloud of dust and pulverized wood. That's when she noticed the telltale aroma of amateur magick—burnt roses.

Bell had broken down her door with magick.

That couldn't be good.

"What is it?" she demanded as she ducked beneath a fragment of the door that hadn't been destroyed.

Sweat sheened his face, and he was breathing hard. His wide-eyed gaze went to her sword. "You won't need that."

"Bell." She sheathed her sword and took him by the shoulders. "What is going on?"

"Do you remember the thing I told you Stolas released when you were in the Nether?"

Her pulse lanced against the tender flesh of her wrist. "His Shadow Wolf?"

"It's loose again," he panted, working to catch his breath. "It's—it's destroying the castle. The Seraphians are too scared to go near it. Even Nasira can't get it under control. You may be the only one who can stop it."

The first sign that something was wrong was the howls. Deep, booming, bloodcurdling howls that sounded more Netherworld beast than mortal wolf. They were in the royal tower, three levels below Stolas's chamber. Bell and Haven made it to the growing crowd of Seraphians and Chosen just as Nasira came rushing around the corner.

Panic whispered through Haven at the sight. The slip of gorgeous silver and black strappy nightgown Nasira wore revealed claw marks raking every available inch of her arms and legs. And while the ghastly furrows were already healing, knitting together before Haven's eyes, it was the sheer size of the wounds that alarmed Haven. If Stolas's wolf had hit a major organ—no amount of healing would have saved her.

Nasira's wings were ruffled and askew, missing feathers in more than a few places. Her gaze darted to Haven, and Haven was shocked by the rare shadow of fear darkening the Noctis girl's expression.

"Where's Stolas?" Haven demanded as Xandrian, Surai, and Ember rushed over.

Nasira shook her head. "Asleep. He must be having a nightmare."

Xandrian scowled as his focus slid in the direction of the howls. "That's the result of a nightmare? Dare I ask what happens when he actually gets angry?"

Nasira hissed, flashing her canines before turning to Haven. "I can't stop it."

His familiar had destroyed the Hall of Light in less than a minute, and that was when Stolas was awake to direct its bloodlust. She could only imagine the devastation it would wreak now. "Nasira, you have to wake him up."

"I can't, Haven. No one can get within a hundred feet of his chamber while he's sleeping."

A roar exploded from somewhere close by, followed by the boom of stone shattering.

Stone.

Goddess Above.

The castle trembled with the force. Dust and loose stone rained over them.

"I think it broke through the floor," Surai muttered.

"The floor?" Haven tucked a rose-gold strand behind her ear, her hair still damp from her bath before bed. She didn't know much about wolves, but dogs only dug downward when there was something they wanted. "Nasira, what is it trying to find?"

"Not find." Her eyes closed, reopened. There was a hollowness in her gaze that Haven had never seen before. "Destroy."

Delphine and Bane had approached at some point during the chaos, and Delphine explained further using signs. Haven could only pick up on a little.

Room. Magick. Secret.

Surai translated. "A few days before Morgryth attacked, the level two floors below was suddenly walled over and warded."

"The entire level?" Haven asked, thinking that was a mistake.

But Surai nodded. "The entire level. Every window was paved over. Every door destroyed."

Xandrian grinned. "Who needs doors when you can use the ceiling?"

Nasira looked a few seconds away from ripping Xandrian's head from his shoulders, so Haven stepped between them and said to Nasira, "If there are wards then the Shadow Wolf can't reach it, right?"

Nasira's ashen lashes lowered as her gaze collapsed to the floor. "It can if the wards were created by its master."

Stolas. What could have been so terrible that he needed such security to keep it locked away?

Another explosion rocked the castle. Another howl pierced the night. The intense rage and grief inside that otherworldly sound cut straight to her heart. Right now Stolas's Shadow Wolf was his pain personified, and every ounce of his emotions was laser-focused on that room.

What the Netherworld was in there?

A pulse of magick flared over them like a band snapping.

The first ward was broken.

"Perhaps it will stop destroying everything once it finds whatever the hell is pissing it off so badly?" Xandrian proposed through a yawn.

The color leached from Nasira's face. "That can't happen. There is a . . . a curse on the thing inside that chamber. An amplifier curse."

Surai sucked in a breath. "Goddess save him then."

"What?" Haven flicked a desperate look to Bell, whose face was stricken. "Bell? What is an amplifier curse?"

He slowly met her gaze. "It means whatever is inflicted upon the object will return tenfold to the aggressor."

She blinked. Still not quite getting it.

"If Stolas's wolf destroys the object," Surai whispered, unable to look at Haven, "Stolas will die."

Another ward snapped over them. For a moment, as the fading magick trekked across her skin, she couldn't quite take in Surai's full meaning. It was incomprehensible to Haven that Stolas could die.

He'd survived so much. Even death.

And then . . . a slice of fear cut through her chest.

Stolas could die.

Would die if she didn't do something.

Everything fell away. Gone.

She was running toward the howls and explosions.

Propelled by a pulsing ache of terror that gnawed at her heart.

That grew more and more painful with every ward that slammed over her, broken.

She darted down the final corner to a room choked with dust and the bittersweet scent of severed magick. Voices called her name, but from so far away. A few Seraphian soldiers huddled in the shadows, watching her as she lunged past.

A yawning hole waited where the floor was supposed to be. She jumped without looking how far the drop was . . .

Legs kicking empty air, she glanced below and realized her mistake. The fall was three stories high.

She just had time to draw a cushion rune before she hit. The floor slammed into her, pain ricocheting through her bones as she rolled over her shoulder to break the impact.

Popping to her feet, she quickly assessed her body—unbroken—before searching the room for Stolas's Shadow Wolf.

She didn't have to look far. Through the cloud of pulverized stone and oily charcoal smoke from the shredded wards, a hulking form emerged. Her mind spun wildly as she tried to categorize the creature.

It was a wolf but not a wolf.

It possessed the same lupine body. Blocky head, long muzzle, sharp swiveling ears meant for catching even the smallest noises. And just like the wolves around Penryth's forests, before they'd been hunted to near extinction, there was a savage beauty to the predator that reminded Haven of Stolas.

But that's where the similarities ended.

True mortal wolves weren't the size of wyverns.

They didn't have fur so black it seemed to devour the light.

And they certainly didn't possess muscles that rippled and bunched beneath the sleekest, most luxurious pelt she'd ever seen. Not shaggy like most wolves.

Soft. A fur hunters the realm over would pay any price for.

Then there were those luminous red eyes. Eyes now trained on her.

Eyes too ancient, too intelligent and knowing to come from an animal.

A spine-tingling snarl rumbled the room as the Shadow Wolf's black lips curled back. Wicked incisors made for tearing flesh and cracking bone greeted her. Frothy foam and saliva hung from its teeth, and its gums were . . . bleeding.

She understood why as she flicked her gaze around the room. In the short amount of time the wolf had been inside, it had left a trail of chaos and destruction. Tearing indiscriminately at everything in its path. Chunks of stone formed countless piles. Debris was pulverized beyond recognition, a few jagged splinters of wood or shreds of fabric the only pieces left to hint at its origins.

Behind the creature rose wooden shelves packed with every manner of belonging. Urns and portraiture busts, books, lutes, tightly rolled wool rugs, even paintings. If she knew which object was the cursed item, perhaps she could possibly wrap a shield around it for protection.

Her stomach sank. There were hundreds of shelves. Even if she knew what to look for, she would never find it in time.

The only option was to distract the wolf until Stolas woke up.

Considering its predatory focus was already locked onto her, that wouldn't be hard to do. Surviving, on the other hand, would prove infinitely challenging.

She smiled at the creature. "You're not so bad, are you?"

An unearthly growl ripped from its slavering maw and stole her breath. Huge paws flexed, its onyx claws puncturing the stone floor.

"Stolas?"

It didn't make a single noise as it leapt.

She had expected the wolf to attack, but still, the sight of such a powerful beast hurtling down on her was near paralyzing.

She dove. White-hot fire sliced across her shoulder.

Not fire. Claws.

Claws that jerked her around so violently her head snapped back. She crashed into a heap of rubble. Stars danced in and out of her vision. Air fled her lungs in the form of a grunt. She rolled and rolled, head glancing off stone. Teeth snapped in the air by her face.

Stolas! She flung his name out into their shared consciousness. Trying to spear into his mind. *You're having a nightmare, and I need you to wake up.*

When the heat of the creature's breath cooled over her skin, she lurched to her feet. Her boots slipped and slid over the dusty floor as she pivoted to square off with the beast.

Twin pools of Netherfire burned from the shadows, searing into her. She searched their depths for a hint of Stolas, something she could connect with, but—

Nothing—there was nothing but molten fury and grief and pain.

A low growl filled the space between them as the creature saw the golden orb hovering above her palm. She must have subconsciously drawn out her light magick.

"Don't make me use this," she pleaded, willing Stolas to hear her.

Wake up, Stolas.

She knew it was going to lunge by the way its hindquarters rippled. Her magick arced across the shadows and broke across its muzzle. The bitter scent of singed hair was followed by a sharp yelp of pain.

She flinched from that horrible sound, scrambling backward through the debris. The shelves rose around her, providing the illusion of safety.

Deep down she knew there was nowhere safe from a creature that could crack stone like it was rotted wood.

But she clung to the illusion anyway.

The shelf to her left groaned, warping inward seemingly in slow motion as the wolf tore into it. Splinters of wood and fragments of clay and glass peppered her face, her injured arm. Throwing up a temporary shield, she managed to deflect the worst of it. White fangs gnashed against the golden bubble of magick between her and the beast, but the magick wouldn't last for long.

She needed to distract it. What could distract a wolf?

The answer had barely formed in her mind before she was throwing out sparks of magick. A rune was drawn over each one, and the sparks flared into glowing field rabbits that scampered across the floor around the wolf's giant paws.

It snapped its teeth over the magickal creatures. The impact rattled her bones.

The wolf wouldn't be satisfied with such empty prey for long. Her heart lodged in her throat as she sprinted through the maze of shelving.

Stolas's familiar was worse than she imagined. A frenzied beast of nightmares. There was no reaching it. No bond that she could see to Stolas.

Blood soaked the sleeve of her tunic and dripped to the floor. Her back stung where it must have caught her earlier. Adrenaline turned the pain into a relentless throb, but her gut said the cuts were deep.

A thud jerked her attention to her right. She took in the approaching shadowy figure—

"Bell?" she hissed. "How?"

He bent over, positioning his hands on his knees as he sucked in air. "I just . . . climbed my way down. It was a combination of . . . gravity and . . . falling."

"Idiot," she muttered.

Another light thud revealed Surai, who landed much more elegantly. A magickal rabbit darted between her legs, its apricot-colored light gliding up the blades of her twin katanas.

"Thought you might need some help, *Soror*." Her lavender gaze slid to Haven's wound, the destroyed shelves behind her, and the flaming rabbits scuttling around the room. "Looks like we were right."

"Nasira and the others are trying to get past Stolas's wards to his chamber," Bell explained. A golden orb tinged and feathered with red danced between his fingers. It was perfectly constructed, an offensive display the most distinguished lightcaster would be proud of.

"Someone's been practicing," she whispered, not that she expected anything less from her studious, overachieving friend.

Bell's pearl-white teeth flashed. "I mean, not to brag but—"

An ear-splitting howl cut him off. Too far—the howl was too far away. Which meant . . .

The object! Runes.

Haven darted around the shelf and searched the darkness for the creature, following the sound of cracking wood and shattering to the far side of the room. Every crash was punctuated by frenzied inhalations.

Any moment the wolf would discover the object it hunted and destroy it, sealing Stolas's fate.

She ran toward the creature. Her frantic pulse lashed her skin.

Don't find it. Don't find it. Don't find—

A booming creak, like metal being warped, echoed off the walls, and then a massive crack sent her heart into overdrive. She leapt across an overturned shelf in time to see what was left of a large iron cage rent in two. The Shadow Wolf had peeled back the iron bars just enough that it could fit its giant head inside, but not enough to allow its shoulders access.

The focus of its rage was something oblong and around her height, covered in a lacy black shroud.

The wolf's jaws snapped and tore the air trying to get to the item. One more push. One more swipe at the iron bars . . .

"Hey!" she yelled. The wolf was too frenzied to notice her, but it couldn't ignore the spear of light magick she sent sailing into its haunch.

A blink. That's all the time it took before the wolf was upon her. It moved so fast she didn't even see the swipe of its paw until it was already connecting with her side. Her head snapped sideways as she slammed into a nearby shelf.

The force blanked her mind. She came to on her rear, back slumped against the shelf. Twin flaming red eyes blinked inches from hers. The wolf was so close that she could pick out the bits of fabric and wood caught between its razor-sharp teeth. Silver tufted its sharp ears, which were constantly pivoting back and forth.

Slobber dripped to the floor between her legs in soft, methodic *plops*.

A velvety growl stirred the air. She resisted the urge to close her eyes as hot breath rolled over her cheeks.

Holding the creature's predatory stare, she willed it to recognize her.

A low whine crawled up the beast's throat. She stiffened as it suddenly jerked its head forward, pressed its warm nose over her, and began to sniff.

Silken fur stroked her jaw. It smelled strange . . . like smoke and something else. A spice she knew but couldn't name.

"Haven!" Bell's voice came from somewhere behind the wolf, but she didn't dare move her head to look. Surai would be with him. Both willing to die protecting her.

"No, Bell," she whispered. "Wait."

If Bell and Surai provoked the wolf, there was no doubt in Haven's mind the creature would seriously injure them—or worse. But her hesitation was more than that.

Something was happening. A deep fluttering behind her ribs that seemed connected to Stolas's familiar somehow.

All at once, an invisible chain inside her jerked taut. She gasped. A whine trickled from the wolf's soft muzzle as its head shot up. It stared into her eyes for a long, strange moment, and that's when she understood that it was her Shadow Familiar reacting to Stolas's.

She didn't know why or what that meant. Perhaps Stolas felt her familiar through his wolf even while asleep?

All she knew was that everything in the predator's demeanor changed. Gone was the terrifying beast. In its place was a docile, affectionate creature sitting on its haunches, tongue lolling as it watched her with the adoration of a loyal hunting dog.

"Haven," Surai whispered. "Are you okay?"

The wolf's dark ears flicked back as a warning growl built deep in its chest, but once it took in Haven's calmness, it decided Surai was harmless and went back to . . . what?

Protecting her. It was protecting her. And its eyes—its eyes were changing.

Silver was overtaking the bright red striations. Silver eyes rimmed in amber.

Stolas.

As recognition flooded those familiar eyes, so did understanding. His horrified gaze went to her shoulder. Another whine, as if in apology . . . and the wolf faded into a dark mist that ebbed away.

THIRTY-FIVE

Even wounded and in pain, the moment the threat was gone, Haven's curiosity took over. Her shoulder protested as she used the shelf to pull herself to her feet. Her head throbbed with every beat of her slowing heart. But as she spun in a slow circle, allowing herself to finally take in the room and its contents, her wonder eclipsed any other thoughts.

Bell and Surai rushed to her side.

"What the Netherworld was that?" Bell demanded.

"Hmm?" She forced her gaze from a golden flute with fire runes that lit when her fingers neared.

"The wolf should have killed you," Surai added. "Instead, he reacted to something."

"Stolas recognized me." It was basically the truth. The rest was too . . . confusing to explain. What would she say?

My inner Shadow Familiar reacted somehow to his?

It probably recognized another beast similar to itself.

That hardly seemed worth mentioning anyway.

Her friends accepted that explanation and succumbed to the same awe she felt as they walked around, cataloging the ancient and powerful items.

Although there were very few outwardly expensive jewels or treasure, each item was imbued with enough power to fetch a king's ransom in coin and runestone.

This was the Darkshade heirlooms, at least, the stuff not looted or kept in the vaults below. Which didn't make a lot of sense considering how rare and coveted the objects littering the shelves were. And there were so many of them.

An entire level of the tower bursting with so much collective magick it made her bones hum.

"What was it trying to destroy?" Surai asked, and they all directed their attention to the shrouded oval-shaped thing in the center of the warped cage.

Haven approached the mysterious item carefully, knowing any second now Nasira or Stolas would appear and force them out. It was because of that very secrecy that she was interested.

Surai whistled beside Haven. "Stolas's familiar snapped spell-reinforced iron bars like they were twigs."

"I wonder what's inside?" A cold, icky sensation seeped into Haven as she drew nearer to the object, and her body instinctively recoiled. "Do you sense that?"

Surai made the sign of the Goddess. "That thing has a wrongness to it, *Soror*. Let us leave it and be done."

But Haven's curiosity had been replaced with a strange enthrallment. "Do you hear a voice?"

A distant keening song trickled from behind the shroud. Calling to Haven. Begging her closer. Begging her to lift the veil. Bile clawed up her throat as she drew even nearer. The thing was repulsive. The decaying wrongness of it sending violent shivers over her skin.

And yet she couldn't stop.

Haven reached through the gaping hole between the iron bars, her fingers brushing the black lace—

"Get back!" A sharp gust of wind swept through the room.

Haven was torn from the warped cage and sent hurtling backward onto her ass along with the others.

Scuttling to her feet, she whipped her head to see Stolas striding to the cage. He flicked his fingers and the misshapen iron bars creaked and moaned as they began melding back together under his expert touch.

She was so busy watching him reshape the cage that she almost didn't realize the shroud had slipped away. It must have happened when he flung them back.

Curious, she crept closer to the mysterious object, a tall, oblong mirror framed in exquisite jade carved to look like monstrous creatures were escaping from another world. Held up by a pair of crooked silver legs ending in beastly paws, it stood the height of a man.

Although in excellent condition, it was obviously old, the silver legs tarnished with age and frame fissured with cracks and chips.

Which made the perfectly flawless surface of the mirror . . . strange. Stranger still was that the surface didn't seem to reflect their surroundings at all but another place entirely.

Squinting, she picked out what appeared to be a . . . a room.

Not just a room but a cavernous chamber filled with opulence and luxury befitting a palace. Dust and something else—possibly spiderwebs— clung to everything. From her vantage point on the floor, she could make out the art on the walls. Most were dark, gruesome depictions of violent battles or demons tearing into mortals, but one piece in particular caught her eye because of how different it was from the rest.

A woman on a golden settee nursing a baby.

Done with the cage, Stolas finally realized the shroud had fallen. With an elegant sweep of his hand, he positioned the veil over the mirror once more.

He had worked quietly, efficiently, but all the while she felt a simmering rage just beneath that polished veneer. Now he turned that fury on her. "How could you be so foolish?"

His voice was like a thunderclap, and it dredged up everything that had happened earlier.

In all the madness, she'd nearly forgotten.

Hot anger swept through her, clumping in her throat and preventing any words from coming out. Which was probably a good thing as she strode toward him, considering what was running through her mind.

Bastard. Inconsiderate, black-hearted bastard.

She halted a few inches away. "What did you expect me to do? Let you die?"

"Yes."

She flinched. "Then you obviously don't know me as well as I thought you did."

"Do you not hate me enough yet?" He flashed a razor-sharp smile, the savagery hewn into his features piercing straight to her core. "Do you need another lesson?"

A whisper of fear flickered to life—

No, she wasn't doing this. Playing this game. "I know what you're doing."

"And what is that?"

"Trying to make me despise you. Is that what you want?"

The strong column of his throat dipped. "Want and need are two very different things."

"Then what *do* you want?"

Silence.

The others were frozen around them, busy pretending they weren't listening. Even Nasira, who was rifling around in the shelves for

Goddess knew what, had half an ear pointed in their direction as she eavesdropped.

Haven didn't care. "I know I will never understand the trauma and hurt you feel after what happened here, Stolas. Maybe I don't have a right to understand. But I do have a right to know what you want . . . from me."

There. She'd cleared her heart in front of the Goddess and everyone.

"I want nothing from you." The softness of his words were at odds with the sharp pain in her gut—as if it had been kicked.

Given what happened earlier, his callous behavior shouldn't have come as a surprise.

But it did. And it hurt, the pain just as fresh as it had been earlier.

"Stolas," she whispered, wishing she could reach him. Wishing she could run her fingers over the hard line of his jaw, or through the silky bone-white hair that desperately needed a cut. Just *reach* him. "I could never hate you, no matter what you do. How can you not see that?"

He blinked, an unreadable emotion rippling across his dark expression. His gaze trekked to her shoulder, and his jaw flexed. "You're injured."

"I'll be fine. Surai can help heal me."

"No. This is my responsibility." Before she could protest, he brushed his hand over her wound. All Seraphians possessed a modicum of healing magick. Thousands of years ago, that skill was used to mend injuries made after they'd blood-letted some poor Solis or mortal slave.

She assumed there was usually a touch of euphoria involved to smooth the otherwise painful process, but not this time. She gritted her teeth as his magick worked into her broken skin, drawing the ragged edges together like the iron bars from the cage.

When he was finished, thick ash-colored lashes lifted as his eyes met hers. The same eyes that had peered at her from the wolf right before it disappeared.

"You saw me, didn't you?"

He gave a stiff nod.

"What was that between your familiar and mine?"

A soft exhalation drew Haven's attention to Nasira only a few feet away. Her hand was in her pocket as she flashed a dark look at Stolas and then stalked away.

Haven's shoulders sagged. Somehow she'd managed to anger both Stolas and Nasira. *Wonderful.*

When she turned back to Stolas, she found his expression had gone hard. But there was a conflicted emotion in his eyes . . . a raw brokenness that sent cold rivering from the top of her head all the way to her toes.

"There may come a day when you have to let me go, Beastie. Promise me you will."

Her throat clenched. "I don't . . . I don't understand."

"I hope you never have to." His gaze darkened as it darted over the covered mirror.

She followed his stare. "Where did you get such an awful thing?"

"It was a gift from a Demon Lord. All of it."

"In return for what?"

His voice was distant as he said, "It doesn't matter now." He turned to her, eyes guarded and unreachable. "We leave at dawn. You need to look every bit the daughter of Freya. I'll have Nasira bring you something."

His massive wings shot out and he took to the air. There was no apology. No explanation. Nothing beyond a coldness in his wake that terrified her more than his wolf's rage or the unsettling darkness she felt spilling from the mirror.

THIRTY-SIX

They had just secretly entered a kingdom openly hostile to Haven, to enter a contest where half the contestants probably wanted Haven dead, and all Bell could talk about was seeing a Valkyrie in real life.

"So a Valkyrie's wings never come out unless called by the horn?" Bell asked, his bottom lip caught between his teeth as he waved his acrum over the fading portal. The harsh glare of the sun flashed across the jewel on the wand and made Haven blink. "Do the wings sprout from their backs?"

A few moments ago, they had threaded straight into one of the lower courtyards in the palace gardens of the Morgani Queen, and now they hunkered down among an overgrown bed of giant banana leaves.

She could almost feel Stolas's smirk as he watched them from somewhere above.

The archery tournament was held on the Island of Kieri, which literally meant the color green in Solissian. The jewel of the Morgani Islands, the heart-shaped landmass was a tropical paradise of crystalline blue ocean and lush rainforests. It was also the largest island and home to the famed Morgani Valkyries.

Ember finished scanning a palm tree lined walkway before cutting her eyes at Bell. "Yes, their wings were gifted to them from Freya herself, only to be used in battle. And no they don't *sprout* from their backs, they just . . . appear."

He grinned as he glanced over his shoulder, completely impervious to Ember's mood. Sweat beaded his upper lip, the humidity here making Veserack seem pleasant and dry in comparison. "And only your mother has the horn?"

Ember sighed. "If you keep us waiting here any longer with that portal visible, we'll get to meet them up close and personal. And I promise you, even without wings, you don't want that."

Bell chuckled under his breath as he slipped his acrum into the sheath at his waist. "Done. It's invisible to all but us. More importantly, only we can enter."

Xandrian arched a bored eyebrow as he checked the portal's structure. He was grumpier than usual, and he kept jerking on the hood of his plum-colored cloak. "When can I take this blasted thing off?"

"As soon as your face stops being so damn pretty," Surai remarked.

"So never," he grumbled. "Wonderful."

Even here among other Solis, Xandrian's exquisite features were easily recognizable.

Finished with his check, he begrudgingly admitted, "It will do."

Haven shoved an oversized gold-and-orange leaf out of her face as she followed the others to the graveled path. The coliseum waited in the distance. The tan stadium was a fifteen story high structure centered in the middle of a turquoise cove. White gulls circled above the training grounds, ready to scavenge food leftover from the crowd.

Overlooking the water was the queen's palace and barracks, carved into the white cliffs surrounding the cove.

The sight dredged up old childhood longings. One of Damius's traders had mentioned how every Morgani female left their islands at twelve to come to Kieri and train. The best ended up serving in the queen's personal guard, one of the special fighting units, or as Valkyries.

The notion that females could become warriors had sparked something inside her. She didn't understand until now what that feeling was—hope.

Now that emotion was nearly overpowering as the shouts and cheers from the coliseum grew louder. Nine palm-tree lined bridges spanned the cove, all leading to the main event. The crowds became near impossible to push through.

Surai and Ember flanked Haven, Bell behind her and Xandrian in front so that she was hardly visible.

Few revelers paid any attention to them. Everyone but Haven was dressed in loose, light clothing, their weapons hidden and runemarks dulled with magick.

When the occasional citizen happened to look past the circle of Haven's guards to the woman inside, they stared. And stared. Their gazes sharpening as they took in the sleek bow at her back, mapped with runes. They gaped at her rose-gold hair, uncovered and crafted into the elaborate braided hairstyle the Morgani preferred.

Ember had added two golden serpent clips to hold it all together.

They were trying to figure out which nation she hailed from. If they saw what glowed beneath the tan cloak she wore . . .

Gripping the soft edges, she pulled her cloak tighter around her body, sure the light from her fleshmarks was seeping through the too-thin fabric.

Haven herself had trouble looking away from her fleshrunes earlier, and covering the elegant swirls and marks had felt wrong. They had never appeared so luminescent. Especially when paired with the gown clinging to her body.

Made from a delicate material she could only guess at, the dress had looked simple at first. So much so that she suspected Nasira had given her a plain gown out of spite.

That is, until she touched the material. An emerald swath of slippery fabric that was airier than silk but sturdier than gauze, it was like touching cold mist. It was even colder on, but in a pleasant way, and it molded to her every curve, draping almost intelligently to flatter and tease.

Other than a delicate dusting of black diamonds along the low neckline, the fabric itself was all that was needed to draw the eye. When sunlight fell upon the gown, a rainbow of colors undulated beneath the rich, vibrant green to create a dazzling display of prisms and light.

But it wasn't just the hair and the bow that caused them to stare. Haven could see it in their faces when she finally met their eyes. They didn't know who she was. Not yet. Most were citizens from surrounding nations who had never heard of the mortal who claimed to be Goddess-Born.

But they knew she was *someone.*

That was the point of the ensemble, of course, and why Stolas had insisted she look the part. It was also why Haven was grateful when the crowds turned so thick that people were too busy fighting their way through to notice her.

Near the first entrance, Xandrian and Bell broke off to take their seats in the stands. It only made sense to split up. Bell and Xandrian would blend in, and if anything happened—like the Morgani Queen deciding to imprison Haven to give to Archeron—they could help free her unnoticed.

Surai touched Haven's wrist. "Are you sure you want me to come with you? I can join Stolas and Nasira in the sky if that would be better."

Stolas. Even now, caught in a crowd of thousands, she could feel the weight of his stare from wherever he watched, hidden behind layers of impenetrable magick. He was the one who insisted on being a guardian from above, and Nasira—who had looked close to wilting the moment they entered the wet, tropical climate—was more than happy to keep him company.

The two Seraphian heirs were much better suited above anyway. The Solis still had no reason to trust Stolas or Nasira, and many believed the lies Archeron had spun about the *Lord of the Netherworld*.

Things would be . . . easier without them publicly present. Especially Stolas.

But that didn't mean he wasn't ready to protect her. If anyone so much as approached Haven wrong, he would intervene.

Violently.

Of that she had no doubt.

For a breath, she recalled his face when he saw her earlier in his mother's dress. He had almost looked *stricken*. As if seeing her in the dress had dredged horrible memories to the surface. Only it felt as if his reaction was more than that—

"Haven?"

Haven refocused on Surai, her heart twisted as she recognized the pain darkening her friend's eyes to cloudy amethyst. The Morgani Queen might not welcome Stolas Darkshade, but like hell would Haven let the queen make Surai feel ashamed and unwelcome here. "Surai, you're my sister, my best friend, and my most loyal protector. Do you really think I'm going to let anyone shame you into feeling less than? Especially when your only crime was loving someone?"

"But the queen—"

"Let me deal with her."

Surai threw Ember a pleading look. "Tell her what your mother is like."

Ember shrugged. "She's a cold-hearted bitch with claws when she needs to be, but so am I. Let's see her try to kick us out."

"And I thought Rook was brazen," Surai muttered as she shook her head, the jagged tips of her black hair flicking her jaw. Ignoring Surai, Ember snatched two roasted spits of . . . something from a passing vendor. Something with long knobby legs and toes—

Shadeling Below, those were frog legs. The man flashed his teeth as he whipped around to demand payment. One look at Ember, the green band tattooed across her eyes marking her as a Morgani warrioress, and he fell into a curt bow instead. "Have as many as you'd like."

Ember took two more skewers and handed one to Surai. "Try it. A festival specialty." She waggled her golden eyebrows at Haven. "Want one? They're crunchy and salty and—"

"All yours," Haven murmured, wrinkling her nose as she pushed toward the first gate.

Any hope that they could just sneak into the tournament died as she took in the Solis females near the entrance. Tall, athletic, and bronzed skinned, they wore golden breastplates over leather skirts that barely covered their long, muscular legs. The metal shields slung across their shoulders carried the Morgani emblem, a harpy carrying a sword in its claws.

Four soldiers were hunched over a makeshift table, getting in a round of cards while they waited for the last entrants to straggle in.

"Aren't they supposed to be guarding the gate?" Haven asked Ember as they approached.

"Who says they're not?"

"But they're . . ."

"Playing cards, probably rather poorly?" Ember smiled wistfully, and Haven wondered how many times she'd done the same with her friends. "If trouble starts, every single one would put a spear through ten men before most could blink."

Surai chuckled under her breath as she cast a sidelong glance at Haven. "Didn't you know, Haven? The Morgani do everything better."

"It's not bragging if it's true," Ember amended.

Fair point. And her statement looked every bit the truth as the female soldiers raised their battle-hardened gazes to appraise the late entrant.

Her fingers loosened around the edges of her cloak, ready to drop to the twin swords on either side of her waist at the first hint of trouble.

Before Haven could say a word, Ember ambled over, clapped the closest girl on the shoulder, and said, "Hey, Lena, how's the competition looking?"

The girl, apparently Lena, gave Haven a once over. Then she shrugged. "Fair. I have my money on an Asgardian archer from Tyr."

"Well, add a mortal to your betting pool because this one's going to win," Ember said, and Haven prayed her friends didn't notice how Ember's casual demeanor didn't match her tight eyes.

"Sorry, you're too late," Lena said, looking back to the cards in her hand. "They just closed entry to the tournament."

Haven's heart dropped, but Ember just laughed. "We both know late entries can still get in, with the right . . . incentive."

Lena dealt a hand without looking up. "Not this time. Security is tighter today. Too many pompous asses in attendance, if you get my drift."

Ember leaned over Lena's shoulder, tapping the card she should play. "Which pompous asses are we talking about?"

Lena sighed. "Let me do my job, Ember. You're not even supposed to be here."

Casually, Ember slid something from her pant pocket into Lena's lap. Then she folded her hands over the item. "I wasn't here, remember? And you didn't see us come in late." She whipped her head toward Haven and Surai. "Let's go."

Haven averted her face as she passed the table.

"Wait." Lena's sharp focus settled on Haven as she took a harder look this time. "That bow is nearly bigger than you are, mortal girl. Think you can handle such a powerful weapon?"

How should she play this? Most mortals would be terrified of a Morgani warrior, but if the girl thought Haven was weak she wouldn't bother risking her neck to let her through.

Haven grinned. "Bet it all on me and find out."

She didn't dare breathe again until she heard the gate shut behind her. Surai slipped her arm inside Haven's as they entered a dim tunnel. "You should have been Morgani with that arrogance, *Soror*."

Haven felt herself laugh despite the tangle of knots in her belly. "What did you say, Ember? It's not bragging if it's the truth?"

"Damn right," Ember said as she thumped her chest.

Haven kept that confidence—right up until they emerged from the tunnel into the sun to face a stand full of thousands. Years of hiding her attention-catching hair had her throwing her hood over her head. Her heart skipped as her pulse lanced her skin.

Breathe. Just breathe.

Shielding her eyes from the glaring sun, she searched the crowd for the queen. There. Sitting in a shaded box with a retinue of her finest warriors and the rulers from participating nations.

The Morgani Queen looked so much like Rook that Haven almost gasped. An older, harder version of her friend, the beautiful woman had the same amber eyes and strong, regal features. A rich gold band stretched across her eyes, the highest color a Morgani warrior could reach. Instead of a crown she wore a snarling panther's head.

Sapphires glittered in place of the poor creature's eyes.

"The panther headdress?" Surai whispered. "That was the queen's sister."

Rook had mentioned once that her aunt tried to take her mother's throne, but wearing her sister's dead shifter pelt felt like overkill.

"Go," Ember whispered. "Hurry."

Surai squeezed Haven's hand. "Remember who you are, Haven."

Haven jogged across the sand to the line of contestants while Surai and Ember waited with the other attendants under a shaded awning. She scanned the crowd until she found Bell's face, his features tense and bright blue eyes tight with worry. Xandrian's scowl could be seen beneath the shadow of his hood.

All too soon, it was time to present herself. Haven was the last entrant, and the crowd was already restless. The queen wasn't even looking at Haven as she chatted and laughed with someone to her left. Haven couldn't quite see who is was because of a guard. The gulls had already descended, their squawks as they fought and scrabbled for scraps reverberating over the walls.

All of the major contenders had been introduced already. She was an afterthought. A nobody.

Even the announcer who approached Haven had to stifle a yawn as she impatiently said, "Name, lineage, title—if any"—she flicked a disdainful look over Haven at that—"and the nation that you champion."

Boisterous chatter and laughter from the crowd muffled the woman's words. Haven's fingers clenched and unclenched over her cloak, her palms damp. The wet air grew thinner by the second, every inhalation less satisfying than the last.

"I am . . ." No one was listening.

The coliseum was too loud. Her voice too soft.

She hesitated. Never before had she publicly declared herself. Not like this. After spending her entire life pretending to be small . . . to be less than, leaving the shadows was terrifying.

Hid—that's what she had done for countless years. From Damius. From the royals and nobles in Penryth. From the life she was supposed to have.

She'd covered her hair, masked her talents, stifled her voice. She'd recoiled from the magick that even Damius felt swelling her veins. Pushed it so deep inside herself that it only broke free on Bell's runeday.

That's why she'd dedicated her entire life to Bell—because by the time he saved her life, she didn't understand how anyone could think it was a life worth saving. Why she'd given her heart so quickly to Archeron, the first male who didn't recoil from her strength.

And why now, knowing who she was and the untold magick she and she alone could access, a part of her still desperately longed to stay hidden. Small. Unremarkable.

But she wasn't small. She wasn't unremarkable. She wasn't no one.

And she was tired of hiding.

She flipped her hood back. The moment the cloak slipped from her shoulders and pooled on the sand at her feet, her runemarks flared with pure golden light that made the sun seem dim in comparison. A hush fell over the crowd. The announcer's mouth was agape as she stared at Haven, at the runes and symbols like starlight painted across Haven's flesh.

She understood now why Nasira had chosen this particular gown; her runelight reacted with the material somehow to create a mesmerizing display of colors and light that could make anyone look like a Goddess.

Silence choked the air. She certainly had their attention now. Head held high, she met the Morgani Queen's intense stare and called out loud and clear, "I am Haven Ashwood, descendant of the Goddess Freya and the God Odin, Goddess-Born, the child of prophecy, and I represent the newly restored nation of Shadoria."

For a wild beat of her heart, an inhuman stillness came over the stadium. Or perhaps time simply slowed as Haven waited to see what the hundreds of trained Solis soldiers would do. What the *queen* would do. The contestants gathered beneath the queen's viewing box waited too, each one slowly drawing their bows in preparation for the queen's command.

Haven flicked her gaze toward the Morgani Queen. Understanding slowly dawned in her eyes, followed by a dangerous sort of cunning that sent a wave of dread crashing over Haven.

Steeling her mind, Haven prepared herself for battle.

And then the sound of clapping drew Haven's focus to the Solis the queen had been chatting with moments earlier. The Solis royal male now fully visible and staring down at Haven behind one half of a golden mask.

THIRTY-SEVEN

Even with his face partially hidden behind the golden mask, Archeron still looked every bit a God. A beautiful, vengeful God. He was draped in purple and gold, the largest sword she'd ever seen strapped to his back. Light caught in the jewels of his sword and mask and fingers like little stars dancing all around him.

Staring down from above with that half-sneer, he seemed so much bigger than she remembered.

So much crueler.

As if someone had taken the Archeron she loved, the soldier whose only desire was to return to his homeland, and molded him into a darker, corrupted version.

He smiled as he lifted from his seat to his full, towering height. "Look at you, Little Mortal. All dressed up like a shiny present. Are you *my* present? Because I'm going to be very disappointed if you say no."

"Don't worry," she growled, grabbing her bow and slipping an arrow from the quiver at her back. "I do have a present for you." When she felt the bowstring go taut, she aimed the arrow at Archeron's head. Bright blue magick danced from the iron tip. "Where would you like it?"

She swore a few of the Morgani soldiers snickered.

A hint of fear clumped beneath her sternum as she caught the hidden rage behind Archeron's smug expression. His nostrils flared, his smile stretching beneath cold, almost vacant eyes.

She knew what lurked beneath that arrogant veneer. She'd witnessed the infection that twisted his once noble soul into the depraved king before her.

Sunlight flashed inside the ruby and gold ring he wore as he flicked his fingers. In the span of a blink, at least twenty Gold Shadows entered the arena—

And were obliterated in a spray of blood and pulverized bone.

Instead of screams, the stands went utterly silent. Ember and Surai rushed to Haven's side, weapons drawn. Xandrian flipped back his hood as he and Bell readied themselves to fight.

Finally, a lone scream pierced the awful quiet. But it wasn't for the twenty perfectly round spots of blood in the sand.

Archeron's jawline was like jagged marble as he whipped his head up.

She followed his hateful gaze to a dark streak hurtling from the sky—

Stolas landed so hard she swore she felt the ground rock, sand shifting at her feet. A wave of sand and dust rippled outward as his wings snapped taut to form a protective shield between her and Archeron. She counted three more impenetrable shields shimmering in the air around them.

If Archeron was a vengeful God, Stolas was a wrathful monster of shadow and death. With his horns and wings and those merciless bright red eyes, the cowering audience had no choice but to see Stolas as the villain.

And a part of her hated them for it. She didn't care anymore what they thought. She didn't care that blood clumped the sand all around them. Didn't care that Stolas was the people's nightmares come to life.

If they tried to hurt him—if anyone tried to hurt him—she would end them.

She found Archeron's gaze, held it as she replaced her arrow, slung her bow onto her back, and strolled to Stolas's side. She could feel Stolas's stare as she ducked beneath his wing, and there was something in his intense focus that made her chest burn and her throat catch.

Still holding Archeron's furious gaze, she teased, "Did you have to kill all of them?"

Stolas's lips tilted wickedly. "Have to? No, but it was extremely satisfying. I told you, Beastie, I will protect you always, no matter what."

A tremor rippled across Archeron's taut jaw.

Every muscle in her body clenched as she stared down the king who so cruelly made her experience the horrendous death of everyone she loved. The friend who betrayed her. The male who would see her on her knees before him, a captive once more. Knowing it would kill her.

Just like Damius. Like the Shade Queen. Like her father. All of them wanted to use her for their own dark desires, to drain her of power and life until she was an empty husk, a mindless weapon. And Archeron was no different.

No, he was worse because she had trusted him. Loved him.

Unblinking, her gaze still clinging to the male she would have once died for, she leaned into Stolas. They might never be lovers. Might never be more than two wronged heirs to broken kingdoms and fallen Gods.

Hated. Despised. Hunted. Misunderstood.

But when Stolas looked down at her, surprise and pleasure sparking in that predatory gaze, she knew he would battle to the ends of the realm for her. Would destroy anything and everything that threatened her.

And she for him.

There wasn't a word for something like that.

Anything left between Haven and Archeron died in that moment, replaced by an icy, seething, abject hatred that pitted behind her sternum.

"She looks thin," Archeron said softly. "Perhaps you should let her off her chain once in a while, at least enough to eat, Darkshade. Or is that only for fucking her?"

Fury blasted from Stolas—

She brushed his waist, her touch like water dousing flames. *Ignore him*, she whispered into his mind. *He's trying to provoke you. Make you act like the monster they think you are.*

Maybe that's what this realm needs, he answered back, mirroring her own thoughts from the other day.

Not yet. She had to believe they could still gain allies through peaceable means.

The harsh lines of Stolas's features softened as her words took hold, his lethal powers receding.

Despite the tension choking the air, the queen was still casually reclined on her throne, lithe legs crossed at the ankles as she lazily swept her gaze over the scene. "So this is the famous Lord of the Netherworld. I thought you would be . . . uglier. How the dead must have loved waking from death to find *you* standing over them."

Haven swore she caught a shudder pass over the good side of Archeron's face. A face that would never again be called beautiful or handsome.

Stolas performed a graceful bow, a wavy strand of silver-white hair tumbling over his forehead and making him look almost boyish. "I aim to please, Queen."

"As do I." Her amber eyes turned hard. "Currently, there are one hundred crossbows with poisoned bolts pointed at your heads, and I can think of nothing that would please this crowd more than loosing them on you."

A quick look revealed arrowslits in the wall. Countless bolt tips— glittering and sharp and ready—flashed from the thin holes. The guards must have assembled the moment Haven cast off her cloak. Adrenaline flooded Haven in a surge of prickly fire, her senses coming alive as she waited for the telltale scream of bolts slicing through the air.

Her power greedily rubbed against its cage of flesh and bone as it prepared to annihilate everything in its path.

If this queen thought they would go down without a fight, she was dangerously mistaken.

Stolas didn't look at the bolts.

He didn't cast a single glance at Archeron.

But he did grin, and it was a wicked, beautiful thing indeed. "We have so much in common, you and I. Currently, my sister, the Seraphian Empress, waits above you, ready to unleash her absolute rage on this melting cauldron of a kingdom. She would love nothing more than to start with you, Queen." He examined his fingernails. "She fancies heads as trophies, and yours would be the jewel of her collection—if it wasn't too badly damaged, of course. I have my doubts."

A muscle ticked in the queen's jaw. "I had heard there was a Seraphian girl claiming to be the last female heir—"

"I can assure you that she is not only my sister, but a Noctis every bit as powerful as my mother once was. Her temperament, on the other hand, is far more . . . *mercurial*, but no ruler is perfect—except you, of course." He fell into another bow, but this time his eyes never left hers.

Only Stolas could manage to both threaten and seduce the Morgani Queen in one breath.

The queen's lips parted to respond, but then . . . hesitated.

Archeron looked to the queen, aghast. "Surely you know every word this Noctis spews is a lie? He's a serial trickster and manipulator. For all we know, that *girl* above is a Seraphian slave he's parading as his sister in order to hold the Seraphian throne. If—"

His words cut off as a long, serpentine shadow slid over the stadium and coasted across the sand. The seagulls squawked in alarm as they fled.

Muffled cries of terror followed.

The queen managed to remain calm as that huge shadow darkened her shaded box, but her focus darted to the sky. And when she took in Nasira's familiar, the magnificent beast with glossy scales the color of onyx and midnight wings that nearly blotted out the sun, a tiny tremor rippled across her composed visage.

Lips tilted upward, Stolas cut his silver eyes at Archeron, and the look between the two males chilled her blood. "Please, Sun Lord," Stolas drawled, "explain how a *servant* would possess a Shadow Dragon when that particular familiar has belonged to the royal Darkshade lineage for longer than you've existed."

Every eye was drawn to Nasira's dragon as it glided across the clear azure sky like strokes of charcoal against canvas. Even Haven had trouble looking away.

That was the creature Nasira had hidden from Haven in Penryth. She could only imagine the fear and chaos Nasira would wreak when the dragon reached full size.

"You could have forced the poor girl to share your bed," Archeron growled. His nostrils were flared, the vein above his temple engorged. "Everyone knows a Seraphian female's familiar can take on their lover's form."

Haven blinked; she was apparently the one person who didn't know that.

Stolas's voice was soft, lethal as he said, "My Shadow Familiar was cast years ago, and it is the same as my mother's."

"And we are just supposed to take your word for it?"

Stolas shrugged, but Haven caught the violence in that small act. "Or I could prove it."

By the way the queen's throat dipped, his mother's Shadow Wolf must have been formidable. Still, Haven knew the queen would never capitulate to the promise of violence. If anything, the more Stolas and

Haven publicly threatened her, the more she had to fight.

Haven craned her neck to the top of the coliseum where a female clad in silver and gold armor perched. *Valkyrie.*

The name filled Haven with awe and a twinge of fear.

More Valkyries silhouetted against the sky, waiting like gargoyles for the horn to give them wings. If Haven didn't do something, this would turn into a bloodbath.

Haven looked to the queen. "I must be mistaken. I was told you offered your protection to everyone? That I would be safe during this hallowed festival to honor my mother's sister?" Her gaze lingered on Archeron. "Or do your rules not apply when male kings decide they're inconvenient?"

A few of the Morgani women in the box with the queen gave quiet nods of approval.

The queen's golden lashes lowered as she appraised Haven. One finger tapped her bare stretch of thigh. That heavy stare slid to her daughter to Haven's left. Back to Haven.

Haven didn't dare break that gaze. If she did, she knew her attention would wander to Archeron. Even now she could feel his eyes boring into her, his hatred like a living, breathing thing between them.

Everything she said and did was viewed by him as a betrayal. As a confirmation of his suspicions about her.

Finally the Morgani Queen uncrossed her ankles, resting her hands flat on the arms of her throne. "Why are you here, Haven Ashwood? And do not tell me it's for the glory of winning this tournament."

Haven lifted her head to meet the queen's unflinching gaze. "I'm here because a king is so threatened by my powers that he won't accept the truth—a war is coming. One that will decide the future of our world forever. I'm here because I seek an alliance between all our nations, mortal, Solis, and Noctis to fight this threat." She felt Stolas's powers follow her as she stepped forward. "The Sun Sovereign sees me as a weapon to be broken, enslaved, and harnessed against his enemies."

"If you are not a weapon," the queen asked, "then what are you?"

"That depends. Ally with me and I will be your salvation."

"If not?"

"Then I am your ruin."

Nervous laughter peppered the air, but the queen wasn't smiling. "No Solissian ruler will ever ally with a mortal who possesses forbidden magick. Surely you realize that?"

"And if I were like you? An immortal? If my flesh were impervious to time and my bones didn't snap like twigs, if my face stayed firm and beautiful and my hair never grayed . . . would you believe then that I was Goddess-Born?"

The queen blinked. "Foolish child. To become—"

"Would you follow me, Queen? If I could prove to you I was *her* daughter?"

Another blink. Hesitation and something else flashed across the queen's face.

Then the queen waved her hand. "Since its inception, this festival has offered safety and refuge to all, and there will be no violence while it lasts. Whoever you are, you will be protected during your stay here, mortal girl."

Not quite a commitment to an alliance—that had been a long shot. But . . . relief swept through Haven. She still had to win the tournament and find the painting, but this was good.

Once she discovered the message her mother left, once she became immortal—everything would become so much easier.

"And my friends?" Haven pressed.

Don't get greedy, Stolas warned in her mind, but she could feel his approval.

The queen glanced at Surai and Ember, and Haven's hands fisted at her sides as the queen made her disdain more than apparent. To their credit, both women refused to look away from the queen's cold sneer.

Finally the Morgani Queen lifted her shoulders, every muscle rippling in her defined arms, and said, "All members of your party, however ill-bred or otherwise foolish"—her sharp eyes lingered on her daughter—"will be guaranteed protection for the duration of the festival. But I do not recommend overstaying your welcome."

They were safe. All of them. Even Archeron wouldn't flagrantly challenge the queen's rule and cause a war between their nations. She heaved a long sigh as the tension eased from her shoulders, prepared to join the archery contestants waiting across the arena, when another shadow fell over her.

She turned to Stolas. "Tell Nasira to stop—"

Her words died as she recognized the warning expression twisting his features. His wings snapped out.

She jerked her gaze up in time to see why.

Dark, twisted shapes choked the clear blue sky, so many that they became one massive wave of churning black occluding the sun. The snap of leathery Golemite wings and otherworldly screech of Gremwyrs rumbled to a loud roar as the sky filled with them. The nearest Golemite soldiers held wicked black bows, and the gremwyrs appeared to be holding smoking buckets.

Somewhere high above the writhing mass of darkness, a shrill command split the din of claws and wings and bellows. "Now!"

Haven would recognize that voice anywhere. The Shade Queen.

Stolas's low warning snarl became a roar of warning as the sky lit up with glittering red fire the color of blood. Arrowheads flickered ominously with the eerie flame. Buckets became fireballs consumed.

"Netherfire," Stolas snarled. "It will burn through anything it touches."

It hit Haven a half-second later what was about to happen. Oh, Goddess Above. All the innocent people. They were swarming from the

THIRTY-EIGHT

The sky was a red sea of chaos and death. Surai and Ember joined with Stolas to create a thick shield over them. Casting out her powers, Haven merged her magick with the others . . . and then flung it wider to cover the stadium on the far side.

A visceral jolt as someone slid their shield to layer hers.

Her magick roiled at the intrusion until she recognized the signature—a whisper of brine and crashing waves.

Xandrian!

Bell's powers were next, the frail shield he contributed hinting at dahlias and burnt roses as they combined their magick to cover the stands.

"Brace yourself," Stolas warned as the first wave of fire hit.

The explosion shredded the air and nearly knocked Haven off her feet. Flaming arrows smashed into the shields, hundreds all at once, the impact rattling her teeth as they bounced off. She could feel the Netherfire eating away at the magick like acid.

Burning flesh and sulfur hit her in a wave, and she fought the urge to double over and vomit. Despite the shields, violent, searing heat whooshed over them, so hot it hurt to breathe. Acidic, smoky air burned her throat.

A cacophony of death followed.

Jagged screams sliced the smoky coliseum, only to cut off abruptly. Stone sizzled and cracked as the Netherfire consumed it. Outside their shield, Netherfire popped and hissed over the sand, rivers of flame eating away at the ground to form deep smoking trenches. The sand not fully consumed became sharp, brittle glass.

Red—everything was red. On fire. As if a pit had yawned open and dragged them into the deepest depths of the Netherworld.

Surai fell to her knees, her face twisted into a grimace as she held the shield. A red glow cast from the flames danced over her high, rounded cheekbones. Haven staggered against Stolas as the Netherfire ate away at everything not protected by a shield.

And then, just like that, the heat faded. The Netherfire seemingly consuming the world turned to a smolder and then fizzled out.

In its wake was devastation. Absolute, incomprehensible devastation.

Whole sections of the historic coliseum . . . gone. Burned to cinders. The few areas of the structure that remained stuck up like the jagged bones of a long-dead creature.

People spilled over the sides like ants, some climbing down, others pushed, their clothes aflame.

The blare of an ancient horn echoed across the arena. Three Valkyries perched on the highest edges of the coliseum took flight, their glorious white wings beating the air. More rose in the distance, the gold of their armor reflecting the beams of sunlight that managed to pierce the smoky veil like shards of light magick.

The queen's stadium box remained untouched. Where was Archeron? He must have fled at the first sign of attack. The queen and her soldiers were in various states of shifting, many bent over on all fours, backs arched as their bodies elongated and fingers shortened into paws.

Fur replaced skin.

Some golden. Some spotted. Some pure black.

Haven barely had time to blink before every Morgani warrior had transformed into their feline forms. Leopards, panthers, mountain cats.

And the queen . . . it was impossible to look away as the massive lion perched for a stretched-out moment along the bannister overlooking the arena, all golden fur and ferocious amber eyes. Bits of ash drifted around her as her feline gaze snagged on a Gremwyr that landed in the arena. Haven could have sworn the lion queen grinned.

With a snarl, she leapt thirty feet and landed on the creature.

Her claws sank deep into its leathery back, hindquarters shredding wing and bone. It squealed—

Teeth flashed as the queen ripped open its throat. The Gremwyr went limp in the sand.

It was all over in less than a second.

Surai appeared beside Haven. "See, cold hard bitch with claws."

"Get Haven back to the portal," Ember growled. Her voice was like gravel, her shoulders already hunching.

"Are you staying?" Haven asked.

Ember's rounded pupils lengthened into a slash as she dropped to all fours in the sand. "I can't leave my home when it's under attack. You understand, right?"

Haven knew if she ordered Ember to go back to Shadoria with the others, she would. But even if the Morgani Queen wasn't ready yet to accept Haven as an ally, there was no way Haven would leave the kingdom during a surprise assault.

Especially by the Shade Queen.

"I understand because I'm not leaving either," Haven said. "I plan to stay and fight."

Shouts drew her attention to Bell and Xandrian rushing toward them. They had to jump over gaping holes in the arena where smoke still drifted, the edges smoldering red hot.

Glass crunched beneath Bell's boots as he neared. "We're staying too."

Xandrian looked less than pleased about that, but he nodded. "I'm just here to make sure he doesn't do anything stupid."

Haven craned her neck to look at the sky. "Where's Nasira?"

"Follow the fleeing Golemites above and you'll find her," Stolas said dryly.

Haven did and found the girl in the midst of the aerial battle. Lightning-blue streaks of magick slammed into the dark horde, dropping five at a time. The ones that didn't drop immediately fell prey to her Shadow Dragon.

Distant screams drew their attention to the palace atop the cliffs in the distance. A swarm of gremwyrs and Golemites circled above, the Netherfire they carried like one giant flame from here.

"Oh, Goddess no," Ember whispered.

"They're destroying the palace," Stolas murmured.

Ember's voice trembled with rage as she said, "Why would they do that?"

Haven met Stolas's stare. "They know about the painting. Somehow they know that's why I'm here."

"It's possible, or they're punishing the Morgani Queen for your presence. Making it known that anyone who gives the Shadeling's daughter shelter will be punished. It would be a good way to isolate you and make you come to him." But by Stolas's hesitation, he suspected the former.

"Take me there." When Stolas didn't move she added, "Please." She needed to save the painting before they destroyed it.

Grinning, Bell swaggered forward to reveal a bandolier glittering with daggers. "I knew there was a reason I brought these beauties, freshly sharpened and tipped in *blight*."

Surai cut her lavender eyes at Bell. "Blight?"

"Yep." Somehow Bell's swagger grew, if that were possible. "That's what I named the poison I've developed for the Noctis. Soon it will stoke fear in the heart of every single winged darkcaster"—Bell slid an apologetic look toward Stolas—"except you, Stolas. Obviously."

Stolas arched a brow. "Obviously."

Haven cleared the humor from her face as she shook her head. "No. Bell, I need you, Xandrian, and Nasira to go back to Shadoria and ensure the Godkiller is safe. Then you must go straight to the mortal lands to prepare King Eros for battle against Renk. The Shadeling is up to something. We don't have time to get more allies before we take back Penryth."

Bell's jaw gritted, drawing attention to the dark stubble she'd never noticed before, but he nodded.

"If you can," she continued, "reach out to Ashiviere for an alliance. Without a Solissian kingdom fighting alongside us, we'll need every soldier we can muster."

"I won't let you down, Haven."

She embraced him. "I know. The next time we see one another, I'll be immortal and you'll have a massive army waiting for me."

She shifted her focus to Xandrian as Bell pulled away. "Let anything happen to him—anything at all—and I'll hold you personally responsible."

Xandrian flashed a dark grin. "Noted." His focus shifted to Stolas. "Think you can handle this alone, Shade Lord?"

There was an undercurrent of warmth in Xandrian's teasing tone, and Stolas's response lacked its usual bite. "It will be easier now that I don't have to worry about saving your ass, Sun Lord. Oh, and don't underestimate the mortals. They're much trickier than they appear."

Xandrian gave a mock salute. "Always."

Haven felt her lips tug into a smile. That was probably as close as Stolas and Xandrian would ever come to friendship.

As soon as Bell and Xandrian had safely crossed the arena, Surai changed into a raven and Ember fully shifted into a steel gray panther with white markings.

Stolas slipped behind Haven, his arm a steel band around her waist. "Ready?"

"Yes."

Surai would lead them directly to the vaults inside the palace where the painting would be. The sky was clogged with oily black smoke as they rose over the ocean toward the cliffs. The winds high up blasted the heat from the fires all around them, the acrid air stinging her eyes and lungs. Fires smoldered all over the island, but the worst of it came from the palace.

Once a long, meandering ivory structure that hugged the cliffs, it was now pitted and deformed. Gaping holes spewed tongues of fire and tendrils of smoke. As they neared, winged shapes rose from the destruction.

Ash and soot clung to the Valkyrie's cloud-white wings as they fought the Golemites. Some of the Valkyrie rose from the palace, dipping and lurching in the air, their beautiful wings singed. One emerged with wings covered in flaming red Netherfire.

Haven nearly cried out as the Valkyrie plummeted down the cliffside into the still turquoise waters below. Two Gremwyr dove after the Valkyrie, and Haven had to look away when they began fighting over her body.

This was what they were fighting against. Ruthless, depraved evil. The attack was a tiny taste of what was to come if the Shadeling escaped the Netherworld.

Most of the Gremwyrs and Golemites were concentrated around the palace, but a few lingered in their path. Before Haven could so much as lift a finger, the deformed Shadowlings burst apart in a spray of dark blood.

That Stolas could so easily destroy a living, breathing being—it should have bothered her. But it didn't.

Not a bit.

"Get ready," he murmured as he landed on what once had been the top floor of the palace but was now a jagged ledge of marble overlooking a gaping hole. Sparks and cries of battle surged up from the depths of the palace.

Her bow was in her hands and an arrow nocked before she made out the first winged creature hurtling from the smoke.

As she released her weapon, she inflamed the end with light magick wrapped in threads of dark. The flame grew as the projectile pierced the shadows and sank in a Golemite's throat.

It clutched at the shaft as it plummeted into the dark chaos below.

Stolas flung out his arm and three Gremwyr tumbled into a wall. The force killed them on impact.

Picking through the sifting layers of darkness, she leapt to another ledge. Mid-jump, a Gremwyr appeared with its hideous mouth yawned wide open, fangs glistening.

She put an arrow through its open mouth and landed, spinning in time to see the creature spiral into the thick plumes of smoke and ash. She felled two more Gremwyrs and a Golemite before Stolas landed across the divide on what was left of a grand staircase.

Shadows unfurled around him as his powers stretched out. His eyes glowed nearly as red as the Netherfire in the dim half-light. When his lips curled up in a delighted smile, she didn't even flinch at the fangs there.

Surai appeared, changing back into her Solis form. The slender blades of her swords flashed as she twirled them. "Try to keep up."

On some unspoken signal, they all dove into the murky chaos. The upper levels of the palace were destroyed, and Haven had to jump across the strips of flooring still clinging to the skeleton of the once glorious building.

Finally they reached an undamaged portion of the castle, spreading out as they raced down the hall. Haven traded her bow for a short sword, her other hand cupping light magick, ready to unleash it.

The wait didn't last long. Two Golemites streaked around the corner toward them. Before Stolas could react, her magick flared across their bodies. They screamed in rage.

That is, until her sword parted their heads from their bodies.

Stolas glanced over at her. "I didn't know it was a contest."

She grinned. "It's not."

But it most certainly was.

Rolling her eyes, Surai rushed through the corridors, leading the way to the vaults. She didn't even have to bloody her swords. Every Golemite and Gremwyr they encountered died before they knew what happened, cut down by Haven and Stolas.

Haven lost count after twelve. Her magick seemed to take on a life of its own as it leapt from her hands and consumed the Shade Queen's soldiers. The ones that didn't die right away she finished with her steel before Stolas could claim them.

The sounds of snarls and metal on metal drew them down the final hallway. On the other side was a large, airy ballroom with mirrored ceilings and a parquet floor of white and gold. Ferns sprouted from enclaves, and arched open windows spanned the walls. Dark smoke drifted in the spears of sunlight.

"The vaulted gallery is just beneath," Surai said, katanas held low at her side as they entered the room. "There's a stairwell on the other side of the dais that leads there."

That explained why the fight had ended up here. A formation of

Valkyries, panthers, and leopards fought alongside the Morgani Queen. Still in her shifter form, the queen's huge size made her easy to spot among the fighting.

Countless Golemites soared above in the high ceiling, flinging their powers down at the group. Only the Valkyries could reach them, and Haven gaped up for a moment at the skilled warriors as they fought two and sometimes three Golemites at a time.

But there were just too many of them. They were funneling in from the windows. Thudding the floor as they landed, talons scraping loudly. The sound of leathery wings flapping in the air grew louder with every passing second.

A Gremwyr happened to notice them standing at the entrance and charged. Stolas snapped his fingers and it collapsed at their feet, neck obviously broken. "Poor dumb thing," Stolas murmured. He arched a wicked brow at Haven. "You know, this would be the perfect time to search for the painting."

The words he left unsaid hung between them. While the Morgani Queen was occupied and the Shade Queen's forces distracted, they would be free to look for the piece.

A roar drew Haven's focus back to the battle. The Morgani Queen had just felled a Golemite and whipped to face two more . . . but she was limping. Blood darkened her tawny fur. Too much of it—and it was too bright to be anyone's but hers.

Haven readied an orb of light magick. "I can't leave her to die."

"Neither can I," Surai said, joining Haven. Golden light flared down the curved blades in each of her hands. "Even if she is a cold-hearted bitch who abandoned and hurt the love of my life, Rook would want me to help her."

"Wonderful." Stolas procured two perfect orbs of dark magick with elegant sweeps of his hands and held them up. "Not that we're still counting, but this puts me up by three."

The electric blue spheres hurtled toward the battle and slammed into two Golemites who were about to finish off a wounded leopard.

Showoff.

Haven followed with a volley of her own magick. Sheathing her sword, she drew her bow and began picking off Golemites and Gremwyrs in the air.

Time slowed and warped.

Her senses picked up everything. The steady thump thump of her heart. The screech of talons over marble. The whoosh of wind and wings against her skin. The metallic bite of blood in the air.

As Haven and the others fought, they slowly drew closer to the nexus of battle. Bodies thudded the floor after every pull of her bowstring. At some point Ember found them and joined in the fray, taking out enemies with a ferocity that rivaled her mother's.

A yelp of pain came from Haven's left. She whipped around. Two Gremwyrs had a fallen Morgani guard in their mouths. One had her by the ankle, the other by the shoulder. In her injured state, the soldier had shifted back to her original form. They were pulling in opposite directions, each one trying to claim its prize.

The queen let out a roar as she leapt, eviscerating the first Gremwyr before it had a chance to respond. The second one refused to let go of the soldier's shoulder. The greedy creature tried to scuttle backward with its meal.

Injured and fatigued as she was, the queen refused to back down. She leapt so fast the Gremwyr didn't have time to flee. After making quick work of the beast, the queen bent her lion head down to lick the injured soldier—

A streak of something drew Haven's attention to the smoky shadows behind the queen. A flash of metal and a wavering form.

Her breath hitched. There was no time to warn the queen. Haven lifted an arrow and released, whispering the rune to imbue the iron tip with light and dark magick. The queen's golden eyes flicked to the projectile and she jerked her head up with a growl . . .

The Golemite's weapon, a curved sickle, halted an inch from the queen's neck. He stared in disbelief at the arrow that rested fletching-deep in his chest as the magick consumed him from the inside. The curved sickle blade he held clattered to the floor, and cracks of golden light appeared on his skin.

He burst apart in a splash of light, leaving only his armor and shoes intact.

Haven lifted her eyes to the queen, and something passed between them. Not quite trust, more like . . . respect.

There was no time to think about that as the fighting resumed. For every Golemite they killed, three more flooded in from the windows. When Stolas threw up a shield to cover the windows, they peeled back the roof, the walls, destroying anything in the way of entering.

But Stolas couldn't hold the shields for long—not when every ounce of his magick was needed to fight.

Outside the windows, the sky churned with Golemites as the Valkyries tried to protect what was left of the castle. A Valkyrie wrapped around a Golemite male tumbled in through an open window and rolled across the floor. The Golemite was dead, his wings splayed limp at an odd angle, dark eyes unblinking at the ceiling. The poor Valkyrie was too injured to move from beneath the much bigger Golemite corpse, and she gasped for breath.

Haven joined Ember and Surai as they aligned their backs together near the circle of the queen's guard. The queen limped over, her paws imprinting the smears of blood that slicked the floor all around them. She was panting. The wounds on her haunch and chest seeped bright red blood.

They wouldn't last this way much longer.

Morgryth's voice rose above the shriek of battle, followed by muffled thuds on the roof as things began to land. Through the tears in the ceiling, Haven made out Golemites in night-black armor.

Each one held . . . a bucket.

A whoosh split the air as Netherfire came to life in their hands. Hundreds of soldiers all about to drop that deadly substance directly on top of them.

"Goddess protect us," Surai whispered.

The shield they constructed bubbled outward, growing until it covered their circle. So few were left. The Valkyries fighting above dove toward that protection. Most made it, but a few were caught mid-air as the Netherfire fell. Gritting her teeth as she held the shield, Haven watched the ceiling disappear in a flash. Watched the molten red flames come for them in seemingly slow motion.

A Valkyrie inches away from the shield was incinerated right in front of them. For a breath, as the Netherfire clung to their wall of shield, eating away at the layers, hissing and popping, Haven's world was fire.

An inferno of unnaturally dark red flames that consumed everything they touched and never burned out. The gut-twisting smell of singed hair and flesh filled the hot air. And then, just as the heat began to soften and the fiery light dim, she turned for Stolas—

He wasn't with them.

THIRTY-NINE

Dread snatched the air from Haven's lungs. How was that possible? She felt his signature on the shield, layering his powers with theirs to strengthen the boundary and . . . and protect them.

Protect *them*.

Where had she last seen him? She jerked her head to the left of the doors. He had been right there fighting three Golemites. She tried to peer through the layer of magick but the fire had warped it, and with the smoke and flames—

Covering her face with her free hand, she rushed from the protective bubble. Surai tried to grab her but Haven moved too fast. She pierced the transparent curtain of magick, quickly brushing away embers of Netherfire before it caught on her hair and dress, and . . .

Halted. Her stomach clenched wildly as a chasm yawned open at her feet. Everything in the ballroom not protected by the shield was gone. The thick spelled stone that once separated this level from the vaulted gallery below had been eaten away.

And the wondrous artifacts and items stored in the alcoves, the painting—

Everything, *everything* was gone. Incinerated. Her stomach lurched. The stench of the burned magick released into the air made her nauseous.

But she didn't care. Not about the painting or becoming immortal. None of it compared to the panic she felt as she searched for Stolas.

Please be alive. Please.

Panic rolled through her.

Sucking in lungfuls of ash-tinged air, she scanned the divide and noticed an area in the corner near where she last saw him. The floor was still intact as if he'd used some of his powers for a shield. Boulder-sized chunks of rafter and debris piled high, little pockets of fire still burning.

Meaning his shield had collapsed at some point.

His name scraped up her raw throat—

And then she heard her name called on the other side.

Archeron kneeled at the chasm's edge as smoke curled around his boots. He was covered in gore and blood. The royal jacket he'd been wearing earlier had been removed, and his hair had fallen from its restraints, making him look so much like the Archeron she once knew that her heart tugged.

How many times had she seen him just like this? Filthy after some battle, hair messy and pushed to the side, sleeves rolled up. Even his smile felt similar, that teasing arrogance on full display.

But it was only half a smile. The other side was covered behind the mask she'd quickly learned to despise. To fear, even. Flames danced across its sleek surface, making the jewels glitter and flash.

Embers rose between them like fireflies.

"Haven." His voice was unusually soft as he held out his hand. "Haven, come to me. I can protect you."

She shook her head, her words catching around the lump in her throat. His voice was too familiar. His smile too like the old Archeron.

Stolas—she needed to find Stolas.

"Look around you. You don't stand a chance." Against her will, she obeyed. Her pulse spiked as she took in the Gremwyrs swarming down the walls, a wave of death. Golemites hovered in the sky above, their wings too susceptible to fire to descend.

The moment the last of the fire burned out they would join their Shadowling brethren to finish the remaining Solis off.

There was no doubt in Haven's mind that Morgryth would take Haven alive to her father—after torturing her first, obviously. And the things her father would do would make the Shade Queen's torture seem pleasant.

"Come to me now," Archeron continued in that deceptively gentle tone, "and I promise my men will protect them. You have my word. I will be gentle with you, Haven. As long as you bend to my will, you have nothing to fear."

Her gaze darted to the rubble where Stolas had been, desperation clawing her chest.

"Haven, please. Am I really that loathsome that you would prefer to be taken by the Shadeling than me?"

The vulnerability in his voice startled her. He wanted her to come willingly to him. Needed her to for some inexplicable reason.

She met his pleading stare. His hand still outstretched, fingers curling as he beckoned. Bits of ash had caught in his hair and collar. The side of his mouth that she could see lifted hopefully, his emerald green eye bright with expectation.

With . . . longing.

She glanced back at Surai and Ember. Both women were injured. They wouldn't last long against the approaching onslaught. But they would never give up. And if they were given the option to give Haven to Archeron and survive or fight and die, she knew which option they would choose.

Her focus flitted back to Archeron. To his outstretched hand and false offer of safety. But it was an illusion, and he was just as bad as the Shadeling.

Maybe worse.

At least the Shadeling knew what he was. Archeron still thought himself righteous and good. Could still somehow justify his abominable actions.

She met his gaze and snarled, "I would rather die than willingly give myself to you."

The light inside his one good eye flickered and then guttered out. The flash of pain and surprise in his face slowly transformed into a malice so dark it nearly buckled her knees. "On second thought, why don't I sit back and wait until Morgryth and her ilk have showered you in the blood of your friends? Maybe then when I slip my leash around your neck you'll be grateful."

"You would risk war with the Morgani Queen just to have me?"

His focus drifted to where the Morgani fought behind her. "How can I start a war with someone who's dead?"

Snarls drew both their attention to the corner where—

Oh, Goddess. Stolas.

Horror coiled in her gut at the sight of him. Bloodied. Feathers singed and charred, a few smoldering and spewing smoke. His tunic hung in tatters over his body, revealing terrible wounds and blood—so much blood.

His? Others? Her mind whirled as she tried to make sense of what she was seeing. Figures dashed around him, their quick movements hard to pin down.

Five, no six, no *countless* Golemites and Gremwyrs had descended on him and were tearing at him with teeth and weapons and claws.

He fought back with the strength of a God. Tossing Gremwyrs aside like they weighed nothing. Ripping limbs and wings from his enemies.

Slashing his sword in impossibly fast, measured strokes.

Why wasn't he using his magick?

And then it hit her. He hadn't fed before they came, and then with the shield and battle . . . his vast powers were depleted.

He'd used the very last of it to shield her.

A Gremwyr dove from high above, catching Stolas in the upper back with its talons. The pain in his gritted jaw as he held back a cry pierced her core. Stolas somehow managed to fling the beast back and then sever its head with his sword, but more were descending. He slammed his horns into a male Golemite's face, cratering it on impact. He rammed the butt of his sword into another Golemite's temple, dropping him.

But there were too many. This was Morgryth's revenge. If the orders were to take Haven alive, they would be the opposite for Stolas, the male who murdered Morgryth's only daughter.

A Golemite female darted from behind, clipping one of his wings—

This time he grunted, every muscle trembling as he whipped to face the threat. His tormentors were laughing.

Laughing.

At the male who had saved her countless times. Who had endured torture for her. Who had somehow, *somehow* held on to a shred of hope for centuries despite unimaginable cruelty. Who had bet everything on her, a rash, impulsive girl who tried to end her life.

A life he saved. Over and over again.

Even when she didn't think she deserved it.

Even when she probably *didn't* deserve it.

Wrath like she'd never felt before split her open—a torrent of fire a thousand times hotter and greedier than the Netherfire.

Pain cracked her knees—she had fallen. The pressure in her chest was building and building and . . .

Oh, Goddess, she was going to break in half.

The air punched from her lungs as the pressure released. The fire sizzling her skin softening to a soothing heat.

She must have shut her eyes, and when she opened them, she had trouble understanding what she was seeing.

A great beast of golden light cut through the black smoke as it leapt toward Stolas. His tormentors were too enthralled in the attack to notice the creature. That is, until it roared.

That roar turned into a howl that was soon matched by another creature.

Stolas's Shadow Wolf. Their plaintive howls intertwined to create an ethereal song that reached deep inside her, filling the yawning pit of emptiness she had felt her entire existence. Warmth cascaded through her, over her. A euphoria of belonging, of *rightness* she didn't understand.

The Golemites pivoted to face the new threat, oblivious to Stolas's wolf behind them. Haven watched, transfixed, knowing deep down what this was.

Her familiar had released.

And it had chosen a form.

A wolf—a majestic golden wolf to match Stolas's black one.

It circled Stolas's tormentors, and she could feel it waiting for her command.

She didn't make it wait long.

Kill them all.

The Shade Queen's army scattered—or tried. Her wolf snapped its giant head down, teeth cracking bone as it took them out in threes and fours.

Shrieking in terror, the Golemites and Gremwyrs tried to take to the air, but her wolf snatched them down one by one. Breaking their necks. Tearing off their heads. Eviscerating them. Ripping them in half.

A part of her said she should have looked away. Should have felt a twinge of horror.

Instead, she felt a deep, primal satisfaction.

It was all over in a few seconds. Her wolf had become corporeal, the golden filaments of light becoming luxurious platinum fur tipped in rich gold. She was slightly smaller than Stolas's wolf, lither, her fur thicker when compared to the onyx wolf's silky pelt.

Whining, her wolf padded over to Stolas, who had just finished off the last remaining Golemite. He was panting slightly and favoring his ribs, but when her wolf leaned down to sniff him, he went inhumanly still. The golden beast licked the wound over his chest before nuzzling her head against his cheek.

For a strange moment, Haven imagined sketching the scene. Stolas, his wavy bone-white hair fallen over the side of his forehead, thick ebony horns curved back against his skull like a crown. His glossy wings were held aloft behind him, one slightly more outstretched than the other.

And her wolf, radiant, almost glowing from within as it checked his wounds.

Stolas's gaze went to hers, and she felt that same connection she had when her familiar had recognized his yesterday. A taut jerk low in her belly, but a hundred times stronger than before.

And when Stolas's lips curled upward—her breath hitched.

His wolf howled, the sound beckoning Haven's familiar.

It was a call to hunt.

Together, the twin wolves descended on the room, creatures of light and dark working in tandem. Their movements seemed almost coordinated as they pounced and lunged, sending Golemites and Gremwyrs fleeing in every direction.

As Haven watched, she couldn't help but think of earlier when she and Stolas had cleared the corridors together. That same sort of bond between them as they hunted and slaughtered everything in their path.

"When did that happen?" Surai asked as she made her way over to Haven.

Haven lifted her bow and reached for an arrow. "Just now."

Something, a flicker of movement, a noise, drew Haven's focus to Stolas. There was a strange, almost bittersweet look in his face as he watched his wolf and hers clear the room. As if their pairing brought him both pleasure and pain.

Another movement drew her eye to a shadow rising behind Stolas.

And when she spied the golden mask, fear plunged straight into her heart.

FORTY

Stolas had never seen any creature quite as beautiful as Haven's familiar. She seemed to be made from frost and starlight and molten amber, her lupine eyes a mosaic of silver and gold. He could feel his wolf snarl in delight. His familiar had been restless since the moment it recognized its mate in Haven's familiar.

Which meant there was no denying anymore who Haven was to him.

Not that he had doubted.

His injured wings gathered close to his body as he assessed his injuries. Most of his power had gone to shielding Haven, but he'd left a small reserve to erect the shield that protected him from the extent of the Netherfire's wrath.

His powers had given out shortly afterward, his wings suffering the brunt of the damage. The pain was unfathomable, and he had stupidly let it blind him to the approaching Golemites until they were already upon him. He would never let himself live that down. Any other time, even without his powers, he would have wiped them from the face of the realm.

Instead, they'd managed to wound him. Some injuries were bone-deep and ragged where talons had carved into his flesh—but already he could feel the deep itch that meant his skin was mending. Without his wellspring of magick it would take longer, but he would heal.

In the meantime, he would make the Golemite bastards pay for his wings. One death for each perfect feather the fire singed.

It only seemed fair.

He lifted his gaze, prepared to take to the air and join his wolf, when he saw Haven—

Her panicked expression sent him whirling, but too late. A light prick settled in his left flank, just below his rib cage.

A jolt of icy-cold agony followed.

Archeron's face resolved from the smoke, his teeth bared and eyes burning with pure malice. In his hands were two weapons: the glorious longsword of his mother and a small dagger.

By the pain surging through his body with every pulse of his heart, the dagger was tipped in some type of poison.

He was immune to most toxins in this realm, but this felt different.

Fighting against the wave of pain spreading through his body, Stolas stalked toward the Sun Sovereign. "Using poison? I would expect nothing less from a coward such as yourself."

Archeron roared as he brought his sword down on Stolas.

Stolas slipped from the blade's reach, dancing between Archeron's strokes. Toying with him. If he had his choice, he would prolong Archeron's death for days. Make him feel every agonizing sensation, every ounce of shame for what he'd done to Haven.

But, as lovely as that would be, they didn't have the time for such pleasures. Snarling, Stolas slammed his fist into Archeron's face, his knuckles connecting with the edge of the mask.

Archeron staggered.

A growl of pleasure ripped from Stolas's chest as he hit him again. The feel of bone and metal shattering beneath his knuckles was so damn satisfying.

The mask split with a booming crack. Archeron's dagger clattered across the floor and into the abyss. The Sun Sovereign stumbled back, clawing at the ruined mask, powers converging as he tried to meld it back together.

But it was destroyed beyond repair, and the jagged bits slipped through his fingers.

Now his monstrous face was on full display. One side flawless, so perfect it might have been carved by the Gods themselves. The other hideous and ruined.

Something about the contrast of beauty and horror was deeply unsettling.

Panting, Archeron lifted his free hand to map the disfigurement.

Any remaining light in the Sun Lord's eyes faded. "You forced her into your bed."

Like most Solis, Archeron misunderstood what it meant when a Shadow Familiar paired to another. The truth would enrage him. Stolas flashed a taunting grin. "If you believe Haven can be forced into anything then you don't know her at all."

"You are an animal, a barbaric monstrous creature. She would never be with you unless you hadn't enthralled her somehow."

"Enthralled?" Stolas asked, stepping closer. "Perhaps I simply accept her for who she is, every part of her." He closed another inch of space between them. "But you should know, that's not why her Shadow Familiar chose a wolf form."

Stolas knew the exact moment Archeron understood his meaning. The Sun Sovereign's mangled face twisted in a rage-filled roar as he lifted the sword—

Stolas struck with lightning speed, wrenching the heavy weapon from

Archeron's grasp. "The big blades might make fools soil their pants, but in true combat, they move like shit."

A flash of light formed in Archeron's palm—

Stolas rammed the butt of Archeron's sword into the soft part of his throat.

The king's magick snuffed out. He clutched his neck, gasping, wide eyes watering. That was going to sting a bit.

"The big ones are good for blunt force, I suppose," Stolas drawled as he examined the beautiful sword, famously gifted to Archeron's mother from an Asgardian king. "But I find sometimes a good steel-toed boot works just as well."

Stolas lifted his knee and slammed his foot into the center of Archeron's wide chest. The impact punched the remaining air from Archeron's lungs, and he tumbled backward over the edge and into the vaulted gallery below. A earth-rattling boom followed as his body smashed into a wall.

Now that was fun. Stolas took enormous pleasure in Archeron's groan as he dove to finish him.

Ground bits of stone and rubble crunched beneath Stolas's soles as he prowled toward Archeron, who was back on his feet. Pockets of fire still crackled in the alcoves. The Netherfire had burned away almost everything, although a few bits of frame or chunks of what had once been statues remained.

Stolas let the tip of that magnificent sword scrape against the ground as he approached. An insult for a weapon as exquisite as this one.

"You know," Stolas purred, "your mother was cruel to a fault, but she at least deserved such a finely crafted blade. Then again, you have a habit of coveting things that don't belong to you."

The rubies inlaid inside the hilt caught the light of the dying fires as Stolas snapped the blade over his thigh and tossed both pieces onto the floor.

A small circle of magick formed over Archeron's palm. "My mother lost her way. She would have ruined Effendier if I hadn't . . ."

"Hadn't what?"

Archeron's throat dipped, and he lifted his hand.

Stolas arched a brow as he regarded the ball of light spinning between Archeron's fingers. "I have to say, I am a bit disappointed. Where have your powers gone, Sun Lord? I could blow that sad little display out with a single breath."

Archeron's nostrils flared, and he retreated into an alcove littered with the burnt remains of what were probably once gorgeous tapestries. *Such a shame.*

"Tell me, Sun Lord." Stolas stalked soundlessly after Archeron. "Did you rip the sword from your mother's hands before or after you killed her?"

It was a hunch, but the way Archeron flinched, Stolas knew he was right.

Coward.

"Interesting," Stolas continued as he circled Archeron, the heat from the flames warming the air. "That you would just happen to be here during Morgryth's attack. Tell me. When did you sell your soul to the Shadeling, hmm?"

With a choking growl, Archeron released the golden sphere. Stolas ducked beneath the magick, plucked a melon sized chunk of rubble, and hurled it at Archeron's head.

The movement was so quick Archeron didn't see the projectile until it was upon him. He flung his hands up, the rock shattering into pebbles and dust against his forearm.

Stolas canted his head as he watched Archeron struggle to conjure his powers. "When you shattered your magickal enslavement to King Boteler, the ancient dark magick inside that ring entered your soul. But the unfortunate thing about dark magick, Sun Lord, is that it needs an energy source. That's why your powers are a shadow of what they once were." He tsked softly. "If anyone in your court knew how weak you really were, your reign would be over."

Archeron's face was unrecognizable as he sneered at Stolas. "You have no idea what you're talking about."

"Don't I? I am a lot of things, but fool is not one of them."

Stumbling, the king managed to right himself before sending a volley of desperate magick toward Stolas.

Stolas evaded the offensive light magick again and again. Each time slipping around the orbs of power with startling ease. It was disappointing to watch a lightcaster as powerful as Archeron once was use such pithy magick.

That would dull the pleasure of killing him, but not enough that he still wasn't going to draw this out. Toy with the king, just a little, savoring the sweet scent of his fear.

He deserved that and so much more for what he did to Haven.

Another wave of light magick left Archeron's hands. He was growing desperate.

"I spent half a lifetime enslaved to the bitch-queen that just destroyed an entire palace using Netherfire," Stolas drawled, strolling around a mound of smoldering ash. "The things she used to do to me would make you tremble with fear, *King*. Do you really think the flimsy spheres of magick you're producing are going to do anything but piss me off?"

Desperation formed in Archeron's visage, his gaze glossy and wild eyed as he snarled, "I've seen your death."

Stolas shrugged. "We all die eventually. Trust me, I've done it once already."

There was something depraved flickering beneath Archeron's panic. The feeling it gave Stolas was akin to passing a lake where a demon lurked just beneath the surface, its putrid and rotting flesh infecting the water.

"I made Haven see it too," Archeron rasped. "Over and over and over. Made her watch you die in a hundred different ways, so that when you finally do, it will destroy her."

Stolas froze as the fear he kept hidden came to life on that bastard's lips.

"You're not the only one who has access to the Demon Lords' dark . . . talents. Eventually she will see you for what you are, and she will end you."

Stolas tilted his head as he murmured, "Did you know, after she returned from the Nether, she cried so hard I thought she was going to break apart in my arms?" The memory of her moans of anguish sliced through his own pain. "You took her extraordinary love for others and you twisted it, *weaponized* it against her."

Archeron retreated a step only to find a wall in his way. A strange look of finality settled over his features. "You only see her goodness. I did too, once. She is quite charming in a stubborn, naïve sort of way. But such immense power cannot be trusted in a mortal. It needs to be broken, chained, and controlled. Harnessed for the good of Haven and the realm."

"By you?"

"Better me than you, Noctis filth."

"That's where we differ, Sun Lord. You see her fire and it terrifies you. You want to smother those luminous flames until everything that makes her wondrous and amazing becomes small and dim and ordinary, a spark you can ignite at will."

"And you don't?"

Stolas chuckled darkly. Such ignorance. "No. I want to stoke that magnificent inferno until this entire miserable realm is aflame and the greedy tyrants like you are nothing more than forgotten piles of ash."

"And if she burns you too?"

A wicked grin flickered across Stolas's lips. "Then I'll die fucking warm and content." His wings began to unfurl as a blinding rage took hold. "You, on the other hand, are going to die cold and alone, and much sooner than you anticipated."

Archeron appraised Stolas, a cunning glint in his gaze. "Your magick is gone, you are grievously wounded, and you have no weapon."

"Doesn't matter." He stepped closer, moving stealthily now. "I'm going to tear you apart with my bare hands for what you did to her. But first I'm going to drain the little magick you have left."

Archeron gave a soft laugh. "Feeling the poison, are we?"

"Nothing your magick can't remedy," Stolas murmured, his attention riveted to the artery pulsing in Archeron's neck. He hadn't blood-let from anyone in a long time, but he would make an exception for Archeron.

"Are you sure about that?" Stolas dragged his gaze upward to see the working side of Archeron's lips wrenched into a sneer. "I should thank you, I suppose. Once she's mine, Shade Lord, her wolf will be too. Think of the armies she and that beast will destroy under the banner of the Sun Court."

A flash of movement filled Archeron's palm as he conjured what appeared to be another weapon.

Not a weapon—

Stolas lunged for the king just as Archeron activated the device, a circular gold disk engraved with demonaic runes.

A portal whooshed to life between them.

Instead of Stolas's fingers closing on Archeron's neck, they curled uselessly over smoke and ash.

FORTY-ONE

Haven was mired in smoke and blood and worse. Her throat burned, her eyes stung, every muscle in her body ached. As soon as she'd spied Archeron behind Stolas, a final wave of the Shade Queen's forces had descended on their tiny group. It was a half-hearted attempt, fueled by desperation and malice, and with the help of the two Shadow Wolves, Haven and the others repelled the attack.

When she'd turned back to Stolas, heart in her throat at what she imagined seeing, he was only feet away. An overwhelming panic threatened to swallow her at the sight of his wounds.

So many jagged tears in his flesh. So much blood. Streaks of dark crimson clung to strands of his pale hair, and his poor wings . . .

At least one had been severely injured, blood caked and drying along the apex, and he held it gingerly the way a cat would an injured paw.

But it was the pain in his eyes, pain he tried and failed to hide, that settled like rocks in her gut.

She'd witnessed that agony once before, in their shared dreamscape

337

after the Shade Queen tortured him mercilessly.

Concern propelled Haven into his arms. She forgot she was still angry with him. Forgot the deep wounds he'd inflicted when he threatened to take away her freewill in the Hall of Light.

Her need for him to be safe and out of pain eclipsed everything else. He trembled as her fingers rushed over his body. Each time she came across another injury her insides contracted as if she were the one hurt.

"Beastie . . ." His raw voice shivered in restrained agony. "I am fine."

A huff of air rushed from her lips as she lifted a bloodied strip of his shirt to expose a gaping wound. "You call this fine?"

"A mere . . . flesh wound."

"Liar." Gathering a clean strip of his tunic, she pressed the cloth into the most troubling injury, a gash that trenched across his chest and down his stomach. Blood soaked the fabric immediately.

He flinched, his eyes never leaving hers. "I am surprisingly . . . resilient."

"No, you are bleeding out like an idiot." She focused on conjuring gauze and bandages to hide the way her eyes rolled. "Why didn't you feed before we came?"

"I am going to ignore the disdain in your tone and take your concern as a sign of your undying devotion to me."

Annoyed, she ripped what was left of his shirt from his torso and began applying the clean bandages.

Amusement sparked inside his eyes. "If you wanted to undress me, I would suggest waiting until we don't have an audience."

His gaze tightened as it shifted behind her.

The others were watching. The queen and the remaining guards and Valkyries had changed back into their Solis forms the moment Haven beheaded the last Golemite, as if staying shifted took more energy. Now they had regrouped into a loose circle over the oval of floor left standing, and were tending to the wounded.

The white, turquoise, and canary yellow tiles—once a mosaic of some sort depicting large cats gathered around a throne—were mired in blood and death.

Two Valkyries hovered over the queen, ignoring their own injuries as they used their magick to mend her various wounds. Ember and Surai were helping staunch the bleeding from a Valkyrie who had lost an arm.

They had all stopped what they were doing to stare at Stolas and Haven, their battle-weary gazes trekking to the two wolves standing guard at opposite sides of the ballroom.

His hand was shockingly cold as she guided it to the gauze at the center of his chest. "Hold this while I secure the bandage."

"Haven."

"I don't care what they see."

"Haven—"

"You are important to me, Stolas, and I will not hide that from them or *anyone.*"

The hard lines of his features softened. "Your brave devotion is appreciated, but we need to shift our focus to escaping. Archeron knows my magick is gone. Our portal back to Shadoria will have been destroyed. His forces will be waiting the moment we leave the queen's presence."

"What about her protection?" Haven asked, already knowing his reply.

"It ended the moment the tournament did," a steady female voice answered behind Haven.

Haven turned to appraise the Morgani Queen. Even after such a devastating attack, she possessed an unflappable regality Haven had only seen once before, in Rook. "So you would let him take me, knowing what he would do?"

She clutched her side as she laughed. Gone was the finery from before: the panther headdress, the jewels and gorgeous gown. In its place was a naked, bleeding queen who Haven knew would happily go down fighting for her kingdom and people.

Surai had once said most Morgani soldiers shifted without the magick to retain their clothes afterward. It was considered purer.

"In this state," the queen said, pointedly dragging her gaze over the injured and dead, "he could take whatever he wants with very little opposition, and he's smug enough to know it."

Brushing aside the two Valkyries, whose wings had disappeared as soon as the sky cleared of their enemies, the queen limped toward Haven, head held high. The only thing she wore was the Valkyrie horn around her neck and blood.

And yet Haven doubted any queen had ever looked so magnificent.

"He won't do it openly," the queen continued. "He's not ready to publicly challenge my authority—not yet anyway, so that buys you a little time."

Haven managed to keep her voice steady as she asked, "Any chance one of you can thread portals?"

"We do have a few threadcasters in our court—if they are still alive— but I'm afraid *our* talents lie elsewhere."

Frustration welled inside Haven's chest. The moment they left the rubble of the palace, Archeron would be waiting.

"Now," the queen purred, "tell me, Haven Ashwood, what is it about the alcoves below that interest you?" Haven's surprise must have been obvious because the queen added, "You looked stricken when you witnessed the destruction of the private gallery beneath us, and I imagine there was something you wanted. Something you planned to ask for if you won the tournament."

There was no reason to lie—not anymore. The gift her mother left her was destroyed.

Haven nodded, burying her disappointment with the other raw emotions from the last hour. "It was a painting."

The queen arched a blonde eyebrow, wrinkles forming in the half-dried smear of blood on her high forehead. "All of this for a painting?"

"It would have been special somehow. Perhaps odd."

The queen winced as a soldier slid a red cashmere cloak over her body. "I have a . . . weak spot for art, as most rulers do. There are—were countless canvases stored below. Some in the private gallery and others tucked away in the alcoves. It could have been any one of those. Perhaps I would recognize it by the artist?"

Haven brushed a loose strand of hair from her face and sighed. "My mother."

The queen's dry lips parted slightly as understanding dawned. "Your . . ."

"Freya. Before her death, she created three paintings. We think one was destroyed, but there are still two out there."

Were. Haven's heart contracted a little at the reminder. All her hopes of becoming immortal, of finding something tangible of her mother, something created just for her . . .

The loss was too much to think about.

Haven pushed through her pain to see the queen staring at her quietly. "You really believe it, don't you?"

"What?"

"That you are her child."

"I don't just believe it; I know it." She might not feel deserving of the honor, but for the first time since the prophecy was revealed to her, she knew it was true.

"Only a daughter would mourn for such a thing." The queen finished tying her cloak around her shoulders, her gaze distant. "There was a piece years ago that was noteworthy, but there was only one, and I sold it shortly afterward."

Fiery hope swept through Haven. "Sold it?"

The queen's amber eyes, so much like Rook's, refocused on Haven.

"It was an . . . odd thing. Plain but entrancing in a way I cannot describe. The night after I purchased it, I dreamt I was inside the scene. There was a—a black pit viper on the back of the settee the woman and her baby sat upon, poised to strike. A terrible venom dripped from its curved fangs. I tried to warn them, but they couldn't hear me, and then I awoke with the strangest feeling that I should sell the painting." She shook her head as if trying to dislodge the dream from her mind. "I did the very next day to a Demon Lord passing through."

The breath caught in Haven's chest. That meant the painting was safe. "You said a mother and child. That's the illustration on the canvas?"

"Yes." The unfocused look faded as the queen regained her composure. "It was so simple. Bizarre, even. I could have sworn the first time I saw it, the mother was nursing the child. And yet, when I looked upon the painting before it changed hands, the baby was swaddled and sleeping."

"I've seen that somewhere before," Haven whispered.

The image flickered across her mental landscape, building upon itself in nebulous layers as her mind slowly constructed it. The beautiful woman whose face was mostly obscured as she looked down with adoration at a child.

A baby.

Her.

FORTY-TWO

"As have I." Stolas's breath caressed Haven's neck. She'd almost forgotten he was behind her. "By chance, was this Demon Lord called the Prince of Ash?"

The queen managed to hide her surprise behind a saccharine smile. "Yes, although he introduced himself as Raziel Nightfell. I only learned of the peculiar nickname later." Her smile deepened. "He made quite an impression on many in my court. If he had not insisted on leaving so soon, I fear he would have caused a severe disruption between my soldiers."

It was impossible to miss the way the queen's personal guard—the Valkyries in particular—grinned.

The queen cut a steely gaze toward Stolas. "How could you know such a thing?"

Stolas met Haven's eyes as he said, "Because he gave that painting to my court along with a number of illicit items shortly before Morgryth's betrayal."

"How fortuitous," the queen murmured. "The painting, not the betrayal."

Stolas shifted his attention to the queen, staring for a heartbeat too long. "Indeed."

A chill swept over Haven, raising goose bumps along her bare arms. "But the painting's not *in* the castle, Stolas. It's inside that . . . that thing."

She wouldn't say mirror, because whatever was locked away, fortified behind that spelled iron cage, was not a mirror. It was something else.

Something wrong. Not of this world.

A muscle flexed in Stolas's sharp-edged jaw. "It was in my possession until a few days ago, although I didn't know what it was at the time." He released a ragged sigh. "What you saw inside that jade frame, Haven— that is the home of the Keeper."

Surai sucked in a breath. "The blood augur from the Demon Lands? That's who's inside the mirror you nearly died trying to destroy? The one whose curse would have ended your life?"

Stolas's eyelashes dipped as he nodded.

"Why is she called the Keeper?" Haven asked, knowing full well the answer would be awful.

And it was.

"Because when she tells you your future," Surai whispered, as if the witch could hear them discussing her, "she takes something in return. Sometimes it's a seemingly random object like a favorite necklace or the button off your shirt. Other times the price is your favorite child or a sliver of your soul."

Haven frowned. "Can we enter through the mirror?"

Stolas shook his head. "The mirror is a one-sided portal that travels into our world. Only the Keeper can pass through from our side back to hers."

"And where exactly is that?" Haven pressed.

"The Demon Realm."

Just like that, Haven's hopes turned to ash in her throat.

The queen tsked. "Only a fool would meddle with such forsaken creatures. They say she is the mistress to a powerful Demon Lord. That she has lived since the ancient times and is part demon, part something else. Tell me you only consulted with the demon witch that one instance, Prince Darkshade."

"Twice." Stolas's voice was raw, eaten up with suppressed anguish.

A shudder coursed through Haven. "We know you gave the Keeper the painting. What was the price the first time?"

Agony darkened his eyes to pewter, and he answered softly, "A sum I could not pay. So she took something infinitely more precious in its stead."

The way every muscle in his body seemed to tense and cord warned he didn't want to discuss the event further. Not that they had time to delve into his past. Every second they wasted without a plan gave Archeron time to amass more of his forces around them.

"Tell me," the queen said. "Besides the sentimental component, why do you seek this piece of art?"

Haven searched the queen's eyes. She wasn't sure what she was looking for, but whatever she saw convinced Haven the queen could be trusted with the truth. "Immortality. That is what I seek."

"Ah. A Goddess-Born whose flesh wrinkles and decays in the blink of an eye does cause a bit of a problem."

Haven reached out and clasped the queen's hand. The cool flesh was flaked with dried blood. "If I succeed, can I count on your alliance?"

The queen's guards rushed to stop Haven, but the queen called them off with a look. She stared down at Haven's fingers over hers. When her gaze shifted up to Haven's, her eyes were bright with emotion. "Tell me, how exactly did my daughter die?"

"She died saving me. I was surrounded by Gremwyrs and she fought them back so that I could escape." She inhaled, breathing through the unexpected grief swelling her throat. "Because of her selfless bravery, I'm standing here today."

Surai let out a ragged breath.

The queen nodded, her features hardening before she crossed to the edge of the smoking chasm to stare into the ruined gallery below. "You should know, there is a one-way portal in the deepest alcove. It hasn't been used since the last Demon Lord visited, but if it's still viable, it will take you straight to Cimmeria, the trading capital of the Demon Lands and stronghold of the Demon Lord, Malik Damir. Rumor has it that is where Malik keeps his blood augur mistress."

The Keeper. Haven's excitement guttered as she glanced at Stolas.

Despite his efforts to hide his condition, he was fading before her eyes. His breathing was labored, his wings drooped as if holding them up was too much effort, and his irises were the color of bleached bone.

Something told her that was not good.

"I need to find him . . . sustenance." There really was no great way to say it.

"There." He lifted his gaze to hers, the act taking way more effort than it should have. "I can . . . find what I need there."

Surai scoffed. "You cannot be serious. The Demon Realm? You know what they will do to Haven?"

"I do," Stolas murmured, "and I have a plan for that."

"Do you?" Surai countered. "Because in your condition, I doubt you will survive the portal."

Haven craned her neck for a better view of the sky. The smoke from the battered city formed a veil that dimmed the setting sun, casting fingers of murky orange and muddy yellow over everything. Somewhere just out of sight waited Archeron and his reinforcements. He would have had time to thread over hundreds if not thousands of men. Haven was confident in her powers—but not that confident.

They had no choice but to go through the Demon Realm.

Haven hated to point out the obvious but . . . "How will we return to this realm?"

"It's brilliant, actually," Stolas rasped, hand pressed into the bandages on his chest—bandages soaked through with dark blood. "The mirror will take us straight back to Starpiercer Castle."

"Assuming the Keeper doesn't kill us," Ember amended. She had an arm around a Valkyrie as she helped the soldier up. "Our light magick doesn't work in the Demon Realm. Not like it does here."

Haven released a disappointed breath. That was a blow, one she wasn't expecting. Still. "I made it a very long time against near-impossible odds without magick. We'll be fine. But you and Surai aren't coming."

Surai and Ember opened their mouths to argue—

"I need you both in Shadoria to ready the troops for travel to Eritreyia. Bell is already there amassing the last of our allies."

As the graveness of their task sank in, they dipped their heads in solemn obedience. In Haven's periphery, she caught the queen watching the interaction with unabashed curiosity.

"And you, *Soror*?" Surai asked. "When will we see you again?"

Haven wanted to wrap her arms around her friend, just in case it was the last time they met. But thinking like that—acting like that felt like a bad omen. So she gave Surai a radiant smile and hoped her friend knew how much she appreciated her.

How much she loved her.

"Soon." Haven turned to the queen. "I take it you have someone trained in the art of threading?"

"Of course, but to create a portal to Shadoria will take half a day, at least."

"Then I humbly ask that you offer shelter to my friends until then."

Haven knew what she was asking. Once Archeron learned of her escape, he would be furious. Enough to take that out on Ember and

Surai? She didn't think he would risk the Morgani's ire to hurt them, but it was still asking a lot of the queen.

The queen arched a brow. "Asking favors? I was not aware our friendship had progressed to that level yet."

"Then consider it repayment." The words she left out—*for saving your life, Queen*—hung in the air between them.

"I thought I already repaid you when I so helpfully made you aware of the portal below."

"Then look at it as a down payment on our future together."

The queen never let down her hard mask as she gave a subtle nod, but the corners of her lips twitched upward.

Long shadows fell over them as the sun finished its descent, and Haven shivered. Soon Archeron would grow impatient. Yesterday she would have said he wouldn't dare attack in the Morgani Queen's presence. But that was before she saw Archeron's wild desperation, his . . . his obsession.

That was the only word that even came close to describing what she saw in his eyes.

After that, Goddess only knew what he would end up doing if she remained here.

She faced Stolas to find him quietly watching her, waiting with a rare patience. "Ready?"

A bemused smile brightened his face. "I would ask for a clean pair of clothes and perhaps a nice cloak first, but . . ." He shrugged, his smile growing devilish. "If you prefer me this way, well, you wouldn't be the first."

Surai muffled her snort behind her hand. Before anyone could notice how inflamed Haven's cheeks were, she quickly conjured dark leather pants and a storm gray tunic she remembered liking on him. She went to conjure her usual outfit—loose shirt and worn pants—when he shook his head.

"Wear that." He indicated her gown with his chin, his lingering gaze burning through the thin fabric straight to her belly. "It will go with the false story we'll use for anyone overly curious about who we are."

"And that is?"

The teasing glint in his eyes didn't bode well. "I'll explain after we cross. You'll need a fur-lined cloak. The evenings get rather cool there."

Rather cool for Stolas meant freezing so she conjured the plushest, heaviest cloak she could recall, a gorgeous emerald-green cashmere piece gifted to her from Bell years ago and probably still in her tiny closet in Penryth.

That left only one detail to finalize.

"Shall I use my powers to get down?" She glanced at the smoldering gallery a floor below. The drop was too high to jump safely and Stolas was in no condition to fly them.

An annoyed growl rumbled his chest. "My wings have suffered much worse, I promise you."

He held out a hand. Was he trying to save face? It didn't matter. She wouldn't force the issue, and she trusted him not to jeopardize their safety for his ego.

She meant to walk the few feet to him, but she nearly staggered into his arms, her tired, achy body longing to relax into his strength. Warmth filled her belly as his arms slid around her waist, steadying her.

She felt him jerk behind her as her head brushed the wound at his chest.

"Stolas—"

"I'm fine." He tensed as his wings slowly spread to their full length, pain radiating from his body. "You forget, I've had thousands of years to learn to embrace agony. To thrive off it. This pain is nothing compared to what I've suffered before."

A deep sadness swept through her at that statement.

Right before Stolas dove into the shadows of the burned out vault, the queen held up a hand.

Her amber eyes met Haven's. "You asked if I would form an alliance with you. Become an immortal and this horn I wear around my neck is yours—along with my entire army. Or what's left of it, anyway."

"Why?"

"Because one of my daughters gave her life for yours, and the other, who won't even take an order from me, her mother and *queen*, just obeyed you without hesitation. Only Freya's daughter could command such loyalty."

Haven watched, speechless as the queen padded over to Ember and slipped the blood-splattered silver horn over her daughter's neck. The queen looked over her shoulder at Haven. "For when you become immortal. I know that, in the meantime, my daughter will keep this hallowed horn, bestowed upon the Morgani from Freya herself, safe."

Ember's eyes glinted with pride as she nodded. "With my life."

"And," the queen added. "My daughter knows if she ever wants to come home, she is welcome."

Haven sank against Stolas. Their wolves howled, leaping after Haven and Stolas as they plunged into the smoky darkness below. Knowing what was at stake now, she was all the more determined to become immortal.

Whatever it took.

FORTY-THREE

The queen was wrong. The portal leading to the Demon Realm didn't take them straight into the city of Cimmeria. Instead, they slipped from that murky darkness into a cool stretch of empty desert at least an hour's walk from the city. Perhaps the portal's magick was failing, or the queen had been confused.

Either way, Haven wasn't prepared to slog across a desert in little more than a strip of iridescent too-thin fabric, a heavy cloak that dragged the sand, and sandals.

After a few quiet minutes of panting and trudging over the endless dunes, it became apparent the sandals were more hindrance than help so she trashed them. The cloak was a nuisance, but the temperature was dropping fast, which meant it would soon be a necessity.

Normally they would have flown the rest of the way, skimming through the dark sky toward the rising oasis crowning the horizon. Normally Haven wouldn't have thought twice about slipping into Stolas's embrace and taking to the air.

But as soon as they entered the Demon Realms, Haven turned to Stolas to complain about the location—and froze.

His eyes were glassy, the color of old bone. His breathing was shallow and labored. And his skin had taken on a waxy pallor that she'd only seen on corpses.

Jaw clenched and brow sheened with sweat, Stolas had reached for her. She hid her alarm with a soft laugh, making some excuse about needing to walk under the stars to clear her head.

He didn't even argue, which was so unlike him that her alarm turned to full-blown terror.

It wasn't continued blood loss. His new shirt was still pristine, and the few cuts she could see were fading pink lines.

He needed to feed. She had no idea how long he could last before he succumbed. But this, whatever this was, felt like more than just a sustenance issue.

And why hadn't he given in to his baser nature and tried to feed on *her* yet? Especially after his cruel warning the night before?

She glanced sideways at him, and her heart raced into a hammering rhythm as she took in his half-closed eyes.

"Can I ask you a question?" she blurted, hoping conversation would keep him awake.

She took his grunt as a yes.

Where to even start? "How often do you need to feed?"

"Every . . . few days."

That often? "So in Shadoria?"

He released a haggard breath. "There are a few lightcasters more than willing to help."

"Because of the feelings of euphoria you give them in return?"

He gave a near-imperceptible nod, eyes cloudy and unfocused as they stared ahead. "Their light magick, like yours, comes from being able to access the energy of the Nihl, so when I magick-let a lightcaster, I'm not actually taking anything from them."

"Because you're using their doorway to take directly from the Nihl."

Another faint jerk of his head.

She caught her bottom lip between her teeth. "What does blood-letting feel like? Is it similar to magick-letting?"

The line of his shoulders stiffened, his wings twitching. "Blood-letting is an archaic custom. It's . . . messier. More primal. Not as pure as magick-letting."

"Then why do some, like your sister, prefer it?"

"Because it satisfies a primal urge that lurks deep within all Seraphians. It isn't the blood itself that gives us pleasure, it's . . . it's all of it."

An icy wind blew back her cloak, and her breath caught as she took in her faded runemarks. They had gone from luminescent swirls of light to a faint flicker against her skin.

Worse, the place where she felt her magick reside was now a barren hole. Whenever she tried to reach for it, a cold, unpleasant sensation, like nerves grinding together deep within, made her stop.

A shiver swept through her. Wrapping the cloak tighter around her chest, she surveyed the landscape. Two enormous golden moons illuminated the night air to a pre-dawn glow, giving the false hope the sun would rise any moment. All around them stretched a sea of sand. Rising like a sea serpent against those choppy waves was the city of Cimmeria, a metropolis of colorful buildings, tents, and a dark palace. Engraved against the first swollen moon, the domed behemoth seemed straight out of a twisted fairy tale.

Above it all, winged shapes churned and dove. Demons? Something else? Did it really matter if they never made it past this endless wasteland of sand and wind?

Stolas's breathing was ragged now, and she pressed a hand to her mouth. He looked a few steps from falling flat on his face. If that happened she wouldn't be able to move him.

Not on her own.

And even if she somehow found a way to drag him, there was no way she could make it to the palace.

"Stop looking at me like that," he rasped.

"Like what?"

"Like I'm . . . dying."

"Are you?" Panic edged her voice.

He arched an eyebrow, the act taking more effort than it should have, and cast a sidelong glance her way. "Your faith in me is . . . overwhelming."

His sarcasm wasn't enough to comfort her. Not nearly. Knowing Stolas, his last dying breath would be reserved for some wry comment.

Desperation kicked in, and she slipped her arm around Stolas's waist. His body jerked at the touch. Thinking he was about to make another sarcastic comment while refusing her help, she prepared to argue . . .

But he didn't seem to notice.

Bad—this was bad. Stolas would never let her help him unless . . . unless he was in serious trouble. Maybe not dying.

Some of the tension lifted as they crested a soft rise and she spotted a long stretch of multicolored tents. The makeshift town converged on a black river that led straight into the city. The river was wide enough to accommodate barges and smaller vessels, and they cut across the twin moons dancing on the water's surface.

Stolas touched her arm and nodded toward a collection of scarlet tents off to the side. "There." A pause. "Haven, do you understand what I have to do?"

Her heart ratcheted into a hammering pace as she recognized the weakness in his voice. "You need a lightcaster to feed from."

His brow furrowed. "Yes, but here there's only one way to drain a lightcaster."

Only one way? Oh—*oh.* "You need to blood-let."

It wasn't a question, but he nodded anyway, his haggard features stilling as he studied her reaction.

"You don't need my permission."

"You say that, but the act itself is . . . barbaric. My basest nature will be released. I will try to keep it contained but . . . your body will instinctively react in ways that may alarm you."

She held his stare. "You don't have to hide what you are around me, Stolas."

"Remember that later," he murmured as, together, they staggered down the dune, grunting and gasping for breath. Sweat rivered down her spine and pasted strands of hair to her forehead. A soft rushing sound drew her focus to Stolas's wings as they dragged along the sand, carving twin lines in their wake. Between the lines unspooled a thin dark ribbon of blood.

His injured wing wasn't healing. A sense of urgency spurred her faster. Stolas was fastidious about keeping his feathers preened and would never let his wings touch the ground.

By the time they reached the scarlet tents, most of his impressive weight was resting on her shoulder. She swung her head side to side, panic eating away at her vision. The tents were arranged in a circle around a courtyard. Divans and pillows were scattered in various places, and people lounged in every available space. Fires roared from gravel pits.

A sweet, metallic scent haunted the air, and something about it made her go cold all over.

"What is this place?" she whispered.

Stolas slowly managed to lift his head. His eyes were faded slits. "Demonai."

That one word meant nothing to her. Demonai? Was that different than the Demon Lords? Shifting on her feet, she glanced around. Patrons were beginning to stare, but no one came forward to offer help.

Anxiety turned to anger as she swiveled around, stumbling, searching for someone to offer assistance.

A female wearing a sheer silver gown uncurled from a large magenta cushion and approached. Black hair fell to her waist, a pair of misshapen horns twisting around her head. Her eyes were purely feline, the slashed pupil surrounded by a startling yellow.

"Let me guess," Haven whispered to Stolas. "This is a demonai."

The demonai's disturbing eyes lingered on Stolas. "Drenat immortium da moi taiga."

Haven frowned as she tried to place the melodic language. Even the way the slippery words trickled from her lips, melded together like a whispered chant, felt foreign. "I don't—I don't understand." Haven grunted as she shifted Stolas's weight, bracing against the pressure. "He needs to feed. *Feed. Now.*"

"Mortalisium or Solisati?" The female's eyes glinted with a newfound cunning as the female realized Haven didn't speak her language. "Mortal or Solis or both?"

The demonai's command of Solissian was paltry, at best, her thick accent jumbling the words. But Haven understood her meaning.

As far as how to answer the demonai, Haven was completely clueless. The truth was, she didn't know how any of this worked. She didn't know what Stolas needed or if he had a preference.

She hated how powerless that made her feel, but she hid her emotions behind a casual smile. "Whoever has the strongest light magick."

The female lifted a dark brow as she appraised Haven. Then she said in her thick, choppy accent, "That would be you, blood slave."

Blood slave? So that was their cover. Haven would have a discussion with Stolas about that later . . . after he survived.

"Sorry, I'm all out of magick to give."

The female shrugged and nodded to a nearby tent. Then she grinned darkly at Haven, revealing a mouthful of sharp silver teeth and two larger incisors. "I can join you—"

"Rasati corath!" Haven flinched at Stolas's gravelly voice.

She didn't need to understand the demon tongue to translate the dismissal. At least she knew he was still coherent.

To a degree. A fading degree that wouldn't last much longer.

The female shrugged again before sauntering over to a couple on a divan.

Haven struggled under Stolas's weight as she guided him toward the tent. "So we don't have to pay?"

He made some noise that sounded like a grunt. "No, they will be . . . overjoyed to have me . . . drain them."

She truly couldn't tell if he was being arrogant or telling the truth.

"Tell me they're not slaves."

"The only true lightcaster slaves are inside the Demon cities. The rest are . . ." He dragged in a breath. "Former slaves turned addicts or . . . or free Solis trapped here after the war."

Many blamed the Demon Lords and their demon trade for the war and the Shadeling's fall. Portals that had connected their two worlds for countless millennia had been destroyed.

Or so they had been told.

If the Morgani Queen still had an active portal to the Demon Realm then others surely did as well.

Somewhere nearby a flutist began a haunting tune as they neared the large tent. The same cloying metallic aroma drifted from the half-open flap leading inside. As they crossed the threshold, the scent became near overpowering. Incense smoke layered the room, illuminated by the remnants of a dying fire inside a brass chimenea and hanging sconces that harbored a sage green flame.

Two females reclined on a large couch. Just like Haven, the faint shimmer of fleshrunes appeared on their arms and legs, only visible when the light hit at the right angle.

Solis.

"Leave," Stolas growled.

She thought he was addressing the second Solis female until he turned to her, his face near unrecognizable. His features had hardened, shadows trapping in the severe hollows beneath his cheeks. His pupils were so dilated that only a thin band of silvery-white remained. The tips of his fangs glinted softly, their size swelling his upper lip. "This is going to be unpleasant, Haven."

She shook her head. "I can handle it."

Like Netherfire she was going to leave him alone and defenseless in this state.

He moved so fast he became a blur.

When he resolved from the shadows behind the first Solis female, Haven realized her mistake.

There was nothing defenseless about him.

His wings instinctively stretched to form a wall around the bed, either for privacy or to keep the females corralled, she didn't know. Not that they needed much corralling. Their eyes were slits of need as they rubbed against him.

Stolas's arms held the female tight to him, one arm banded across her upper chest, the other around her waist. He had held Haven the same way hundreds of times before, but there was nothing affectionate in this embrace. More like the way a cat held down a flailing bird with its paw before burying its teeth into the bird's breast.

But the only distress the female in his arms displayed was impatience as she moved her long dirty blonde hair to bare her neck—

Stolas's fangs sank deep into the flesh below her jaw. Her mouth peeled wide, but instead of a scream, a moan of pleasure slipped from the Solis female's throat. She writhed seductively against him—or tried, but Stolas growled, arms tightening until she relaxed and gave herself to a different kind of pleasure.

Haven knew Stolas was trying to make the event as civilized as possible. Every time the female in his arms moved, even a tiny bit, he growled low in warning. The female's lips were parted, eyes dazed and pupils swollen.

And her runemarks were burning brighter and brighter in tandem with her growing ecstasy.

Gathering her courage, Haven let her gaze drop lower to where Stolas's lips pressed flush against the wound. She thought it would be messier. Louder. But he drank with a quiet efficiency that was undoubtedly for Haven's benefit.

The other female tried to touch him—

He snarled, sending her scuttling back to wait her turn, and Haven found herself glad.

Glad.

Her stomach clenched oddly as heat swept through her. Heat and a whisper of anger—of jealousy. Not that he was feeding from the Solis females, although a part of her was bothered they could offer him the life blood she refused.

No, she remembered the brief taste of euphoria he had given her. How absolutely wonderful it felt. Like liquid sunshine.

She remembered and she longed to feel that ecstasy again. To experience that inside his arms. Which was incredibly confusing because at the same time she was repulsed by the thought.

A soft cry of pleasure drew Haven's focus to the female in Stolas's arms again. Pure white light swirled inside her heavy-lidded eyes as Stolas's euphoria filled her.

Sweat cropped Haven's skin. Sweltering—the room was suddenly sweltering, as if a fire blazed to life somewhere nearby. She sucked in gulps of the metallic too-sweet air as the tent slowly started to spin.

Wiping her sweat-stained palms on her dress, she looked from the female's face to Stolas—to see his gaze locked on her as he drank.

He was silent, and the only reason she knew he was actively draining any blood was by the way his throat rhythmically bobbed.

Every dip was followed by a surge of dark golden light inside his eyes.

A shock of fire speared her middle, filling her the way the golden light swelled inside his irises. Even with his lips pressed against the Solis female's throat, Haven caught the way the corners of his mouth lifted in a wicked, inviting smile.

Her body responded in kind. Coils of heat tightening in her belly. Her pulse lashed against her neck, throbbing almost painfully as her flesh began to ache.

If she didn't leave she would do something regrettable. Darting toward the door, she lurched beneath the flap. The cool winds washed over her in an icy wave and she nearly stumbled before finding purchase against a sturdy wooden pole. She leaned back as she willed her heart to slow and her breathing to calm.

Raw emotions knotted behind her breast, but no matter how hard she tried to disentangle what she felt, the only thing she could pinpoint was frustration.

She wasn't even sure why she fled. Was it the savagery of the act itself? Or the fact that it didn't disgust her like it should?

That she had stared right into his eyes as he fed from another being and she'd felt . . .

Nope. Thumping her head back, she exhaled, watching her milky breath spill into the courtyard.

You're in love with a monster.

She dipped her chin to stare at her bare feet, and when she looked back up, the demonai female from earlier was watching her across the fire, her primordial eyes glinting above a sharp grin.

The glow of several pairs of eyes watching Haven around the courtyard soon became too many to count, and her hand went to the sword hilt at her waist, fingers curling and uncurling against the cool steel.

The Demon Realm was a land of unfathomable mysteries, but one thing was becoming alarmingly clear.

Here there were only two categories one fell in: predator or prey.

And her light magick cast her squarely in the latter.

FORTY-FOUR

Despite the frigid temperature, the greedy eyes all around her, and the knowledge of what was happening inside the tent at her back, Haven struggled to keep her eyes open. She hadn't slept more than a few hours for days, possibly weeks. She would just sit until Stolas came out.

The sand was soft against her legs. With half-frozen fingers, she settled the fur-lined cloak over her body, tucked in her icy toes, and closed her eyes.

Just for a moment.

She immediately fell into a half-sleep, disrupted by nightmares where she would awaken to find herself surrounded by demonai with demented eyes and fangs and tails.

It could have been minutes or hours later when she flicked her eyes open to Stolas leaning over her. It came to her that he could have been one of the demonai with his horns and wings.

At the same time, caught in the murky grip of dreams and waking, it came to her that she didn't care.

"Are you better now?" she murmured.

"Yes."

"I'm glad you don't have a tail. Horns I can handle, but . . . I don't think I could deal with that."

Amusement played over his lips as he stared at her quietly for a few breaths. His fangs had yet to retract, moonlight glinting the curved points. He slipped an arm beneath her knees and another around her waist. Cool air assailed her back as he lifted her up, resting her against his chest. Her legs ached, her feet throbbing and numb, and she couldn't feel her butt.

He, on the other hand, was warm, unusually so, especially given the cold outside. He must have just left the tent.

A surge of bitterness welled inside her at the memory. "I can walk."

"You're freezing," he murmured. "I apologize, I should have made sure you had shelter before I . . . fed."

"You were dying so I forgive you. But this dress was a mistake. I've worn sashes that were warmer."

"I was *not* dying." He shifted her in his arms. "And this dress will never be a mistake on you."

"Where are we going?"

"I've secured us a small tent for the night. It's not glamorous, but there's a fire and blankets."

"And I need to be carried there?" she asked, tilting her head to meet his eyes. They were swollen with magick, the luminescent golden glow seeping out of them brighter than the moons above.

"Carrying you into my tent tells the demonai out there who have been watching you all night that you're mine."

Mine. Something fluttered inside her chest. "My, aren't you a greedy Shade Lord?"

A dark smile curled at the edges of his mouth. "You don't know the half of it."

Her heart sped up. "You can't possibly still be . . . hungry."

"Can't I?" he taunted softly. "Beastie, darkcasters are ravenous by nature. We drink from lightcasters for two reasons: necessity and pleasure. Every demonai in this camp has been sated ten times over this evening, and yet they still burn with the primal need to drain your essence."

She shivered. *And do you burn with that same need?*

The unsaid question hovered between them, along with a million more. Questions she might never dare ask for fear of the answer.

Her hair slipped over her shoulder as he dipped into a tent barely a quarter the size of the one before. Stolas had to stoop to keep from brushing his horns on the pitched ceiling. Haven's entire body shivered as the warmth from the brass chimenea in the center met her cold skin. Her limbs were stiff and achy as he settled her onto a pile of soft tan and black furs.

He turned to hang their cloaks on one of the tent poles, and she let her eyelids drift shut as the heat rolled over her.

When her eyes blinked open, she found Stolas watching her beneath heavy lids. Firelight caught in the dress's strange metallic sheen, highlighting every curve from the cliff of her collarbone to the dip between her breasts.

His ashen-silver lashes dipped as he let his gaze roam lower.

"Definitely not a mistake," he murmured, voice thick with sarcasm and something else as he dragged his attention to the fire. The new logs shifted, flames leaping from the chimenea, crackling and popping.

She curled into a ball beneath the furs, eyelids drooping, and watched Stolas settle in front of the fire. He stretched out his long legs. His wings were facing her, their normally glossy sheen dulled by dust and sand. One hand rested over his side, pressed as if to quell pain.

Haven propped up on an elbow. "So you're all better now?"

The memory of him stumbling, wings dragging in the sand, was hard to shake.

"How do you define better?"

"Are you going to die?"

"Not tonight."

Smartass. "Are you not going to sleep?"

It felt like a silly question. Noctis slept as much as Solis did, which was very little. But they did need at least a few hours a night.

"I can rest my eyes here," he answered without looking back.

"Are you worried the demonai will come for me during the night?"

"No. They know you belong to me."

"Belong?" She lifted a sleepy brow, suddenly far from tired. "To you?"

"Semantics." She could tell by his lilting tone he was grinning. "They *assume* you belong to me because I just carried you into my tent. Normally a lightcaster of your rare powers would be the property of a Demon Lord, but that fits into our story."

"Which is?"

"That I am here to sell you to Lord Malik."

She tensed beneath the covers. Sell. That word flooded her veins with violence. Violence and shame and a powerlessness she swore to never feel again.

"If that bothers you, we can make a new strategy."

She shook her head. Stolas knew how she felt about slavery, and he wouldn't have made the plan if it wasn't their best option. Pretending to be a blood slave, however reprehensible, gave them the highest chance of infiltrating the palace and taking back the painting.

"So I'm safe—for tonight, at least?" she pressed.

His shoulders dipped slightly as he gave a heavy sigh. "From them? Most likely. Although your intoxicating scent of magick is probably driving them half-mad with bloodlust as we speak."

"You said I was safe from *them*. Does that mean I'm not safe from you?"

"Bed," he growled.

She rolled onto her side and closed her eyes, but tired as she was, she couldn't sleep. His warning about what to expect when he fed came to mind. Was he purposefully staying away from her because he thought she was disgusted by what she saw?

Perhaps she was, in a way. But beyond the instinctive fear she'd initially felt watching him blood-let, there was a new intimacy to their relationship.

He had let her see him at his most terrifying. A tiny shiver swept through her as she remembered how he had dared to hold her stare as he drank from the Solis female.

And the look that passed between them . . .

She lifted her head. "What did it feel like earlier? When you fed?"

He froze. "Why would you ask me that?"

"I'm . . . curious. I want to know what it is about the act that Seraphians crave."

"No, you don't."

"Try me. I may not be as squeamish as you think."

He sighed. "It's feeling a weaker creature trapped beneath us. The power of holding their future in our hands. Having complete control. It's feeling their heartbeat weaken as we slowly drain their life. It's making someone moan with absolute, mind-numbing pleasure one second and fear the next."

He was trying to upset her, but there was truth in his words. Her dry throat convulsed as she tried to swallow. "So the high comes from the act itself?"

"It comes from both. The magick in the blood we drain reacts with our deep-rooted predatory instincts to form a release, if you will. Call it bloodlust or something else, there's truly no name to accurately describe the experience."

Bloodlust. Considering what she witnessed in the tent, that name seemed more than fitting . . .

"And you enjoy that?" she whispered, already knowing the answer. "The power and control, the savagery?"

He stared quietly into the fire. "Do you want me to lie?"

"I want you to trust me with the truth."

"Yes, I enjoy it."

"All of it?"

The tips of his wings curled. "All of it. Deep down, beyond the veneer of manners and civility, that is who I am, Haven."

She managed to stifle her shiver. "I don't believe you."

"Then you are a fool."

"Stolas."

He stilled at her voice.

"Come here."

He was quiet for a long time. Every wild beat of her heart that followed reminded her she was playing a dangerous game. But the way that he had looked at her as he fed, the powerful longing in his face . . .

That wasn't duty that passed between them. It was something so much more.

He unfolded to his feet. She watched him beneath heavy lids as he prowled over, moving with that fluidity and grace that once unnerved her and now . . . what?

Made her feel safe? No—not safe. She would never be truly safe around him.

There was a soft patter of sand falling against the ground as he shook out his wings, the play of firelight against his midnight and indigo feathers mesmerizing.

The flames at his back cast deep shadows over his features. "Haven, being this close to you so soon after feeding—it could be dangerous."

"I won't hurt you."

He didn't laugh. "For you."

She lifted the fur, noting the way his gaze darted to the curve of her neck. "I trust you."

A low chuckle more growl than laugh vibrated his chest. "You shouldn't. You really, really shouldn't."

"How about this? I am going to tell you what I do know about you. For each statement that's true, you come a step closer. False, you take a step back."

"Are you sure you want to play this game, Haven?"

She stared directly into those luminous, teasing, *dangerous* eyes. "Yes."

"Your naivety is alarming," he murmured, but he nodded.

Her pulse was lashing her wrists. Every part of her felt raw, exposed— but he'd bared his soul, dark and savage as it was, and that trust resonated deep inside her.

Now it was her turn.

"You use your savage nature as an excuse to push me away."

He didn't say a word as he took a step closer.

"You push me away because you are afraid of hurting me."

Another step forward.

"You crave my blood, my magick, and you feel guilty about it."

He retreated.

"Okay, you crave my blood and magick and you don't feel guilty, but you worry you will act on those impulses and that I will hate you."

He reclaimed his step.

She dragged in a deep breath. "In Solethenia, after the ball . . . that wasn't out of duty. You . . . enjoyed it."

Even with his lips steeped in shadow, she knew they were grinning as he drew closer. He was at the foot of the covers now. His familiar scent of irises and blood mandarin rolling over her.

Gathering her courage, she tilted her head to stare up at him. "When you looked at me while feeding earlier, you wanted me."

Her stomach fluttered and churned as she waited for his answer.

He loosed a soft breath. "Haven—"

"You want me still. Not out of duty. Not because of an oath. Not to feed on me—although that craving is still there as well. You *desire* me."

A slight tremor of anticipation and nerves swept through her, and she suddenly found it hard to breathe. It came to her that she had no idea what she was doing. That Stolas was probably right, this was dangerous, but not for the reasons he thought.

Giving her heart to Stolas Darkshade was foolish for about a million reasons.

But she was done being ruled by fear. If today had taught her anything, it was that the future did not belong to them. They only had the promise of this moment.

And she refused to live one more precious second of that borrowed time afraid.

Refused to be the girl without a voice.

The girl who accepted a smaller life because it was easier.

Who didn't take what she truly wanted because it was safer.

Who dimmed her wants, her needs, her magick to make others comfortable.

She finally knew exactly what she wanted, and he was standing right in front of her.

Lifting the fur covers, she said, "Come here, Stolas."

And he did.

FORTY-FIVE

Stolas let out a frustrated snarl. "This will end badly."

She was startled by how bright his eyes still were. The golden glow was turning brassy yellow, the center already fading. By tomorrow, she would bet the light would be the yellow ring she was used to. "Define badly."

He went inhumanly still.

Propping on her side, she slowly reached over to touch his face.

His hand shot out, capturing her wrist. The flesh was still tender from where his fingers clenched the night before, and she winced.

He caught her reaction, his magick-swollen eyes sliding to her wrist. "Why did the Goddess make your kind so damn fragile?"

"Then don't break me."

"Haven—"

"No." She brought her other hand up. A low growl started in his chest as she dragged her fingertips softly down the ragged cliff of his cheek—

In one quick movement, he rolled on top of her, his hands pinning her wrists to the soft ground. "Enough."

"No."

He was staring down at her, his eyes riveted to her lips. His fingers around her wrists were gentle, so very gentle.

"I want you, Stolas." Her confession broke open her hard surface to the vulnerability beneath, but she managed to hold his stare. "I know now that you want me too but you're afraid you will hurt me."

"I *will* hurt you."

She didn't know if he meant physically or otherwise. "No, you won't. Let me prove it to you."

She tugged a hand free and slipped it through his tousled hair.

He froze, a puff of air trickling from his parted lips. A low groan followed. "Do you know why my fangs are still retracted, Haven? I am still in the thralls of bloodlust. Every beat of your heart, every flicker of fear you try to hide arouses the greedy monster inside me."

Those soft strands slid through her fingers as she grasped the base of his horn, and then she pulled him to her. Surprise flashed in his eyes, followed by something darker.

Something that should have terrified her, but didn't.

"And what about this?" she whispered. She let her teeth graze his bottom lip. Let her tongue flick out. "Which part of you does that arouse?"

She felt the last of his restraint melt away as he settled on top of her. His mouth crushed hers. His tongue parted her lips, first claiming and then softer as he explored her. The tips of his fangs pricked her bottom lip, metallic warmth filling her mouth.

Growling, he kissed her harder, the taste of her blood mixing with the taste of him.

"This is agony," he whispered.

Heart racing, she curled her legs around his waist. "And now?"

"Such a wicked thing," he half-chuckled, half-growled. He lifted back to look at her, his eyes luminous, spilling magick straight from the Nihl. "What shall I do with you?"

"Take off my dress."

His jaw flexed. Still holding her gaze, he caught the slit of her gown, his knuckles scraping up her thigh as he dragged the fabric up. She closed her eyes as he tugged the silky material over her head, and when she reopened them, he was drinking her in.

"And now?" he murmured.

"Your turn."

She watched him undress. First his shirt and then his pants. In the low firelight, shadows trapped in his muscles, highlighting every ridge and curve. Runes, he was beautiful. A dark God risen from the Netherworld.

"Now?" he asked, his husky voice settling low and warm in her belly.

"Come here."

He did as told. "So demanding. What else?"

"Kiss me."

He did, sliding over her as his mouth captured hers. And the soft, caring way he kissed her this time, as if she might break, was almost enough to undo her.

Her lips parted in a moan as his hands began to move over her body. Fire followed his caresses, inflaming every inch of her flesh as he stroked closer and closer to where she wanted.

"Tell me," she rasped against his mouth. "When you looked at me earlier, what were you thinking about?"

His growl tickled her wet, swollen lips. "Would you like me to show you?"

"Yes."

He tsked. "Where are those manners?"

"Yes, *please*."

Her back arched as his fingers finally went where she wanted them to. Wicked, throbbing heat surged to meet them, rolling down her middle in searing waves.

His growl rattled the tent, and he stilled for a moment before resuming, only this time slowly. So damned slowly.

At the same time, his mouth coasted down her throat.

Tasting her. Gliding against her skin so very softly. She could feel his primal need to use his fangs. Could feel them dancing over the tender areas of her flesh.

"Such exquisite torture," he murmured. "I think it only fair you suffer a little too."

Her hips were moving in frustrated circles. He snarled, pinning her with one hand while the other continued building the pressure inside her with slow, halting strokes meant to torture and tease.

Her belly tightened as she remembered last time, but—

"More," she whispered. "I need to feel you. *All* of you."

Something dark and greedy rippled across his features. She went to lift her legs around him, but his hand gripped her thighs. "Slowly, Haven."

Holding her stare, he slid his hands behind her knees and then guided her legs until they locked behind him. His jaw was clenched taut as he settled low and began to kiss her. The sensuality of that kiss lit a fire inside so hot she half-expected to open her eyes and see flames dancing off her skin.

She felt his length press against her. "When I looked at you, Haven? This was what I imagined doing."

A moan parted her lips as he began to fill her, slowly—so damned slowly. The muscles of his neck and jaw trembled as he fought to control his darker instincts. Pressure swelled to fill her. She tried to quell that ache as she tightened her legs around his waist. Tried to force him deeper.

"Such a greedy Beastie," he growled as he kissed her.

She slipped her arms around his neck and closed her eyes, drowning in the feel of Stolas. His scent, his lithe, powerful body, his amused growl. His hips were moving in maddeningly slow, teasing circles. That deep wire of tension growing tauter down her middle, sharper, until it felt razor-edged.

"Is this what you meant by belonging to you?" she whispered.

He snarled, moving faster, and she quickly angled her hips so that he plunged deeper—

She cried out, and his fangs clamped down softly on her bottom lip in warning.

But she was moving against him now, that exquisite pressure building and building.

She felt something primal and raw take hold as he whispered, "Someone needs a lesson on how to behave."

His mouth covered hers. And when his tongue slid between her lips, he buried himself all the way inside her. She moaned, his tongue spearing deeper as he rocked against her. That exquisite ache became a coiling sensation of pleasure that tightened with every thrust.

She lost herself in what followed. The tortuous dance as he dragged her to the edge of pleasure again and again only to rip it away.

Cruelly, wickedly. Over and over and over until—

That razor-edged tension whipsawed through her like lightning, followed by wave after wave of pleasure. As the last wave crested over her, Stolas shuddered, letting out a soft groan. They lay there for what could have been minutes or hours, entangled together, not saying a word as her legs trembled and sensation slowly returned to her body.

When he finally rolled onto his side and pulled her to him, a part of her longed to stay like this forever. In this moment, she wasn't the Goddess-Born and he wasn't a Seraphian Prince.

They were simply . . . lovers.

He brushed his finger over a flaky spot on her hip. "Is that Golemite blood?"

"Goddess Above," she groaned, surprised by how hoarse her voice was. "I hope this Demon Lord likes his slaves bathed. I don't think I can take another night covered in sweat and gore."

"But being covered in the blood of your enemies suits you." He propped onto his elbow, a lock of moon-white hair sliding over his forehead as he looked down at her. Firelight glinted inside the glossy black surface of his horns. "Say the word and we will find another way to enter the palace."

"No. This is the only way." She tilted her head to stare up at him. "Told you that you wouldn't hurt me."

He chuckled darkly as his thumb began lazily circling her navel. "Gloating, on the other hand, doesn't suit you."

"Doesn't it?" As she smiled, she thought she could see all the different facets of him—monster, broken prince, protector, friend, and now lover—struggling for purchase. "Then what does?"

"I can think of a few things," he purred as his fingers stroked lower. *Lower.* "Like . . . this."

She gasped at his touch, and when he brought his lips to her neck, kissing her collarbone, her shoulder, his hand still moving so gently . . .

"That's better," he murmured.

This time, they made love while half-asleep, moving together in a slow, sensual rhythm until they shattered together. And afterward, as he kissed her cheek with a tenderness she would have sworn him incapable of a few hours ago, she couldn't escape the sensation of something clicking into place.

This felt *right*, righter than anything she'd ever done before.

Wrapped in the self-proclaimed monster's arms, she tumbled into the most deep and restful sleep she'd had in months. She dreamt that she was a white and gold-tipped wolf hunting across the dunes alongside a midnight-black wolf with yellow-ringed eyes.

The dark wolf howled, and she answered it with a resounding call of her own, so loud that it reached into the heavens and shook the stars from the sky.

FORTY-SIX

Haven had sworn she would never let herself be taken as a slave again. Never let herself be bought and sold like property. And yet, here she was, shackled to a group of Solis slaves in front of the Cimmerian palace. A soft silver mist clung low to the ground, obscuring the wide onyx palace steps that led up to an imposing iron gate. Serpents were carved into the doors, their hissing heads twisted around the sharp gold finials.

Ignoring the bite of magick seeping from her shackles into her wrists, she craned her neck to study the palace. An architectural wonder of arches and towers, the dark stone structure was capped by three enormous gold domes.

It was perhaps the largest palace she'd ever seen, which made the poverty and sickness surrounding it even harder to fathom. Beggars lined the dark cobbled streets, and pickpockets hid in alleyways, waiting to filch what they could from demonai nobles leaving the palace.

In that way, she supposed, the Demon Realm was similar to her own world.

There were other similarities. There was a sun that rose and fell—although it was a distant orb muddled by layers of dense clouds that gave everything a faint chartreuse glow. Or perhaps that was the pale green runelight lanterns and lamp posts positioned on every corner and building. The same light flickered from the palace windows and archways.

The markets were also much like the ones in Penryth. The vendors haggled. The patrons claimed they were being robbed. The thieves grabbed what they could.

It all felt so very normal.

At least until she took a closer look at the objects being sold. Monstrous skulls the size of watermelons, jars filled with reptilian eyes that tracked movement, and herbs she couldn't begin to pronounce. Then there were the demon markets where everything from demon horns to actual demons could be purchased.

But it was the similarity of the people of this realm that was the most jarring. They looked like mortals in nearly every way. Contrasted against the demonai, the nobles who claimed demon blood and possessed some degree of dark magick, they almost seemed two different races.

The palace gates creaked as they slid open, tendrils of mist curling in their wake. A demonai servant appeared, cloaked and stooped. Her heart sped up as he hobbled down the stairs toward the slaves, and for once she was glad she missed breakfast, her stomach churning.

Remember the reason you let Stolas pretend to sell you to the demonai slaver this morning. Remember why you tolerate the shackles and leering grins. Remember who you are.

But her flesh remembered too. It recalled years ago when Damius had placed an iron shackle on her ankle and staked it deep into the sand. It could still feel the searing pain as weeks turned to months and her flesh turned raw and infected beneath the metal.

Fighting through her panic, she managed to lift her dry lips in a timid smile, mimicking the expression of the other Solis chosen to be presented to the Lord Malik. Most were probably already addicts, and yet it was hard to reconcile their hopefulness with her rage.

Harder still to stand there looking grateful as the hunched demonai servant appraised her, when what she really wanted was to take the dagger hidden along her thigh and ram it through his misshapen skull.

But she wanted immortality more, and somewhere in the recesses of this dark palace, in a tower built just for her, was the Cimmerian Demon Lord's mistress—and her mother's painting.

So Haven looked obedient instead of murderous. She even twirled a little for the small, hunched demonai with pointed ears and a bat-like nose.

And leaned against a column close by, she felt Stolas's stare. Her cheeks heated, and last night's events came back to her in a fiery flash. If not for the subtle ache between her legs, she might have thought it all a dream.

Haven flexed her wrists, trying not to stare at the faint red marks her shackles had rubbed into her skin. She was settled inside a large chamber, one of hundreds tucked away in a forbidden area of the palace. Only female mortal servants and the Demon Lord were allowed to roam the halls.

If Haven managed to become the Demon Lord's favorite, she might even get a nicer room with her name on the door.

A fresh round of disgust filled her as she realized how much the arrangement resembled the royal stables back in Penryth. Except, when one of King Boteler's prized stallions became lame, the poor beast was killed.

Here, the women were simply thrown outside the palace walls to fend for themselves. Most were addicts by then, and they ended up in the camps.

Killing them would have been more merciful.

She clenched her jaw until her teeth ached, focusing on her surroundings to temper her growing rage.

The room was large and airy, with a scattering of furniture—a couch, a loveseat, a few cushions. Brass chimeneas were placed near the couch and the bed, flames crackling behind their grates. A dark teak wardrobe sat in the corner, it's parted doors revealing countless dresses. The bed itself was small, barely large enough for one person, which bolstered her hopeful suspicion that the Demon Lord entertained his blood slaves in his own private chamber.

A door clicked shut, and Haven turned to see the woman who removed Haven's shackles holding a pile of colorful silks in her arms. Her name was Imara, and Haven watched the tiny woman flit around the room, gathering all the lotions, soaps, and tints that were supposed to prepare Haven for the Demon Lord tonight.

Haven sighed as Imara approached with a wide comb made of ivory. She had been surprised to learn the leathery woman was from Haven's realm. Haven had immediately peppered Imara with all kinds of questions, the first being how Imara ended up here.

But the wizened woman, who had to be approaching eighty years, refused to discuss anything beyond the most basic questions.

Was this Haven's room? It was.

Was she locked in? Another yes.

When would she see the Demon Lord?

Imara had stopped jerking at a stubborn rose-gold knot and laughed, revealing a sum total of three teeth.

According to Imara, all new blood slaves were shown off their first night after dinner. The Demon Lord had to *choose* Haven. Otherwise, she would be dragged back to her room and locked inside until she was summoned, which could be days—or years.

The way Imara raked her gaze over Haven, lingering on her tangled hair, crusted with a lovely mixture of blood, ash, and sand, she was going to be in this room for a very long time.

The other option, Imara mentioned offhandedly, was being given tonight to the Demon Lord's friends.

Neither of those options could happen. She needed to be chosen tonight. The Keeper's tower would be near the Demon Lord's rooms for easy access. Once there—well, Haven didn't yet have a plan for how to deal with the Demon Lord.

Stolas was working on that delicate aspect.

After brushing as many of the tangles as she could from Haven's hair, Imara led her to an adjoining bathing chamber. The room was also large, the claw-footed tub big enough for two and somehow already filled with steamy, bubbly water. Floor-to-ceiling windows splashed the city's ethereal light across the dark marble walls.

The dusky light made it feel closer to evening than early afternoon.

Beyond the windows stretched the city, a vast tapestry of interconnected buildings that stretched to the horizon.

Haven sank into the hot bath, sighing as the heat worked into her tired muscles. Imara's knobby fingers shook as she set soaps and oils onto the bath's ledge. A basket of what had to be bread came next, the familiar yeasty smell making her stomach tighten. Along with the bread came a platter of fruits—figs, pomegranates, dark red strawberries, and perfectly ripe peaches. A cup of fragrant tea steamed beside the small feast.

Imara took her job very seriously. Haven needed to somehow be cleaned, painted, and fatted by tonight.

With a fierce nod, the woman left the room. A few seconds later, Haven heard her chamber door close and the lock click. Haven was reaching for a loaf of bread when the faintest prickle of magick made her pause.

"I thought the old crone would never leave," came a familiar voice.

Stolas. The breath caught in her throat as he resolved from the shadows of the far corner. She wasn't the only one who had cleaned up since they last met. His wavy hair was freshly washed and brushed, the pale strands so silken that she imagined running her fingers through them again. The fitted sable jacket he wore was embroidered with silver to match his shirt. It showed off his wide shoulders, muscular chest, and tapered waist.

She couldn't take her eyes off him as he strolled around the side of the tub. His attention drifted to the bathwater. She noticed with alarm that the thick layer of bubbles had melted into a few flimsy islands.

Considering what they had done last night, her modesty felt silly. And yet . . .

His lips curled faintly at the edges, and she exhaled when he shifted that predatory focus to the food on the bath ledge. Plucking a strawberry from the platter, he sat on the edge of the tub, lifted his eyes to hers, and bit into the fruit.

She frowned at the way her heart fluttered. "Did you come here just to eat my food?"

"Oh, did you want all of that?" He jerked his chin toward the platter. "I suppose it is important that you smell delightful tonight."

"You can tell what someone has eaten by scent?"

He took another bite. "Not everything, but certain fragrant fruits have a particular scent. You would be surprised how well strawberries and figs pair with blood."

Goddess Above. The meal was meant to make her *taste* good. "What about the tea?"

His nostrils flared. "That's simply to drug you so that your primal instincts are dulled. Everyone panics their first time."

"How do they know it's my first time?"

He inhaled once more. "Your scent. During your first blood-letting, you are marked."

"Forever?"

He shrugged. "It's a territorial thing."

Pushing the food aside, she crossed her arms over her chest and changed the subject. "How did you get your powers back?"

"Demon blood." He caught her look of disgust and added, "It's the only way to access dark magick inside this realm. Even with what I consumed, my powers are a shadow of what they normally are."

Haven lifted her arm. Bubbles slipped away to reveal the faded glint of her runemarks. "And my powers?"

He shook his head. "Even a drop of demon blood can corrupt a lightcaster's magick."

Her arm splashed back into the water. "And here I was so excited to sample demon blood. Is there anything I *can* consume in this place that won't ultimately harm me?"

"Not likely. But if we play our cards right, we will be gone by morning." He pulled something from his jacket pocket, and she thought she caught him wince slightly at the movement. Was he still injured?

The item clinked as he carefully set it on the platter next to a pomegranate. "This will put the Demon Lord into a very brief compulsion."

She stared at the dark thimble-sized jar. "What is it?"

"Very expensive, that's what it is."

"Did you steal it?"

One side of his mouth quirked. "No."

"Then how?"

"I can be very charming when I need to be."

She nearly laughed . . . until the hungry way the demonai female last night looked at Stolas came to mind, followed by a hot rush of jealousy.

With the females of this realm, he wouldn't have to control his true nature.

He could be himself without apologizing.

Exhaling, she slid her focus back to the elixir. "Do I put it into his drink?"

"Ideally, you would consume it and then . . ."

She would *become* the drink. Bile soured her throat. "I don't think that I can."

"That's good, because if he touches you like that, I will kill him, and that would be very bad for us."

"What about slipping it into a cup full of blood?"

His jaw flexed, and he released a slow breath. "When you're in the room, his entire being will be hyper-focused on you, nothing else. Do you understand?"

Unfortunately, she did. The only hunger the Demon Lord would feel was for her. "Can you tell me anything about him that might help me?"

"All I know is that the Demon Lords all made dark bargains with high level demons. Each one takes on that demon's traits. It's rumored that Malik's demon resembled a serpent."

She wrapped her arms tighter around herself to hide her shiver, but he noticed anyway. His eyes held hers as he kneeled, and again, she noticed a slight wince.

But then he reached out and cupped her chin, and her thoughts zeroed in on the feel of his long, cool fingers pressed gently into her flesh. The way his wings twitched.

He stared at her for a stretched-out beat of her heart. Then he tilted her face up to his. "You don't have to do this. Say the word and we will find another way."

The offer was tempting, but . . . "I can't. Every day that I remain mortal puts us in danger, and I refuse to lose anyone else. By doing this, I can protect those I love."

A fleeting emotion passed over his face, too brief to catalog.

"What?"

He released her chin, hesitated, and then brushed the back of his hand over her cheek. "The way you love others, Haven, it's extraordinary."

He rose before she could respond, his focus drifting over the jar. "Do you still have the dagger?"

"Yes. I hid it beneath my mattress."

"Coat the blade in the elixir. You will have to stab him, and it must be deep for enough of the potion to enter his body. Do you think you can do that?"

She grinned. "With pleasure. Will it kill him?"

"No. Demon Lords are protected by ancient, demonic spells and blood magick. You could stab him a thousand times and the demented bastard would laugh in your face."

Her grin became a pout. "That's disappointing."

"There's a reason the same Demon Lords have existed for countless millennia despite hating one another. Their demented magick makes them practically untouchable."

"But not immune to that." She nodded toward the tiny jar.

"Everyone has their weaknesses."

Her head thunked back on the tub. Stabbing a Demon Lord who kept a harem of slaves was easy. Getting that Demon Lord to choose her over the countless other delectable options so she *could* stab him was . . . trickier. And completely out of her wheelhouse.

"How do I make him choose me tonight?"

"How?" Stolas's face softened. "Do you really not know how marvelous you are?"

She didn't know what to say to that.

He turned his back on her, one hand pressed to his flank. "You will be presented to the Demon Lord and his favorite courtiers late tonight." He studied the outfits Imara had hung along the wall for Haven before holding up a sumptuous gown of pure black. Light caught in the hundreds of diamonds clinging to the deep neckline and sparkled like stars against the night sky. "Wear this and every male—and female—in that room won't be able to tear their eyes from you, including me. If at any moment you feel uncomfortable, find me in the crowd."

"You'll be there?"

"From this moment forward, I won't let you leave my sight."

She arched a brow. "Even when I get out of the bath?"

His grin could only be described as lupine. "Especially then."

She watched him meld back into the shadows. Then she washed her hair and oiled her body, taking her time. Only when the bath was tepid going on cold did she finally rise.

And from somewhere nearby came the faint but unmistakable sound of a low, wicked laugh.

FORTY-SEVEN

Imara came for Haven around midnight. Haven had spent hours after her bath transforming every inch of herself into a vision worthy of a Goddess. Her skin was oiled into a supple sheen. Her hair brushed and styled so that it fell in rose-gold waves down her back. Out of all the jewelry presented to her, she chose two diamond-encrusted black clips in the shape of serpents to hold her hair out of her face.

The style bared the elegant curve of her neck.

Stolas was right; the black gown clung to every curve she possessed, and even Haven had a hard time looking away from her reflection in the full-length dressing mirror.

If Imara thought Haven's chances had dramatically improved, it was hard to tell. She could have been grimacing or smiling as she herded Haven down the runelighted steps toward the dining hall. The dagger—coated in half the jar of potion—was strapped tight to her right thigh, and she welcomed the chafing as it rubbed between her legs.

The pain reminded her she wasn't totally helpless.

A cool weight pressed just beneath her sternum. She'd used strips of the sheets to tie the jar around her chest. Just in case.

Haven was too caught up in the dark beauty of the castle to feel anxious. The walls were created from onyx marble veined in gold, the ornate carpet runners made from strange patterns. Jade chandeliers hung from the arched ceilings, their runelight tinted chartreuse. Demonai servants and nobles strolled the halls.

They passed a demonai girl no older than ten walking a leashed panther. Only when the panther's green eyes met Haven's did she realize the pet was probably a Solis shifter. But it was the pitying look in the panther's eyes that made Haven realize she was leashed too.

Even if her chain was invisible, she was a pet. Groomed and fed and ready to perform for its master.

They had just descended a majestic stairwell leading into a foyer when a figure caught her eye. She wasn't sure quite what drew her attention to the pale blue skinned male in the corner. The deep hood of a lovely silver and turquoise cloak cast most of his features in shadow. But even without being able to see his eyes, she felt him tracking her every move.

"Imara." Haven turned to the hunched woman. "Who is that male?"

But when Haven looked back, he was gone.

Haven let the odd encounter drift from her mind, her growing nerves all but erasing the memory.

The long hem of her gown swished around her legs as she entered the banquet hall. A smoky haze of incense and strange magick layered the air. Demonai of every kind filled the rows of tables. Some were dressed in finery that rivaled Solissian rulers. Some wore travel-stained tunics and breeches. All had the yellow eyes and silver teeth that marked them as demonai, tails and horns and other beastly features hidden beneath cloaks and hoods.

And every single one was filled with a terrifying bloodlust. But it was the quiet figures in the mezzanine above the dais that chilled Haven's blood. It was *their* stares she felt crawling beneath her skin as Imara prodded Haven toward the dais in the center of the room.

Several other Solis females were already lined up. They wore similar form-fitting gowns, cut to reveal as much flesh as possible. By the glazed sheen of their eyes they had all sampled the tea. Goose bumps swept over Haven, and she fought the urge to wrap her arms over her chest as she climbed the steps to join them.

Where was Stolas?

She scoured the crowd for his face, only to come across what had to be the Demon Lord, Malik, looking down from the mezzanine. Her heart stumbled into a frantic pace as she took in the enormous throne he reclined on. The high back resembled a hooded cobra, complete with two giant rubies for the eyes. A crown of fang and bone jutted from his jet black, shoulder-length hair, along with the mostly hidden points of his ears.

That was all the confirmation she needed. Stolas said every Demon Lord could be marked by two attributes: startling beauty and unnaturally pointed ears.

The ears were real, but the rest was an illusion, and she wondered what face this Demon Lord hid behind his pleasing mask—although pleasing might have been a stretch.

Every feature was just a little too sharp, a little too severe to be considered alluring. Then there were his yellow serpentine eyes.

Something in his cold gaze hinted at unfathomable cruelty. Her hand fluttered nervously to where the dagger hid, comforted by the cold bite of steel against her thigh.

And when the Demon Lord's eyes shifted to her and lingered, his razor-sharp focus brimming with insatiable hunger, she knew she would have no problem putting the blade through his heart.

But first she had to convince him to choose her. Acting on instinct, she widened her eyes with feigned fear, letting her gaze flick from the

Demon Lord to the door, like a trapped rabbit. Her chest rose and fell in rapid bursts, the diamonds clinging to her plunging neckline throwing sparkles over her cheeks and arms.

It was easy to act petrified when true fear curdled in her marrow. Runes, she would probably have nightmares about this horrifying realm for years to come.

On some silent signal, a portly mortal servant came and took all but Haven and three of the others away. Haven didn't have to fake the rapid beat of her heart as the lights dimmed. She should have been triumphant that she was still on stage, but her survival instincts had taken over, her body primed and ready to flee at the slightest noise.

Strange, enthralling music slithered through the air, unlike anything she had ever heard before. The slow, haunting tune seemed to surround her. Stroking her skin, warming her flesh, easing her panic as it slowly penetrated deeper and deeper inside her.

She struggled against the magick, especially as her inhibitions began melting away. A restless, pent-up energy spread through her chest, her legs, the pressure growing. Every muscle in her body begged to align with the beat.

The others had already started to dance, rocking in lazy circles, moving in a suggestive way Haven had never seen before.

Despite the pull of the music, a part of her still couldn't bear to dance for the Demon Lord. Her pride refused.

This is what you're here for. But she couldn't do it. Couldn't dance for a bastard like Lord Malik. And it was going to cost her the painting.

Remembering Stolas's words to find him, she swept her gaze over the crowd of demonai, searching for that familiar teasing grin. She found him near the front of the circle, so close she could leap down and touch him.

But he wasn't grinning. Not even close. His features could have been cut from marble as he watched her. Perhaps it was the spelled music affecting him, or the dress, but there was no mistaking the desire burning inside his eyes.

Molten heat blasted down her core. Something jerked taut between them, and the others faded into muffled darkness.

Her world shrank to the music, her body, and Stolas. No one else existed.

Before she knew what was happening, her hips began to sway. Then her arms. Lifting and floating above her as she rocked and drifted with the melody. She took a strange fascination in the way Stolas's focus riveted to her every movement. The way his full lips parted slightly and his pupils swelled as her hips traced little circles over the dais. The hunger in his eyes was like last night as he watched her, but different.

Almost . . . bittersweet.

As if every twist of her body drove a sharp blade of agony and pleasure deeper into his heart.

Their eyes were still locked when the enchanted instruments stopped playing. A rush of cold reality broke through the spell, and Haven froze in place. Stolas's head whipped to the mezzanine, lips peeled in a silent snarl.

She followed his stare, knowing what she would see. But that didn't prepare her for the icy fear that slithered down her spine as Lord Malik pointed at her. The gesture was flippant, as if he was deciding which dessert to have sent to his room.

In a way, she mused darkly, he was.

An icy trickle of horror dripped down her spine, and she met Stolas's eyes. His expression was hard, jaw set, but she caught the near-imperceptible nod meant only for her.

Behind him, a flash of silver and turquoise cloak and ice-blue skin drew her attention. Why was the same odd figure standing so close to Stol—

Cold, bony fingers wrapped around her bicep, the talons indenting her goose-pebbled skin.

She jerked around to find a demonai with patches of dark green skin and limp, skeletal wings clutching her arm.

"Aren't you the lucky one?" he said in guttural, broken Solissian.

Accent or not, his sarcasm was perfectly clear.

She was not lucky. In fact, given the way the demonai looked at her, odds were good that most of Malik's blood slaves never survived the night.

The demonai halted in front of an iron door carved to look like a nest of intertwined snakes. *Moving* snakes. A few of the diamond-shaped heads turned their way, forked tongues tasting the air. They bared their venomous fangs in a hiss.

If a door covered in deadly vipers wasn't a sign to run, Haven didn't know what was.

The demonai whispered a word in Serakki, the demon language, and the snakes settled back into the door as the lock clicked open.

The demonai turned the iron knob, shaped like a viper's head, and jerked his pointed chin beyond.

Even he knew better than to go inside.

As Haven slipped over the threshold and the door slammed shut, a wave of fear rolled over her. She had just willingly entered the private chambers of a ravenous Demon Lord armed only with a dagger, a half-full jar of potion, and her wits.

FORTY-EIGHT

The room was veiled in shadows. Haven breathed through her panic as she worked to still her thundering heart. That would only drive the Demon Lord into a frenzy. She needed him interested, but just enough to distract him from the blade with his name on it.

Her eyes picked through the darkness as they adjusted. The room was large, probably for the times Lord Malik decided to share his prey, lounge furniture strewn across an enormous fur rug. A huge fireplace crackled to her left. Despite the flames licking into the air, the room was freezing.

There was no bed, which meant this probably wasn't the Demon Lord's chamber. She turned in a slow circle as disappointment pinched in her chest. The potion would only work for an hour, two at most. In a castle this size, everything hinged on the Keeper's quarters being nearby.

She went to catalog the rest of the room when something caught her eye. A translucent webbing draped over a navy settee.

Curiosity became alarm as she finally understood what the webbing was: snakeskin.

The size of a large man. Or a Demon Lord.

The sensation of being watched fell over her like an icy wind, the hairs on her body lifting one by one. Sticky dread clumped beneath her sternum, making it hard to breathe. Sweat slithered down her shoulder blades.

A soft laugh came from behind her.

Instinct begged her to whip around to face the threat. But that would only provoke his savagery. Her mind screamed as she turned to face Lord Malik using careful, slow movements.

It took every ounce of her willpower not to grab the dagger at her thigh.

Or worse, run.

His features were even more disturbing up close. Inky shadows collected in the deep recesses of his eye sockets, and his mouth twisted in a malicious smile.

The Demon Lord's head ticked to the side, the quick predatory movement sending her heart into a tailspin. "Are you afraid, little mouse?"

There was no reason to lie. "Yes."

His throat dipped, those yellow eyes dropping to her neck. "I cannot decide what I would enjoy more. Letting you try to run first while I hunt you, or taking you immediately. What do you think, little mouse?"

She took a step back, her hand inching toward her thigh. "Why put off pleasure that can be had now?"

"Pleasure?" He bared two curved fangs the length of her pinky. "I apologize if you have been misinformed. Only one of us will be feeling that. You, on the other hand, are going to scream. Loudly. Can you do that, little mouse?"

She held his stare, refusing to flinch. To give him the fear he craved. "You have no idea what I can do."

He was closer—when did that happen? Her heart slammed into her throat as she blinked and he was only a few feet away.

"Then show me."

He became a blur and then disappeared from view. *Where is he?*

Her hand closed around the dagger as he grabbed her by the shoulders from behind. His grip was tight enough to crush bone. White hot agony flared where his fingers jammed into her flesh.

"This is going to hurt," he promised, breath hot on her neck. "A lot."

"So will this." Blade sweaty and cool in her palm, she slammed it backward, bracing for the impact of metal meeting flesh and bone.

Pain exploded in her wrist. She was jerked around. The Demon Lord's hand crushed her wrist in a vise-grip, twisting her arm as he brought the knife up to examine. "Oh, you're not a mouse at all, are you?"

She lashed out, striking him in the face with a fist. He didn't so much as flinch. Something cracked as he twisted her arm even farther. Fire lanced up her forearm. The dagger clattered to the marble floor.

She tried to hit him again but he caught that hand. Instead of anger, his eyes burned with wicked delight. "And you said you didn't want to play."

"No, I said I didn't want to delay the pleasure of ramming that knife through your skull."

She jerked her knee up but he twisted out of reach.

His cruel laugh reverberated over the high marble walls. "Did you really think you could hurt me?"

Enraged, she flung her head foreword, headbutting him in his hideous face. A satisfying crack followed.

She jerked her head back and flashed a ferocious smile. "Yes."

"You really shouldn't have done that." The pressure released from her wrists, and then he bared his venomous fangs. "Run, little mouse. Run so that I can find you."

The dagger. She scoured the marble floor—

Too far—it was too far away, resting beneath an ivory ottoman. She would never make it in time. Running wasn't an option.

Horror swept through her as his illusion shed like the snakeskin on the settee. When he was finished, only his eyes remained the same. His mouth was a long scar that reached ear-to-ear, his broad nose now two raised holes, and his pale skin had transformed into onyx and green scales.

A forked tongue darted out, flickering over her face and neck.

Running was what he wanted her to do. What he expected.

She cringed from his real face, making sure her eyes stretched wide in fear and her breathing became labored. His diamond-shaped head began to slide back and forth, his reptilian gaze locked onto her.

She let a tremor rock her otherwise frozen body, as if she was too petrified to do anything but tremble in fear.

Her fear was like a drug washing over him. He drank it in, relishing her abject terror, savoring it as he prepared to strike.

All he needed now was one final push . . .

Eyes glassy, she forced a high-pitched cry from her throat, like a rabbit caught in a trap.

He had no idea she was the bait.

The Demon Lord's mouth snapped wide as his too-long fangs plunged straight for her neck.

Just like she wanted him to. She took the half-full jar of potion, which she'd grabbed while Lord Malik was distracted by her act, and hurtled the bottle into his open mouth.

He hissed and stumbled back, coughing, clawing at his throat. "What did you . . ."

Translucent eyelids snapped over his eyes as he blinked, and then his expression softened, his focus blurring.

"That took longer than planned," a male voice murmured from the right.

She whipped around to glare at Stolas. "You were here the entire time?"

"As I said I would be."

"So you could have grabbed the knife, you could have—could have stopped this at any time!"

"Yes," he answered as he strolled up to the Demon Lord and waved a hand in his face. "But I thought after what he called you, you would want to prove him wrong . . . little mouse."

All the pent up terror and rage exploded. The things the Demon Lord planned to do to her . . . the things he had already done to countless females—

The glint of the dagger caught her eye. She picked up the weapon, stalked toward the Demon Lord, and slammed the blade hilt-deep into his heart.

Lord Malik let out a low moan.

Stolas looked to her. "Done?"

She yanked the blade free, dark syrupy blood flinging through the air, and chose the opposite side of Lord Malik's chest to bury the weapon.

Pain rippled inside the Demon Lord's eyes, but he didn't move. The gaping wound visible beneath the hole in his shirt was already mending together, which seemed unfair considering what he had planned for her. The pain and torment.

She grasped the dagger, twisting, before rehoming it in his thigh. A muffled grunt slipped from Lord Malik's snake-like mouth, his eyes tracking her.

"Finished," she declared.

"You sure?"

She exhaled. "Yes."

"A shame. The hideous coward deserves so much more." Stolas lifted the Demon Lord's lip and ran a curious finger over one of his fangs. "Interesting. I would guess the venom in his fangs acts as a paralytic to keep his victims from fighting back."

Fury swept through her. She took no small pleasure in the way Lord Malik's eyes peeled wide as she took the weapon, twirling it viciously in front of him. "This is going to hurt. A lot."

She drove the blade under his sternum.

He gasped, choking on the pain.

"Who's the little mouse now?"

Stolas arched a brow.

"*Now* I'm done."

"Are you sure? Because your violence is almost as sexy as that dance you performed earlier. Tell me. Was that for me, Beastie?"

Fiery heat tumbled through her. Something knowing flashed behind Lord Malik's expression, and she shook her head, hoping her cheeks weren't as red as they felt. "We should probably hurry. I really don't want to be here when he wakes from the compulsion."

Stolas gave a disappointed sigh. Then he jerked his chin at Lord Malik. "You inflicted the potion so you are the one who can compel him."

She squared off in front of Lord Malik, trying and failing not to gloat at their switch in positions. Now she was the one in power. "How do we reach the Keeper?"

Lord Malik swallowed. Blinked. He was fighting the compulsion. His gaze slowly coasted behind Haven. "Take the tunnels behind the hidden doorway there. When it branches off, take a left. Her chambers are just beyond."

"There will be some kind of lock or spell to prevent entry," Stolas warned.

She looked into those horrible eyes once more. "How do we enter?"

"I have . . . the key." Beneath his stupor she could see him fighting every word.

"Where."

"My neck."

Stolas snatched the key and slipped it over his head.

"Anything else we should know?" Haven asked.

"It has been too long since I fed her." His lips twisted into a grin. "She will be so delighted to have company."

Goddess Above. Haven couldn't wait to be done with this nightmarish realm.

"You are going to forget what happened here," Haven added. "Forget everything about us. You won't remember me or my companion. Understand?"

"Yes." Malice glinted inside Lord Malik's eyes, and she knew he was aware now of everything that was happening, even if he couldn't do anything to stop it. "The little mouse and the dark wolf."

Haven froze as a shiver rolled through her. Did he know who Stolas was?

They were running out of time. The compulsion would only last so long. "Stay in this room. Don't leave it all night, and if anyone knocks, tell them you're busy."

She crossed the chamber, firelight glinting off the diamonds at her neckline and dancing over the room, when something made her look back. Stolas had taken the knife out of the Demon Lord and stabbed him again, in the side this time.

She realized why a second later as he whispered something into the Demon Lord's ear. Now Stolas could compel him.

Jaw clenched and eyes burning with hatred, Lord Malik removed the dagger from his side, positioned the blade longways with the sharpened edge over his chest, and sliced deep. A grunt followed as oily black blood poured from the cut.

Stolas caught up to her, grinning, but the smile didn't reach his eyes.

"What did you make him do?" she asked as they found the tunnel behind the hidden panel.

"What is the saying, death by a thousand cuts?"

Haven flicked up her brows. "Is it wise to provoke him further?"

"You mean, beyond drugging him, overriding his will, stabbing him—four times, I might add—and forcing him to give us access to his most prized possession?"

"Point taken."

Stolas closed the panel with a soft click and then turned to her. Torches flickered from somewhere just beyond, the air cool and dusty. "Lord Malik deserves to be flayed alive for what he did to you. But, for now, I'll settle for a few removed parts."

"You didn't?"

A muffled groan of pure agony came from the Demon Lord's chamber, and Stolas's lips curled in a devious grin.

He *did*. Shadeling Below.

A garbled scream followed, so loud that anyone on this side of the castle would hear it. But Haven knew screams from that chamber were a nightly occurrence.

No one would come to Lord Malik's aid.

FORTY-NINE

Haven thought after dealing with Lord Malik, the Keeper would be tame in comparison. She was wrong. When they approached the final passageway to the Keeper's quarters, silky white spiderwebs blocked their way. The webs were intricately woven patterns that ran floor-to-ceiling, bigger than any normal spider could make.

The door to the Keeper's quarters was even more ominous. Spiders scuttled across the iron surface, thousands of them.

Haven made a face. "And here I was thinking Lord Malik was the worst thing we would encounter tonight."

Stolas released a ragged breath. "The Keeper is an ancient blood augur, the oldest in existence that we know of. She's part demon, part witch, and part something insidious that's not of this world."

"She can tell the future?"

"In a way. Some say she weaves the strands of destiny on a giant web. That she can even manipulate fate."

"What is she like?"

His mouth twisted in disgust. "Vile. Hideous in every way. The first time I met her, she came in the form of a beautiful, naked Seraphian female. She claimed she was being held captive by a Demon Lord. That—that if I would just give her what she wanted, it would save her. In return, she would let me see my future."

Haven swallowed. "What did she want?"

"Me in her bed." Loathing rippled across his expression, a powerful, raw hatred. "But after she showed me what I wanted to see, I refused my end of the bargain. I was young and stupid, and by then I had glimpsed the repulsive creature lurking beneath the seductive glamour."

"But she is Lord Malik's captive, or was that a lie?"

"Yes. He tricked her with a clever bargain years ago, and now she is his mistress. That was her price. He must visit her bed once a month. In return, she feeds him bits of the future. Enough that he has gained an edge over all the other Demon Lords."

"Does he know about the mirror portal?"

"Doubtful. He hardly seems the sharing kind."

So it must have been another Demon Lord who gave him the mirror.

"Why did you go to her a second time?" she asked, searching his face. If the Keeper truly were as hideous as he described, it didn't make sense to bargain with her again.

Something passed over his face, there and gone. "Because I was desperate to hear that my fate had changed."

"And had it?"

His jaw flexed. "We should hurry before Lord Malik's compulsion wears off." He turned his back to her, lifted the key from his neck, and inserted the dark brass object into the keyhole. Black spiders scurried from the door handle as the ward fell away and the lock turned.

Loudly.

"There goes the advantage of surprise," Haven whispered.

"Oh, she knew the moment we entered the last corridor."

The spiderwebs.

"Is this the right time to mention I abhor spiders?" she murmured, just as the door creaked slowly open.

On its own.

Stolas turned to her, his face overcome with an emotion she couldn't quite catalog. "Wait. I just need to look at you for a moment." His lashes dipped as he slid his gaze over her, slowly, hardly breathing. "When I close my eyes, I see you dancing still. That was for me, wasn't it?"

This was hardly the time, but . . . "Yes."

He met her stare. There was something so bittersweet in his eyes, and she didn't understand why. "What happened last night between us . . . it wasn't a mistake." Then he turned his back to her, murmuring, "It's time."

She was still reeling as they entered a large chamber that must have once been a gorgeous sitting room, but was now covered in years of dust. Moonlight flooded the huge windows and illuminated a filmy set of couches and chairs. Paintings covered the walls, and odd knickknacks and personal items were piled in corners. A man's brown moth-eaten jacket. Spoons and forks and every manner of cutlery. A woman's tortoise-shell brush still tangled with black strands.

Pearl bracelets and gold cuffs piled on low tables next to worn boots and a dingy whale-bone corset.

Cobwebs covered everything. All of the silver threads led into the next room, a larger grand entertaining hall where Haven glimpsed more art.

"What's the plan?" she whispered as they padded quietly into the next room, ducking the thick strands of webbing. Their feet left prints in the heavy layer of dust covering the ground.

"I thought I could distract her while you go for the painting," he murmured.

His wings twitched violently against the cobwebs sticking to his feathers, and she thought she caught him wince. He pressed a hand to his side—the same area he was favoring last night.

"Stolas—"

Scuttling noises came from somewhere high above, like giant spider-legs clicking over marble. A thick canopy of webbing obscured the high ceiling. Her stomach dropped as she saw the complex tangle of strands begin to twitch and shiver.

"Are you gifts from Lord Malik?" came a whispering voice, like soft feathers brushing together.

"Not exactly," Stolas said. He gestured silently to a wall full of paintings across the room, and Haven snuck toward the gallery as Stolas continued, "Do you remember me, Keeper?"

Dust rained over the floor as the Keeper's nest shivered with movement.

"Come closer so that I may look upon you," came the Keeper's seductive voice.

A soft thud drew Haven's gaze behind her, and she was surprised to see a woman standing in a shaft of moonlight. She was naked, her body reminding Haven of the voluptuous statues of the Goddess that dotted the temples. Sleek onyx hair cascaded down her back.

Stolas appraised the Keeper. "I didn't know this was that type of party."

Her laugh was enchanting, mesmerizing even. "Hello, Seraphian Prince. Did you come to finally fulfill your end of our broken agreement?"

His gaze flicked to Haven and back to the Keeper. They didn't have much time.

"No, but I have brought you something you will like even more."

"The mortal girl poking around my things?" the Keeper murmured, and Haven froze. "How you spoil me."

Stolas could only distract the Keeper for so long before she realized their plan. Haven searched the canvases on the wall, cringing at the macabre depictions of demons feasting on mortals. The disquieting, otherworldly creatures locked in graphic scenes of battle. Many of the canvases were cracked and dulled with age, their ornate golden frames rotting.

Where are you? Something drew her gaze to the center of the gallery, and her heart wobbled strangely.

There.

The painting was smaller than the others, but still larger than average, the size of an ordinary window. The frame was a simple unvarnished wood. Inside the frame, a pretty woman with long blonde hair was holding a newborn baby.

Creeping as quietly as possible onto a threadbare silver and red rose-patterned couch, she reached for the frame—

She jerked her hand away from the dark magick just as archaic symbols glowed over the frame, burning a pale blue.

The frame was spelled against thievery. By the cold magick she felt coming from the runes, one touch would have probably incapacitated her. Maybe there was a way to disarm them?

She squinted at the bizarre symbols engraved into the frame, but the runes didn't look familiar.

Her heart sank. To come all this way just to see the painting and not be able to touch it . . .

There had to be another way. Breathing hard, she looked for clues that would point to immortality. But there was only the mother and her baby inside a plain, sparsely furnished room. The couch was brown and spotted with age and use. The side table beside it was empty. And the only décor was a painting on the wall behind them—

A painting. She peered closer at the canvas. Compared to the poor furnishings and plain room, the art was expensive. A heavy golden frame of ivy enclosed what looked like, from here, a woman with floating white hair spewing golden light from her mouth.

Flowers were strewn in a neat arc over her head. Above that, a river flowed.

It was strange, and yet . . . she couldn't take her eyes off the image.

A painting—inside a painting.

Something tugged at her memory. Another piece of art, this one created by Stolas's mother.

What if this was the same? What if she could enter the art itself? What if the true painting was disguised inside this one, hidden in plain sight?

That would explain where the second painting went.

Before she could overthink it, she slid off the couch and backed up. Then she sprinted onto the couch and leapt into the frame.

Her eyes squeezed shut against the expectation of hitting the wall. Instead—instead she tumbled into another room.

Into the painting.

It couldn't be possible, but it was. Somehow it was. Instead of cold, dusty marble, the floor pressed into her cheek was worn wood. The suffocating stench of vile magick was gone, replaced by the smell of honeysuckle and freshly-baked bread.

The room wasn't glamorous by any stretch, but someone cared enough about this place to keep the floors swept and clean. Soft warm light spilled from open windows onto a ragged scarlet rug.

Humming drew Haven's attention to the couch. The woman wore a shawl over a gray sheath dress, and she was rocking her baby in her lap. Her golden eyes sparked with endless love.

Haven's throat clenched as she stood and drew closer. The song the woman sang was familiar. Demelza hummed the same tune. It was a lullaby.

Haven froze as the woman's voice filled the air.

"The stag in the wood, the bear in the field, they will all bow down to you. The ravens up high, the Shadowlings of nigh, they will all swear oaths to you. The mortal kings, they will fall one and all, to worship at your feet. But those that don't heed the shadow of wings, the bite of fiery eyes, your wrath will come and swallow them whole, the girl of fire and ice."

This scene had happened. Somehow Haven understood that, just as she understood her mother had preserved the memory for Haven so she would know how much she had been cared for once.

That her mother had sang to her. Had *loved* her—enough to willingly die so that she could live.

A part of Haven longed to stay here. To soak in the pure adoration she felt radiating from her mother like sunshine, an exquisite type of warmth she might never feel again.

It would almost be enough, she thought.

Almost, but not quite. Her friends waited on the other side, and they had given up everything for her. Then there was Stolas . . .

Stolas.

"I think you would like him," she whispered to her mother, who couldn't hear her, of course. "And I think he would adore you."

The baby cooed, and the blanket swaddled around it pulled back so that a vibrant rose-gold hair peeked through.

Time to get back. Haven carefully grasped the frame and lifted, the painting heavy in her arms. She took in the scene one final time, engraving every single detail to memory, and then she leapt through the darkness into the other side.

FIFTY

Stolas fought against the deceptively soft pull of the Keeper's beauty. The magick in her enchantment had grown even more powerful than the first time he bargained with her. He found his gaze drawn to her large, dark eyes. The feigned innocence appealed to his predatory side, as she knew it would.

Her night-black hair slipped over one breast as she ignored Haven completely. Such was her confidence that both Haven and he were caught in her web.

Tendrils of her vile powers slithered over his inner magickal walls, testing, searching for a weakness. A way to influence him.

He grit his teeth against the searing wound puckering his side, the black poison seeping into his bloodstream. Haven had been right. The poison did nearly kill him. He had hoped feeding last night would slow the vile toxin enough that his magick could do the rest, but whatever it was, it was too powerful.

Soon the little bit of magick the demon's blood allowed him would recede, and then he wouldn't be able to keep the poison contained any longer. It would fill his arteries, his heart pumping it to every part of his body.

"Why are you here?" the Keeper purred. "The last time I saw you, you were very disappointed. Don't tell me you want to confirm your tragic destiny again? The answer will be the same, but the price this time will be much steeper."

Stolas kept an eye on Haven in his periphery. She was up on a couch examining something on the wall. He met the Keeper's otherworldly gaze, his face emotionless as he said, "What if I told you there were two reasons for this visit?"

"Two reasons?" She arched her back a little as she strolled closer. "Now I am very curious, Prince. Very curious indeed."

The loud thumping of footsteps came from across the room. The Keeper's head whipped toward Haven just as she jumped onto the couch and . . .

Shadeling Below. The fool jumped into the wall—

And disappeared. He blinked, head tilted. That was unexpected, but he trusted she had a reason.

The Keeper slowly twisted her head back to him, the insectile movement corrupting her innocent illusion. "Oh, someone is being very naughty." Her bowed lips wrenched into a malicious smile. "That's her, isn't it? The immortal you are destined to love?" The Keeper's nostrils flared as she inhaled deeply. "Ah, but she is still a mortal, and the mating bond between you has not been secured. Is that why you thought it was safe to love her?"

Stolas pulled out a blade. The dagger was carved from obsidian, the first weapon his mother had ever given him. He had worn it every day of his life.

The Keeper's too-wide eyes slid to the dagger, her lips forming a fake pout. "My feelings are hurt, Prince."

"I have had this weapon hidden at my side since my court fell." His throat ached as he held the dagger up to the delicate moonlight. The cool obsidian handle hadn't touched his fingers for centuries, and the familiar weight cracked open memories—black, nightmarish memories he had blocked. "It has been waiting patiently."

"For what, sweet Prince?"

"Vengeance."

He struck so quickly that even she couldn't move before the blade slashed over her chest. An insectile squeal split the night as she reeled back, her beautiful illusion bleeding away to the demon-hag beneath.

"There you are," he whispered, shuddering in revulsion.

Clumps of coarse gray hair hung from a skeletal head, egg-sized black insect eyes staring back. Her nose was two slits above two arachnid fangs that curved to her chin. Eight spider-like legs were attached to her body, and they clicked against the dusty marble floor as she scuttled back up her web.

"Fool." Her enraged whisper reverberated through the room. "Stupid fool."

Agony rippled up his side, and he slammed a hand against the feverish wound. All of his concentration went into using his magick to keep the poison from spreading. To hide the injury just long enough—

Molten agony radiated from the wound. He staggered, biting back a groan. The poison was moving too quickly. Rustling sounds came from all around.

Darkness eroded his vision as he searched for the Keeper. He needed her to attack before Haven returned. "You came into my home and took something that didn't belong to you."

Chilling laughter echoed all around him. "You broke the Goddess's law when you refused your end of our bargain, Prince. I had every right to take whatever I wanted then. Although if I had known the power of that feather when I traded it to Morgryth, I would have asked for so much more."

His mother's feather. Caustic poison flooded his mind now, his vision blurring. Pain tore through his chest.

Archeron's poison had entered his heart.

Every breath now brought on deep, wracking agony. He plunged forward, cobwebs clinging to his face, his wings, his hair. He swung the blade wildly, the honed edge cutting through the Keeper's nest.

A streak of black to his right. He pivoted to face her, blinking against his fading vision at the monstrous creature. "My mother helped me craft this dagger, and then Morgryth forced me to put it through her heart."

"You cannot blame me for that," the Keeper crooned.

"Oh, but I do." He lunged but she skittered just out of his grasp.

He staggered as red-hot fire pulsed over every inch of him.

"Come on, you bitch," he snarled.

He heard her behind him, but he was too far gone to turn before she struck. Twin rods of pain slammed into the flesh between his neck and shoulder as the Keeper slipped her fangs into him. The bite of her venom came next.

Followed by a dull ache as she started to *feed*.

He supposed there was some dark justice in that.

He waited until he was sure she'd taken enough, until there was no doubt the poison flooding his veins was inside her too—and then he used the last of his energy to fling her off him.

He rolled onto his back. His wings were spread out beneath him on the dusty floor, his chest heaving and lungs rattling with every inhalation.

It was done.

Her spindly legs tapped the marble as she approached. "You said there were two reasons you came here, Prince. Humor me with the second one before I finish killing you."

A violent cough wracked his torso. So this was what it felt like to truly die. "I came . . . to help someone I love."

She brought one of her legs up to caress his face. "This is the infamous Lord of the Netherworld? The Seraphian Prince who once spurned me? What a disappointment you are. You failed at both."

"Are you . . . so sure about that?"

Even half-dead, Stolas was still lucid enough to catch the moment when she understood what he had done.

She hissed. Cool air assailed his inflamed skin as she jerked up his shirt. Whatever she saw on his flank, it must have been terrible because she shrieked, skittering away from him. "What have you done?"

"Poison," he groaned. "Not sure . . . what kind, but it's not pleasant. Can't find an . . . antidote." His dry lips stretched into a pained grin. "Too bad you couldn't foretell your own death."

Her shrieks became screams as the poison took hold. "This isn't how you were supposed to die," she gasped. "I saw you fall from the sky. I saw her *kill* you."

"Well I'm changing things up . . . a bit." He found himself chuckling, despite it all. After everything he had survived, it was Archeron's poison that would finally end him.

Closing his eyes, he pushed the sound from his mind and focused on the memory of Haven dancing.

Just for him.

FIFTY-ONE

Haven came out of that magickal world to silence. A grim, awful quiet that resonated in her bones. Cobwebs were broken and strewn everywhere, furniture upended. And on a bare spot of floor, lying on his back with his wings outstretched behind him, rested Stolas.

He wasn't moving—not even his feathers, which never quite stilled.

No.

Panic bloomed in her chest as she made out the creature on its side a few feet away, clearly dead. She tossed the painting onto a chair and rushed to Stolas, calling his name.

One of his wings twitched, lighting a spark of hope inside her.

He was still alive—

Her hope shattered as she took in his face. His eyes were rolled back in his head, his mouth twisted in pain and flecked with black. One hand rested over his chest, clenched knuckle-white over a black dagger she'd never seen before. "Stolas, what's happening? I don't understand."

She grasped his shirt, startled by the feverish heat of his skin radiating through the fabric. Desperation made her clumsy as she ripped it off, buttons flying.

A soft moan parted his lips.

"Oh Goddess," she breathed as she took in the wound at his side. The injury itself was small, the size of a pinky-tip, but black veins snaked out from the hole, slithering over his ribcage and around to his back. "What is this? Stolas, please."

Two nasty, coin-sized puncture wounds seeped fresh blood just above his collarbone. That had to be where the Keeper bit him. His chest shuddered with every shallow breath.

Fighting against the waves of hysteria threatening to drown her, she reached out for her magick but came up empty. Frustrated, she tried again and again. Slamming up against that hollow emptiness. Clawing at it in fury. In terrified desperation.

Nothing.

She couldn't help him. Couldn't do anything but watch as he gasped and faded.

She looked again to his festering wound, trying to understand. To grasp what was happening.

It was the same flank he had been guarding.

The injury was old.

"Why?" she demanded, begging him to open his stupid silver eyes and look at her. Just look at her. "Why didn't you tell me?"

Shock was taking over. A numb, helpless shock. She didn't know how to help him, and he was dying.

Dying.

She slammed her palm into the floor, suddenly furious with him. "You don't get to leave me, Stolas. Not like this."

"Touching, but your anger will do nothing to stop that particular poison from killing him, I'm afraid."

Haven scrambled to put herself between the threat and Stolas. The figure stepped from the shadows—

"Your cloak," she said, confusion adding to her wild array of emotions. "I saw you earlier. Twice."

"Yes." He flipped back his hood and knelt beside Stolas.

Haven gasped. "You're a Demon Lord."

The sharp prick of his ears poked from his short, silver-gray hair, but it was his beauty that confirmed her suspicions.

Large yellow eyes rimmed in charcoal lifted to hers. "I suspect you have a lot of questions, but we simply do not have the time. All you need to know is that my name is Raziel, and yes, I am a Demon Lord. A foolish one who once bargained with a Seraphian Empress and lost nearly everything."

She didn't have time to be skeptical. "So you're here to help Stolas?"

"I am here to save his life. Three times do I owe him that favor before my obligation is fulfilled."

"If that's true, where have you been all the other times he nearly died?"

He shrugged. "My obligation didn't begin until he entered the Demon Realm."

Haven exhaled, her mind spinning. "Let's say I'm going to trust you because I have no other option. What do I need to do?"

Raziel frowned down at Stolas's wound. He sniffed the air and his frown deepened. "I suspect the poison is rotmire, a particularly wicked venom procured from a high level demon."

"When would he have . . ." Her words trailed away as a vision of Archeron sneaking up behind Stolas surfaced.

Had he poisoned him then? Stolas should have said something . . .

It didn't matter. She would deal with that later. "Is there an antidote?"

"The blood of a God. A few rare vials do exist somewhere, but they would be nearly impossible to find, and by that time, he would be very, very dead." His gaze settled on her neck. "Unless you know of another source?"

He knew who she was. There was no point dancing around the truth.

She nodded. "My blood." He didn't even bother feigning surprise. "How do I—I don't know how to make him drink from me."

"Give me your wrist," Raziel commanded.

Any other time his soft voice would have terrified her. But if he wanted to drink from her, or worse, there was no need for such an elaborate story.

She offered her arm, hand turned palm up. She nearly yanked it back when she saw the razor-sharp talon slide from his fingertip. In a flash, he had opened a deep wound in her wrist.

His gaze lingered on the blood a second too long—but then he growled and forced his attention on Stolas.

"You don't have to stay," she said as she edged closer to Stolas. His chest had stopped moving, and her heart clenched. But then his breath fluttered over her wrist as she pressed it to his lips, and she sagged against him in momentary relief.

"Who will stop him from draining you to a husk?" Raziel mused.

"He won't hurt me."

"You do realize who this is, right?"

"He won't hurt me," she repeated.

"I think I will stay, just in case."

She tensed, unsure what to expect as her blood smeared Stolas's lips. He stirred.

Pressing harder, she called his name.

His eyelids fluttered open, all black eyes unseeing as they roved side to side. His hand shot up, trapping her forearm, his fangs sinking deep. She bit back her cry of pain as he sucked—*hard*—the pressure in her veins matching the aching throb where his teeth penetrated.

She shifted on her knees against the pain. He snarled, holding her wrist so tight she had no hope of breaking free.

"Stolas."

The oily black veins were slowly receding back into the wound as a golden spark of light grew in the center of his eyes.

"Stolas."

The wound was healing now, all signs of the festering poison fading away. The puncture wounds above his collarbone were mending too.

"Stolas."

"Tell me when you want me to force him to stop," Raziel said in a bored tone.

"Stolas."

"Preferably before he kills you—"

"Stolas!"

Stolas's pupils constricted back to their normal state, his eyes darting to her face. Recognition settled in those magick-filled depths, followed by something else. A deeper bond that was both confusing and startling.

The deep ache in her wrist faded to a stinging throb as his fangs retracted. Stolas's brow furrowed as he looked from her to Raziel and back, and then he gave a guttural snarl. "Do you have any idea what you've done, Demon Lord?"

Raziel smiled. "Saved your life?"

She tore her wrist away and wrapped her fingers around the wounds.

"He will probably be slightly out of it for a few minutes," Raziel murmured, and she noticed he was backing away.

She frowned at him. "Where are you going?"

"Oh, did I not mention he despises me with every fiber of his being?" Raziel flashed a dark grin. "He blames me, among others, for his court's untimely fall and the Empress's death."

"Wait." She peered closer at him. "You're the Demon Lord who gave him the mirror?"

"The one and only."

Stolas wobbled as he propped onto his elbows, his eyes dazed as he tried to focus on Raziel. "You," Stolas growled.

"Me." Raziel gave a little bow. "Until next time, Darkshade."

Stolas roared as he stumbled to his feet and lurched toward Raziel, but the Demon Lord simply . . . disappeared.

Stolas was breathing hard, his eyes darting around the room. She needed to get them back to Shadoria. Shredded cobwebs masked the furniture and belongings, and she yanked the sticky strands away from everything she could until . . .

There. A sliver of jade peeked from beneath the silk webs. She ripped back more to reveal the exact same mirror that was in Starpiercer Castle.

She rushed back to Stolas, slipping her arm under his, and together they limped toward the mirror. Last second before they crossed into the portal, she remembered.

Goddess Above and everything holy, she almost forgot the damned painting.

Once that was safely in hand, she joined Stolas. His drunken gaze raked up and down her body, a wolfish grin lifting his lips—lips still wet with her blood. "Why did you stop?"

"What?" She forced him toward the mirror's surface.

"Dancing. You stopped dancing."

Rolling her eyes, she shoved him through the portal. She was about to follow when she sensed someone watching just over her shoulder. Raziel.

The Demon Lord grinned. "It *was* a nice performance."

She sighed. "When Stolas recovers from his stupor, there's a chance I'm going to kill him all over again. You might want to be ready."

"I look forward to it, Goddess-Born."

With that, she stepped through the mirror and left the nightmare world of demons behind.

FIFTY-TWO

Haven was sitting on the cold floor of Stolas's tower chamber, staring at the painting propped against the side of his bed, when she heard Stolas land behind her. They had arrived back in Shadoria only a few hours ago. The magick of the portal had sobered Stolas immediately.

He hadn't said a word as Haven went to find Surai and Ember. It was early morning here, but they were already awake, preparing supplies for travel to Eritreyia.

Haven was disappointed to discover Bell already gone. He and Xandrian had left last night for Ashiviere.

He would have loved trying to interpret the painting with her.

They had decided for now the painting was safest in Stolas's chamber. After checking on Demelza, Haven had made him take her here, lured by the mystery of the painting. While she searched the canvas for clues, he had left to meet Nasira.

Now Haven was sitting cross-legged in front of the art, her back stiff and achy as she frowned at the confusing scene. Her Shadow Wolf was stretched out a few feet away. The wolf whined as Stolas approached, but Haven couldn't tear her focus from the painting.

Nothing about the illustration made sense. The woman in the canvas had her back turned so her face wasn't visible. She was on her knees in a field of poppies, arms flung out and head back. Everything about the woman was luminescent—her hair, her skin, her flowing crimson robe.

But it was the pure white magick spewing from her mouth that Haven found the most fascinating.

The plaque at the bottom was titled: *The Light Singer.*

"What do the flowers above her mean?" Stolas asked, and she startled at how quickly he'd closed the distance between them. Sometimes she forgot he could move with such quiet speed.

She exhaled, lifting from her knees to a stand. "I don't know yet."

"You have been through a lot in the past few hours. Rest. It will be here in the morning."

She turned to face him, shocked to see a fresh scratch running down his cheek. It was already healing. "What happened?"

"Nasira." He pinched the bridge of his nose. "We had an argument, but you don't need to worry about that. Not tonight. Rest."

"I can't. Not until I've bathed every bit of ick from the Demon Realm away. But Demelza is snoring loud enough to wake the Shadeling and I'm too weary to bathe myself."

His eyes were luminous as his lips tilted into a dark grin. "I can help with that."

"You can help me bathe?"

"Why not? It's not as if I wouldn't enjoy it."

Her throat clenched at the intimacy in his voice. The promise of continuing what started in the Demon Realm was alluring. And yet . . . "Why did you lie to me?" She met his gaze. "Why not tell me you were poisoned? That you were . . ." Her voice wavered. "Dying?"

He held out his hand. "Sit down and I promise to explain."

Her heart was racing as she let him lead her to a dark couch in front of the fire. But instead of sitting, Stolas paced in front of her, the firelight catching in his feathers. "At first, I didn't tell you what Archeron had done because I knew you would have insisted on finding the antidote instead of the painting. I thought—hoped feeding from the others would be enough that my magick could do the rest."

"But it didn't."

"It helped, and I was hopeful. But by the time I met you in your bath that night, I knew the poison Archeron used was more potent than I anticipated. Toxins from the Demon Realm are highly effective, even against me."

A ragged breath lifted her chest. "Why not tell me then?"

"Because we were so close to your goal, and—" He raked his fingers through his pale hair. "You were willing to sacrifice so much to protect your friends, how could I not do the same?"

She closed her eyes against the tears she felt building. Did he not know how important he was to her? "Did you know my blood could heal you?"

"No. I suspect that was Archeron's final blow. He assumed I would either die or drink from you and lose all control."

"Except you didn't. You stopped." Her gaze slid to her wrist, the bandage covering her wounds. "So you decided to use the poison slowly killing you to kill the Keeper?"

He shrugged. "It was rash, I'll admit. But I was dying anyway and she would never stop hunting you for taking what belonged to her, Haven." His jaw hardened. "I won't lie—killing her was a type of vengeance."

"What did she take from you all those years ago?"

Haunted eyes lifted to meet hers. "The Demon Lord that saved my life, Raziel? He and his father came to our realm to negotiate. In return for promising them sole access to blood slaves, he would help my mother achieve peace, an end to a seemingly endless war. The Keeper was one of the gifts he supplied, but my mother refused to bargain with the hag."

"So you did?"

His gaze was bleak as he nodded. "But instead of helping predict the war, she told me *my* future. One that I did not want to hear. In my hubris and ignorance, I thought I could deny my end of the bargain, not knowing that gave her the right to enter our home and take what she wanted."

Haven was strangely breathless as she asked, "And what was that?"

"A single feather. My mother's." His hands fisted and relaxed at his sides. "Every female empress is gifted the powers of this land, the same powers that eventually will go to Nasira. But a Seraphian's magick is rooted in our feathers, which is why my mother was meticulous in making sure every single errant feather of hers burned." His head tilted back as a jagged sigh fled his lips. "When she discovered I had bargained with the Keeper, we fought in front of the mirror. Neither of us noticed the feather she lost in the skirmish. But the Keeper did, and she took it to give to Lord Malik. He had discovered our agreement to trade with only Lord Raziel's court, so he gave the feather to Morgryth and made his own deal."

Haven swallowed. "The feather . . . that was what allowed Morgryth to steal your mother's powers?"

Even with only his profile visible, she caught the flash of agony in his expression. "Yes. The spells needed to extract such strong magick are rare, but they do exist in the Demon Realm."

She was alarmed to discover her hands shaking in her lap. "If that is true, why go to the Keeper a second time, Stolas?"

When he met her gaze, she nearly gasped at the raw emotion in his eyes. "Because I was desperate to hear that my future had changed. I should have known that fate bends to no one, not even me."

That had been right after they returned from Veserack, and it suddenly seemed no coincidence that his moods blackened right after. "Is that why you suddenly tried to push me away? To protect me from this dark future?"

His throat dipped.

Another thought came. "In the Demon Realm, in our tent—you only came to my bed because you knew you were dying."

"As I recall, you would not take no for an answer."

"Would any of that have happened otherwise?"

Her breath caught as he suddenly approached. He kneeled between her legs, slipped his hands behind her knees, and pulled her toward him. "I apologize for hurting you. For pushing you away. I thought—I thought I was protecting you from something worse. I thought I could somehow change the future, but what's done is done." His fingers sent shivers of pleasure skittering through her flesh as they slid up her thighs. "I see now I could no more stop this thing between us than I could prevent the sun from rising every morning."

The muscle low in her abdomen jerked taut. "And what is this thing between us, exactly?"

"I want you, Beastie. I have for months, and every second not acting on that desire has been prolonged torture." He leaned forward. She thought he was going to kiss her, but instead he rested his forehead against hers. "Do you have any idea how many nights I've replayed that hour in Solethenia? The way you glowed? The exquisite sounds you made?"

Goddess Above.

"We make our own future, you and I," he rasped, tugging her legs around his waist. "Whatever consequences arise from loving you, Haven Ashwood, they will be worth it."

Her arms curled around his neck as her mind whirled in dizzy loops. "Loving me?"

He kissed her nose. "Yes, and I'm now going to spend several hours proving that to you until I'm satisfied you believe me."

"What about the bath?" she squeaked.

"Who said there wouldn't be water involved?" he purred, sliding an arm around her waist and lifting her into his arms. "But I won't make love to you until you are in my bed. I want to look at you bathed in the silver glow of the moon, still wet from your bath, and know that you are mine . . . " He released a long breath. "For as long as fate allows."

Mine. Warmth spread over her entire body, her heart racing in anticipation. And yet, something else still bothered her. "What about Lord Malik? What will he do to you for taking what belonged to him?"

Lord Malik would have broken from his compulsion by now, and even if he didn't remember past events, once he discovered his most prized possession, the Keeper, dead—well he wouldn't overlook such an insult.

"Let me worry about him."

And then they were in Stolas's personal bathhouse, steeped in the steam and moonlight and their desires, and she forgot about the Demon Lord. Forgot about the Keeper and the painting and becoming immortal.

She lost herself in Stolas for what felt like an eternity. When finally she lay warm and spent in his arms, their wolves guarding them at the foot of his monstrously large bed and his chest rising softly at her back, she replayed his words again.

Whatever consequences arise from loving you, Haven Ashwood, they will be worth it.

EPILOGUE

Nasira slipped quietly down the runed steps spiraling deeper into the underground vaults, passing rooms full of gold and silver, heirlooms that had been around since the time of the Gods. None of them held her interest. Her focus was riveted to the thing below. She could feel the Godkiller's curiosity as it cast out its net, searching for the intruder it felt approaching.

Hello, Empress, it whispered into her mind. *I was hoping you would return.*

Heat from the molten lava below lapped at the shield she'd erected as Nasira approached the edge. The ancient weapon drew her eye. Just like every other time, a shiver of wonder swept through her at such ancient, unchecked power.

You smell of blood, it purred.

In a daze, she looked down at Stolas's blood half-dried beneath her long fingernails, and the same emotion she'd felt while they argued bubbled up inside her. That anger and desperation hotter than the magma below.

It hadn't started as an argument. She had been engulfed in relief when she first saw him and realized he was back from the Demon Realm. But then she'd questioned him about the rumors.

"Is it true?" she demanded. "Did Haven's Shadow Familiar take on your wolf form?"

He hadn't tried to hide the truth. "Yes."

Panic had engulfed her. And when she asked, "But you haven't consummated the bond?" and saw his crestfallen face, it felt like a dagger rammed into her heart.

"Nasi," he said, using her childhood nickname. "I was dying when she gave me her blood. I did not know what was happening until it was done."

"No. There has to be a way to stop this. *No!*"

"It's too late."

She knew he told the truth. There were three requirements to consummate a Seraphian mating bond. Shared dreams, shared blood, and a shared Shadow Familiar form.

When Haven freely gave Stolas her blood, she locked the final piece into place.

Tears stung Nasira's eyes as she shook her head. She hadn't cried when the Golemites ripped her from her bed. She hadn't shed a single tear when she watched first her siblings die and then her parents.

But now—now she couldn't keep her emotion in check. Stolas was all she had left. And even if she never found the courage to tell him, he was everything to her.

A wild desperation came over her. "Then you have to keep Haven from becoming immortal. Destroy the painting—"

"Stop!" he growled before his face had softened. "I will not take this from her and neither will you."

"Have you forgotten what the Keeper told you?"

His eyes lifted to hers, bleak and forlorn and resigned. "How can I forget? I will find a lover who is my equal in every way, an immortal mate who burns brighter than the sun. I will love her more than I have ever loved another—and she will kill me."

"If you let her become immortal, the prophecy will be complete and she will turn on you."

"Then I can only pray that when she does, it does not break her the way killing our mother nearly broke me."

She had struck him then without thinking, her talons slicing an ugly wound down his cheek. He hadn't reacted, hadn't moved an inch as blood dribbled down his jaw and fell between them.

And then she had fled here.

The Godkiller stroked its insidious claws of power over her, that fathomless magick promising so many, many things.

Tell me, the Godkiller whispered. *What is it that you want, Empress?*

Part of her knew once she spoke the words, there would be no turning back. But the other part understood she would do this and far worse if it meant saving the only family she had left.

So Nasira Darkshade leveled her gaze at the most powerful weapon that had ever existed and made a bargain.

THE END

Book five, D A R K   B R I N G E R , will release August 2021.
You can pre-order it on Amazon.

In the meantime, you can keep up with Haven and Archeron's world and all things Kingdom of Runes by signing up for my monthly author newsletter!

W W W . K I N G D O M O F R U N E S S A G A . C O M

GLOSSARY

• **The Bane** – The central region of Eritrayia and a barren wasteland, it acts as the buffer between the Ruinlands destroyed by the Curse and the untouched southern kingdoms protected by the runewall

• **Curseprice** – The items that must be collected and presented to the Shade Queen to break the Curse

• **Dark magick** – Derived from the Netherworld, it cannot be created, only channeled from its source, and is only available to Noctis. Dark magick feeds off light magick.

• **Darkcaster** – One who wields dark magick

• **Devourers** – Mortals with Noctis blood who practice demented dark magick and worship the Shade Queen; live in the bane and guard the rift/crossing into the Ruinlands

• **The Devouring** – The dark magick-laden mist that descends when the Curse hits and causes curse-sickness and death in mortals

• **Donatus Atrea** – All-Giver, or runetree of life where all light magick springs from

• **Eritrayia** – Mortal realm

• **Fleshrunes** – Runes Solis are born with; the markings tattoo a

Solis's flesh and channel their many magickal gifts

• **The Goddess** – Freya, mother of both Solis and Noctis, she is a powerful and divine being who gifted mortals with magick and fought on their side during the Shadow War.

• **Heart Oath** – Oath given before an engagement to marry. Can only be broken if two parties agree to sever the oath and at great cost

• **House of Nine** – Descendants of the nine mortals given runeflowers from the Tree of Life

• **Houserune** – Rune given to each of the Nine Houses and passed down from generation to generation

• **Light Magick** – Derived from the Nihl, it cannot be created, only channeled from its source, and is only available to Solis and royal mortals from the House Nine.

• **Lightcaster** – One who wields light magick

• **Mortalrune** – Runes mortals from the House Nine are allowed to possess/use

• **Netherworld** – Hell, where immoral souls go, ruled over by the Lord of the Netherworld

• **Nihl** – Heaven, ruled over by the Goddess Freya

• **Noctis** – Race of immortals native to Shadoria and the Netherworld who possess dark magic, they have pale skin, dark wings, and frequently horns

• **Powerrune** – Powerful type of rune forbidden to mortals

• **The Rift** – Chasm in the continent of Eritrayia caused by the Curse that leads to the Netherworld and allowed the Shade Queen and her people to escape

• **Ruinlands** – Northern half of Eritreyia, these lands are enchanted with dark magick and ruled by the Shade Queen

• **Runeday** – The eighteenth birthday of a royal child of the Nine Houses, where he or she receives their house runestone and potentially come into magick.

• **Runemagick** – Magick channeled precisely through ancient runes

• **Runestone** – Stones carved with a single rune—usually—and imbued with magick

• **Runetotem** – Tall poles carved with runes, they are used to nullify certain types of magick while enhancing others

• **Runewall** – A magickal wall that protects the last remaining southern kingdoms from the Curse

• **Sacred Heart Flower** – Given to the Solis at birth, this sacred bud is kept inside a glass vial and worn around the neck of one's intended mate

• **Shade Lord** – A powerful Noctis male, second only to the Shade Queen

• **The Shadeling** – Odin, father of both Solis and Noctis, he once loved Freya but became dark and twisted after fighting against his lover in the Shadow War. He now resides in the deepest pits of the Netherworld, a terrifying monster even the Noctis refuse to unchain.

• **The Shadow War** – War between the three races (mortals, Noctis, Solis,) sparked by the Goddess Freya giving mortals magick

• **Shadowlings** – Monsters from the Netherworld, under the control of the Lord of the Netherworld and the Shade Queen

• **Solis** – Race of immortals native to Solissia who possess light magick, they are more mortal-like in their appearance, with fair eyes and hair

• **Solissia** – Realm of the immortals

• **Soulread** – To read someone's mind

• **Soulwalk** – To send one's soul outside their body

• **Soulbind** – To bind another's will to yours/take over their body

• **Sun Lord** – A powerful Solis male who enjoys special position in the Effendier Royal Sun Court under the Effendier Sun Sovereign

• **Sun Queen** – A powerful Solis female who enjoys special position in the Effendier Royal Sun Court under the Effendier Sun Sovereign

SOLISSIAN WORDS AND PHRASES

- **Ascilum Oscular** – Kiss my ass (maybe)
- **Carvendi** – Good job (more or less)
- **Droob** – Knob/idiot
- **Paramatti** – Close the door to the Nihl, used during a light magick spell
- **Rump Falia** – Butt-face
- **Umath** – You're welcome
- **Victari** – Close the door to the Netherworld, used during a dark magick spell

THE NINE MORTAL HOUSES

- **Barrington** (Shadow Kingdom, formerly Kingdom of Maldovia)
- **Bolevick** (Kingdom of Verdure)
- **Boteler** (Kingdom of Penryth)
- **Courtenay** (Drothian)
- **Coventry** (Veserack)
- **Halvorshyrd** (unknown location)
- **Renfyre** (Lorwynfell)
- **Thendryft** (Dune)
- **Volantis** (Skyfall Island)

KINGDOM OF RUNES PLAYERS

Mortal Players

- **Haven Ashwood** – orphan
- **Damius Black** – Leader of the Devourers
- **Prince Bellamy (Bell) Boteler** – House Boteler, crown prince, second and only surviving heir to the king of Penryth
- **King Horace Boteler** – House Boteler, ruler of Penryth
- **Cressida Craven** – King Horace Boteler's mistress
- **Renk Craven** – half-brother to Bell, bastard son of Cressida and the King of Penryth
- **Eleeza Thendryft** – Princess of House Thendryft of the Kingdom of Dune, House Thendryft
- **Lord Thendryft** – House Thendryft of Dune Kingdom
- **Demelza Thurgood** – Haven Ashwood's Lady's Maid

Noctis Players

- **Stolas Darkshade** – Lord of the Underworld, husband to Ravenna, son of the last true Noctis Queen
- **Avaline Kallor** – Skeleton Queen, Ruler of Lorwynfell, half Noctis half mortal, promised to Archeron Halfbane
- **Remurian Kallor** – Half Noctis half mortal, brother of Amandine, died in the last war
- **Malachi K'rul** – Shade Lord, Shade Queen's underling

- **Morgryth Malythean** – Shade Queen, Cursemaker, queen of darkness, ruler of the Noctis

- **Ravenna Malythean** – Daughter of the Shade Queen, undead

Solis Players

- **Bjorn** – Sun Lord of mysterious origins

- **Archeron Halfbane** – Sun Lord and bastard son of the Effendier Sun Sovereign

- **Surai Nakamura** – Ashari warrior

- **Brienne "Rook" Wenfyre** – Sun Queen, outcast princess, daughter of the Morgani Warrior Queen

GODS

- Freya – the Goddess, ruler of the Nihl, mother of both Noctis and Solis

- Odin – the Shadeling, imprisoned in the Netherworld pits, father of both Noctis and Solis

ANIMALS

- Aramaya – Rook's temperamental horse
- Lady Pearl – Haven's loyal horse
- Ravius – Stolas's raven
- Shadow – Damius's wyvern

WEAPONS

- Haven's Sword – Oathbearer
- Stolas's Dagger – Vengeance

ABOUT THE AUTHOR

AUDREY GREY lives in the charming state of Oklahoma surrounded by animals, books, and little people. You can usually find Audrey hiding out in her office, downing copious amounts of caffeine while dreaming of tacos and holding entire conversations with her friends using gifs. Audrey considers her ability to travel to fantastical worlds a superpower and loves nothing more than bringing her readers with her.

Find her online at:

WWW.AUDREYGREY.COM

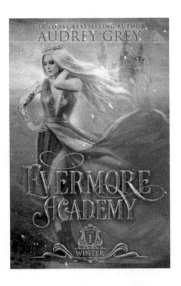

**Welcome to Evermore Academy where the magic is dark,
the immortals are beautiful, and being human SUCKS.**

After spending my entire life avoiding the creatures that murdered
my parents, one stupid mistake binds me to them for four years.

My penance? Become a human shadow at the infamous Evermore
Academy, finishing school for the Seelie and Unseelie Fae courts.

All I want is to keep a low profile, but day one, I make an enemy
of the most powerful Fae in the academy.

The Winter Prince is arrogant, cruel, and apparently also my Fae
keeper. Meaning I'm in for months of torture.

But it only gets worse. Something dark and terrible looms over the
academy. Humans are dying, ancient vendettas are resurfacing, and
the courts are more bloodthirsty than ever.

What can one mortal girl do in a world full of gorgeous monsters?

Fight back with everything I have—and try not to fall in love in
the process.

CPSIA information can be obtained
at www.ICGtesting.com
Printed in the USA
LVHW101738090622
720900LV00016B/477/J

9 781734 947946